The Betrayal of Guy Maddox

To Jill, with my very best
wishes for 2021.
  Hopefully you will enjoy
this novel as much as you
did the boy in the red boat.

Michael Seirton

JAN 2021

Michael Seirton

Publisher - STA BOOKS

www.spencerthomasassociates.com

ISBN: 978-0-9933957-3-4

Cover image of Paul Greaves © John De Vere Brown

Editor – Jennifer Smith

Dedication

This book is dedicated to the memory of Jennifer Smith

Our lifelong friendship began at The Castle Theatre, Farnham, and we never lost contact with each other from that gloriously creative period of our lives, even though our careers took different paths.

Although this wasn't the first story of mine that (Zen) – Jenny edited, this manuscript was her favourite. While in hospital towards the end of her illness, she insisted on editing the final chapters. Her beautiful spirit slipped away three weeks later in September 2016.

God bless you, Jenny, for being such a kind and wonderful human being, for always being there when family, friends and re-homed dogs needed you most. XXX

Acknowledgements

In chronological order are those people, without whose kind encouragement there would never have been any film or theatre career and, this novel would never have been written.

Arthur William Chambers, my late uncle, who encouraged me from childhood with all of my creative interests.
Irene Chambers, my beautiful and supportive mother, who suggested the theatre as alternative employment to working in a scrap metal yard.
Ian Cooper, an Artistic Director at The Derby Playhouse, who gave me the opportunity to design sets for the stage.
Paul Greaves, was my main strength, mentor and life partner. Without his understanding and belief in my ability, there would never have been a Michael Seirton.
Dick Tuckey, the Artistic Director, who gave me in the most creative job I've ever had, designing for the stage at The Castle Theatre, Farnham.
Caroline Smith, The Director, whose adventurous playbill stretched my creative ability to the limit and unknowingly, prepared me for the many difficult film locations ahead.
Jennifer Smith, the Stage Director, who became a lifelong friend and latterly, edited the manuscript of Guy Maddox.
Kate Fleming, a voice coach at The National Theatre, persuaded me to write for an interview with an Oscar winning designer at Pinewood Studios.
Terence Marsh, was this Production Designer who took a chance and gave me a job. This interview opened a new chapter in my career.
Ken Court, the Art Director, who insisted I applied for the position of Set Decorator on the feature film Agatha.
Shirley Russell was the Production Designer and Simon Holland her Art Director who gave an unknown the chance to work on that important BBC/Warner Bros production.
Sandra Marsh, my friend and agent, guided my film career in England and America.
Diana White who, having read one of my manuscripts, recommended me indirectly to -
Fiona Spencer Thomas, who became my agent and friend.

Chapter One

To the eye of a newcomer, the arid scrub and sparsely wooded valley belonging to the Navajo reservation in New Mexico would have seemed an uncharitable place to live, being hemmed in on either side by the sheer walls of a canyon. Alongside the north face of the canyon, separating the reservation from a narrow strip of road linking the settlement of Fort Laverne with the larger town of Santa Rowena, was a fast-flowing river. Each spring, when the snows melted, the Rio Via tended to flood, submerging the road and preventing any movement either in or out of Fort Laverne.

The Navajos had been allocated their seemingly useless parcel of land in 1895, but in 1902 the isolated settlement of Fort Laverne underwent a rebuilding programme to include an extension of the railroad from Santa Rowena into their town. This stretch of railroad was expected to run through the reservation. When negotiations between the railroad company, the government, and the Navajo elders broke down, the proposed railroad was never built, and the rebuilding work in Fort Laverne ground to a halt.

By the year of 1953, Fort Laverne was little more than a ghost town with a poorly attended church, a meagerly stocked General Store, a Methodist school, and an ever-thinning population.

The General Store was located at the edge of town. It was here that Jake Velasquez was loading up the few items he could afford for the arduous journey ahead. Aged twenty-five, Jake was tall and lean. His clothes, although clean, were threadbare. Pulled down on his head was an old felt hat that was possibly the same age as he was but the most extraordinary thing about him that morning were the freshly applied Navajo symbols across his face, which were made even more incongruous, given his need to wear spectacles.

Before Jake cranked up the engine on the old truck, he took a long hard look along the deserted street he had known all of his life, a street that he never wanted to see again, but even more so was the crumbling masonry of the loathsome hotel that had once been his home, a sight which made him determined to unearth whatever unpleasant secrets his father had kept hidden for so many years.

Back in 1928, there had been two run-down bars in the town; the less frequented of these had been located on the ground floor of the Grand Hotel. Over the years the unfinished construction had gradually fallen into a state of disrepair. The occupants of the dilapidated first-floor apartment were Ivan and Louise Velasquez, and their only son Jake, a scrawny pale skinned boy with poor eyesight and a shock of unruly fair hair.

Jake's father, Ivan Velasquez was a morose man of low intelligence, trapped in a bad marriage to a selfish and vindictive woman who had shown him even less consideration than she had for their son who, ironically, was the only subject on which they were compatible in their mutual dislike of him. She had never offered the boy any affection and had barely acknowledged his existence.

A few miles north of the town was the ranch owned by Doctor Maxwell from California, who attended Jake's ailing, mean-spirited mother until the day she died.

Louisa Velasquez had become bedridden when Jake was seven years old. There were no neighbours to help, and because of his father's unwillingness to do anything, being fully occupied behind the bar of his failing business, Jake was taken out of school to help out, and he never returned.

He'd never known why his parents were always so secretive about the registered mail that arrived each month, after which there was always more food on the table for a while. It also allowed his father to spend more time in the bar attending to his regulars.

As he grew older Jake began to question why his parents' vicious arguments, inexplicably, were directed towards him. And why they gave no explanation for the headstone, tucked away in a neglected area of their adjoining paddock, with its simple inscription:

J Velasquez
September 1928
Age three weeks
An irreplaceable loss

Whenever he questioned his mother, she became hysterical, wailing and shrieking for him to get out, hysteria which brought his father into the room in a futile attempt to pacify the frantic woman. When Jake repeated his query, he got a severe thrashing. The only conclusion he could reach was that, as he had been born in the same month and year, he was the survivor of twins.

On that occasion, because Jake was in agony with an excruciating pain in his shoulder, his father reluctantly drove him to Doctor Maxwell's ranch.

When the old truck spluttered through the entrance, an athletic young man, repairing one of the large gates, narrowly avoided being hit by Ivan's erratic driving. Although the truck missed Dr Maxwell's companion by a matter of inches, Gilbert's stepladders and tools were not so lucky.

"Pa, you could have killed him," Jake yelled, momentarily forgetting his own pain. Hearing this, Ivan Velasquez had roared with laughter as the old truck crunched over the wooden stepladders beneath.

"D' you think anybody except Maxwell would have missed that dummy if I had?" he'd snarled, slamming down hard on the squealing brakes until the truck stopped inches away from the wall.

The house was built in the style of a Spanish hacienda. This had a grand fountain in the central courtyard, surrounded by a cloistered walkway. Each room had been beautifully furnished from the doctor's previous home in California.

"What's brought you here at this ungodly hour, Ivan?" the doctor had asked, allowing them inside.

"It's the boy again," he'd said, pushing Jake forward.

"What seems to be the trouble this time, young fellow?" he'd asked.

"He fell off the pickup," Ivan cut in sharply. "It's his shoulder, doc. It makes him cry. He never does much of that."

"Then it's as well that you brought him along when you did," Doctor Maxwell said. Yanking on the shoulder, he clicked it back into place. "He must have fallen badly to do this?" he said, angling the lamp into the child's face. "So what can you tell me about this bruising? This couldn't have happened at the same time?"

"He took a bad tumble down the stairs; he's always doin' stuff like that. That's the sort of kid he is, larkin' about where there ain't no need. I can't be watching him all the time, doc. Not a wild sod like this, with Louisa being so demanding. I can't be in two places at the same time."

"And how is Louisa?"

"Not much change there, doc. Still as sickly and bad-tempered as ever," he said, his clothes reeking of stale sweat and cheap perfume.

"The boy is undernourished," the doctor commented, accompanying them out.

"Things are a bit tight, doc. This brat has to make the best of it, like me and the missus."

"He needs feeding properly. See to it, Ivan."

"The thing is, doc, I'm a bit low on cash."

Jake recognised the underlying threat in his father's voice, and was surprised when the doctor handed over a wad of dollar bills.

"Don't think you can try this nonsense with me again, Ivan. That's all the cash you're getting away with this month."

"Very kind of you, Doc," he answered smugly.

Breaking the silence on the way home, Jake asked why Gilbert hadn't mentioned the incident at the gates.

"He can't talk that's why. He's as dumb as a mule."

Over the years, Jake never understood why his mother put up with a self-opinionated brute like his father. Often, during their volatile arguments, she threatened to reveal some unpalatable event to the authorities, which inevitably ended with his father leaving in a rage.

Louise Velasquez died when Jake was eight years old. After that, the responsibility of looking after one ailing parent passed to the other, since his father never could, nor would do anything around the house. After a night's heavy drinking he was barely able to get himself dressed, and so the task fell to his son to do everything.

On the times when his father was incapable of driving the truck, Jake used an old pram to collect anything his father wanted from the General Store, located at the far end of Main Street.

On the day Jake ran the gauntlet between two gangs of boys pelting each other with rubbish. Ignoring the jeers and comments about his drunken father, his temper snapped when a stone cut into his temple and knocked off his glasses. With blood streaming into his eyes, and barely able to see, Jake charged into the boys with fists flailing.

When the boys scattered, Jake assumed that he'd beaten them off, but only until Gilbert knelt against him and wiped the blood from his face. Saying nothing, he bound up the cracked arm on the glasses with a piece of string and drove Jake back to the hotel. That evening Doctor Maxwell called to arrange for Gilbert to pick Jake up in his truck once a week in order to collect any supplies.

Because of Jake's missed education, and the timely intervention of Doctor Maxwell, Ivan Velasquez allowed his son to attend a school on the nearby Navajo reservation over the next four years. It was a period that changed his young life forever.

"Can the boy ride a bicycle?" Doctor Maxwell had asked Ivan.

"Sure, though he's better astride a horse, but we ain't got one of those either. What's your point, doc?"

"Well, I've been thinking, the reservation school is too far for the boy to walk there and back each day."

"Well, I ain't forking out any cash for a bike, if that's what you're after."

"Far from it; Gilbert found an old one at the ranch. All it needs is a couple of tyres and a replacement chain, to make it as good as new."

"Well, I ain't forkin' out fer any of them either. Let the kid walk. The exercise will do him good."

"These items won't cost you a cent. It's all taken care of. Gilbert will collect everything from Santa Rowena. Until then, I suggest you allow him to run the boy to and from the reservation." It was an offer Ivan Velasquez could hardly refuse.

Jake remembered his delight when Gilbert had delivered the bicycle a few days later, oiled and ready to ride, once the seat and handlebars had been lowered. He got Jake to help tighten up the chain.

"This is going to be absolutely brilliant, Gil. I would never have left this behind." It was an enthusiastic comment, causing Gilbert to give a rare smile as Jake examined the initials scratched into the crossbar." Was J.M. who this belonged to?" Not expecting an answer, Jake knew instantly, by the way Gilbert turned sharply away from him with a shrug of the shoulders, that he knew a lot more than he was willing to admit.

The reservation school was a crumbling adobe building, where lessons were given by Tyn Louf. The building was incorporated into the Mission clinic, which was open for surgery every Thursday afternoon by Doctor Maxwell.

Jake's rough initiation into the classroom began even before the dust had settled on the doctor's departing vehicle after dropping him off. Cornered by four older boys, Jake fought them off until Cloud Bird, the chief's son, appeared at his side and the fight came to an abrupt end.

Okuwa Tsire (Cloud Bird) was three years older than Jake. He was the only son of Chief Oglala (American Horse). After his rescue, the boys became inseparable friends.

It was Cloud Bird who taught Jake to ride bareback and track any living creature with stealth and cunning. He helped him overcome his fear of heights by teaching him the skill of diving into a shallow rock pool. For the first time in his young life Jake felt safe and wanted, treasuring every moment he could spend with his Navajo companion. The only irritant was Cloud Bird's six-year-old sister, Moon Spirit, who insisted on tagging along whenever she could. Although she couldn't run as fast as Jake, infuriatingly, she was able to ride any horse better than he ever could.

By the end of Jake's first year on the reservation, an inseparable bond had developed between the two boys, despite their differences: where Jake was a small and skinny nine-year-old, at twelve, Cloud Bird was maturing with the physique of his warrior ancestors.

By this time, Moon Spirit was seven years old, and just as irritating with her competitive challenges. In Jake's opinion, she was the wildest creature he could imagine. On numerous occasions, challenging him to a race, and although he could now ride a horse bareback as well as any of the boys on the reservation, invariably she would win.

At sunset on the night of Cloud Bird's thirteenth birthday, the boys climbed up to the sacred burial ground, where they sat cross-legged on a flat rock, stripped of their clothing. Only Moon Spirit witnessed old Nykodema, the medicine man, initiate Jake with the ceremonial name of Pale Horse, from his darkening blond hair. He then performed the ritual of brotherhood on the two boys: first cutting and then binding their wrists together in front of a blazing fire. At dawn when he cut the bindings, Moon Spirit was fast asleep.

"Shall we wake her?" Jake asked.

"That would be impossible now."

"We can't leave her here, Okuwa?" Jake said, using the tribal name of his friend.

"I can carry her most of the way if you steady me."

"Then we shall carry her between us... brother," Jake said, smiling happily.

They lifted the sleeping girl against his shoulder, and together they carried her home, where they were greeted by their mother, Gia. They lived in a larger adobe building, built into the side of the cliff, slightly apart from the others. Unlike the other utility vehicles on the reservation, parked outside was a Model T Ford, seldom used, given the chief's traditional preference for horses. Because of Cloud Bird's importance within the tribal community, Jake had never been allowed inside the chief's home until that morning.

"My father says you are most welcome in his house, Pale Horse, for you are now my brother."

Given his close friendship with Cloud Bird, except for Gilbert, Doctor Maxwell and the store owner, Jake was shunned by the rest of the white community around the reservation. Inevitably there was relentless abuse from his father, but despite this, Jake refused to end his friendship with Cloud Bird, and the boys' closeness continued to flourish over the years.

When Jake was eleven years old, Ivan Velasquez took up with Marsha Freeman, a widow from Santa Rowena. Jake had refused to live with them, choosing instead to stay in the run-down apartment. From then on, Jake saw his father for a few days in each month when he collected the postal delivery from California.

In his absence, Gilbert would call by to clean the carburettor's filter, check the oil, and change the sparking plugs. Although it was never stated between them, Jake guessed he only did this out of his consideration for his safety.

"When I'm ready, Gil, will you show me how to get Pa's truck started when the engine conks out? I've seen you get it running when no one else could." It was a suggestion that made the silent young man smile.

His father had been gone for three weeks when the first incident happened. Jake had been riding alone when Moon Spirit's pony galloped past without a rider. He found her near the burial ground, unconscious, beside a battered snake, a bloodied stick clenched in her hand. In his haste to protect her from a second attacking snake, Jake trod on his spectacles, but still he killed it. Quickly, he made a cut on the snakebite the way her brother had taught him, and sucked out what venom he could.

With a Herculean effort Jake got the unconscious girl onto his horse, struggling to maintain control of the skittish animal up the narrow mountain path to old Nykodema's cave. He was crumpling to his knees with exhaustion when the medicine man appeared and lifted her down from the horse.

In the small hours of the morning her condition worsened,

threshing wildly as a fever raged. Unable to do anything, Jake feared she was about to die. He left Moon Spirit with the medicine man and scrambled down the rock to where he'd abandoned his horse, only to find it gone.

There was a considerable distance between the burial ground and the chief's home. It was almost impossible to run in pitch darkness, and without his spectacles. Somehow, he covered the distance in good time, returning with Cloud Bird and Gia.

As Gia was employed as housekeeper to Doctor Maxwell, he offered to attend to Moon Spirit's injuries, but the chief courteously refused the offer. For a week, it was impossible to predict whether or not she would pull through and survive. As Moon Spirit was the daughter of the chief, it seemed to Jake that the medicine man was obsessed, chanting ancient rites as he cast a set of bones onto the ground, studying the shape in which they fell. He then cast them onto the girl's stomach, where, strangely, they fell in the same formation as they had upon the ground. Chanting and wailing constantly up to the heavens, the old man then lit tiny fires mounted on stones, each stone set carefully on crossed eagle feathers.

To most of the Navajo, old Nykodema was thought to be involved in the black arts, more of a warlock than a medicine man, and someone to be avoided, except when contact was deemed absolutely necessary. Seeing him make a poultice of crushed insects, herbs and dung, Jake could understand their reasoning.

Nykodema applied and reapplied the stinking pads of goo. To have moved her in that condition would have been fatal. Throughout, both of the boys remained with her in the cave, and never once did either one of them look away from her.

"It is spoken of in tribal legend that if someone you love unconditionally dies, their spirit can be returned through a ritual of fire," Cloud Bird told Jake.

"She won't die, will she? She can't. Moon Spirit's too strong."

"If she does, I swear by my ancestors, I will try and bring her back."

"Could you do that?"

"I would try. She is part of me, just as you are, Pale Horse."

"But if you did this, how would she know it was you calling her back?"

"Through chants telling secret things only the two of us would know."

"And you really believe her spirit would come back?" Jake asked in awe.

"Yes, I do, but only if there was a purpose on earth in need of her spiritual return; if so, the ritual is said to open a gateway."

"But what if the chants didn't work, what then?"

"Then I would die like many others before me," Cloud Bird answered simply.

"You should tell me everything you know about this ritual," Jake insisted. "I am your brother now. I should know about these things."

"If that's what you want brother, I will."

On the night Moon Spirit recovered, Jake got a black eye and a bruised throat from his outraged father because he wasn't at the apartment when he'd returned unexpectedly. But Jake would willingly have taken that beating many times over to see the faint smile of recognition when he returned to the cave. Though now little more than a shell of her former self, Moon Spirit was on the mend.

"Thank you, Pale Horse. I will never forget what you did," she said, falling asleep in Cloud Bird's arms.

"I prayed Nykodema's telling of the bones had to be right." Cloud Bird said.

"What did they say?"

"At her birth the bones formed a ceremonial triangle. This foretold Moon Spirit was born for a spiritual purpose. She has an important destiny on earth. I believe we are here to support her in whatever this is, Pale Horse."

"If you are with me, I will do anything you ask," Jake said.

In the late spring of the following year, the swollen Rio Via burst its banks, and the strength of their bond was cemented. The boys had arranged to meet in the cave at Shadow Rock, a hideaway they used in bad weather. Cloud Bird had been unusually preoccupied for days and had taken to wearing a feathered armlet. Below this were inked symbols, marked from

bicep to wrist.

"Are you going to tell me what these are?" Jake asked.

"It's nothing for you to worry about."

"Then tell me. We don't keep secrets from each other."

"They are protection. It was Nykodema's decision after he interpreted my dream."

"What kind of a dream?"

"I was flying above Shadow Rock and saw an omen predicting my death."

"A dream can't be an omen. It wasn't real."

"It is if what I dreamt is really there. I saw it clearly the next day." Cloud Bird said with conviction. "If I wear this for seven days and nights, it will protect me from evil."

"You can't die. I won't let you go anywhere without me," Jake exclaimed, bringing the glimmer of a smile to Cloud Bird's troubled features.

"We can't alter our destiny. I saw a formation of rock in the shape of an eagle on the cliffs above the river. It wasn't there before. That's why I went to Nykodema."

"Well, if I get rid of that eagle rock you can't be harmed, can you?" Jake said, leaping to his feet.

"Where are you going?" Cloud Bird called after him, but Jake was already making his way towards the heights of Shadow Rock through the driving rain.

Ignoring Cloud Bird's warning of danger, Jake edged his way across the slippery surface until he reached the loose section of rock, which he could see even from his restricted vantage point, formed the shape of an eagle. Braced against the cliff, Jake pushed against it with his feet.

"Come back, you idiot, before you fall into the river and drown. You can't change fate. Come back, please. Do it for me, Pale Horse.

Nothing good will come from this."

"It will if I can save your life."

"I wouldn't want that, not if you lost your own. Listen to reason and come back."

"Not until I get rid of this." Jake could barely see through his glasses in the driving rain. With some difficulty, he passed them to Cloud Bird's outstretched hand, instead of taking hold. Unable to see properly without his glasses, Jake slipped badly, missed his footing, and plunged into the raging torrent beneath.

Struggling against the undertow, he felt Cloud Bird's strong arm grab hold of him and haul him to the surface. Barely conscious, he had no recollection of how he'd been dragged from the river, or how his companion had carried him back to the cave.

Stripped of his clothing Jake was wrapped in a blanket but, even after Cloud Bird lit a fire, he couldn't stop shivering. Over recent months there had been a noticeable maturing of his body. Embarrassed, Jake pulled the blanket around him, but even so, he was unable to stop the shaking.

"You're frozen, Pale Horse. You must get warm," Cloud Bird said. Within moments he'd removed his own sodden clothing and wrapped the blanket tightly around them both. "You are truly brave, my brother, risking your life to save mine."

"I would do anything to save you, you know that," Jake said, warming through from their bodily contact which, although comforting, was distractingly intimate. "I meant to ask, what happened to my glasses?" he asked, not really caring where they were, but needing to concentrate on something else.

"They're probably where I dropped them when you slipped," Cloud Bird said tentatively. Only the sound of rain slashing against the rock outside the cave cut into the following silence. For a teenager who was seemingly in control of any situation, Cloud Bird appeared to be less than confident. "You won't forget me, Pale Horse, if the omen is true?"

"How could I? You are a part of me; you always will be."

"As you are a part of me too." Cloud Bird enfolded his arms about him tightly. Neither of them noticed that Cloud Bird's armlet was missing, or that many of the protective, inked symbols had blended into each other.

"Are you troubled by what happened?" Cloud Bird asked the following morning.

"Was it wrong what we did?"

"No. How could you think that? You and I are two halves. Together we make a whole. Without one, the other would be a half of nothing."

"I never thanked you for saving my life," Jake said, getting into his dry clothes.

Already dressed, Cloud Bird examined the only clear symbol on his arm. "It was something I had to do," he said, re-examining the smudged design. "I can't make any sense of this symbol, can you?"

"I'm not sure... they look like a bird's wings."

"If they belong to an eagle, that means you are meant to save my life too."

"See – Nykodema was wrong. If I don't save you, you can't die."

"That old man is never wrong," Cloud Bird said. "None of this makes any sense."

It was to be a week later before Jake faced the tragic end to Cloud Bird's life.

It happened when Cloud Bird was sent by the elders of the tribe to the County Offices, in Santa Rowena. Outside he was set upon by a gang of white youths who beat him relentlessly, leaving him unconscious.

Jake knew something was wrong when Cloud Bird didn't meet him at the cave as they had previously arranged. He waited for an hour before he went to his home, where Gilbert and Doctor Maxwell were about to set off in the pickup.

"You must prepare yourself for the worst, Jake. Cloud Bird has taken a severe beating. The boy is in a coma. There is nothing I can do for him. It is now in God's hands."

"But you're a doctor. You've got to make him better. You must."

"I can't do anything. No one can. The boy needs specialist care. I'm a country doctor."

"Then, please, take him to the hospital, where someone can help him."

"You know that's impossible. He's Navajo. Be thankful he wasn't left bleeding to death in the street. There is still a chance he might recover at home."

Jake spent the night at Cloud Bird's bedside but saw no improvement. Reluctantly, he left at midday, to find Gilbert waiting in the truck, where he'd been all night, looking as if he hadn't slept either. Without being asked, he drove Jake home.

When Jake entered the apartment he could smell his father's stale sweat even before he saw him sprawled in a chair with an empty whiskey bottle.

"Where have you been you little bastard?" Ivan bellowed, struggling to sit up.

"Cloud Bird's been injured."

"And that's your bloody excuse, is it? I've told you not to mix with that scum."

"I couldn't get away any sooner," Jake said. There was no reasoning with his father in that frame of mind.

"Well not soon enough. Where the hell is my dinner? You've got ten minutes to get me something hot before I take a strap to that scrawny hide. And don't get any ideas about goin' back to the reservation again. From now on, I want you here where I can see you."

"Well I'm going anyway. Like it or not," Jake said, squaring up to the menacingly bunched up fists, protecting his head until the blows eventually stopped.

Locked in his room, Jake treated a split lip with witch hazel and dabbed more on a half-closed eye. There was nothing he could do for the cracked lens in his glasses, which had taken the full force of Ivan's fists. Thankfully he could still see through them. Later, Jake climbed out of the window and slid down the hostelry roof.

On foot, it took almost two hours to reach Cloud Bird's home.

When he arrived, Gilbert was already waiting outside for Doctor Maxwell in the pickup.

I'll come back at midnight and run you home, Gilbert wrote in the notebook. It was an offer Jake gladly accepted.

Cloud Bird did not die immediately. He clung onto life for three months, lost in a deep coma. Through all of this time he was never alone, being attended by his parents, his sister, or Jake, who was with him at the moment of his death. Cloud Bird was fourteen years old.

Throughout this period, Gilbert insisted on driving Jake to and from the invalid's home every day without arousing Ivan's suspicions. When it became apparent that Cloud Bird would not recover, and his parents wanted time alone with him, Gilbert would drive Jake to the ranch, where he would let him help in the stables.

Even though working with horses eased some of Jake's distress, when Cloud Bird died, he wanted to end his own life. Aware, of this, Gilbert devised a scheme for keeping a watchful eye on the distraught teenager.

After the burial, Jake was employed at the Maxwell ranch with an unexpected arrival of horses for breeding stock.

One afternoon, he opened up the one-sided conversation by asking: "Will you teach me to drive, Gil?"

When you are older, Gilbert wrote in his notebook; a useful habit which Jake later adopted for his own use.

Although Gilbert barely set foot outside of the property except at night, he drove the doctor to emergency calls if the older man had been drinking in the evenings. He never got lost in the surrounding wilderness of tracks, a remarkable achievement even for a local driver, and yet Gilbert, a stranger to Fort Laverne, managed to arrive easily to any address. Like Doctor Maxwell, Gilbert had also relocated from California. When he first arrived at the hacienda in 1930, he was driving the old pickup which Jake's father later acquired.

Even though Jake never heard Gilbert speak during the years he worked at the ranch, he doubted if the man was completely mute. Gilbert was the only name that he was ever known by, and Doctor Maxwell never revealed if that was his Christian name or his surname. He was above average height, with a swimmer's physique. Occasionally, when he grew tired of wearing a beard, he would appear clean-shaven for a few days. It gave him the square-jawed appearance of a comic strip hero, which suited him very well. However, this never lasted very long before the stubble was allowed to grow back again.

Regardless of his apparent inability to speak, Gilbert's influence was always at the helm of any decision-making at the ranch. It was he who insisted that Jake should be hired as a ranch hand, to break in the colts, given his Navajo-like affinity with wild horses. At the age of eleven, he had proved to be an excellent horseman.

During these years, Jake could not remember either of the two men having any friends amongst the local community. No one ever visited them from California. It was as though a barrier had been drawn down behind their past lives.

Apart from Jake and Gia, everyone else employed at the ranch was from out of town. Carla, the maid, and her husband, José, were from Mexico. Lee Wong, the Chinese cook, came from San Francisco. Alongside Jake, there were two other ranch hands: mixed-race drifters from Santa Fe.

At the age of twelve, Jake still needed to wear spectacles, and the prospect of ever seeing without them was no longer a possibility. He was as thin as a Navajo lance, all arms and legs beneath a wild thatch of darkening blond hair.

The last time he had seen Moon Spirit at the reservation she had been a feisty nine-year-old and fully recovered from the snake attack. Although clumsy and boyish when competing with him, her wafer-thin body altered like magic the moment she mounted a horse. It made him breathless to watch her transformation into a superb rider, exactly like her brother, for whom he still grieved deeply.

Moon Spirit had been a quick learner under the schoolmaster, Tyn Louf: "Tin Roof", as she nicknamed him. By the time she had reached the age of ten, the schoolmaster could teach her little more. Therefore, Doctor Maxwell used his influence with the education committee in Santa Rowena to secure her a place at the teacher training college in Flatley, San Marco, where, even at her age, she would continue with her studies, and eventually train for a position as a resident teacher on the Fort Laverne reservation.

After Cloud Bird's death Jake seldom went onto the reservation, and he saw nothing of Chief Oglala. Once, however, because of a nagging pain from the brotherhood scar, which had kept him awake all night, Jake went to the cave at Shadow Rock, where he thought this might ease the pain, and perhaps, make contact with Cloud Bird. It was a reassuring and welcoming space where Cloud Bird had shared everything he'd known about the "Sacred Ritual of Fire".

Jake was meditating near the entrance, barely moving in a supreme effort to make spiritual contact with Cloud Bird when the silhouette of the old medicine man momentarily blocked out the sun, bringing Jake back to his senses. "How did you know I would be here?" he asked.

"This is not your time." Nykodema squatted in front of him and removed a leather pouch from his belt. Pressing the pouch against Jake's forehead, he began chanting. Emptying out the contents between them, he studied the position they had fallen. "You cannot do this, Pale Horse."

"I don't understand why not. Is it because I'm white?"

Nykodema took hold of Jake's wrist, turning his arm to display the inflamed brotherhood scar. "You can, but not yet."

"Then when will it be my time?"

"The passage will not open until you become a man. If Cloud Bird is woken before his
time, and your body is not fully receptive, then his spirit will be lost for eternity."

"But how will I know when that time will be?"

Nykodema pressed his fingers against the brotherhood scar. "You will know your time has come when this old wound bleeds."

"But an old scar can't bleed, can it?"

"It will, but only when the passage is preparing to open. Pale Horse and Cloud Bird are one. When you call, your bond will call him back."

No longer having Cloud Bird to inspire him, Jake's love and admiration transferred to Gilbert, who became a surrogate father-figure in an otherwise bleak existence. It was during this period that Gilbert taught Jake to drive. He also gave him instructions on how to treat the temperamental engine, writing the information into the notebook on how long to let the engine cool before firing it up again, and how to make any simple repairs.

Because of Ivan Velasquez's lengthening sessions of drinking, his bouts of depression, and spates of bad temper, his attraction to women lessened considerably —-except for one who was overweight and mean-spirited; she also had a passion for alcohol equal to his own, and, an unhealthy interest in teenage boys. Her stay at the Velasquez apartment was cut short when she awoke Jake's father while trying to force entry into Jake's barricaded room.

Banned from taking the truck in case Ivan needed it for himself, Jake would ride to work at the Maxwell ranch on a horse Gilbert had loaned him.

He was now working there full time. When the other ranch hands and staff were being fed by the Chinese cook, Jake ate separately in the hacienda kitchen.

"I don't know how you make food like this, Gia," Jake commented one time as he cleared every scrap from his plate of baked chicken. "That was really tasty."

"Massa Gilbert, he make for you."

"What? Gilbert cooked this, for me?"

"He wants you to grow strong. Like Cloud Bird."

"No one could be like him, Gia," Jake said ruefully. "I'll always be thin and weedy."

By the end of the first year working for Doctor Maxwell, Jake had the appetite of a horse and suffered fewer headaches and dizzy spells. Also, Doctor Maxwell had arranged new spectacles.

Even though he laboured long and hard in the stables, there was little alteration to his lanky physique; instead, he just grew taller –all knees and elbows. The other work hands would laugh at him. As Jake matured, his mop of bright unruly hair darkened rapidly. What troubled him a great deal was that his voice remained high-pitched until, to his immense relief, it deepened soon after his thirteenth birthday.

Whenever he was in Gilbert's company, Jake would chatter endlessly, never expecting an answer, content to make do with a shrug or a faint smile. Gilbert was in perfect shape due, in part, to his habit of swimming countless lengths in the pool at the end of each working day. Sometimes he helped with the manual labour but usually insisted on working alone, communicating with the other men through a series of hand and head gestures.

Over the next year, Jake split his time between the Maxwell ranch, and spending grimmer times with his father in the dilapidated hotel, now rotting about their ears.

Working at the ranch, Jake was allowed into Doctor Maxwell's book room, where there was a fine selection of periodicals devoted to the motion picture industry which he read avidly, absorbing every piece of information about making movies. He returned to the room frequently.

"You spend a lot of time in the book room, Jake. What is it you find so interesting?" Doctor Maxwell asked him one time.

"It's interesting to learn how motion pictures are made. Why do you have so many books on the subject?"

"Probably because I, like most people from California, find it a fascinating subject. Many people from Los Angeles are connected to moviemaking in one way or another," Doctor Maxwell answered.

"But why would a doctor have more books on movies than on medicine? Did you work at one of the studios when you lived in California?"

"Certainly not; what possible interest would a man of the medical profession have in such a transient occupation?" he said, ending the conversation just a bit too abruptly, to stop Jake's curiosity on the subject.

Occasionally, because the nearest cinema to the ranch was in Santa

Rowena, sixty-five miles away, Doctor Maxwell would arrange for a film to be shown at the hacienda for Jake and the two other ranch hands. After Gilbert loaded a reel of film into an old movie projector, this would be screened onto a taut sheet stretched over the fireplace. For these events, Gia would never sit with them, but watched through the kitchen doorway.

For a man of medicine, Doctor Maxwell had a surprising collection of movie reels, all silent and shot in black-and-white. While most were entertaining, the one that Jake found most interesting was one with the title *Napoleon* that had been filmed in 1927; parts of it had been shot in France, at the Palace of Versailles.

Initially, the projector was skilfully operated by Gilbert. When, on numerous occasions, the brittle celluloid snapped, he would repair the break with swift efficiency. This would inevitably be followed by Jake asking "Can I have a go next time, Gil?" Each time Gilbert refused, until one evening he allowed Jake to try his hand at repairing a scrapped section of film.

Whenever time permitted, Gilbert would show him how to edit out a faulty or damaged section of the film, and most importantly, how to make an almost invisible repair.

One evening, when everything was prepared for another picture show, Doctor Maxwell was called out on an emergency, and Gilbert needed to drive him. At Gilbert's suggestion, Jake took over the operating of the projector and showed the film before they returned.

"You are a natural at this, Jake. You might think about taking this up for a profession, if ever you decide to move away to Santa Rowena," Doctor Maxwell had said on his return; thereafter, Jake was allowed to operate the projector every time. When the celluloid film snapped, and Gilbert wasn't around, Jake strived to make the repairs as close to perfect as he'd been taught. Along with his editing skills, he learnt how to collate each one methodically, using a useful cross referral system devised by Gilbert.

One day, when Jake had returned to the hacienda unexpectedly, he'd heard the high-pitched voice of a young person in conversation with Doctor Maxwell. The voices were heavily muffled by the door so he had no idea what was exchanged between them, but it sounded important. He was debating whether to go in when Doctor Maxwell raised his voice in anger. It made Jake pause at the library door as he turned the handle; the door was now slightly ajar. Although the last thing on his mind was to eavesdrop on the confrontation going on inside, he had no alternative but to wait.

"There is absolutely nothing to get so bloody worked up about. I have no idea why this seems all wrong to you. It's a fact of the reproductive system that throwbacks do happen on occasion. It probably happens more so out here in this interbred community than anywhere else in this county."

Although Doctor Maxwell was angry, what he was saying didn't quite ring true to Jake and, because there was no response, possibly the other person was also unconvinced.

Given that the exchange between them didn't continue, Jake waited a few moments and then rapped on the door. As he entered the room, the opposite door slammed shut. Doctor Maxwell was alone with an empty film canister in his hand. Beside him, yards of crumpled film had been unwound and rammed into a waste bin.

"An unfortunate accident," Doctor Maxwell said. He was clearly angry, but also upset, fingering sections of the crushed celluloid film with care. "What did you want here, boy?"

"I came to return this," Jake said, handing him a repaired reel.

"Well done, Jake," the doctor said, examining the marked section of the repair. "You're wasted out here with such a talent," he said, inspecting the neat repairs.

Jake pointed to the film in the waste bin. "Shall I take this away and edit the damaged sections out?"

"Perhaps not, not this time, Jake. Just take it away and burn it: every inch. Make sure it all goes," he said, attempting to conceal the lid of the film canister, but not before Jake read: *The Devil of Fontainebleau* scrawled on the label. He made no mention of who he'd been speaking to.

Wisely or not, Jake kept a few undamaged lengths of the film, which he hid away in a battered tin trunk under his bed, intending to go through the sections when he had time, but with his own fairly intense workload it soon went out of his mind, and he forgot all about it.

It was Jake's fourteenth birthday when the disruptive letter arrived for his father. He caught only a glimpse of the registered envelope before Ivan went into the study in a rage. This disastrous information sent his father on a drunken bender for an entire week. After that, the long drinking sessions happened more frequently, and the registered mail stopped arriving.

By the age of fifteen, although Jake had put on some weight, he was late developing into the well-built young man he would eventually become. Still of medium height, he despaired of ever getting taller. The only noticeable change was that his now dark hair needed control to straighten out the waves. His features were still thin and boyish, but nevertheless, he caused heads to turn on those rare occasions when he was sent into Santa Rowena in the old pickup. Even his spectacles didn't stop folk from staring, which he found irritating.

It was something Gilbert also did on rare occasions. It was after one of these incidents that he caught Dr Maxwell off guard by asking: "Why does Gilbert stare at me the way he does. Have I done something to annoy him? "The question took the elderly man by surprise.

"An actor will always weigh up the competition. It's the way they are. It could be that when you have fully matured, you will be quite photogenic," the doctor responded absently.

"It isn't like Gilbert is looking at me, but as if he was trying to peer into me, if that makes any sense."

"None at all, boy" the doctor replied, failing in his attempt to appear jovial. "It's probably because, apart from me, you are the only man here who shows Gilbert any respect. You don't think of him as a freak because he doesn't speak to anyone?"

"Of course I don't." Jake answered indignantly.

"Well then, that answers your question," he said, expecting to have brought the conversation to an end.

"Not completely. What did you mean by implying that Gilbert was an actor?"

"I don't remember saying that?"

"You said Gilbert could have been looking at me as competition," Jake said, needing to know more, and what accident had rendered him mute. "Where did he perform?"

"I honestly can't remember. It was so many years ago," he blustered.

It was so out of character that Jake knew he was lying. But even though he was cornered, the doctor wasn't prepared to say more.

"But sir, there must be another explanation of why Gil studies me. He probably knows me better than anyone else. It doesn't make sense that he would consider me as competition in anything."

"Perhaps it's because you have a lot more going for you than any of the other young men in this town. You should consider yourself flattered, Jake. Gilbert generally pays no attention to anyone else. However, if you dislike being noticed so much you would be well-advised to grow a beard."

"A Navajo wouldn't grow a beard," Jake exclaimed indignantly.

"I agree, but a Navajo is what you are not. You might ride and act like one, but that doesn't alter the fact you are as white as I am, and no initiation into the blood brotherhood can ever change that. Take my advice and grow that beard if you are unsettled by the attention. You have been blessed with exceptionally good looks so you may as well get used to the admiration. Either that or become a hermit. In a few years, you will probably be much too handsome to go anywhere unnoticed, even out here in this godforsaken dump," he concluded vehemently.

"But sir, I still don't get why Gil would bother about my appearance. There must be more to it than that?"

"You ask too many questions. Hell knows why I ever got talked into giving you a job. We didn't need any help," Doctor Maxwell snapped.

"But sir, I was employed to help out with the new intake of breeding mares."

"The ranch hands are employed to do that."

"But Gil wrote that I was needed here."

"Damn you, boy, do you need to question every damned thing?"

"I'm only asking why the note said that?"

"Well that wasn't the case, even though your contribution has been admirable."

"If you didn't want me here, who asked you to give me work, sir? Was it my pa?"

It was only when Doctor Maxwell turned to face him in anger that Jake realised this man had, for years, avoided looking at him directly with those pale, staring eyes which had the look of a hunted animal –as if Jake was the hunter.

"God damn it, Jake, leave this alone. Consider this subject closed. Understand?"

"Yes Sir."

Given his youth, Jake didn't bother shaving again for some time, but the little fair hair that grew over the next three months did nothing to alter his appearance and so he shaved it off.

Soon after that curious conversation with the doctor, Jake stopped working at the ranch, to look after his father, who relied on Jake for everything. In his rare sober periods, Jake had to stop him from smashing up everything they owned. The unpredictable outbreaks of temper became increasingly difficult, and Jake needed to be on his guard to prevent any attacks against himself.

Looking after his father might have been easier had there been any affection between them, but looking after the raging alcoholic was difficult. Even though he couldn't stand having the man anywhere near him, Jake couldn't justify leaving him on his own as no one else would care for him; he felt morally obligated, which was like a prison sentence.

Because of his father's alcohol dependence, Jake couldn't afford to restock the empty bar as there was no cash available, his father having systematically depleted most of the spirits himself. Jake closed down the bar and boarded it up along with the rest of the ground floor.

Having nothing left of any value in the apartment from which he could raise cash, Jake was at a loss about how the two of them could survive, no longer having a job at the ranch.

All they owned was the battered, run-of-the-mill furniture and fittings, and an old Rolliflex camera which was kept on a dresser shelf, an item that was so out of character, Jake could only assume that the camera had been won over a game of cards. Engraved onto a brass disc riveted onto the body were the words: "Tom Brice, Silver Lake Herald". Having no financial help from his father, Jake used what was left of his earnings from the ranch to survive. Frustratingly, had they been living in Santa Rowena, given his skill of repairing any damaged film stock, Jake was convinced that he could have made a living at the local movie theatre, which was always advertising for staff.

When Doctor Maxwell called by one afternoon to examine his father's condition, Jake was unable to say how much alcohol his father kept stored in the locked back room. Once the doctor understood their dire situation, he offered Jake a modest amount of financial help, to put food on the table, an offer that Jake accepted, having no alternative.

The alteration in Doctor Maxwell was shocking. Hunched, and with nervous fingers, the doctor searched aimlessly through his medical bag for something that was clearly not there. Jake felt it was another ploy to avoid looking at him directly. It was clear from his breath that Doctor Maxwell was drinking heavily.

Although Jake proposed a scheme to repay the loan in full, the doctor refused to accept any repayment. What didn't make any sense to Jake at the time was the old man's expression of gratitude when he had no alternative other than to accept. It was as though the doctor was actually grateful that he was being allowed to help. As if he was seeking forgiveness.

Chapter Two

Six months after the regular payments had begun they ended abruptly when old Doctor Maxwell died from a heart attack. Gilbert wasn't at the funeral service, nor was he at the graveside, but since he never mixed with strangers, Jake thought it was perhaps in some ways understandable.

Jake had problems getting his father out of bed and dressed that morning, and he arrived late for the funeral, out of breath and sweating, having run all the way. Because it was impossible to push his way through the crowd to see anything of the service from the ground floor, Jake made his way up to the chapel gallery, where he found a seat at the front to observe everything through the rails.

There were too many people to gather inside the small Methodist chapel, all of whom Jake recognised, except for two strangers who looked glaringly out of place, wearing pinstriped suits, grey spats, and patent leather shoes. The taller of the men had sleeked back, greased hair. The other man, who was considerably shorter, had ginger hair that had been carefully combed over a thinning patch.

The two men were much better dressed than anyone else in the congregation. Nor were they seemingly interested in the funeral service, never bothering to open a hymn book. All they appeared to be interested in was to scrutinise every face at the funeral gathering; they paid little attention to anything else.

Jake got a closer look at them when they were leaving the graveside. The taller of the two men tripped while readjusting his sunglasses and missed his footing on the running board of their gleaming black Rolls Royce saloon.

"You bloody idiot, Frazer," he shouted, before getting into the back seat alongside his shorter companion. The liveried chauffeur then closed the door and started up the engine, the sound of which was barely audible from the graveyard, and drove away as smoothly as a phantom along the rough dirt road. In virtual silence, the vehicle soon vanished leaving a cloud of brown dust in its wake. When the dust cleared, the luxury vehicle might never have been at the burial at all.

On his way home from the chapel, Jake called at the General Store to get a supply of beef jerky and tobacco for his father, delaying his return by half an hour, as the owner's wife needed Jake to change out three overhead light bulbs and fit a new plug on the floor-standing fan.

By the time Jake returned to the hotel, his father was on the back porch nursing a split lip, two black eyes, and a missing a front tooth.

"Don't say I never did good by yah, Jake, 'cos I played dumb see, and this is all the thanks I got." he growled, spitting out blood and a second broken tooth before draining the remainder of whiskey from the bottle. "If yah ma knew what them guys gone an' done to our mite out back, she'd turn in her grave."

"Who did this to you, Pa?" Jake asked the ox of a man. No one in the right frame of mind would have tackled his father, not even when he was half sober.

"I knew that you'd be a bad 'un the moment I first seen that pasty white face of yours, bawling your eyes out. I said jest as much to the wife, and I've been proved right," he slurred. After spitting out more blood, he took a long swig from a bottle of tequila. After that he barely made any sense at all. "I said you were a dead 'un, but they took a look out back anyway." His father was crying for the first time that Jake could remember. "They smashed it up; them bastards made me watch them break up that headstone. That's all we had to remember him by."

It was some time before Jake could get another sane word out of him; not until his father had drunk every drop of tequila.

"Did they take anything?" he asked, uncertain about whether there would be any sensible response. He was taken completely by surprise at the vicious surge of anger when his father flung the empty bottle through the window, showering fragments of glass everywhere.

"Them bastards might think I'm a piece of crap, but I ain't that. Far from it, 'cos I outsmarted them jerks. They might have got Brice's camera but they couldn't find anything else," he said.

Lurching to his feet, he dragged everything out of a cupboard in the kitchen dresser and grabbed another, half-empty, bottle of whiskey. Trampling everything underfoot, Ivan staggered over to the broken window pane and began weeping uncontrollably. Taking a long swig from the bottle, he stared into the backyard at the smashed granite.

Whenever Jake's father had been drunk or in one of his senseless rages, Jake had been able to stand up to him, but not this. To see him vulnerable and lost gave Jake nothing to offer except pity, and the very thought of offering pity made him sick to the stomach.

Needing to get some air, Jake went outside, where he found the sledgehammer. He sat for a time on the back step trying, without much success, to make sense out of what his father had been saying. After some time, he returned inside and found his father seated on the floor, drinking.

"Where are these men now, Pa?" he asked.

"With luck, they'll be beating Maxwell's pretty boy to a pulp for them pictures, 'cos I ain't got none here. All I got is a useless piece of crap like you," he slurred before he passed out.

With a sense of urgency, Jake drove the old pickup towards the Maxwell ranch. The engine was screaming as if about to explode, but he kept the accelerator pedal forced to the floor, maintaining its top speed of 40 mph. The combination of rigid suspension and narrow gauge tyres bumped the truck with bone-shaking regularity along the rutted dirt road.

A short time before Jake arrived at the ranch, the Rolls Royce had been driven away from the hacienda erratically, accelerating at speed towards the iron gates and colliding against one of the columns. Although this severely damaged the car, the driver didn't stop, regardless of the bumper being dragged underneath the vehicle – a few yards beyond the gate a jagged section of metal punctured the tyre, which immediately went flat. This drastically slowed the vehicle down, but even then, the driver refused to stop, allowing the vehicle to swerve crazily along the dirt road with a flapping, shredded tyre, causing more damage to the wheel rim.

When Jake noticed the dust cloud being thrown up by the vehicle heading towards him, he maintained his own speed, familiar with the width of the road ahead, and also with the width of his truck, knowing that he could pass the oncoming vehicle with room to spare. As it bore down on him, he realised that the driver had little control over the vehicle, and he was forced to steer off the dirt road to avoid a head-on collision.

The windscreen of the Rolls was severely cracked, and one of the chrome headlamps was shattered and dangled loose by the wiring. The driver's door was so badly dented that the fourteen applications of enamelled paintwork were chipped and cracked, exposing the raw metal. Because of the slow speed of the car, Jake was able to see the occupants quite clearly.

The chauffeur wasn't driving. Instead, he was seated in the passenger seat holding a bleeding head. In the back seat, the taller of the two men at the funeral had his head tilted back, a bloodied handkerchief pressed tightly against his nose. His smaller, ginger-haired companion, called Frazer, was driving. He was no longer dapper as he had been at the funeral; instead, his shirt was torn and bloodied. His necktie was pulled chokingly tight against his throat, giving him the appearance of a drunk after a rough night on the town.

When Jake pulled up at the hacienda and raced inside, fearing the worst, the main entrance hall resembled a battle zone. Antique furniture, and a collection of fine porcelain, had been smashed in a frenzied attack. Doctor Maxwell's prized long-case clock lay face down in its partially shattered case having been caught up in the curtains when the pole that held them had been yanked from the windows. But what shocked Jake most were the smashed canisters and trampled reels of celluloid film, damaged in the fury of a frantic search through Gilbert's neatly filed racks of old movies.

With dread, Jake searched amongst the wreckage, fully expecting to find Gilbert's dead body; instead, he appeared through the doorway brandishing a shotgun, and seemed fully prepared to use it. Apart from a torn and bloodied shirt, a nasty cut on his cheek, and bleeding knuckles, Gilbert offered the same dynamic image of a hero of storybook legend, ready and able to do battle.

"Gil, are you alright?" Jake asked instinctively, never expecting any verbal response from the mute.

He was shocked when Gilbert replied. He was obviously dazed from the attack and still recovering from the fierce onslaught by the three men. He spoke in a voice that was so light it could have been Jake's own when he was ten years old. But to hear a child's voice coming from the mouth of a forty-year-old man was devastating.

When Jake looked up, Gilbert was staring back at him, gauging his reaction to hearing his voice.

"It's a bloody shock for you to hear such a ridiculous voice, isn't it?" Gilbert challenged. His back and shoulders were straight and rigid, facing Jake with a proud military bearing; clearly preparing for any ridicule that his weak voice might provoke.

"I'd be lying if I said it didn't take me by surprise, Gil, but it won't put me into a coma," Jake responded more easily than he actually felt, quickly gathering his wits to avoid hurting his champion's feelings, wanting to put Gilbert at ease.

"Eugene was able to deal with the way I spoke, that was his way. But I never could," Gilbert began to explain. "My voice never broke. I could have lived with that, I suppose, but not the ridicule that went with it."

"And so you played mute."

"Can you understand that?" Gilbert said, massaging an aching jaw.

"If you think back, Gil, mine didn't break for a long time, so I do understand what mental suffering that causes," Jake said. He looked around him at the wreckage in the place that he had come to regard as home. "Why would anyone in their right mind do such unspeakable damage here? What on earth were those men after?"

He followed him into the kitchen, where Gilbert took two beers from the fridge.

"The only fragment I have of a past life, and proof of what might have been the beginnings of an alternative career," he said. Uncapping the bottles, he offered one to Jake.

"No thanks, Gil."

"Then you are a wise man, Jake. I should have thought: the last thing I would want for you is to become like Ivan."

Now that Gilbert appeared more relaxed and was talking more easily, there was something Jake needed to clear up.

"If you don't mind me asking, Gil...why do you keep staring at me, like that?"

"Like what?" he asked.

"The way you're doing now. It's...like when you look at me, you want me to be someone else?"

"I'm sorry, Jake, I didn't realise that it showed. It is just that when I see you at certain angles, you remind me a lot of my brother, that's all."

"If you cared for him, Gil, then that makes me happy," Jake said lightly, which caused Gilbert to give him a glimmer of a smile through his swollen mouth.

"You always brighten up my days, Jake, and today is no exception."

"Who were those men, Gil?"

"Crooks, in the pay of an unscrupulous individual I knew many years ago in California. I know exactly why they were sent here today, but what I don't know is how Stanford, that's his name, could know that I have what they want, or why in God's name he wants it."

"Who is Stanford?"

"You don't need to know anything about him, Jake; he's a bad lot. I hope you'll never be tempted to go to California when I'm gone. It isn't a good place for anyone as genuine as you."

"Are you going back, Gil?" he asked, sensing the reply.

"I must, after this. I'm not hiding away any longer. I need to get to the bottom of some unfinished business. I can only do that if I go to California."

"Will you come back?" he asked, but Gilbert shook his head adamantly.

"Apart from you, Gia, and Moon Spirit, in truth, I loathe this place more than you will ever know. I always have."

To learn that Gilbert would be leaving was disastrous news. In that moment he almost begged Gil to take him along but, given that his father was totally reliant on him, there was no choice other than to stay.

Pulling off the dirt road on his way home, Jake sat in the cab for the longest time, unable to imagine any future without Gilbert's guidance; his mind was a jumble of unanswered questions, questions that needed to be asked if Gilbert was returning to California. Jake scribbled them down hastily into his notebook.

A few days after Doctor Maxwell's funeral, Jake was invited back to the hacienda for a meeting with Gilbert. Every trace of the earlier damage had been cleared away, and had it not been for the old clock, which had been carefully glued and bound tightly in position with rope, it would have appeared as though nothing had happened.

When Jake arrived, he found Gilbert in the study, systematically going through masses of files and paperwork. His grazed knuckles were bandaged, making him clumsier than he would have been normally. There was some adhesive tape across a deep cut in his cheek, but that didn't spoil his handsome features. His unfashionably long hair was sleeked back.

"I asked you here, Jake, to inform you of your bequest in Doctor Maxwell's last will." Gilbert angled the desk lamp onto the document before him. "Eugene has instructed that you are under no obligation to reimburse this estate with one cent of what he loaned you." Gilbert smiled warmly. "We were both aware of your high principles, but I have to insist that you accept his generosity exactly the way he requests in this document."

"Sure, but only if you're convinced that's what Doctor Maxwell intended."

"In this copy of his will, he doesn't appear to have made any provision for a cash settlement on you, which surprises me, but once all the legalities have been cleared, I will send you a cheque each month, until you are settled into some regular employment."

There was a terrible sinking feeling in the pit of Jake's stomach as Gilbert spoke. His life as he knew it was coming to an end, and it was impossible to prevent it. Gilbert was equally as headstrong as himself, and Jake knew that when Gil's mind was made up, there was no turning back.

"You've been very kind to me in the past, Gil. It just wouldn't seem right taking money from you as well."

"I don't understand why not? If you were able to accept the cash from Eugene, then why not accept the same from me?"

"I don't know, Gil. I just can't. It wouldn't be right. I had no other choice than to accept Doctor Maxwell's generosity to help out, but I did that only because of his and my pa's insistence."

"I sure wonder how a boy like you ever grew up to be so principled, with that old reprobate for a father."

Referring to the notes in his book Jake asked, "Gil...do you know what connection there was between my pa and Doctor Maxwell?"

"It's odd that you should ask me that. I could so easily have asked you the same question. I always felt there was something left unsaid about that relationship. I could sense it every time Eugene came back after a visit to your pa. Any question I asked about Ivan was always avoided but there had to have been something." He indicated the pile of documents and papers on Doctor Maxwell's desk. "I thought I might unearth a clue amongst those, but nothing has surfaced. Not yet, anyway."

"You will tell me if you do find anything, Gil...however bad it is? I would like to know what secrets my father thinks are best kept hidden."

"I can promise you that, Jake," he said.

Gilbert continued reading. "In accordance with his will, you are to be given the old movie projector and all of the editing equipment. There will also be included some of the black-and-white movies which you have enjoyed showing over the years. However, I shall be taking a few of the talkies in the collection when I leave for California."

"You have talkies?"

Gilbert was barely able to restrain a smile at Jake's reaction. "There are few, but fortunately these were under lock and key in the back room when Stanford's men came looking."

It came as a shock to Jake to learn there was a more up-to-date collection of movies. He noticed the pile of film canisters neatly stacked on a table behind Gilbert in readiness for packing, and wondered why he had not been forthcoming on what the men were after.

"Are those movies what they wanted?"

"Maybe, although I can't be sure. If so, it's definitely not one of these here, but quite possibly another; in the confusion, it's hard to be certain what they were after, unless it was some important photographs they seemed to think your father had left here for safekeeping."

"Pa said they were after some pictures. That's why he sent the men up here. Maybe they're the photographs the intruders meant."

"That could well be the case, except that I don't have any wretched photographs. But if I haven't got them, why would they imagine Ivan would have them if they were so bloody important?" Gilbert seemed oddly relieved.

"Pa did have a reporter's camera, but he never used it, not once."

"It doesn't make sense to me. Ivan is the last person I would expect to be interested in photography. I guess what was on the photographs will have to remain unexplained, at least for now," he said with the glimmer of a smile. "At least we can assume they are what the men were after, and nothing else."

The thought of his father having a collection of photographs was a bizarre idea, but Jake wondered if he'd inherited his own interest in the art of editing motion pictures from him.

"Maybe they were in a collection of Doctor Maxwell's?"

"It's a thought, but unlikely. You shouldn't concern yourself with this incident," Gilbert said. "Are you sure you're OK? If there's anything else troubling you, you only need to ask."

"There's something I've wanted to ask you about Doctor Maxwell for some time."

"Go ahead, I'm listening."

"It's just that I can't work out why his attitude changed towards me recently. Did I do something to offend him?" Jake asked.

"Jake, you couldn't offend anyone. I know in the latter years Eugene might have distanced himself from you, but trust me when I say he really did care about you, quite a lot."

"Maybe; I shall always be grateful to Doctor Maxwell for his kindness, and for leaving me the projector. But most of all, Gil, I shall miss not seeing you again," Jake said with a weak smile, desperate not to show how empty he was feeling at the prospect.

Jake also thanked him for the compassion that Gilbert had showed to Gia after Cloud Bird died. Not wanting to overstay his welcome, Jake got ready to leave, but Gilbert had other ideas.

"I appreciate you saying that, Jake. I only wish circumstances had been different. I could have spoken freely with you during those years. It was to my own detriment."

"Mine too, Gil, since we share an interest in moviemaking. I would love to know more about how they were made."

"I know. It's sad, but c'est la vie." Gilbert smiled. "I hate to rush this time we have together, Jake, but we must get on with it. I have a lot to do before I leave, and you have a very demanding father waiting at home. Just so that you know what is happening, I have arranged for Gia to continue working here until a suitable buyer can be found. That could see her employed for some time to come," he said. "At the moment, not all of Eugene's bequests can be fulfilled, not until my lawyers are able to find a loophole that will allow Moon Spirit to inherit the stables and all of the mares. So you must have no fear on her account either."

"What — all the horses?" he asked, horror written all over his youthful face.

"Except for the dappled grey mare and her foal; I remember how long it took you to break her. Did you imagine Eugene would ever separate you?"

Jake wanted to say something, anything at all, to express his joy. He knew the gift of the mare and her colt could only have been arranged by Gilbert, as Doctor Maxwell's interest in the breeding stock had waned considerably over recent years. Fearful of having an emotional breakdown, Jake said nothing more. He was about to leave, when Gilbert took a canister that was set apart from the other reels and tentatively handed it to him.

"I want you to keep this reel of film safe for me, Jake, but I must ask you not to watch it until you're older."

It was a curious request, and one that prompted him to ask: "Is this what the men were after?"

"I'm sure it is, but it wouldn't have been of any use to them because the other two reels were destroyed in an accident that also took my brother, many years ago. To view this reel on its own would mean nothing to them, or you, not without the rest of the footage."

"Then what should I do with it?" Jake asked. He could see the doubt that was forming in Gilbert's troubled eyes as he let go of the canister.

"Promise me that you will keep it safe, Jake. I would never entrust it to anyone else."

"I promise you, Gil, I'll take care of it." As he took it, he noticed the label on the side of the container: "End Reel: *The Return of Xavier Gérard*".

"If you keep it, there is no chance of it falling into the wrong hands. If anyone hears of my return to California, and they suspect that I have it with me, this footage might well be destroyed, and that would be a terrible thing. If you keep it safe, it will give me great peace of mind."

What Jake did wonder was whether Gilbert had once been an actor. As handsome as he was, he couldn't have performed on the stage with such a light voice, not unless he'd acted in silent movies.

As Jake's pickup started to move away, Gilbert stopped him in the drive. He was carrying a pile of records and a wind-up gramophone.

"I thought you might find these useful if the evenings get too lonely at the hotel," he said wryly, putting the portable gramophone on the floor of the passenger seat. He then handed him a pile of 78 rpm records, and a very short reel of film.

"That's a really nice thought, Gil. Thanks." Jake smiled.

"It gives me a lot of pleasure to think of it being used again. I also suspect a young man with your keen sensitivity might enjoy this collection of South American music from the pampas. In particular, this top one," he said.

"Why is this one so special?" Jake asked.

"It's the music to accompany this short reel of silent footage," he said, indicating the film stock. "This record belonged to my brother. He died when his truck came off the road in the hills above Hollywood."

"Then I shall treat this with great care."

"As I know you will…" Gilbert hesitated before he continued. "How old are you, Jake?"

"Fifteen and a half; why?"

"When you are twenty-one, I have asked Gia to give you something to remember me by."

"I could never forget you, Gil, not ever."

"Well that goes for me too."

"Will you let me know where you're staying when you've found somewhere to live?"

"Sure, but not for a while. I'll contact you when the time is right."

Within days after their final meeting, Gilbert moved back to California. When he left Fort Laverne, the removal truck was only half full of furniture and personal stuff. He left no forwarding address, but Jake felt sure that Gia might know where he would be living; though she never said.

After Gilbert left, and with only a few dollars to his name, Jake was desperately in need of an income, but he failed miserably in finding work as a projectionist with editing skills in Santa Rowena. Instead, he put Doctor Maxwell's projector to good use by opening a movie theatre in a partitioned-off section of the derelict ballroom at the back of the hotel.

He made a screen out of a framed cotton bed-sheet, tightening the makeshift screen with a solution of watered-down fish glue that he pasted on to the back, and painting the front with white distemper. The projection room was made from a collection of screens and shutters taken from the main dining room.

When the movie theatre first opened, there was keen interest from most of the townsfolk, happy to buy a dollar ticket for a night out in what was becoming a ghost of a town. But after the first few weeks of opening, the demand for the latest colour releases almost brought an end to him showing Doctor Maxwell's black-and-white movies, as it would have cost too much to hire equipment and furnish the theatre with a proper sound system.

However, after reading an article in the local newssheet. He drove into Santa Rowena to collect some free antiquated projection equipment from a run-down cinema being converted into a bowling alley.

After that, he made a monthly excursion to the town and rented whatever cheap movies he could, but even then, the Picture Palace barely made enough cash to exist on given the increasing popularity of television. At the weekends, the younger generation went into Santa Rowena. To cut down on the electricity bill, Jake reduced the opening times to three nights each week, from Wednesday until Friday.

Throughout the following five years, any spare time Jake had was taken up looking after the horses, and helping out with any odd jobs on the ranch. During this time, no "For Sale" board ever went up, and he never once met a prospective buyer.

Expectantly, every year on the anniversary of Cloud Bird's death, Jake would examine the brotherhood scar for any evidence of bleeding, but never found any sign.

When Jake reached the age of twenty-one, the only gifts he received were a woven blanket from Gia, a Navajo belt and a beaded pouch which Moon Spirit had posted from the training college in Flatley, and an inscribed gold wristwatch from Gilbert, three precious gifts that he would treasure forever.

When he strapped on the watch it gave him good reason to smile, wondering if Gilbert would actually recognise him given the drastic alteration to his appearance since they last met. Jake was no longer as thin, but had developed an athletic build. Nor was he small, probably almost Gilbert's own height. His once blond hair had now bronzed, and he shaved every day. On the downside, he still couldn't see properly without wearing glasses, and he had no real friends. There was no gift from his father, which he was secretly glad about as it made his other three gifts all the more special.

With Gilbert on his mind, on the afternoon of his birthday, Jake sorted through the canisters of black-and-white film until he located the short reel that Gilbert had given to him, which he loaded onto the projector. A clapperboard appeared on which was chalked: "Screen test for Isabella & Franco". The production was called *The Return of Xavier Gérard*. The director was Jon Miller, and it was dated "1928".

Jake rewound the screen test and put Gilbert's record onto the turntable, synchronising the sound with the two dancers that appeared on screen. Both characters were masked, gliding effortlessly around a Spanish courtyard. The dance was hypnotic, as if they were a single person, with not a foot or any alignment of their bodies out of place.

What he watched that afternoon altered any earlier perception he'd had about how the natural rhythm of Latin music could be captured on screen: it was more than just a tango, it was a living art form. Barely able to take his eyes off them, the music continued playing on the gramophone, but the celluloid film had been cut: the mesmerising footage was brought to an abrupt end, leaving the empty reel clicking around on the projector. Jake stared at the blank screen, even after the final strains of the music had died out on the gramophone record, and the needle was sticking in the groove.

Running the Picture Palace had been an unlikely project for anyone to consider in a ghost town like Fort Laverne, and unless he did something drastic, Jake realised the enterprise would be doomed to fail regardless of whatever movie was being shown.

Although Gilbert had arranged for Jake to get payment for any work he did at the ranch, he accepted nothing. Instead, needing to supplement his irregular income from the Picture Palace, he did odd jobs at the General Store, arranging with the owner to collect an order of periodicals, and supplies from a warehouse in Santa Rowena on a regular basis, when he was able to arrange these collections to coincide with his own movie returns and the renting of other reels. This meant Jake needed to service and to maintain the old truck regularly, even so, given its unreliability: he usually couldn't get the engine fired up again until a good half an hour after it had been switched off.

The store owner didn't pay much, but through Jake's unwavering perseverance, the Picture Palace struggled on for the next four years. At the age of twenty-five, having split his time between looking after an impossible father, exercising his two horses, and maintaining the stables at the hacienda for Moon Spirit's return, even with all of his youthful pessimism, he had to admit his movie theatre had been a commercial flop. He barely met the cost of the half-weekly screenings, and so, finally, he closed it down.

Ironically, just one week after its closure, Ivan Velasquez was on his way back to the apartment after a drunken night out, when he tripped over a sleeping dog and died where he lay from chronic liver failure.

Unlike the large crowd who attended Doctor Maxwell's funeral, only one elderly ranch hand came in support of Jake. Ivan Velasquez was buried in the same grave as his wife in the Methodist cemetery.

On the following day, Jake had a simple inscription carved into a headstone to his parents. He also arranged for a replacement memorial stone for his unknown twin.

The brotherhood scar had at this time become red and swollen as if infected. Once traces of blood began to seep through the old wound, Jake realised the time for the ritual was getting near. It was three weeks before the anniversary of Cloud Bird's death.

A week after his father's funeral, at sundown, Jake made his way to the cave at Shadow Rock, in the hope of making contact with Nykodema. He had no need for concern, as the medicine man was already waiting there with Chief Oglala.

"We have been expecting you, Pale Horse," Chief Oglala said, indicating that Jake should be seated next to him at the mouth of the cave. "Are you here to open the passage for Cloud Bird's return?" Chief Oglala asked, as old Nykodema cast the bones into an intricate set of markings chalked on the rock floor.

"I am here to do your bidding, sir," Jake said, showing the inflamed brotherhood scar oozing blood. "This is the sign Nykodema spoke of."

"At his birth, it was cast in the bones that my son was destined to achieve greatness in our nation," he said, examining the bleeding wound on Jake's arm. "If Nykodema's predictions are correct, then you, Pale Horse, are the only one who can guide him back to fulfil that destiny."

It was clear that old Nykodema agreed, but only after a careful examination of the chalked lines where each of the bones had fallen.

"If you are in agreement, Pale Horse, then I will inform the elders of my decision. Gia will select a suitable squaw for the ceremony. This will take place on the anniversary of Cloud Bird's death. However, you must be aware that by doing this you will be involved in an outlawed ritual."

"I fully understand the implications, and the risk involved, sir," Jake said.

For three whole days and two nights, Jake was voice coached by old Nykodema in the phrasing of ancient chants that he would be required to make on the night of the ritual. Although Jake had an advantage over other white males in his delivery of the Navajo words, he found it difficult to get the correct, tongue-twisting inflections at the correct pitch, but his perseverance paid off. When he departed from the cave, he left old Nykodema happy.

Jake knew that once he left the town of Fort Laverne, like many others before him, he would never be tempted to return. Having learned the skill of editing from Gilbert, and now free of any moral obligation to care for his father, he intended using that knowledge to earn a living and perhaps by doing that, make his way to California, and find Gilbert.

With barely any cash to settle his father's debts after the funeral expenses were paid, Jake emptied the apartment of anything of value for the auction house in Santa Rowena. The auctioneer refused to accept the reels of black-and-white film, and advised him to burn the lot.

Before he loaded the pickup with furniture, Jake emptied every drawer and cupboard but found nothing of value, not until he searched through his father's roll-top desk. There, he found a grubby folder hidden beneath a sliding compartment under the writing surface. It revealed a perplexing trove of information.

The first document he discovered was his birth certificate: it made little sense. The place of his birth was not given as Fort Laverne, as he had always assumed, but at a hospital in Pasadena, California, where, according to the attached maternity report, it had been a difficult birth from which neither he nor his mother had been expected to survive.

The report was a duplicate copy, typed on a hospital form. To his surprise, the signature on the document was that of Doctor Eugene Maxwell. Something that added to Jake's confusion was that he could only find one birth certificate. There was no mention of his twin's birth in the attached report.

But that was only the start of his confusing finds. When he scanned through the papers of his father's property in Fort Laverne, it became glaringly obvious that it would be impossible for him to put up the hotel for sale, as Ivan Velasquez had never been the owner. He had leased the property in the same month that Jake was born from a man named Jon Miller, who was listed as residing at an address in Pasadena. This was a name that had never been mentioned throughout his entire life, but Jake was sure that it wasn't the first time that he had seen it written down. However, at that precise moment, he just couldn't remember where. What was perhaps most surprising was that, although it had been natural for him to assume his parents were local to Fort Laverne, in the rental agreement, Ivan and Louisa Velasquez were listed as living at a smallholding on the outskirts of Pasadena.

There were two faded sepia photographs of his parents amongst the paperwork which seemed to confirm this. One was of them together at the gate of a dirt farm. In that photograph, his mother was heavily pregnant. In an earlier photograph, taken on their wedding day, his father was barely recognisable: he was slim, with a mass of black hair. it made his skin appear swarthier than Jake could ever remember it. In contrast, his mother was fair, small, and pretty. She was smiling happily, holding onto his father's arm, and she too was barely recognisable as the bitter, unhappy woman that he had known in her later years.

Wrapped in a handkerchief was a grim photograph of a dead infant; not of himself, either as a child, or older. This didn't surprise him as there were no photographs of him either with or without his parents anywhere in the apartment. It was as if he had never existed.

Separate from these photographs, there was a collection of professional stills in a large Manila folder. These were pictures which, rightly or wrongly, he assumed, had been taken on the Rolleiflex camera that had been stolen after Dr Maxwell's funeral.

There were five 10x8 black-and-white photographs in total. All of them had been taken at night in heavy rainfall. In the first photograph, a burly man was chopping down a substantial tree. Seen close up under a magnifying glass, Jake had no doubt that the man was his father, taken many years earlier. In the second photograph, he and another man were hauling the felled tree onto the road. In the third picture, they were positioning this tree to block the road off to any oncoming traffic. In the fourth photograph, there was a close-up of the other man's hands positioning the log. On his finger was a large, square-cut diamond signet ring. It seemed strange to Jake that a wealthy man would be associating with his unscrupulous father. The fifth and final photograph was of a vehicle with its headlights at a sharp bend in the road. Picked out by the headlight beams, there could be seen an isolated tree on high ground above the road – ominously twisted.

Sifting through a collection of crumpled envelopes, all postmarked California, Jake found only one with anything inside, but what he read was a significant find. It contained the letter that had sent his father off the rails so many years earlier: an official notification, typed on headed notepaper –brief, and to the point:

Dear Mr Velasquez,
It is my unfortunate task to inform you that since the Silver Lake Studio has been taken over by Clandestine Productions, a privately owned television company, our directive has since been to stop your monthly pay cheques with immediate effect. Please find enclosed the final payment.
Yours sincerely,
Barbara Jeffords, Head of Accounting.

Because Jake already knew that his parents had a private income, the letter didn't come as a complete shock. Instead, it served to pose more questions when he examined the address of the headed notepaper: "The Silver Lake Studios, Hollywood Land, California." This extraordinary information of his father's connection with a movie studio, although shocking, solidified his decision to set off for California and find work as a film editor – that was, if he survived the imminent "Ritual of Fire" on the Navajo reservation, due to take place in less than two weeks.

In preparation for his trip to California, Jake wrote a detailed account of his editing and projectionist skills to the Silver Lake Studios, applying to be considered as a trainee in the editing department. Unsure about his father's connection with the studio, he addressed the envelope as a work application to the editing department, and posted it from the General Store on the same day.

As previously arranged with the auctioneer, Jake packed furniture and anything else from the building which he thought might be of value on to the back of the pickup and delivered them to the auction house in Santa Rowena. The increased load caused the steering rods to creak as if they might snap in at any time. Equally nerve-racking, was the squealing of rivets from the worn-out brake shoes whenever he applied the brakes. Although any spare cash was limited, it made sense to get the steering rods fixed and the brake shoes replaced before he set off for California; unfortunately, the proceeds from the sale were barely enough to pay off what his father owed the bar owner and so any repairs were out of the question.

"What are you going to do about the interest I'm owed, Jake? I'm running a business here, not a charity," the owner said. "Ivan ran up a hefty tab over the years."

"That's the amount I've paid you in full, Mr Jackson. Until I get work, I have nothing else to offer you."

"And how many years will that take to earn in a ghost town like Fort Laverne?"

"I don't plan staying here, Mr Jackson. As soon as everything's settled, I'm leaving for California. I'll find work there, and mail you what's owed as soon as I can."

"California? What type of work? There are no horse ranches down there, son."

"Maybe not, but there are a lot of movie theatres. I'm a good projectionist."

"I'm aware of that, Jake, but you're not trained. You can't just walk into a job off the street without any professional experience to back you up. The wife's got a few movie magazines out back. You can go through them if you like. You might find one of the studios down there are offering openings for trainees."

"Not to worry about the magazine, Mr Jackson. I've already sent an application off to one of the studios. Thank you for the advice. I'll send you the amount owed as soon as I can."

"I know you will, son. Unlike your father, I trust you."

Prior to his departure, Jake cleared away any weeds from the new memorial stone, where he planted a young rosemary bush, for remembrance, whether the saying was true or not. He felt more affection for that tiny plot than he would ever feel for where his parents were buried.

Chapter Three

Since the untimely death of Cloud Bird, Jake had tried to gather more information about the "Sacred Ritual of Fire" than Cloud Bird himself had passed on to him. Having failed to get any answers from anyone else on the reservation, all he knew was that only three warriors in all of Navajo history had survived this terrifying ritual. Scores of others had attempted to succeed, but had failed, suffering an agonising death. Because supernatural power was invoked during the ceremony, and not because of the many deaths it had caused, the ritual had been outlawed by the American central government a century earlier. Jake remembered how Cloud Bird had once told him he believed the successful end of the ritual to be true.

On the evening before the ceremony, Jake was granted a second audience with Chief Oglala and Nykodema at Shadow Rock. It was a meeting which lasted the length of a night.

"The stakes are much higher than you might have imagined in your desire to return Cloud Bird to his rightful place on earth. If this attempt fails, there can never be another opportunity," Chief Oglala warned. "Once his spirit has been detached from the heavens, if you fail to deliver him through his rebirth, his soul will be lost and will never be at rest."

"I understand the risk, sir," Jake said.

"Perhaps you do, but are you resigned to the possibility of failure, because I am not? In the event of that happening, you can be assured I will damn your soul for eternity."

"I realise what is at stake, sir. I will do everything that is required of me to make this happen. I am aware that Cloud Bird's destiny could not be fulfilled because of his untimely death."

"And are you willing to risk your own life to rectify this, Pale Horse?" Chief Oglala asked, studying the formation of the cast bones.

"Yes, sir, I am, totally."

"Bravery is not all that is required of you. To summon down his spirit to enter your own body, you need to have loved my son unconditionally."

"And I have. I would willingly have given my own life to have prevented Cloud Bird's death."

Chief Oglala exchanged a look of confirmation with Nykodema, prompting him to recast the bones amongst the chalked symbols.

"The reading is good for tomorrow," Chief Oglala said. "If you have any doubts before the ritual, you must withdraw immediately. Once started, there is no turning back. The same will apply to the woman who has been selected."

"Has she been made aware of the dangers involved?"

"She has, but like you, is equally as determined to help instigate my son's return. All I ask is that you are considerate with her body during intercourse. Remember, she is also risking her own life and has never laid with a man before. Although the casting of the bones has shown your pairing is compatible, nothing is certain, and that is a risk to you."

"What would happen if the reading is incorrect, sir?" Jake asked. "I am not concerned for myself, but for this woman involved."

"Once the spirit has entered your body, and if, for some reason, it is unable to pass unhindered into the host's womb, the probable outcome would be that you will both suffer an agonising death."

Late that afternoon, in preparation for the evening ceremony, Jake shaved off every trace of hair and stubble from his face and body. He scrubbed clean every inch of his skin in the brook until he was close to bleeding.

He'd arranged to meet with Gia at sunset at the edge of the reservation. When he arrived, Jake found that she had been true to her word and wasn't alone. Seated on a dappled mare was a young and very beautiful Navajo woman. He failed to recognise her until she got down from the horse to greet him.

"Moon Spirit, why are you here?" he asked, becoming

unexpectedly embarrassed, fearing that she would not only be watching the events as they happened from below with her mother, but also that she must know what would happen between him and the woman on the mountain after the ceremony.

"I am here for the same reason as you, Pale Horse, to honour my brother's rebirth."

Her nearness made Jake nervous. "You shouldn't be here," he said, worried the time for the ceremony was drawing near. He turned to her mother in desperation. "Where is she? The squaw you promised, Gia?"

"She is here," Gia said, taking the reins of the horse from her daughter.

"It can't be Moon Spirit," he exclaimed, barely able to comprehend that Cloud Bird's sister was expected to take part in the ceremony.

"I am here of my own free will. I know what is expected of me."

During the years since he'd last seen her she had transformed from a gawky, high-spirited girl into someone heart-wrenchingly lovely, standing proudly before him as her mother, Gia, handed Jake the ceremonial blanket she had woven for the ritual.

A short distance away was her father, Chief Oglala, seated motionless on his horse. The only movements of his silhouette against the darkening skyline were the feathers of his headdress and lance in the wind. He sat as rigid as stone, every sinew in his body taut in readiness for the battle of elements which he knew would come. His eyes focused on the flat ceremonial rock that, shelf-like, projected over the sacred burial ground where the ritual was to take place.

"I can't allow you to sacrifice your reputation, Moon Spirit. You can't accompany me any further than where you are now when I go to Nykodema. What would your father say if he knew what you were intending? He would never allow it."

"You think my father doesn't know that I am here? How can you be so considerate to others, and yet be so dense about yourself? Do you imagine any thoughts of my reputation would prevent me from being with you tonight? When you are prepared to honour Cloud Bird in such a way? You are not even a warrior from my own people, and yet you are willing to risk your life in an effort to return my brother's spirit here. No warrior on the reservation would take such a risk."

"Even so..."

"You couldn't have stopped me when I was a child, and you cannot tonight. My mind is made up," she said, and he knew by her face that it would be impossible to argue.

Although he admired Moon Spirit, and was genuinely fond of her, the prospect of what was expected of them from the ceremony was disturbing. He would have cut off his right arm rather than select her for the ritual ahead. For the first time in his life Jake felt an overpowering resentment well up inside him towards Gia for having made such a choice. To him it was the worst imaginable. From the tentative look in the girl's eyes, he could tell this would perhaps be a bigger ordeal for her.

Aware of the danger that lay ahead Jake felt like a trapped animal, aware too of the transference ritual that must happen immediately afterwards. With her changed appearance, Moon Spirit seemed to be a complete stranger, but he knew she was not. It worried him about the intimacy required of them if, against all-odds, he did actually survive the ordeal. He knew that he needed to remain calm and focus only on the ceremony, his mind clear of everything else. Otherwise he would never stand a chance of succeeding, and like so many others, he would be dead by morning.

Leaving Gia behind, they walked together in silence, side by side, the way they had done in the past when he was a gawky adolescent, neither of them wanting to exchange a word during the arduous climb.

There was an outburst of angry muttering from the gathered elders when her identity became known as she accompanied Jake towards the burial ground – noises that were instantly quelled when her father lowered his lance threateningly in their direction.

They reached the sacred burial ground and came to the cave of old Nykodema.

"I bring Pale Horse," Moon Spirit said simply. Carefully she removed the blanket from around Jake's shoulders, folding the blanket carefully so that the irregular symbols within the pattern merged into a single image of an eagle. She handed this to Nykodema. In the flickering light cast by the flames the wings gave the impression of an eagle in preparation for flight.

Once he was stripped naked in front of the fire, Jake sat as still as death, cross-legged, on the floor of the cave. The medicine man carefully painted his body with more of the ancient symbols. He painted a swooping eagle over Jake's heart. On the opposite side of his chest the old man painted a ray of light beaming through a cloud. Lastly, Nykodema painted three warrior bars across each side of Jake's face. The first stage of the process was complete.

The old man offered a bowl of liquid that Jake had to drink down in a single draught without taking hold of the earthenware vessel. It was a nauseating concoction, which although cool as it went into Jake's mouth, quickly gave the sensation of scalding the inside of his throat. But Jake kept the thought firmly in his mind that if Cloud Bird's spirit could return through him, then any pain would be surmountable. He glanced at Moon Spirit before the branding ceremony began and saw she had faith in his ability to succeed.

Nykodema removed a glowing arrowhead by the shank from the fire, and branded immediately above Jake's heart two eagle wings without a body connecting them. The pain was excruciating, and Jake struggled hard not to pass out from the stench of his own burnt flesh. To distract himself, he stared through the mouth of the cave into the night sky, biting down on his lower lip to prevent himself from crying out.

Then, wrapped in Gia's blanket, and barefoot, Jake accompanied Nykodema to the shelf of rock over the burial ground. There, the old man lit a fire that he'd prepared for the ceremony. Nykodema removed the blanket from Jake's shoulders and spread it out on the flat rock behind the fire, and he bade Jake sit down. On either side of the blanket, and built above Jake's head height, were two mounds of stones. On top of each mound was a pierced earthenware pot containing incense which the old man then lit. Straddling the two mounds was a slim bough of wood that had been stripped of its bark. Dangling from the centre of this, immediately above Jake's head, were three eagle feathers tied together.

For two long hours, Jake sat in front of the fire, staring directly through the flames into the storm clouds gathering low over the town of Santa Rowena, where on this same date and night, Cloud Bird had been attacked, and many weeks later had died from his wounds. Jake's eyes were watering copiously from the swirling incense and smoke, but he didn't move his position, concentrating hard on keeping the palms of both of his hands perfectly still and upturned, his forearms resting on his bare thighs for support the way he had been instructed. Giddy from the drink that Nykodema had given him, he was amazed how the intensity of the pain from the tribal branding had eased.

Jake concentrated on what he loved and missed about his long-departed companion. He drew great strength from recalling the times they had spent together. Cloud Bird had seldom been out of his mind during those lost years, and it gave Jake the will to survive this mission to make contact with his departed spirit.

At the entrance to the cave, Nykodema was drumming out the slow beat of a heart. At a distance, across the dying fire, Jake was aware of being watched by the tribe elders. He was now entering into a transcendental state and was only partially aware of Moon Spirit close by, loading more wood onto the fire. And then she was gone, just as silently as she had come.

As the drumbeat intensified, Jake began to chant, in a clear and resonant tone, the slow incantation he had memorised by heart. His strong voice echoed across the canyon. Using the Navajo dialect, Jake uttered each word exactly the way Nykodema had coached him.

The passionate incantations were thrust beyond the high ridges of the canyon. Each of the echoing sounds caught in a growing wind that was whipping up clouds of swirling dust all around him. It was as if the spirals were conveying those sacred chants up into a gathering cloud formation above the canyon. The immortal world into which he must enter, providing a route back for the spirit of Cloud Bird to return.

Wafts of smoke from the incense burners gathered about him in a dense cloud. The three eagle feathers on the bent sapling lowered in front of him making a dark configuration that swirled around in the haze before his eyes.

Nearing total exhaustion, Jake was finding it almost impossible to keep awake and yet he did. As dawn approached, his flesh chilled to freezing as the fire died down, and it was then that a sign appeared in the storm clouds above Santa Rowena. He knew that contact had been made when he saw the flight of a grey eagle appear through the dense clouds. Moments later the clouds lit up with jagged spears of lightning.

What he thought at first was a falling cloud was, in fact, the grey shape of an eagle, flying, not towards him, but directly at him. Remaining perfectly still, Jake didn't flinch as the shape hurtled downwards, swooping low at speed, its fierce talons outstretched in preparation for attack. But Jake was steadfast in his resolve and stared challengingly into the eyes of his assailant. When it closed in on him, everything went into slow motion.

With a blood-curdling cry, the mystical bird folded its wings, arrow like, and headed directly towards him. Jake felt an ice-cold rush of air as the image blurred and the savage shape of its head pierced into the taut flesh over his heart.

Lurching backwards, Jake screamed from the intense rush of pain. It felt as if he had been penetrated by red hot coals. Somehow, he forced himself back into the same upright position that he knew he must maintain if he was to see this through. The pain was unbearable, as if molten lava was coursing through his veins, but he was prepared, knowing the passage for Cloud Bird's rebirth had opened, and he would have to endure the agony.

Moon Spirit screamed, and he knew the test of his endurance had begun in earnest when his naked body exploded with flames. His eyelids were scorching, and he believed he would be dead in moments. He also knew that if he took fright and scrambled away to douse the flames then he, like so many warriors before him, would be burnt to a cinder. Accepting his fate, he remained perfectly still until the flames engulfing his body died down. At the same time, the searing heat that had all but incinerated his being, lessened, and he felt his body begin to cool.

Resolute, he stared ahead, still in his position on the blanket, with the sure knowledge that he had succeeded where so many before him had failed. And he knew why. It wasn't because of any superior strength of character, or of moral courage. What had occurred on this night was because the only true ingredient for success was unconditional love.

He stayed in that position until the cyclonic wind had eased; then he got to his feet. His flesh was completely numb; his vision blurred, and it was impossible to walk without stumbling. Moon Spirit guided him into a cool, dark cavern where Nykodema had made preparations for them to sleep.

Bloated and dizzy, he was shivering uncontrollably when they entered the cave. He could see nothing of the interior except for a strange phosphorous light that encompassed him as she helped him onto the buckskin cot and lit the prepared fire. She lay, naked, against him, and covered them with Gia's blanket.

Jake remembered very little of the three days and nights they spent together alone in the cave, except for the tenderness they shared, and the eye-watering smoke from the fire, and the taste of wood-ash on their food, and the welcoming smell of rain.

It was dawn on the fourth day when Jake came down from the flat rock with Moon Spirit at his side. Only the blanket Gia had woven covered his nakedness. Silently, the chief, his elders, and gathered Navajos, parted ranks in respect, allowing them passage to reach the cave of the medicine man. Jake was shaking from the cold, and he desperately wanted to retrieve his clothes.

When Jake removed the blanket, old Nykodema gave him a toothless smile of approval, indicating where he had branded the eagle wings. The branding had healed, and the shape of the branding was no longer a pair of wings but a complete eagle with head, body, and tail.

"Will you ever come back?" Moon Spirit asked him when they parted at the edge of the reservation.

"There is nothing for me here," Jake responded, uneasy at the firm touch of her hand.

She tied a narrow-beaded covering over the brotherhood scar on his wrist, which was still seeping blood. "I made this to keep you safe – until you come home."

He was about to say that he never would, but when he looked into her beautiful eyes, he faltered and said nothing. There was no tearful farewell as she mounted her spirited horse. She didn't turn to watch him leave the reservation; instead, she urged the dappled mare into a gallop, handling the horse as if they were one being. He realised how much he had underestimated Gilbert's insight when handing over all of Doctor Maxwell's horses into her capable hands.

It was a desolate morning when Jake prepared to set off. He felt no tug of remorse at leaving, except for the freedom of riding bareback over the reservation. There were dark storm clouds bellied low over the town. The street was deserted except for a mangy dog searching for scraps of food. Balls of tumbleweed gusted along the potholed road. It was a bitterly cold wind, swirling gusts of grit and dust made it difficult to see anything properly. Battling against this wind, Jake forced open the barn door and reversed out the pickup. On the floor of the cab were his few possessions packed into a tin trunk. Amongst them was Gilbert's end reel, the test for the tango with the essential recording. A beaten-up briefcase contained the letter from the Silver Lake Studio, his birth certificate, his father's copy of the rental agreement for the hotel, and the black-and-white stills. Folded neatly on the passenger seat was Gia's woven blanket, and the worn halter Cloud Bird had given him.

Because the old pickup didn't do much mileage to the gallon, there were four and a half cans of gasoline covered with a tarpaulin. Under here he packed a box of Doctor Maxwell's reels, amongst them was *Casanova*, released in 1933, and the 1927 silent classic, *Napoleon*. Together with these he packed a battered suitcase of clothes and a valve radio. With them was a farewell gift from the owner of the General Store. This comprised a partially empty sack of dried beans, five duck eggs, and two strips of beef jerky. Uncertain if he would find a decent water supply on the journey,

Jake filled three large containers of spring water. He packed a frying pan, and also a billycan to make coffee.

With Cloud Bird's felt hat pulled down on his head, having checked the time on the treasured gift from Gilbert, Jake drove away from Fort Laverne.

Chapter Four

The first night, he parked on a dirt track somewhere near the Petrified Forest to get a few hours' rest before daybreak. At dawn, he filled up the near-empty fuel tank with gasoline from two of the containers in the back of the truck.

The second night's stop-over was after filling up at a remote gas station and where, just in the nick of time, he also filled up his overheating radiator. Given the alternative of being bitten to death by mosquitoes, he settled again for the cramped position across the front seats.

On the final night of his journey, he parked high in the hills above the sprawling city of Los Angeles. The heat was sweltering, and he got no sleep at all.

It was barely dawn when he got the truck revved up. With the map open on the front seat, he cranked the engine into gear. He was desperately tired and in need of a shower when he drove off, wanting only to reach his destination and give the struggling engine a well-deserved rest before it gave out completely or, worse, exploded.

On the map, he followed the best route out of the hills, and soon came to a fork in the road. He knew that he had chosen badly when the tarmac came to an end, becoming a badly potholed dirt road. Because the road was narrow and offered no place to turn and go back, he continued along what soon became a rough single-track road. There were a few passing bays cut into the irregular rock face on his left, but on the right-hand side of the road there was nothing but a sheer drop into the canyon below.

Although he had both of the cab windows fully wound down, the air was stifling. He steered the clanking old truck along the narrow ledge of a road, doing his best to avoid potholes. Aware of the poor state of the truck's brakes, and the steepening decline of the road ahead, he kept far away from the edge of the ravine.

As he approached a nasty curve in the road, Jake began to shiver. A sharp pain pierced his heart, and his vision became increasingly distorted. There was nowhere to pull over. Fortunately, the need to concentrate on keeping the truck away from the edge of the ravine helped him to keep going.

A few moments before, the cab had been unbearably hot but the temperature had now gone icy-cold. However hard he tried, it was impossible to wind up the window. The tyres screeched wildly as he yanked hard on the steering wheel to get the truck safely around the sharp bend.

Previously, the sun had been blinding him through the rear-view mirror but it was now blinding him directly ahead. When he had cleared the bend, the brilliant light was being reflected towards him from a bank of low cloud lying across the road.

Automatically Jake slammed on the brakes when he saw a fallen tree straddled across most of the lane, giving him no choice other than to stop or go careering over the edge of the cliff.

Not having a vehicle with efficient brakes, and given the steep incline of the road, the rivets on the worn brakes shoes squealed unnervingly as the truck slowed down, but he was unable to stop. With clenched teeth Jake drove directly into the obstruction.

At the moment when the collision ought to have happened, he felt no shuddering impact. The pickup had driven through the obstacle as if it never existed. There was no mistaking the solidity of the fallen tree so it was senseless to assume that it was a mirage.

He looked back through the rear-view mirror expecting to see the tree hadn't fallen in the way he had thought, but it was straddling the entire width of the road.

Barely visible behind him, through the wake of the disturbed mist, Jake made out the shape of an isolated tree standing high on the rocky bank near the bend in the road, which seemed unnervingly familiar. It was silhouetted dramatically against a backdrop of diffused rays from the sun illuminating the bank of cloud. Winging through the backdrop of light was an eagle in flight.

When the truck rounded the next bend in the road there was

no trace of fog. Gone too was the icy-cold chill in the cab and his uncontrollable shivering and, thankfully, the excruciating pain that had been stabbing into his heart. The temperature in the cab was once again stifling, sweltering, and muggy. It was as if the incident with the fallen tree had never actually happened. But now there was a distinct, lingering scent of pine needles which he hadn't noticed before.

Suddenly, coming towards him was a beaten-up truck that appeared to be in an even worse condition than the one that he was driving. Even though it was daylight the driver had the headlights on, although only one of the headlamps was working.

To lessen the danger for the other driver, who had the sheer drop on the canyon edge of the road, Jake braked hard and drove as close to the rock face as he could.

There hadn't been a trace of rain that morning but Jake noticed that the wiper blade on the approaching truck was wiping away water from its windscreen, and the flapping tarpaulin was saturated with rain. Although there was no sign of any rain on the road, there was a lot of spray from beneath the wheels as the engine screamed in its struggle to get up the steep incline.

As luck would have it, there was a natural passing place just ahead and Jake pulled off to the side of the road. In the brief moment when the cabs of the two vehicles drew level, Jake called out to the man. It was impossible to see the driver's face, nor was he certain the man had heard him, as he was hunched up close to the steering wheel and giving all of his concentration on the road ahead.

There was still a strong scent of pine needles when Jake stumbled out of his cab and ran after the departing vehicle, shouting for the driver to stop. But it cornered the bend and went out of sight. Because the driver hadn't stopped and waited for him to catch up, Jake expected to hear a nauseating squeal of brakes followed by the inevitable crash. But he heard nothing.

When Jake rounded the bend, there was no sign of the other truck or the tree across the road. What had jogged his memory earlier was that he now recognised the isolated tree on the ridge of high ground: it was identical to one of the photographs he'd found hidden in his father's roll-top desk.

Before he got back into his cab, Jake had a good look around to see where the pine trees might be, but apart from the solitary one in the photograph, there were no other pines in sight. Yet the heady scent lingered for the longest time inside the cab and didn't go until, during the truck's laboured descent, Jake pulled over and stopped, worried about the stench of overheated brake-shoes which had been squealing down most of the steep track. He wondered if he would ever reach the bottom in one piece. Although it was a loathsome thought, he did wonder if he ought to just sell the old truck for scrap. But he changed his mind when he reached the sprawling city of Los Angeles.

Jake drove around the city for what seemed like hours, frustrated at being unable to find the old Silver Lake Studio. He could make no sense of the road layout as his map had been printed in 1923. Instead of the tracks and narrow lanes he had expected, he was driving through a rapidly developing city, with many sprawling new developments, and the unforeseen complication of fast-moving traffic.

He was suffering from the onset of a heavy cold and had a blinding headache which he attributed to the smoggy air, so different to the cooler, higher altitude of Fort Laverne. He hated the dry, airless heat of the valley. It was difficult to breathe even when the truck wasn't moving.

Because the pickup had no sun-visor, Jake turned down the brim of Cloud Bird's felt hat. Both of the cab windows were wound down. In an attempt to get cooler, he had opened his collarless shirt to the waist.

Jake parked up the truck and became aware that shoppers and passers-by were staring at him. The sales girls, too, were staring, passing murmured comments when he bought two postcards at the counter. He could only attribute this response to Moon Spirit's gift of the beaded Navajo band tied around his wrist, which covered his brotherhood scar.

After sharpening his pencil, Jake wrote a brief account of the journey and some of the places he had seen en route in his neatest handwriting, but he didn't mention anything about the log straddling the road, nor of the rain-splattered truck. At the hacienda, having addressed the card to Moon Spirit, Jake debated for some time on how to sign-off, given he had spent three intimate nights with a woman who seemed more of a stranger than the girl he had grown up with. He scrawled his name across the bottom and didn't give it another glance. He dropped it into a mailbox with another card to Gia and got back into the truck.

Later, when he caught sight of his own reflection in a store window, he understood why so many people had been staring at him oddly, as he had managed to achieve the ceremonial requirement of leaving the painted symbols untouched on his face for seven days.

After another long hour of driving, Jake became convinced that he would never find the studio at all. He was dog-tired and his cold wasn't being helped by the exhaust fumes in the rush-hour traffic. Tiresomely, his truck was low on gas and he couldn't afford to drive aimlessly around streets that weren't marked on the old map, so he began asking passers-by if they knew where the studio was. Either they didn't, or wouldn't go anywhere near the half-naked warrior shouting at them above the noise of the engine.

With an eye on the fuel gauge and having lost all sense of direction, Jake drove along a fine avenue of trees, which eventually opened out into a much better neighbourhood. He came to a T-junction and, although he was fully prepared to be confronted by yet another spider-like configuration of roads and partially constructed dwellings, he came instead to a gated entrance in a high perimeter wall controlled by a uniformed officer. Over the entrance arch was an imposing sign for the Silver Lake Studio.

Before he drove up to the gatehouse, Jake pulled over to double-check the name of the chief accountant who had written to his father, uncertain if he should ask for her by name; but if so, what to say that would persuade her to reveal his father's connection with that accounts department? He therefore decided that his best option would be a bumbling approach. Ironically, bumbling was a perfectly accurate assessment of his state of mind that morning, as he could barely keep his eyes open, let alone think clearly.

Jake pulled the truck just clear of the gatehouse and waited for the attendant to get back into the empty cubicle. The man, however, had other things on his mind. With a clipboard and a sheaf of paperwork in one hand, he was cautiously guiding the driver of a battered stagecoach through the arched gateway, with barely inches to spare on account of the piled luggage lashed onto the top.

"That's gotta be the last time I can do this, Bill. We all know it's a lot further leaving the studio through the back gate, but rules are rules. That's just the way it is," the guard called.

The coachman responded with a brief wave of the hand as he coaxed the skittish team of horses past Jake's spluttering exhaust and out onto the road.

When the entrance was clear, Jake cranked the engine into gear and pulled up at the gatehouse window. The security officer thrust his head out of the opening in an attempt to hear what Jake was saying above the noise of the engine.

"I can't hear a word you're saying, son. Can you switch off the engine?"

There was steam seeping out from under the hood and through the radiator grill and Jake knew it would be fatal to switch off the engine as it would be impossible to get restarted for at least an hour. He did his best to hear what the security guard was saying above the clanking and spluttering of his truck.

"What department, son?" he hollered above the noise, indicating the long list of names on the paperwork attached to his clipboard.

Jake was making another failed attempt to be heard through the cab window, saying he would reverse the truck out onto the road before he switched off, when a shooting brake pulled up behind the pickup and blocked him in. The driver tooted the horn repeatedly, impatient for Jake to move out of the way.

"Sorry about this, Miss Dawlish," the guard called. "We'll only be a moment here," he said, as a slim young woman got out of the driving seat and came over to the gatehouse.

She had the brim of an unstylish hat pulled down over her eyes to shield them from the glare of the white buildings. There was a no-nonsense look about the way she was dressed in slacks and a woven top: neat, feminine, practical.

"Can you be quick about it, Ray? I've got Adelaide Williams in the car with me."

"Miss Williams? I thought she wasn't in the office today?"

"She's been called in for some urgent re-casting, and her car wouldn't start. I called by to give her a ride." She looked enquiringly at the old pickup blocking the entrance. Behind her, the horn of the shooting brake was being tooted again with irritating regularity.

"Marjory, what the hell's going on? Can't you get Ray to move that heap of junk out of the way? I'm already late," the passenger protested loudly through the open window, accompanied with a final toot of the horn. She then adjusted the rear-view mirror to apply a bright smear of lipstick.

"I'm sorry for this delay, Miss Williams," Ray responded. "I'll soon have this sorted. I need to find out who this guy came to see before I let him through."

"He probably wasn't told about the schedule change," Marjory said, tapping the side of Jake's truck. "We don't need this pickup until next week; Thursday, I think?" she said, doing her best not to squint at the blurred shape of the driver inside the cab. "I apologise if the rescheduling is inconvenient. We weren't informed until late last night. We're shooting the scene you were booked for next week," she said.

"You're mistaken if you think I'm here for any filming, miss," Jake responded, feeling like hell, and wishing that he hadn't slept in the cab for the past three nights. Because it was so hard to hear anything she said above the noise of the engine, he mistakenly turned off the ignition.

"If you're not here for filming, what are you doing driving this truck?" she asked, showing more interest in the vintage pickup than the strange individual who was driving.

"Erm…" Jake began awkwardly. He was uncertain how to answer her; his main priority was to get into the studio. He knew he would only have one chance of getting beyond the attendant and through the gates, so he knew he needed to answer carefully to gain access and locate Barbara Jeffords. Only she could answer his questions about his father's monthly cheques, and what his connection had been with the studio.

Jake almost jumped out of his skin as Adelaide Williams gave another long blast on the horn, shouting impatiently at the attendant: "You there… Ray! Why in God's name aren't you doing what you're being paid for? Get a handle on the bloody situation? If that useless pile of junk is allowed to stay there for much longer, it'll take root."

"So, if you're not an extra, what are you here for, son?" Ray asked, deliberately prolonging the wait, refusing to be intimidated by the Head of Programming or anyone else.

"I was…I was hoping to get a job," Jake said in a moment of panic, praying that he wouldn't have to elaborate.

"If it's studio work you're after, son, then I'm afraid you are out of luck. You've come to the wrong gate. You need to ask for Jeff at the South Entrance; he'll give you the form to fill in and show you where to go after that." He had to raise his voice above another harsh blast from the horn in the vehicle behind. "Now then, son, can you move this truck of yours and let the shooting brake get through?"

Jake knew it would be hopeless to start up the engine so soon, but at least he had to show willing for the sake of the guard. He switched the ignition and tried a few times. The engine turned over sluggishly and refused to start.

"I am really sorry about this, sir. It won't start up again until it's had time to cool down. It's my own stupid fault for shutting off the engine without thinking."

"Then I guess you're gonna need me to give you a push," Ray said, sympathising with Jake's predicament. Ignoring the irritating blasts on the waiting vehicle, he removed his jacket and rolled up his shirtsleeves before he came out of the gatehouse.

"I can't ask you to push, sir, not while I steer," Jake said, climbing out of the cab, uncertain about what to do.

"I can manage this, son. At least we have a bit of a slope in our favour," Ray said amiably.

"Even so, I don't think that will work; it's going to be too hard for one person to push. The brakes got too hot down the canyon pass this morning. The brake-shoes are probably binding."

Ray lifted his cap and scratched his head. "Well, it can't stay here, son. I'd better make a call to the teamster's office, and have one of them come out –if that doesn't go against their union rule book," Ray said reluctantly; brightening when Marjory called out her instructions.

"Don't call anyone in the teamster's office, Ray. That will only make the situation here even worse. Just give me a moment while I reverse the shooting brake clear of the truck. I'll get in and steer, while you and this idiot push it clear of the gate. We need to put an end to this God Almighty farce now or this re-casting will never get done." She removed the unattractive hat, revealing pale olive skin, devoid of make-up.

"Thanks for helping out, Miss Dawlish. This gate would have been blocked for a while if I'd waited for anyone else," Ray said, as she climbed into Jake's cab.

"It's the least I can do. We both know what it's like when Adelaide blows a fuse. We've got to get this truck moved," she said, releasing the handbrake and disengaging the gears effortlessly– a skill even Jake had trouble mastering.

In no time the pickup was neatly parked away from the gate, and the girl jumped out. She was clearly unimpressed with Jake, but not so with the old pickup.

"Thank you for helping, Ray. It's a good thing it's you on duty this morning."

"It's me that should be thanking you, Miss Dawlish," he said, as she dusted off the crumbs from Jake's sandwiches which had attached themselves to her slacks. When the shooting brake drew up alongside the pickup, before going through the entrance, Adelaide Williams made her stop abruptly.

"I say, you up there in the cab, who are you?" she called out through a cloud of cigarette smoke.

"The name's Jake Velasquez, miss."

"Are you an actor?"

"No, Miss," he answered in astonishment. "I was enquiring after a job."

"Then why are those tribal symbols painted on your face? Those markings, Mr Velasquez... are they meant to be Navajo?"

"Yes, they are, miss."

"Then are you...?"

"No, I'm not." Not wanting to discuss his private life, Jake cut her short; perhaps, too abruptly for her liking given the cool response.

"If you are not an actor, Mr Velasquez, then what job were you after?"

"I was... I was enquiring after a position as a trainee in editing. I sent off an application two weeks ago," he said thinking quickly, annoyed by the amused look on her face.

"Well that's probably buried beneath a stack of other hopeful applications in the mail room, and will never be seen again."

The heat was sweltering. He was baking hot, and desperately wanted to remove Cloud Bird's battered hat, but decided against it given the undue scrutiny he was getting from the Head of Programming.

"What did he say, Marjory? I can't quite hear from back here in the car. Is he an actor or a real Native American?" she called.

"No, Adelaide, he's neither, just another hopeful looking for work."

To clarify this, Jake indicated the growth of stubble on his chin, hoping that would satisfy her curiosity.

"Your profile is rather familiar, young man, even though most of your features are hidden beneath that war-paint." She removed her sunglasses and replaced them with a pair of spectacles. "Tell me. How old are you?"

"I'm twenty-five, miss."

"Twenty-five you say?" she said curiously, as the shooting

brake moved forward. Unlike her middle-aged colleague, Marjory Dawlish drove past without bothering to give him a second glance.

While his truck cooled down, Jake sat on the running board taking advantage of the shade from the pickup, enjoying the coffee and bagel Ray supplied between the spasmodic arrivals of staff and studio technicians.

"I'd have thought that an organisation of this size would have a few vacancies?" he said, suddenly aware of Marjory Dawlish approaching with a reel of film in its protective canister.

"Ray, would you be a dear and hand these screen tests over to the courier when he arrives? Tell him it's imperative; Adelaide wants them ready by five o'clock, at the very latest. If I can't collect them myself I will send someone over for them."

"I could go?" Jake suggested, catching her off guard.

"I didn't realise you were still here."

"I am until I've finished with this." He indicated his half-finished coffee. "Ray's been very kind to me."

"Ray is well known for it," she said dismissively, turning to leave.

"I could collect the rushes for you?" he asked, this time using the term Doctor Maxwell had used when relating stories of the movie studios.

"Thank you for the offer, but no, thank you. I wouldn't entrust such errands to someone I don't know."

"I understand your reasoning, miss. I was just hoping for some work here. Anything would do."

"Well, nothing comes immediately to mind; however, I feel sure the Transport Captain would pay quite handsomely to hire your truck for next week's reshoot, and possibly again for filming the week after." Miss Dawlish examined Jake's dilapidated pickup in more detail.

"Well, that depends if I'm still here. If I am, then, yes, I'd certainly hire out my truck, but what I need before that is a job. I am prepared to do anything."

"Then I would advise you to send a letter to the employment office with your address and contact telephone number—" she said, but he interrupted.

"There would be no point, miss. I only arrived here this morning. It wasn't my plan to go back again – if ever."

"Then where do you live?" she asked, still more interested in the pickup. "You must have driven from somewhere that has a name?"

"Fort Laverne, New Mexico." Jake thought she looked taken aback – just for a moment.

"That's some distance to travel in a truck of this age. This isn't just any old pickup. I can't remember when I saw a truck like this on the road. Well, not in this city I haven't. You could have done a lot of damage, travelling so far."

"Apart from the pickup, miss, the only other option would have been to come on foot. As it was, it took three days to drive here. There was no choice." He was irritated by the way she was talking down to him as if he was some out of town idiot.

"So, Adelaide was right; you're an out- of-work actor, like the thousands of other hopefuls who arrive here each week. Well, I hate to be the bearer of bad news, but like everyone else, you'll soon discover the streets of Hollywood aren't paved with gold."

"As a matter of fact, miss, I do have an interest in moviemaking, but only in connection to an enterprise I had in Fort Laverne, and that was not as a would-be actor," he retorted.

To his surprise, instead of reacting badly to his response, she asked: "I see, but why choose Hollywood of all places? Surely, there must be somewhere closer to where you live where you could find work that suits?"

"I drove down here on family business. Until that's been resolved I need to find some temporary employment."

"What exactly was this enterprise in New Mexico?" she asked with more interest than she had shown earlier.

"For the last four years, I've run my own movie theatre as projectionist. I also did a lot of editing and repairing film stock. Old celluloid has a great tendency to snap when you least expect it," he explained. It seemed to impress the woman who was displaying more of an interest in him than his truck.

"Look, I can't guarantee much work, but if you call by here again tomorrow morning, say around nine o'clock, then I might be able to help. We could also talk about hiring this pickup from you for next week's shoot. Naturally, you would be paid the going rate."

"Sure, that sounds great," he said hesitantly. "Except, and I hate to ask, but is there any chance I could get something in advance?" He only had enough cash for a single night's stay at a cheap motel. If he was to be there a week he would need accommodation, and to eat, and to arrive at the studios showered and fresh.

"That would be highly irregular," she responded curtly; but, after making another swift assessment of the vintage pickup, she relented. "Well. Are you willing to surrender the pickup and keys to the Transport Captain until the shooting is complete?"

"But how can I get about if I don't have my truck?"

"That's what public transportation is intended for. That has to be the deal if you expect me to give an advance to a man I met only an hour ago. That's the deal which you take or leave, Mr...?"

"The name is Jake Velasquez. Thank you, Miss Dawlish. I won't let you down. I'll be here tomorrow morning at nine o'clock." He handed over the key, which she then passed to Ray through the hatch.

"If you wait here, Mr Velasquez, I'll send your advance out, and Ray, get the Transport Captain to collect the pickup." With that, she turned and walked swiftly to the glistening white office building.

Jake barely had time to remove his suitcase of clothes from the back of the truck when an officious youth appeared at a run from the white office building and got him to sign a petty-cash receipt for three dollar bills. It was less than he'd been expecting, though Marjory Dawlish had never mentioned any sum so Jake felt he only had himself to blame. The amount was barely enough to get food for the week, never mind pay for any decent accommodation.

However, she had asked him to come back in the morning, and he was sure he would land some kind of work, even do odd jobs or to service the toilets; whatever it was, he didn't mind. He would be working on the other side of the perimeter wall for at least a week, during which time he would be able to do some sleuthing to locate the Head of Accounting and find out her connection to his father.

Added to that, he'd been paid a rental fee for his old pickup, when only a few hours earlier he had been wondering if it was ready for the knacker's yard. It made him feel that somehow his life was turning a corner.

At Ray's suggestion, the tin trunk and Jake's possession were securely locked away at the back of an office provided for the sole use of the security men.

Before he set off, Ray gave him a local newspaper with accommodation listings, some of which he struck through immediately. He was advised against one in particular listed as the Hotel Czardas. Although it offered the cheapest rates in town for a bed, it was one to be avoided.

Chapter Five

There were two other possibilities in Grayel Street, which Ray reluctantly agreed were slightly better but a lot more expensive than the Hotel Czardas, and so, contrary to Ray's advice, Jake rented a single room at the Hotel Czardas. The room contained a creaking bed with a lumpy flock mattress, a badly stained pillow, and a grey threadbare blanket. There were no sheets and towels that he could find. Breakfast was not provided in the price.

Just before midnight, Jake woke to the sound of smashing glass and the splintering of wood as a door was kicked in further along his landing. What followed was a lengthy brawl, with a lot of heavy grunting and thuds amid sounds of breaking furniture, interspersed with bellowing exchanges between two volatile male fighters swearing in an alien language. This was added to by the outraged shrieks of an American woman, threatening to carry out immediate castration on both men if the fighting didn't stop. She yelled out for someone to call Officer Reynolds, and to get there fast.

When he heard the crack of bullets, followed by a thud into the landing wall close to his own door, Jake took the precaution of wedging a chair back under the doorknob. This he removed only when a police officer pounded on the door, demanding him to open up.

Officer Reynolds was a bull-necked brute of a man, and not dissimilar to Jake's father in physique. Not dissimilar either was his crumpled shirt patched with sweat, nor his bullying attitude as he barged his way into the room, reeking with that nauseating stench of stale breath and old sweat.

Officer Reynolds began poking under the bed with his truncheon long before he even spoke. "Any idea what went on out there?" he asked, yanking open the wardrobe door as if he expected to find someone inside.

"What's your name, boy?" Officer Reynolds demanded, dragging the cheap wardrobe away from the wall to search behind it; becoming even more belligerent when he found there was nothing there, except for a bashed-in section of filthy plasterwork, a couple of bullet holes, and a dark smear streaked down the wall beneath them. The disappointment in his face was apparent. His darting, red-rimmed eyes stopped scouring every inch of the room for an alternative hiding place and only then did he close the safety catch on his gun. He cautiously replaced it into the holster. "Ain't you gotta tongue, kid? I asked your name?"

"Jake Velasquez, sir."

"So, Velasquez, you got anything to say about what went on outside? You sure must have heard something," he said, opening his notebook to review a list of names scrawled on the page.

"I could hear a fight happening along the landing from here, which ended after a few gunshots."

"Hear anything else?"

"There was a lot of noise, and a woman shouting above the racket. I'm sorry, officer, that's about all I can tell you. I saw nothing,"

"You weren't curious enough to go out and see the action?"

"It was none of my business," Jake said. It was only then he became aware of the officer staring at his bare torso. He hastily pulled on a T-shirt.

"So, what's with the war-paint, pretty boy?" the officer asked, making himself just a little too comfortable on the edge of the bed. "You gotta be new in town if you imagine that a kid like you needs to dress up what's already on offer. You don't need that to pull any punters. The first lesson you need to learn is not to sell yourself off too cheap. With a bit of help, you could even make the big league. I'm not without influence amongst the movie crowd."

"Sir, you've made a big mistake," Jake said, doing his best to appear unfazed by the officer's interest, and moving well out of his reach.

"Never try and kid a kidder. I know exactly why any of you check in here, and why do I know that? Well, that's because I own

76

half of this joint. I can see you got potential, kid. So, I guess this has gotta be your lucky day," he said, lighting a cigarette. "My advice, kid, is that you leave earning the fast bucks to those desperate creeps who try it on their own. They all burn out fast without a manager. That or they end up in the city morgue. So take my advice before you decide to go it alone on the game. What you need is guidance from someone like me, because it's me that knows all the right places to pick up the right clients."

"I didn't check in here for any other reason than to sleep – on my own. That's all," Jake said. Fearing trouble ahead, he very carefully removed his spectacles and unclipped the wristband on the gold watch Gilbert had given him and placed them on the chest of drawers, in readiness for the fight which he presumed would follow the rejected offer.

"Get real, kid. Nobody with any sense would come here to sleep. These rooms are only rented by the hour."

"That's not why I'm here. All I need is a bed for the night. I'm short of cash, and it's cheap. No other reason than that," he said, wishing he had kept his spectacles on to gauge the officer's reaction.

"You're kidding me, right?"

"No, I'm not kidding," Jake said, wanting to get rid of him and the nauseating stink of stale sweat.

It was clear that it was going to be difficult to get him out of the room. Now that Officer Reynolds had let him in on how he operated in the city, it presented Jake with the huge dilemma of how to get away from there without getting beaten up, or shot as a suspected criminal. He just wished he had taken Ray's advice that morning and stayed well clear of the Hotel Czardas.

"OK, kid, I can see you're new to the set-up we have in the city, and I can help out if you're a bit strapped for cash," Officer Reynolds said. He loosened his tie exposing a grimy undershirt, he'd probably slept in for most of the week.

"I'm fine, officer; honestly, I am."

"Not from where I'm sitting,' he said, waving his hands to evaluate the sordid room. "So, I guess this is a lucky night for both of us, Velasquez; me being called out to my own place on a domestic," he said, and removed a small notebook out of his pocket. He flicked over the pages for Jake to see the list of names inside.

"Seriously, officer, you have me all wrong—" Jake began, but was cut short by Reynolds's leering face. It gave him good reason to think it was quite probable that Officer Reynolds would try it on with him, and the last thing Jake wanted was to get arrested for an assault on a police officer.

"And I've got serious news for you, kid. Take a look at the list in this book. Some of these kids were just like you, but they were doing tricks for peanuts until I got them off the streets and into the big time. You see, I ain't one of them jerks in the force that can't see beyond the next pay check. What I do benefits everybody. I operate a kind of dating agency for a lot of the movie toffs. When a new kid arrives in town, they all want a piece of the action. But that comes at a price. And if someone takes a real shine to you then anything could happen in this town. They're always scouting for new talent and a kid with your looks, well… So waddya say, kid, are you up for it?" he asked, reclining on the bed.

At that moment, Jake's thoughts were disrupted by a sharp clattering of high-heels on the landing coming rapidly towards them. The sound stopped outside his room, and a woman hammered on the door, screaming.

"Officer Reynolds, yah gotta come quick; there's a guy inside my room, bleedin' over my frocks."

"Get lost, bitch, I'm busy." Officer Reynolds snarled back.

"You gotta leave that kid be for now and get out here pronto. We gotta get rid of the body. We can't have another dead guy reported from here in a month. If it ain't gone by morning, this joint will get closed down for good, and then we're all screwed."

"Right, bitch, I'm coming," Reynolds growled. He left a five-dollar bill on the table by the bed as he left the room. "Think of the bill as an advance, kid. I'll be back again tomorrow."

As a precaution in case Officer Reynolds came back, Jake wedged the chair under the door handle again. He gauged how far the drop would be onto the fire escape if he needed to get out of the room in a hurry. Fortunately, it wasn't necessary that night.

Needless to say he didn't get much sleep, and was ready to leave well before daybreak, more exhausted than he'd been when he had arrived. Nauseated by the thought of using any showering facility at the hotel, and having seen the state of the communal toilet, he got out as quickly as he could.

Checking out of the hotel, Jake made a big issue with the desk clerk to give him a receipt on headed hotel paper for payment of the room and made sure he got another receipt for the sealed envelope addressed to Officer Reynolds, returning the five-dollar bill. He misled the clerk by saying it was important evidence which needed to be handed over to the officer when he returned to the hotel that night.

Because Jake checked out at three, there were no buses running, and as he needed to arrive at the studio by nine o'clock, he hitched a ride on a delivery truck and got dropped off at the beach. He took a long swim in the ocean after which, having a clearer head, he decided that he would take his chances and sleep outdoors for the next week at least.

After spending so much time in the water, the brand on his chest was beginning to throb, which made him feel both light-headed and sick, probably made worse through the lack of any substantial food the previous day. It didn't help when he got lost on the walk back to the studio.

Bearing in mind Doctor Maxwell's advice that he should grow a beard if he didn't want to be noticed, and because of the recent proposition from Officer Reynolds, and not wanting to draw any more unwelcome attention, Jake decided to keep the unshaven stubble. Just for the comforting familiarity it gave, he wore Cloud Bird's battered felt hat.

When Jake arrived at the studio gates, there was a single light illuminating the yard outside the white building, but not a glimmer of light showing from any of the office windows.

The barrier was down across the entrance at the gatehouse.

Inside, the security guard on night shift was reclining in his chair, fast asleep and snoring loudly from underneath an open newspaper.

Jake had no idea that anyone else was there until a man who was near the gatehouse moved into a more visible position, and coughed.

"Hi there," the stranger said, opening up the lid of a tobacco tin, and making himself a roll-up. "Fancy a smoke?"

"No, thanks," Jake said, and sat down with his back against the wall, hoping the man wouldn't try to make conversation. He wanted to catch up on some sleep, fearing that, if he didn't, he might mess up his first day on whatever the prospective job turned out to be.

"I suppose the assistant director didn't make contact with you either... about the change to the schedule?"

Jake's legs were tired from the distance he'd walked to reach the studio. His eyes were drooping, and the very last thing he wanted to do was talk. "Sorry, what did you say?"

"Nothing of any importance; you look worn out. I won't disturb you if you want to get some shut-eye. The gates don't open till seven. If you've dropped off, I'll bring over some coffee from the catering truck when I get mine."

"Why aren't the gates opened until seven?"

"The film crew would normally be open earlier but there's a dawn shoot in the canyon. The call here is at seven o'clock. That's when the coaches bringing the extras arrive."

"But how do the guys get in to make sure everything is ready on the set for when they arrive?"

"The studio parking lot is at the other gate. They get in that way. The office staff arrive around half past eight." He settled down into a better position for the long wait.

The little Jake could make out about him in the poor light was that the man was probably just a few years older than himself. He was lean, and above medium height, which was unusual for an American Indian. It was hard to make out his features clearly, except that his skin was dark against the crisp white linen shirt.

When Jake awoke, the man was stooping close by him with two

steaming mugs of coffee, which he placed on the ground between them.

"If you're hungry, pal, I don't mind sharing these with you. In fact, I'd be grateful if you did. I made too many last night. They'll only go to waste if you can't help me out." He offered Jake an opened lunch box of fresh sandwiches.

Feeling groggy and unsettled by the sound of a stranger talking to him, however friendly, wasn't the best way to be woken after the recent incident with Officer Reynolds at Hotel Czardas. Although Jake was ravenously hungry, he couldn't bring himself to take advantage of the other man's generosity.

"Honestly, I'm fine," Jake said, but even so the man placed the tin between them.

"Maybe you'll feel more like something to eat after you drink this coffee," he said, handing Jake one of the mugs. "Please take it, the mug won't bite and neither will I." He spoke with an encouraging laugh as Jake took a hesitant sip. "You need to drink up before the coach arrives and the extras make the early morning stampede to the catering truck."

Jake was actually enjoying the coffee, and he drank it down gratefully.

"I meant what I said about the sandwiches; I really did make up too many last night before I crashed out. The ones on the left are cheese and cucumber. The others are chicken and pickle. Go on, try one. You'd be doing me a favour," he said, with an engaging smile. When Jake took one of the smallest, the other man smiled broadly. "I'd put good money on you being new in town."

"Why say that?" Jake asked.

"Because you've got manners, that's not what I'd normally associate with your typical studio extra. When the regulars get here, they act like a shoal of hungry piranha, especially if the coach arrives late." He nodded to a cook who came through the back door of the catering truck now parked against the wall.

The metal shutter grated noisily as the caterer opened up the side of the truck. Inside, two organised cooks were working feverishly, inserting several containers of piping hot food into place in the steel counter.

Jake turned his attention to his companion. He too wore a worn felt hat. The brim was pulled down low to shade his pleasant features from the sun, which, at seven thirty, was already bright. The young man got a friendly wave from Ray when the security guard took over from the night watch, and slid open the hatch to lean out, calling: "Hi there, Scott, I see you've found our lost stray."

A dusty coach pulled up with a squeal of brakes for the security check. It immediately disgorged an all-male crowd of extras. Each was greeted by an assistant director who seemed to have appeared from nowhere and was handing out call-sheets along with food tokens and studio passes. Without a single exception, the men crowded around the catering truck until they were given breakfast.

"See what I mean about the local extras? "Scott commented, opening his tin of tobacco to roll up another cigarette.

When a second coach appeared, Ray leant through the hatch and called to Jake: "You'd better get through here now, son, before the crush starts in earnest." Then added, "I thought you would be here a mite early, but not before I arrived. Did you have any breakfast?" he asked.

"No, I didn't. I didn't want to be late on my first day, but Scott here was kind enough to share his sandwiches."

"I thought as much. I got an extra bagel for you on my way in. Keep it for later." He handed Jake a brown paper bag. "And before you offer, I don't want money. Just hang onto what cash you have. We all start on the bottom rung. Scott and I both know how it feels to be broke in this city."

"You're very kind, Ray. Thanks."

"It's my pleasure, son. Did you find a decent place to stay last night?"

"I got a room at the Czardas," Jake blurted out, but wished he hadn't when he saw Ray's uneasy reaction. Apologetically, he added: "It was the cheapest place."

"You can't stay in a joint like that, son. It's got a really bad reputation; much worse than any flophouse."

"It wasn't exactly what I expected, but it was fine. Not much to grumble at, really, at that price." Jake didn't want to offer any details about the previous night's events.

"Where was that you stayed?" Scott asked.

"At a rooming house in Grayel Street; it was advertised as a hotel."

"I did warn him about that dump. Anywhere would be better for a new kid in town rather than there," Ray said with a hint of annoyance.

"You did warn me against it, but it was cheap enough and it was a bed for the night."

"Ray's right. The Grayel Street area has got the worst reputation in town."

"Like I said, it was all I could afford," Jake blurted out defensively, wondering if everyone in the city would offer an opinion on his sleeping arrangements. "OK, so the bed wasn't anything to write home about. Anyway, I'm out of there and got a place with a decent view of the beach." He neglected to add that it would be under the pier.

"How long do you plan on staying there?" Scott asked.

"Not long. It depends on my job."

"If you do go back to Grayel Street here, don't be taking any of your belongings with you. They'll be safe enough here for a few more days till you get sorted out properly."

"I won't be going back there, but thanks for the offer, Ray."

Lounging back in his chair, Ray switched on the radio, and Jake got ready to leave.

"Thanks for the coffee and the sandwich, Scott. And thanks for the bagel, Ray. You're both very kind."

They were now being jostled as the second coach load of extras swelled the crowd at the entrance.

"So, if you're not working here as an extra then who are you working for?" Scott asked.

"My job offer is only temporary, and, if nothing else comes along, then I might apply to get some work as an extra."

"It won't be that easy; you need to be a member of the extras union, and there's a long wait for that."

83

"Then I guess my only hope of earning a living is to hang onto this job for as long as I can," Jake said, as he was edged away from him by the crowd.

"Have you any idea where you will be working?" Scott called after him, but his voice was lost amongst the crowd blocking the entrance, making noisy conversation as they showed their day passes.

For two hours, Jake waited in an outer office, endlessly checking the time on Gilbert's watch. He thought how ironic it was that, although they might be in the same city, there was no way of contacting him. To talk with him was the very thing he needed more than anything else.

At the end of that long wait, he was approached by a young man with bad breath and pockmarked skin. He led Jake up a grand flight of marble stairs and down a long corridor with a squeaky linoleum floor. At the end of this was the canteen.

Marjory Dawlish was seated behind two tables that had been pushed together to form a temporary working area. On this were neat stacks of paperwork. Most of these had an actor's photograph attached. She clipped a handful into a binder before giving Jake her attention.

"I see you didn't bother to shave," she commented, handing the completed files to her assistant, instructing him to take them to her office.

"I will, when I can afford a new razor and blades," he said, irritated by her condescending attitude. "I don't have spare cash for non-essentials. Not with the prices they charge in this city to get a bed for the night. Luxuries like shaving will just have to wait."

"It's the studio policy here, particularly in the main office block, to keep a good standard of appearance."

"Maybe I can work out of sight. I'm only here on a temporary basis" he said grimly.

She stood up and beckoned him to follow her through a haze of not-unpleasant perfume along another corridor.

Instead of being taken into an office in the white building, they went outside, down a long alley between two stages, and into an older building connected to one of the stages.

"I apologise for the state of this place. This is all I can offer you for temporary work. You did say you didn't mind what it was."

From her matter-of-fact tone Jake guessed she didn't expect an answer.

He followed her up a bleak staircase encased between walls that hadn't been painted in years, barely white, in parts. There was a dark flaking gloss on most of the woodwork. From the cracked plaster on the walls came an invasive, musty smell of wet sandbags. As they clattered up the echoing stairwell, Jake got the disturbing impression of being in an abandoned military shelter, than a million-dollar studio where many successful movies had been produced over the years.

"I didn't expect a movie studio to be like this," Jake said. He couldn't keep the surprise from his voice. Marjory Dawlish began to laugh, which helped thaw the frosty beginning.

"The sound stage attached, and this building, have not been scheduled for renovation until next year, although some of the spaces are still in use. There is a walkway through from the main building, but as I am rather limited for time, I brought you via a shortcut. Frankly, this has to be the grimmest place I have ever asked anyone to work."

"So I'll be working here then, doing what?" he asked, waiting to be handed a can of paint and a brush.

"Well, to begin with, I wanted to show you what's involved, and then you can tell me whether or not you are up to the challenge. You did say you would consider anything?"

"Sure, and I meant it. What is it you want me to do? Clean this place up, and give it a coat of paint?"

In response, she laughed again. "What I had in mind isn't quite as bad as that." She opened up a room that was lined with cluttered shelves of old film stock, some in canisters, piled in a jumble gathering dust.

"Jeepers, this is a mess in here."

"I couldn't agree more." She grimaced, looking at the chaos of piles on the shelves and floor. "I appreciate it's a challenge for anyone to regain any semblance of order in here. If you decide to give it a go, it will probably take you more than a week to sort through every one of the damaged movie reels, but it is an important job that has to be done."

"Why is it in such a state?" Jake asked. He could tell immediately that his question didn't go down well.

"I didn't bring you here to get your opinion. It was to offer you work. That is what you wanted when you agreed for us to use your pickup. But if you're not interested..." She was about to close the door, until Jake stopped her.

"I didn't mean to offend. It's just a shock to see old film stock being left out where it would easily get ruined."

She seemed appeased and switched on more of the overhead light, and allowed him further into the room.

"The problem we have here is that, because of the damp and length of time the stock has been left here, some of the labels are barely attached, and others have none at all. For anyone to view this old footage everything will have to be labelled correctly."

It wasn't the information that troubled him, it was what she wasn't saying which made him wonder what had been happening when he saw the full extent of the damage in the storeroom. It was an archivist's worst nightmare, and Jake realised what a difference Gilbert's comprehensive filing system would make to what was little more than a trashy dump of discarded film stock.

Everywhere, there were shelves and racks crammed with reels of celluloid film, most of which appeared to be in opened, unlabelled canisters. On the floor were other canisters stacked haphazardly on top of each other. However, it was the old movie stock lying exposed with no canisters at all that appalled him. The damage to the celluloid was unimaginable and, based on that alone, it was clear that the stock had been subjected to some atrocious handling; almost, it seemed, a deliberate act of vandalism.

"If the previous owners of the studio allowed this to happen, it isn't any wonder the place ran at a loss," he found himself saying.

She stepped back quickly to avoid a cloud of dust that billowed towards her as he moved a stack of metal film canisters to see if there were labels on them.

"Has some of the stock been taken away?" Jake asked as they left the room, seeing that some of the racks had very few reels on them.

Marjory switched off the lights and, holding a handkerchief tightly against her mouth, she closed and locked the door.

"This room was used by the old Silver Lake Studios, in its heyday, to store anything that wasn't commercially of value. This isn't where most of the good film stock is now being stored. Drew Walters takes care of the archives in another part of the building. This place is only used as an annex to that."

"What I don't understand, Miss Dawlish, is who would leave that store in such an awful mess?"

"Actually, there's no one person in particular, not since Malcolm was asked to leave. Since then, Drew's assistant has been collecting anything that might be viewable. What they've been unable to catalogue has been left behind. However, before any of this gets cleared out and dumped, I need to make perfectly sure that nothing of any importance has been missed, and that is precisely why you are here today, Mr Velasquez."

"Where are the main archives?" Jake asked.

"In the main building along there." She had stopped at a door with badly flaking paint a short distance away from the covered bridge that connected the building they were in to the main white office building.

"So my job is to catalogue and label any of those reels that haven't been identified?" he asked, with mounting enthusiasm.

"That's why you have been offered the job, Mr Velasquez. Correct me if I'm wrong, but didn't you say yesterday that you worked as a projectionist in your own theatre?" She sorted through a bunch of keys to unlock the door.

"Yes, I did a lot of editing too."

"I will need some evidence of your editing skills before you tamper with any of ours, which may, or may not, be of some value. We don't know what's in that room."

"I understand," Jake said, as she unlocked the door.

"This is where you will be working once you've done the test Drew has set for you." She opened the door into a shabby room. "We have several viewing theatres. This one is hardly ever used, but you should find this adequate for our requirements."

The space to which she seemed so indifferent was much grander than anything Jake was prepared for. However, he did his best not to appear overwhelmed.

"Is there anything else you need to know before I leave?"

"Well, yes. How do I make contact with you if I need more information about anything? Do I need a pass to allow me through the gates while I am working here? And, what time am I to start work in the morning?"

"Well firstly, Mr Velasquez, your temporary position here is dependent on your editing skills." She showed him a collection of split, snapped, and damaged celluloid film on the table. "These pieces of film have been sent here by Drew. When you have finished you might as well go home. Leave the film here, and it will be collected. We can talk again tomorrow morning at nine o'clock."

"Sure, I'll get onto it directly." Jake was paying more attention to the cutting and splicing equipment than he was to Marjory Dawlish as she left, closing the door quietly after her.

There were twelve pieces of archive footage for him to work on. Five of these he very quickly spliced together into one length, blessing Gilbert's patience as he worked, and the hours he spent teaching him that skill, wondering what he would have thought of him now, using that technique in a Hollywood studio, almost ten years later. Three of the other pieces he was able to edit into a single run. The remaining four lengths, however, caused him to work late into the evening, and he missed the last bus.

It was gone eleven o'clock when he set off, but having missed his ride to the beach he called in at a Mexican food store for a burrito and Coke. It was almost one o'clock when he arrived at the pier, tired and ready for a sleep; sleep which didn't happen: the tide was in, and most of the timber structure, where he had planned to spend the night, was underwater.

Luckily, he found a quiet place among the dunes, which suited him perfectly, and within moments of settling down he was fast asleep.

He awoke to the sound of a council worker whistling tunelessly as he collected empty bottles, clattering them into his cart before moving on a few feet.

Unable to sleep, Jake took a long time swimming in the surf, but as soon as the town hall clock struck six o'clock, he set off at a brisk pace towards the studio, having decided not to spend any cash on bus fare.

When he checked the time on his wristwatch, he realised that the town hall clock had been striking an hour late, and it was eight thirty when he arrived at the studio gate, hot and sweaty.

Fortunately, it was Ray on duty again that morning. He opened up the locked storeroom, which enabled Jake to get a change of clothes from his suitcase. Ray directed him to the washroom, and Jake changed his clothes, which although crumpled, were clean.

Probably because it was new to him, the stubble of his beard really itched, but not as much as his hair, clogged up with salt from the morning swim. To prevent himself from scratching his scalp until he could wash his hair, Jake crammed the felt hat over it. Feeling more like a tramp than just being down on his luck, Jake made his way to the Projection Room, where he found Miss Dawlish waiting for him with one cup of coffee, and that was hers.

"This splicing you got together yesterday looks very impressive," she said, holding up the strips of re-joined celluloid against the light to examine them again. "I must get these to Drew in the editing suite. I'm sure what you've accomplished here will meet his exacting standards. He thought you'd have faltered repairing one of these. I'm no expert but they seem to be perfectly well spliced together."

"I know exactly the one that would be." Jake grimaced, reminded of the difficulty he'd had, which forced him to work so late. "That would be this one here. He took the strips from her and attached one of them onto the sprockets of the projector. Switching on, he wound the celluloid through, which was then projected onto the screen for her to see.

"Well done, Mr Velasquez. I'd say you've done a marvellous job. Would like you to stay on and work here. I'm sure Drew will be happy with this."

"Can you do that...? Without his go ahead, I mean? I wouldn't want you to land in any hot water; not on my behalf."

"You needn't worry about that. Drew works for me, not the other way around."

"Great, then I'm ready to make a start. But I need to ask you a couple of questions first."

"Well?" she said looking anxious, checking the time on the wall clock. "I can spare you five minutes. What do you want to know?"

"First off, who will unlock the Projection Room; second, who should I contact once I've viewed a batch of those reels? I assume you'll want me to enter everything I've viewed into a book before I hand them over?" he said, expecting to be given a record book similar to the one Gilbert used in which he detailed every movie at the ranch.

"I'll have the office runner bring over a set of keys. There is a contact list on the wall of all internal telephone numbers. As for making records, that's a question to ask Drew. Is there anything else you need to find out before I return this to him?" she asked, carefully placing Jake's edited footage into a canister.

"There are two things, actually. Because I'll be viewing some footage that doesn't have any title on the canister for reference, would it be possible to get a list of every movie that was made at the studio?"

"You mentioned two things?"

"The other, is that I would like a second book to keep here so that I can keep a record for myself on what I've found, to show whether it's either a complete movie or not."

Assuming that his request probably wouldn't materialize until the day his work at the studio had finished, Jake removed the notepad and pencil from his back pocket, deciding where he would make a start and broke down the first few pages of the notebook into sections with a numbering code for each reel, the movie title (if any) how many reels each movie comprised, when it was filmed and, its release date.

By the end of the day, no record book had been delivered; an error which he had forgotten to mention when he saw Miss Dawlish again that afternoon. She was a lot less impatient with him than she had been earlier, when she saw a stack of twelve viewed reels plus the details of each reel neatly recorded into a book, duplicates of which were taped onto the relevant canisters.

"What are these reels doing here?" she asked, checking the time on the wall clock. "It's almost five; no movie stock should be left unattended after you've gone home."

"The guy I spoke with in the Archive Department said I shouldn't deliver them in person; he said he would prefer to collect them himself."

"Drew said that? I wonder why? That isn't normally the way he works." She dialled his number on the internal phone. "Hi Drew, this is Marjory. I'm with the new guy in the old viewing theatre, and the checked reels are still here. You did, ah, that's OK then. I'll get him to bring them over before he leaves. I'll come with him now to show him the way."

"Sorry, did I get it wrong?" Jake asked.

"No. Drew forgot to ask his assistant to come over."

Before they crossed over the gantry bridge into the main building, they went down a short flight of stairs to reach a lower section of the corridor. When Jake missed his footing, he would most certainly have fallen down the staircase to the corridor below, if Marjory Dawlish hadn't caught hold of his arm until he regained his balance. Steadying the pile of reels, they went up a short ramp to gain access to the gantry bridge. Once in the main building the Archive Department was easy to find.

"I did say I could help with the canisters. You didn't have to manage them all on your own. You could have had a nasty fall back there," she said.

"I didn't expect so many stairs; otherwise, I would have asked."

"Don't try to carry as many as you have there, and for heaven's sake, do watch where you're treading next time. You could have broken your neck if you'd fallen."

By the time they arrived, his arms were aching from the weight of the canisters.

The Archive Department was on the top floor, and Jake rested the pile on a handrail as they waited for the door to be opened, which gave him time to clean the dust off his spectacles.

The clinically clean Archive Department with pale coloured walls came as a big shock. It was the exact opposite to the derelict storeroom and the viewing theatre where he had been working. There was squeaking linoleum underfoot, and a neatly arranged collection of cactus plants on the windowsills. On two of the walls, devoid of shelving, there was a display of neatly framed movie stills featuring elegantly posed actors of the silent era, while other frames had examples of elaborate set designs from the same period.

It was one of these, in particular, which attracted his immediate interest. It was a sepia-tinted sketch of a central courtyard enclosed by cloistered arches and belonging to a grand hacienda. What caught his attention was that it seemed to be a little familiar. Annoyingly, he was unable to look at the sketch in closer detail because he was called over to be introduced. He made his way towards them, alert, hoping there might be something else familiar, before he was obliged to give his full attention to Drew and the other occupant of the Archive.

"Your system is very impressive," was all Jake could think of to say when he met the first of the two men.

The assistant was considerably younger than the man engrossed in a conversation with Marjory Dawlish. He was tall and wafer-thin and had an unpleasant way of squinting through his spectacles. Jake chose to say nothing more. Drew Walters finished his exchange with Marjory Dawlish, and he was finally introduced.

Drew had badly dyed red hair and a greying beard. He stared at Jake curiously, and for just a bit too long for Jake to feel comfortable, but he was considerably more likeable than his silent colleague.

"So I gather you are quite taken with our system?" Drew began, resuming work on the editing table. "This archive wasn't planned this way. Not until the powers that be were made to listen to good old-fashioned logic," he commented dryly, splicing together two lengths of film by using a gleaming piece of cutting equipment.

"I am, sir, very much," Jake responded, admiring the efficient use of space, and the way every piece of equipment had been fitted to make it easily accessible.

"At last, Marjory, a youthful voice of sanity telling it the way it really is. If it's appreciated by the youth of today it should go someway to proving your fight to secure this investment with that Jeffords bitch wasn't all for nothing." Drew said, and threw a length of unwanted film into a linen waste bin.

"You give me too much credit. Barbara Jeffords would have signed the cheque eventually."

"Maybe, but I doubt that she'd have budged on her offer if you hadn't pushed for us."

"You know that we couldn't afford to lose you. Nor Frank," she added quickly, but not quickly enough to avoid Frank glaring in her direction. But Jake was far more interested in the mention of Barbara Jeffords.

"Barbara Jeffords? Who's she?" He was pleased he managed to keep his voice calm, considering she was the woman he most wanted to meet, and question.

"She'll be arranging your pay cheque every week," Marjory said, and Drew laughed.

Putting on a pair of white cotton gloves, Drew handled a strip of film and scrutinised every inch. He examined another strip, and finally another. Jake recognised them as the ones he'd repaired the day before.

"Be warned, young man," Drew said, "she's not someone to get on the wrong side of." He was interrupted by the internal phone ringing, which Frank answered. He then indicated to Marjory the caller was asking for her.

"Honestly, Drew, what are you thinking? You shouldn't be making that sort of comment about a head of staff to a newcomer," Marjory said cautiously, moving away to speak on the phone.

"The kid needs to be told who to avoid and who to trust if he's gonna work here."

"Perhaps, but if she gets to hear of it…." She took the handset from Frank.

"Then I'll take my chances on that score. This isn't the only studio in town," he said. "You need to listen to me, kid, and stay out of that woman's way. That is one nasty piece of work, just like old man Stanford. Either of them would eat you alive."

"Stanford? Is that her husband?"

"Her brother. The pair ran this studio together, which is probably why it went bankrupt."

"Take a word of advice: be cautious of what you say around Barbra Jeffords. No one is safe from her wrath, not even the private life of Adelaide Williams; you've met her, presumably?"

"Yes, she seems very much in control of her department," Jake said, wondering where the conversation was heading, but with Marjory Dawlish caught up in a telephone conversation, he had no alternative but to express some interest.

"Not long after this studio was taken over, it appeared that Barbra Jeffords fired Adelaide's butler without informing her. That old guy was devoted to that woman. He'd been in her service since she was a child."

"How is it possible anyone could do that?"

"Creative accounting, I suppose. The way I heard it, the butler was on the studio payroll; don't ask me why."

"What became of him?"

"He was probably sent back to England, but only Barbra Jeffords and Stanford would know that. So I would suggest you stay well clear of them both."

Throughout this conversation, Miss Dawlish was still engrossed with her telephone call, and Jake wondered how she would react to discover him receiving more studio gossip.

"Were you working in here when this was operating as a movie studio?" he asked.

"If I had been, the old Archive Room would never have been allowed to get into such a state. What you see here is how I work," Drew answered proudly.

"Since our company took over, Drew has worked wonders in the Archive Department to create this new editing suite," Marjory said, putting down the phone. "It has taken him eight months of hard work to achieve this."

"It was ten, actually. A lot of that work was made necessary because that idiot Malcolm had been in sole charge of the storeroom. The place was in an absolute shambles," Drew said bitterly. "God alone knows what went on in that man's head to do that. I can only hope that it was that brute Stanford who broke Malcolm's nose."

"Never," Marjory protested.

"Why not, he only needed to take a look at that movie archive to realise that he had to sell up or go bust."

"Who was this Malcolm who wanted to destroy so much of the studio's movie history?" Jake asked, trying not to show too much interest.

"Malcolm Reynolds was part of Stanford's studio-mafia—" Drew started, but was interrupted abruptly by Marjory.

"We should be getting off, Drew," Marjory said, ushering Jake towards the door. "I'll get Mr Velasquez, Jake, to drop off his work now that he knows the way here."

They left, and she closed the door after them. "It would be advisable when you make deliveries here not to become involved with any studio gossip. Drew is marvellous at what he does, but he is the worst person ever at preventing everyone from getting on with what they have been employed to do."

"I understand," Jake responded. He was comfortable with what he'd learnt during the short time he'd been in the Archive Department, but knew that Drew Walters would be the perfect source for any other information he might need during the limited time he would be working there.

Chapter Six

Before making his way to the beach that evening when he got off the bus, Jake stopped to examine a display of watches in a pawnshop window and, on impulse, because it was still open, he went inside.

"I've got this watch," Jake began, tentatively, uncertain if he should pawn Gilbert's treasured gift for cash. However, his stomach was empty and rumbling and he felt sure that he might pass out if he didn't get something to eat very soon. He had barely ten cents left in his pocket from the three-dollar advance.

"I'm sorry, son. I can't take on another watch just now. There's not much demand for them see," the proprietor said.

"Sir, you don't understand; the last thing I want is to pawn this watch, but I have no choice. I need to eat. It's all I have that's of any value," Jake persisted, uncertain why the owner was scrutinising him cynically.

"If I had a dollar for every time I've heard that, I'd be a damned sight richer than I am right now. The fact is, I've been taken in many times in the past by a guy turning up here with a hard-luck story; but not a single one of those guys ever came back to claim what he'd pawned. That is, if it was his to begin with. So you see my predicament, and I'm not prepared to take that chance again." The pawnbroker shook his head. "Besides, why would I need to if I've got a box crammed full of crap watches out back which ain't goin' nowhere fast. The market ain't what it was."

"I don't want to sell it," Jake said with increasing alarm. "I need to pawn it until the end of the week when I get paid." Carefully, he unclipped the gold clasp before handing over the watch for inspection.

"Well now, ain't this just a little beauty," the proprietor remarked, unable to conceal his astonishment. "I can't remember the last time I saw a dandy timepiece of this quality. If truth be told, I can't recall when I last handled a watch like this. Just in case the law comes calling, I need to ask where a young fella like you got hold of such a great watch?"

"Actually, this was a gift for my birthday."

"Then are you sure about putting it in hock?"

"Not really, but I need to eat," Jake answered. He loathed being so desperate that he needed to leave the watch behind.

Jake bought a fish and chip supper along the seafront, and walked for about a mile towards what remained of a storm-damaged pier. In a surf shop along the way, he bought a towel then searched for a dry, secluded position under the pier, making sure that where he chose to spend the night wasn't in danger of being swamped by the incoming tide.

With $3.65 in his pocket, he wouldn't starve, but nevertheless, he found it hard to relax and get the sleep he so desperately needed, fretting about the pawnbroker, or mislaying his pawn ticket, and wanting to retrieve his watch at the first opportunity. Apart from an itching scalp and dry skin from bathing in sea water, and irritating grains of sand that always found a way into his underwear, given his current financial situation, he expected to be roughing it there until he got paid, particularly when he considered how much cash he would have left – given the three dollars advance from his salary, and paying the inflated rate of interest the pawnbroker expected.

For the first time since his arrival in California, and after being allowed into the studio to begin his second day of work, he felt more in control of his life. He liked working on his own. He went to the storeroom to collect the first stack of reels and gathered up the first pile of canisters. He locked up the store again and took them to the Projection Room.

Left to his own devices, Jake was soon able to familiarise himself with the equipment, which was more up to date than he was used to. However, he soon found that he was hankering after Doctor Maxwell's old projector, which he knew well and had serviced regularly. The problem with the one in the Projection

Room was that no one had serviced that piece of equipment in years. After trying to view the first reel he was unable to bring any of the images projected onto the screen into sharp focus. To try and resolve this, he began to strip down the projector to locate the fault and, at the same time, give the machine a decent clean. He discovered that the fogging wasn't due to a lack of service, but that the inner surface of the lens had been purposely rubbed with an abrasive.

Jake made an extensive search of the Projection Room but he couldn't find a replacement lens in any of the cupboards. When he called the Archive Department and spoke with Drew, he could offer no solution either.

Because it was impossible to work without getting a replacement lens, Jake spent most of the afternoon searching through every drawer and cupboard, and a pile of equipment boxes covered in dust, which he almost missed in the dim light of the storeroom. These boxes had been pushed under the back shelving units and were almost impossible to see. It was in one of these boxes that he found the replacement lens he needed. Once fitted into the projector, every reel of film projected on to the screen was shown in perfect clarity.

It was late when Marjory Dawlish came into the viewing theatre. "I thought I should inform you that we are using your pickup in tomorrow's shoot, Mr Velasquez."

"Sure," he said, annoyed that she'd broken his concentration, and wondering why she needed to tell him if the vehicle was under the control of the Transport Captain. "Is there a problem?"

"None at all, at least, that's what I've been informed. Why, is there something the Transport Captain needs to know?"

"You saw what it was like on the morning when I blocked up the gate. It can be a difficult machine to start."

"Then it might be a good idea if you go down to the back lot where the scene is being shot, just in case you're needed." She was examining the footage Jake had been splicing together. "You are very good at this...I can barely see what you've repaired. Incidentally, I should mention that Drew was most impressed with your work and, from this, I can see why."

Because she seemed relaxed and a lot more communicative than usual, Jake decided to get more information.

"Would you mind if I asked you about the guy, Malcolm, who was responsible for the Archives Department before Drew took over?"

"Why would that be of any interest to you?"

"I just wondered why he got away with leaving the store in such an unholy mess. What kind of person was he?"

"Might I ask what's brought this on?"

"Sure, it's because I am certain the mess he left behind must have been deliberate."

"Then I strongly advise you to stop right there. Granted, Malcolm did leave the storeroom in a reprehensible state. But, however unpleasant I have known him to be on occasions, I'm sure he'd never have behaved in a malicious way."

"That is because you've not been witness to what I have. I've good enough reason to suspect him. There were too many mismatched reels placed into wrong canisters."

"And that justifies your suspicions?"

"No, there was something else. There were a lot of missing labels off the canisters and some reels. You can actually see where the title has been purposely torn away, or that it's been scraped off. Whatever else might have happened to these labels, none of them would have come off without manual help. It wasn't caused through damp, age, or neglect; there's too much evidence against it."

"If what you are suggesting is correct, it makes no sense to me. It would be very B Movie stuff if it came to light that the mess Malcolm left behind was actually deliberate," Marjory said reluctantly.

"Anyone who knows what they're doing would never make such a mistake. This was calculated; but what puzzles me, is why?"

"I'm sorry, I can't help, if indeed that did happen," Marjory said, although Jake felt she might be holding something back.

Later, instead of leaving the delivery of his work until the end of the day, Jake went over to the Archive Department much earlier, when he put his theory to Drew.

"Well, I agree, Jake. Something stinks about all of this. Malcolm Reynolds should never have been allowed to get away with sabotage. He should have been prosecuted, and yet nothing was ever done about it. I made quite a stir in the office about the state of the place when I took over. It ruffled a few feathers, particularly that old hag, Barbara Jeffords. She's still got a stranglehold on the windpipe of the studio, even now, after the place was sold. I would guess that she is involved somehow."

"What do you think his reasons were to behave like that?" Jake asked.

"There was some interesting gossip about a movie made by the old Silver Lake Studio a good few years before; it was never released," Drew said thoughtfully. "I heard about that around the time the TV company was opening up negotiations with Maurice Stanford to buy the place."

"That doesn't make any sense. Why would that cause Malcolm Reynolds, or even this Barbara Jeffords, to go off at the deep end?"

"It just might, if what they said about that movie was to be believed. It was something quite special. Unique, one of them said, which, had it been released, would have prevented the studio from being sold off."

"But how could that affect Malcolm Reynolds?"

"Trashing the archives? What I heard was the final reel had gone missing, and without that the movie couldn't be released. What I do know is that Maurice Stanford is still optimistic about getting the missing reel back. If he did, I'm certain that he'd take a chance and release it."

"Was the movie shot in colour?" Jake was praying that it would have been.

"I doubt that; although, Moira, in publicity, did say that it was advanced in every way – beyond anything else made at that time. If it was shot twenty odd years ago, then I would assume it was filmed in black-and-white."

"And one reel was missing?" Jake asked, remembering what

Gilbert had told him about a fatal accident when two reels were destroyed in the car wreck. Drew must be referring to some other, unrelated, incident. Even though it all seemed a bit too coincidental, Jake never for a second doubted the truth of what Gilbert had told him.

"Yes just one. Why, what made you ask?"

"Well, if this movie is as old as you suggest, why would anyone in their right mind consider releasing a black-and-white movie? I can't see how that would be of any interest to today's audience," Jake said, remembering how difficult it had been to generate any interest amongst the locals back in Fort Laverne and, once the novelty of opening a Picture Palace in the town had worn off, to get them to pay to watch a vintage movie. Even though they were starved of entertainment, they would only pay to see something released within the past five years.

"The age of that movie wouldn't have mattered."

"How could resurrecting an old black-and-white movie bring in any revenue? Nobody back home would give a dime to watch a movie that was made over twenty years ago unless they were movie buffs."

"You have a point, but this was something quite extraordinary. It was a mystery, filmed in the style of a French or Italian classic."

Hearing that offered Jake some reassurance that Gilbert's reel could not have been connected. "Then it would be a classic who-dunnit?"

"Something like that; but this one had what those old dramas lacked. It was a musical. Nothing like it has ever been produced by another studio, either here or anywhere else in America, according to Moira."

"How come she knows so much about it?" Jake asked.

He wanted more information but he was unsure just how far he could push the questioning without making Drew suspicious. Fortunately it hadn't so far, but Drew's assistant, Frank, seemed intent on edging closer, and wasn't paying too much attention to the splicing job he had in hand.

"Moira's worked here forever in the publicity department. If you need to know anything about what's been made here, she's the one to ask. She's got a ton of movie periodicals that go back to the dark ages, which she protects like a mother hen."

"Then you know Moira quite well?"

"As well as anyone can, but not well enough to let me take one of her magazines away to research the movie stock which came with the studio. However, she did show me an enthusiastic write-up about that lost movie. It said the director was a genius, and the production outshone anything made in Europe."

"I still don't see why that might affect Malcolm Reynolds. Why would he risk his position and deliberately cause such chaos? What would make anyone get so riled up to do that?" Jake asked.

Drew finally noticed his assistant's interest and scowled. Frank moved away and seemingly began to pay more attention to his work than their conversation.

"What I heard," Drew said, purposely turning away from Frank, and speaking in a lowered voice, "was that Maurice Stanford intended to re-edit the movie credits and name himself as director and producer."

"Is that legal?"

"Probably not, but knowing how Stanford operates, he would probably get away with it if the end reel ever resurfaced."

"So where does Malcolm Reynolds fit in?"

"Based on hearsay, he would be credited as co-producer. That's only Moira's opinion, but she has good judgement. She's smart and has a good nose for facts."

Jake didn't pursue the conversation any further. He knew that Drew was no fool, and the last thing he wanted was to give him any idea that he might have a personal interest. Only then did he realise Drew had been staring at him for some time. It coincided with a crash as Frank either accidentally or deliberately knocked a canister of film off the work surface.

"I'm sorry, Drew, I missed that. What did you say?" Jake asked.

"Oh nothing of any importance, I was thinking out loud," Drew blustered.

But Jake needed to know. "Are you unhappy with the repairs

I've done?"

"Gee, no, I couldn't be happier about them. No, it was nothing like that. It was about you."

"What about me? What have I done?" Jake asked, wondering what on earth it could be that would cause Drew to flush red.

"It's just that when I was talking, and you were standing in profile against the window, you seemed shockingly familiar to someone I've seen before. I never forget a face, but for the life of me I can't think who, and that's going to bug me till I remember."

"I probably look like a million other young guys in this town," Jake said, attempting to shrug it off.

"You know what? I'd pay good money to see that face of yours without all that stubble. Will you be shaving it off any time soon?"

"No chance." Jake laughed uneasily at the way the conversation was going. He knew he needed to get out of there but Drew insisted they were both entitled to a coffee break, and that Jake must stay and take it with him.

Frank made the coffee. It wasn't very hot so Jake drank it quickly, but not quickly enough as Drew remembered the name, and he was beaming.

"I remember exactly who you put me in mind of. It was a guy called Renaldo, something or other. He was a big name in Hollywood in the Twenties. It was one of those faces you don't forget; he dropped completely off the circuit when talkies came in."

"If it was that long ago, your memory could be playing tricks." Jake laughed, but wished he could let him get back to what he was being paid to do. But Drew was expounding on a favourite subject.

"There must be publicity stills of him in the building. I'll see if I can track one down for you," Drew called after him as Jake hurried to the door.

The next morning, because Jake's pickup was needed for the main shot of that day, Marjory asked him to take a break from his work and be on the back lot by ten thirty when the camera crew was due to begin filming. When he arrived and saw the crowd of extras hanging around the catering truck, he remembered Scott's comment that first day at the gate, and it made him smile. Jake cleaned the lenses of his glasses before he scanned the faces, sure that he would recognise him. It wasn't a face that anyone would forget easily, but with so many extras and crew milling about, there wasn't much hope of singling him out even if he was there.

Some of the extras were dressed in US cavalry uniforms, while others were queuing outside a costume tent, still wearing their everyday clothes, and smoking.

What Jake found particularly interesting was the activity in the corral of horses being saddled up for the next camera shot, which is where he would have preferred to be. Concerned because there was no sign of Marjory Dawlish, Jake asked one of the extras where his pickup might be, but neither he nor any of the other extras could give him an answer. He then asked an assistant who was passing and learnt the sequence of filming had been changed and the pickup wasn't required until after lunch.

Jake returned to the viewing theatre by taking a shortcut between two of the stages. He saw an arrogant-looking man with dyed ginger hair striding towards him wearing the weirdest outfit. Jake could only presume that it was expected to pass for an authentic American Indian costume. Unable to prevent himself, Jake burst out laughing.

Almost immediately, the man, an assistant in charge of the crowd scenes, barked out instructions to a group of extras about what they ought to do on the set: a construction of what barely resembled an adobe village.

"Quiet, please," the assistant director shouted at Jake through a megaphone.

Marjory noticed, and she crossed over to him. "What are you making such a noise about?"

Jake didn't hold back with his opinions of the stage set and the man's costume. Moments later, the fuming assistant director had joined them. When he got up close, Jake was surprised. He recognised him as the sandy-haired man he'd seen at Dr Maxwell's funeral.

"How did this bloody idiot get on the set, Marjory?"

"I apologise, Frazer. Jake has only just begun working here, and he isn't yet familiar with on-set procedures."

"Then either get him off here, or fire the jerk. I don't care which," he snapped and was about to walk away when Marjory stopped him. "I think you need to hear this, Frazer. Apparently, the layout of the set is all wrong. It needs changing."

"Technical advice on the Navajo Nation is not your responsibility. Broken Tooth is our technical advisor. He knows better than anyone what is required on set. After all, he is a Navajo chief," Frazer replied.

"That guy is no more Navajo than I am." Jake said firmly. The rich tone of his voice made the people close by turn and pay attention.

"And how would a four-eyed creep like you know?" Frazer barked back incensed that anyone would dare to question the technical advisor's authenticity.

"This man knows a damn sight more than you might imagine, and his opinion shouldn't be dismissed on a whim. You should listen to him," Marjory said.

"How can he? The guy's white," Frazer sneered.

Jake's annoyance spilled into anger. "Yes, I am white, but I am also a Navajo blood brother," Jake said proudly, undoing Moon Spirit's wristband to expose the ceremonial scar. He then unbuttoned his shirt to reveal the intricate brand of an eagle, not yet healed, and looking incredibly painful. It caught both Marjory and the assistant director off guard.

It was Marjory who rallied first. "Frazer, you should listen to what he has to say if the set's wrong... unless, of course, you want to be bawled out of the theatre when the director gets to hear about it."

"Hey, you, Broken Tooth – or whatever you're calling yourself today. Get your arse over to my caravan now, and wait for me there," Frazer shouted angrily.

When Jake returned to the set at the newly specified time, it was to discover that filming had been pushed back again. There were a lot of craftsmen finishing off work on the fake adobe dwellings; the exposed plywood was frantically being re-plastered for the waiting painters. Closer to the camera position, an injured man was being carried away on a stretcher and loaded into an ambulance. Jake was waiting close by to ask what time he ought to return to the set, but the assistant director was offering apologies to an irate director about the delay in filming.

"What the hell am I expected to shoot if I haven't got a blasted rider to do the scene for me, you blundering idiot," the director screeched, gesticulating with a smouldering cigar clamped between his fat fingers.

"It'll be impossible to get someone from the wranglers' agency to cover for him at short notice, Mr Stanford," Frazer said, his voice faltering.

"Then find someone here, you bloody simpering buffoon. Anyone will do; just make sure they can sit on that blasted horse without falling off, like the last imbecile."

"We can't put just anyone on that nag, Mr Stanford," Frazer tried to explain.

"And why the hell not, horses jump, don't they? Unless they're dead from the neck up, like you, you useless little fart," Maurice Stanford hissed.

"The horse won't be able to make that jump again, sir, because it's lame."

"Then get another, and be quick about it. Any more hold-ups on today's shoot and you can find yourself another job."

"But, Mr Stanford, it's an incredibly high jump and that was the only horse that could clear it," Frazer answered.

"What about using that brute over there?" he demanded, pointing with the cigar. "That crazy stallion with the flared nostrils and bad attitude has been prancing around the corral since I got here. Use your loaf, man, harness that thing." he snarled, chomping down savagely on the cigar. "If that sprung-loaded stallion can jump with the same energy that it can buck, the beast should fly over." He was indicating a fierce-looking grey horse which snorted angrily as it charged any onlookers that got too close to the corral. Across the bridge of its eyes, the horse had the black markings of a mask.

"But, sir, it would be suicide for anyone to ride that fireball except for Scott, and he's not arrived yet," Frazer answered nervously, checking his watch.

"You think I give a brass fart what jerk gets on its back? Just get another rider," Stanford snarled, glaring around him until his eyes focused on Jake. "Try him, that four-eyed extra over there. He'd be about the same size as Clark."

"But the union...he's not an extra."

"I can handle them, Frazer. I want this scene in the can within the hour."

"I don't know if he can ride, Mr Stanford."

"Then damned well ask him. And, Frazer, a word to the wise, don't tell that prick what he's riding. Let him find that out for himself."

"But, sir – what you're suggesting...even an experienced rider would never attempt a jump that high...not without a saddle...and certainly not on that horse—"

"That is precisely why we have insurance. The new rider can break his blasted neck for all I care. I need this shot whatever it takes. Just get to it, Frazer, and make sure he takes that jump. Now get out of my sight, and take that interfering clown into make-up quick."

Being unable to ride every day was something Jake missed more than he could have imagined, and being offered the opportunity to sit astride a horse again that afternoon was a blissful thought indeed, and too good to miss.

Within moments of agreeing, Jake was hurried along into the make-up tent, where he was shaved, and his face and torso darkened. It was only when the make-up artist was about to apply the war paint that Jake protested, insisting that he applied his own.

When Jake came out of the tent, he was barely recognisable, wearing little more than a suede loincloth. He wore nothing on his feet, having chosen to ride barefoot. Covering his hair was a long black wig and a feathered headband. He wore beaded amulets and was carrying a spear. He had a sheath of arrows slung across his shoulders.

Still wearing his glasses, Jake was closely accompanied by a young assistant director with a megaphone until they reached a gated corral. "Make sure they don't get broken," Jake said, handing over his spectacles.

"Don't worry, I'll leave them at the make-up tent," he said, as Jake entered the enclosure.

Although he was unable to see anything clearly, Jake was aware of the tense atmosphere amongst the gathered extras when the wranglers failed another attempt to control the nightmarish stallion rearing up inside the corral. Removing the quiver complete with arrows, Jake handed these and his spear to an extra before he climbed over the corral fence.

For the first time since arriving in California Jake felt a strong connection to his Navajo past, so close to the magnificent animal. Approaching through clouds of swirling dust and the reverberating thud of hooves, he reached out, laying the palm of his hand on the beading sweat of the stallion's neck. At the moment of bonding, Jake felt Cloud Bird's reassuring presence guiding his hand in that first reassuring contact with the animal.

Within ten minutes, he had not only quieted the stallion, but was astride its back. After a spirited bucking session, the wrangler opened the gate at the cue given by an assistant to say the film was rolling. Ignoring the sheath of arrows the extra offered up to him, Jake grabbed hold of the spear just as the stallion charged through the opening. Leaning forward onto its neck, he urged it towards the jump, which the fearless grey cleared magnificently.

Moments later, a mounted warrior galloped towards them from the other side, whooping like a maniac. The warrior's riding skills were similar to the way that Cloud Bird would handle his horse, and it seemed odd how much the warrior resembled him – until he smiled, and Jake took to the stranger instantly.

"Well done, sport. I thought you'd be a goner taking a jump like that," the warrior said.

"I didn't do anything. It's this beauty that should take the credit, not me."

"I've never known Firebrand let anyone on his back before, except me, of course, and that always took time. I can't believe that you tackled a jump like that, bareback." The young warrior offered Jake his hand. "I say, pal, are you all right?"

"Sorry, it's hard to focus on anything properly without my glasses."

"What? You need to wear specs and you took that jump without wearing any? Where are they?"

"One of the assistant directors has taken them to the make-up tent. I'm not sure how to get back there."

"That's OK, I'll show you. We can walk there together, but first I must get Firebrand back into the corral. No one likes him being out these days. I'm Lone Wolf, by the way, and that was my idiot boss who just broke his collarbone attempting that same jump earlier. He should have known better. He's thought to be the best wrangler in movies. I guess now he isn't."

"So you work here then?" Jake asked, wondering who he was, and whether he'd been amongst the extras earlier. Because of their make-up and wigs, it was hard to recognise anyone at all.

"Sure, I can't say I enjoy it that much, but it's a living. So, what's your name?"

"Pale Horse," Jake said, stroking the stallion's neck. "I've only recently got here from New Mexico." He shook the man's hand; he was studying the beaded strap over the ceremonial scar on his wrist.

"You are Navajo?"

"Partially, I was accepted as a blood brother. Otherwise, I'm Jake Velasquez. I own that beaten-up pickup over there," Jake said, indicating the truck when they rode past.

His new acquaintance burst into a peal of laughter. "So you're that Velasquez. I should have guessed as much. My sister told me you rode, but I didn't imagine it would be anything as good as that."

"Your sister knows me?"

"Madge, Marjory Dawlish," he said with a broad grin, exposing a set of very white but irregular teeth. "I can see that you didn't expect that either? The make-up people here do a great job wouldn't you say?"

"They sure do," Jake said. Hearing Marjory Dawlish's name

reminded him he needed to get back to the viewing theatre, just as soon as his truck had been used, and so they agreed to meet up in the bar for a drink later.

"How will I recognise you?" the warrior asked.

"I'll probably be the only guy in there wearing a pair of specs."

Jake was in line with the other extras, waiting to get cleaned up in the make-up tent, when he overheard Marjory talking to one of the girls re-dressing the American Indian wigs onto their appropriate wig stands.

"Any idea where I might find him, Cathy, it's rather urgent I get hold of him directly."

"Delores," the wig mistress called over to the woman who was with one of the extras, "what time did you clean off that new kid from Archives? Marjory is here looking for him."

"Who, Velasquez? The kid's still here. I've been saving him till last," she said with a broad wink. "With a bit of luck, I'm hoping he'll invite me out for dinner." she said, with the raucous laugh of a heavy smoker.

"You and me both," Cathy said. "Say, did that kid remind you of anyone?"

"Come to think of it he did, but I can't for the life of me remember who, can you?"

"I don't know. I can see his face as clear as day. The name will come to me in a minute. It was a movie actor everyone raved about. Damnation – what the hell was his name?"

"Was it that English guy, Olivier?"

"No, it wasn't him." Delores lit up a cigarette and inhaled deeply. "Think American. Think gorgeous with a great body."

"Douglas Fairbanks?"

"It's not him either. He was the leading man in one of the last silent movies they shot here."

"Any idea what it was called?"

"All I remember is a big costume drama, set in France."

"That's got to be *The Devil of Fontainebleau*."

"How stupid of me, of course, Gilbert Renaldo; how could anyone forget him in that movie? I must have seen it at least six times. Every woman in the studio had a crush on him. He was absolutely gorgeous."

"I see now what you mean about the similarity with this kid's profile."

Any embarrassment Jake was feeling by overhearing such comments were immediately forgotten at the mention of *The Devil of Fontainebleau,* and his own similarity to the actor, Gilbert Renaldo.

Jake could see that Marjory was concerned about something other than having to find him, and when he stepped out of the tent, she was noticeably taken aback by the alteration.

"Why the hell are you in make-up?"

"Sorry, I was next to be cleaned up. What's wrong?" Jake asked, wiping the lenses on his spectacles.

Instead of answering, Marjory walked on ahead, making her way back to the set. When she did speak, there was a noticeable softening of the mouth, also, the way she avoided looking at him directly when she spoke, confused him. It was clear that something had altered her attitude towards him, although he couldn't determine exactly what.

"Can you do something about that pickup, Mr Velasquez? The engine isn't firing at all, and that is causing absolute mayhem down here on the lot. They've tried everything possible to get it going, but it simply won't start," she said as he caught up.

"That's probably because the carburettor's been flooded," Jake said, feeling like a stray dog that had followed her onto the set. "It's easy to do with that truck for anyone who doesn't understand the old girl's quirky temperament."

"Then you should get down there immediately," Marjory said, indicating a shorter route between the facility trucks.

He sprinted off towards the group of men offering up alternative solutions, all clustered around the old truck with the side bonnets up.

Instead of following Jake, Marjory made a detour towards the camera crew, where the Transport Captain could be seen loitering near the catering table with a half-eaten doughnut

"Did you find out who this tin can belongs too?" the director complained, as Marjory strode past, seemingly oblivious to the spreading perspiration marks under his armpits. He waved a black cane in her direction, which had the desired effect and made her stop. Peering at the attractive woman from beneath the rim of his panama hat, he asked: "I hope you realise that pile of junk is costing this company a bloody fortune every minute we're held up from shooting this scene."

"Yes, Mr Stanford. Everything is in hand, I can assure you."

"Assurance is not what I want, Marjory. I want to hear that piece of crap running, or heads will roll. Whoever hired this rust bucket needs their head examining. This is twice today I've been held up from shooting by incompetence."

"That would be me, Mr Stanford, and I apologise for the delay," Marjory said through gritted teeth, making her way towards Jake, who was tinkering with the engine.

Some distance away, Maurice Stanford had resumed his seated position on the camera dolly, and readjusted the focus of the lens in her direction.

"Why are we still waiting?" Stanford hollered through the megaphone.

"It won't be starting again for a good half hour," Jake called back through cupped hands. He deftly removed the sparkplugs.

"Half an hour?" the voice through the megaphone screeched back, even though Jake was coming towards him. "That isn't good enough."

"Unfortunately, you have no choice," Jake said, walking past him with the spark plugs in his hand.

"Who the bloody hell are you? And why are you in war paint?"

"I'm the stand-in horse rider, Mr Stanford. I was in the make-up tent when I was told I was needed," Jake said. He could see that his words irritated the director, who seemed desperate to find any comeback at all.

"If you're that interfering swine who thinks he knows better than our technical advisor on-set, then where the devil are you going with those plugs?"

"The pickup's mine. These plugs need to be dried off, and the carbon sanded, before the truck will start, otherwise you'll be here all day."

"Hey, you there," Stanford hollered at a passing technician. "Get that Transport Captain up here now, and get that prick to bring another set of plugs."

"That isn't possible, Mr Stanford. Mr Blake has nothing in the workshop that fits this odd gauge."

"Then where the hell is he?" Maurice Stanford blustered, lobster red, and seemingly about to explode with frustration.

"He's tracked down a set of plugs in a garage in Santa Monica. He's on his way there now. He didn't trust anyone else to fetch them."

"Santa Monica, dear God that could take hours. It will be dusk in two hours, and we'll have lost the shot."

Twenty minutes later, Jake returned to the back lot with the dry plugs. When they were installed, he fired up the engine first time, and the camera rolled.

When Jake eventually returned to the Projection Room, Marjory had coffee and doughnuts waiting. Once again, he was struck by the change in her, which this time was more evident. Her hairstyle was less severe and no longer pulled tightly away from her face; instead, it hung loose, but there was something else that struck him. For the first time since they'd met, she was wearing lipstick.

"Do you remember Adelaide Williams, on the morning you showed up at the gates?" Marjory asked.

"Sure?" he said, biting into the doughnut, not comfortable with her new look, which he hoped was not for his benefit.

"Adelaide was on-set this morning when you took that jump. She was tremendously enthused by the scene. She had no idea that you were the warrior on horseback jumping that perimeter fence."

"It was quite a jump for any horse to make without the risk of injury. I'm surprised any company would be allowed to build anything so high and expect any horse, even without the added weight of a rider on its back, to make a clear jump."

"The longer you remain here, the sooner you will learn

113

anything is allowable in the art of moviemaking, if that's what the director wants – excluding murder, of course," she responded with a smile.

"And is your Miss Williams happy to go along with that? Risking the life of a horse with that barbaric jump?"

For a moment she looked at him oddly. "Aren't you interested in what Adelaide had to say about you?"

"Me? What on earth would she have to say about me? I wasn't the one that cleared the jump."

"That wasn't all she had to say." Marjory laughed. "Repeating her words as best as I can remember, what she said was: 'I cannot believe how beautiful that was to watch.' She asked me to arrange a screen test tomorrow."

"Perfect. That stallion was pretty amazing, wasn't he?"

"The test won't be for the horse, Jake Velasquez; the screen test is meant for you."

"You're kidding me, right?"

"No, I'm not. This is not just for Adelaide, but for most of the women watching you astride that horse today, and quite probably some of the men too. The way you ride and look on a horse is perfect screen fantasy. What you need to consider is this: because of all the Westerns that are being produced for TV, no one should turn down an opportunity to cash in on their good looks. And who knows, with your charismatic appeal, all America could be swooning at your feet – if you were handled properly," Marjory said, just a little too enthusiastically.

"But I don't want to be an actor. I can't imagine anything worse."

"Acting on film is very different to being on stage. All you are expected to do is look into the lens of the camera and say the lines. If you get them wrong, they do more takes until you get it just right. I promise you, movie acting couldn't be easier."

No matter how she might phrase the prospect of standing before the camera, Jake had no intention of staying on at the studio any longer than necessary. All he wanted was to find out how his father had been connected with the studio, and get the hell out of there.

"I'm sorry, Miss Dawlish, I meant what I said. I'm really not interested in any screen test. I'm more interested in the job I'm doing for the Archive Department."

"Wake up, Jake, for God's sake. You're in Tinsel town. That's why everyone comes here, hoping to be discovered."

"Well, not me, that's for sure. Did you come here for that?" He could tell that she was taken aback by the question.

"Actually, yes, I did hope to make a name for myself on the screen, but that was when I first came out here."

"What about Lone Wolf, the wrangler? He's better looking than most of the extras I saw on-set. He thinks it's more like a meat market than a profession."

She seemed uncertain how to respond. "Oh him? Well, he is a bit different, I suppose, but then he is more obsessed with horses than making a name for himself on screen."

"Then I must be different too, because I feel exactly the same as he does."

Because Marjory had given the impression that she barely knew who Lone Wolf was, Jake assumed he'd misheard what the warrior had told him about Marjory being his sister. He could tell by the way she scrutinised him that he'd caught her on the wrong foot by refusing to go along with the screen test. The same way that out of town wranglers had scrutinised him back home.

"It would be unwise to spend more time in his company than you have to. He – isn't attracted to women," she said, watching him carefully.

"He probably hasn't met the right girl."

"That isn't what I meant," Marjory said, with unconcealed annoyance.

Given the warning she had chosen to impart about a man that he barely knew, Jake regarded her with some reservation.

"You seem shocked by my frankness. Sometimes the truth isn't nice," she said bitterly, making herself more comfortable on the stool before launching into the next attack. "We really must re-address this screen test, Jake. Unless you agree to make it, knowing Adelaide, she wouldn't want you to carry on working here, and that would be a shame."

It was paramount to Jake that the issue of his father was resolved. He also needed to get his watch back. The last thing he wanted was to be noticed, but what Marjory intimated by not taking the screen test seemed to threaten everything.

"Surely, there must be some way to avoid this, particularly if I don't want to?"

"Unfortunately there isn't. This industry has no room for modesty."

"Then the movie business is barbaric."

"At last, you finally realise the glamour of the big screen has teeth."

"There must be a way out of this without losing my job?" he asked, but Marjory would have none of it. To Jake, he felt she was there on a mission from her boss, and not in the mood to be rejected.

"Any escape route that you might have had was sunk from the moment the girls in the make-up department began raving about you to Adelaide. To be perfectly honest, to hear such comments from a hard-boiled group of women is quite something when you consider they are in contact with good-looking actors every day."

Jake's mouth had become dry, and felt as unpalatable as the ongoing conversation. "They were only surprised because I looked different after I shaved off the stubble and got rid of my specs."

"You are being too modest. Adelaide is rarely interested in comments about another good-looking face. You've caught her attention and you would be a fool not to seize this chance and take the screen test. What harm can it do? It's a door of opportunity opening. Adelaide thinks you are one of the most interesting men she's seen here, on or off screen, in the past decade."

"This would be very wonderful if becoming a screen actor is what I wanted, but it isn't. It just isn't for me."

She was not listening to anything he was saying. It was obvious that Marjory Dawlish wasn't going to be put off the plan she had in mind.

"Maybe that's what you think now, but you will soon change your mind if, as I suspect, the camera falls in love with you; then, you would need someone to manage your career properly and I'm prepared to take the risk if you are?"

"Honestly, Miss Dawlish, a career acting in movies is the last thing I want. I'd be much better behind the camera, editing. That's what I'm good at."

"Well I'm not giving up on you that easily, Jake. Think it over, and we'll talk again soon."

It rained heavily on the first Saturday he sheltered under the pier, and turned bitterly cold on the Sunday. His clothes were soaked through, which made him think how bizarre his life had become since arriving in California. All weekend, he was saturated through to the skin, he was desperately hungry, and he found it impossible to sleep in the icy blast that surged under the pier at night.

It was approaching nightfall when he was discovered, wet and shivering, by a man and two women in uniform. They were on the hunt for down and outs in need of charitable help. He was offered shelter for the night at the local Salvation Hostel.

To begin with, Jake put up some resistance." I do have a job, sir, at the Silver Lake Studio. I worked there last week. It would be wrong for me to accept your kind offer."

"Then if you have work, why sleep rough in this dreadful weather?"

"I don't get paid until the end of next week. Apparently, that's studio policy. I was given a small advance to get me through, but that ran out."

"Then you must accept our offer of a bed for the night," the man said encouragingly. "We don't discriminate. You're in need of a bed and that's good enough reason," he said, and Jake gratefully accepted.

That night, he slept in a communal dormitory, with vagrants and drunks. Some were ex-servicemen down on their luck. One of these had shell shock from the war in Europe; he screamed hatred towards an imaginary advancing army throughout most of the night. Two other men were amputees from the D-Day landing, less than a decade earlier, who would never be able to readjust back into society: tragically brave outcasts who, after years of fighting for their country, could barely find work, and lived mainly on the charity of others. To Jake, it made the huge salaries the studio paid out to a handsome face seem farcical.

Jake was to sleep in a long room that reeked of unwashed socks and disinfectant. The dormitory was partitioned down the centre to accommodate extra rows of similar cots. Each bed was supplied with a clean blanket and a pillow, but what gladdened him most was the communal showering facility. This was empty when he used it before climbing thankfully into his bed. He was the first to get up and was well on his way to the bus station before any of the other residents were out of bed.

By lunchtime on Monday Jake's stomach was groaning, in need of food. He encountered Marjory as he was delivering a stack of film stock to the Archive Department.

"No one could have reviewed all of those reels this early," she said, eyeing the pile suspiciously.

"Drew had locked up and gone home when I got to the Archive Department on Friday night, so I'm taking them over there now. Incidentally, no one came by with my pay check?" he said.

"Oh, that's normal practice here. Everyone is required to work two weeks in advance."

"Well as my position here isn't permanent, perhaps you could make an exception. My problem is, I had to pawn my watch to get enough cash to live on until I got paid. The guy only gave me a week to reimburse the loan and if I don't collect my watch by tomorrow afternoon, he can sell it on, and I think he might just do that."

"You could easily buy another."

"I could but I won't. It isn't the value. It's the thought behind it. I couldn't replace that."

"The person who bought you this must have been very special."

"I've known him since I was a child. He was more of a father than my own ever was. It was Gil's perseverance that instilled in me the skill of editing."

"Then I understand why this watch means a lot to you. What does he think now that you're using that talent at one of the Hollywood studios?"

"He doesn't know where I am, Miss Dawlish. I haven't spoken to him in almost ten years. I must get this watch back, I really must."

"I will certainly do what I can to help you, Jake, but likewise, I would hope that you would return the favour by taking that screen test. It would mean a lot to me."

"If I agreed, would I get the cash by tomorrow?"

"Leave it with me, and I'll see what I can do."

True to her word, she came back an hour later, but with only half of the amount he should have been paid.

"I'm sorry, Jake. I did try to get you the full amount, but getting half of your salary was the very best I could do. Barbara Jeffords is a hard nut to crack."

"Thanks, Miss Dawlish, for arranging this."

"You seem disappointed?"

"I expected my pay to be more than this," he said, checking the meagre amount in the wage packet.

"Actually, there is no specific category for what you're employed here to do, so you get paid the minimum rate. If you recall, I did mention at the time, work here was scarce."

"Yes, you did, and thanks for getting me this; it'll certainly help," he said, and wondered how he could manage to eat after he'd got his watch out of hock, which was his main priority.

"Will you have enough to live on?" she asked.

"Maybe." Calculating that, if he set off earlier in the morning and walked in, and did the same after work, he could manage on burritos and fruit for the remainder of that week.

He was heartened by the thought that once he had resolved what his father's connection with the studio had been then he could try to find out where Gilbert was now living in California.

Knowing him only as Gilbert, Jake decided that he might possibly track him down through his connection with Doctor Maxwell. He knew from his birth certificate that Dr Maxwell had moved to Fort Laverne from Pasadena, and hoped that maybe Gil had moved with him.

The following morning, Jake had barely started to work when Marjory marched into the viewing theatre and switched off the projector.

"Why did you do that?" Jake asked, and wondered if anyone in that town had any manners.

"It's time to honour our agreement."

"What agreement?"

"Your screen test. You need to come with me to Stage Three."

Disappointingly for Jake, there was no evidence of a movie set. Instead, there were two scenic flats braced together with a window piece, where a cameraman and a small crew were setting up for the test.

As soon as they arrived, Jake was ushered into the make-up department where a steely-eyed woman was waiting, business-like and focused on her job. Unlike the girls who'd been in the make-up tent the previous week, this woman knew exactly what little was needed, and Jake felt a lot more at ease, and much less like a painted marionette.

"Is that all he needs, Beatrice?" Marjory asked.

"I can't improve on what nature has already provided. The camera will love this boy. He will photograph beautifully. You can take my word on that," Beatrice said, packing away the make-up box. "This could be a new star in the making." She shook Jake's hand. "I would normally say 'good luck', Mr Velasquez, but there is no way you'll need it."

Although Jake liked the woman, he felt sickened by what she'd said, and was quite determined that after the test was done it would be an end to it. He needed more time to get the answers about his father so he played along, but had every intention of getting away from what was more of a farce than real life as soon as he possibly could.

The set, such as it was, was supposedly the corner section of a dusty European book room, full of clutter; an untidiness which helped to detract from the high starched collar, and the flamboyant coat he had been made to wear. Marjory had already given him a two-page script, which he found easy to memorise.

Playing opposite him was a professional stand-in, a stout, bombastic character who'd been a stage actor before breaking into movies – a would-be hopeful, who saw the screen test as an opportunity to land a decent part with the production company. Unfortunately, the man had a voice that could only be likened to a loudhailer.

Although Jake wanted the session to be over as quickly as possible, it was hard to speak his lines sensibly in response to the over-projecting voice of the stand-in, and Jake forgot what he had to say. When the camera was re-set for the second take, Jake imagined that he was having a natural conversation with Gilbert, instead of the stand-in. The take went smoothly and the cameraman didn't feel the need to do anymore, and called it a wrap.

"What's happened, have they cancelled?" Marjory asked, taking his arm when she met up with him in the corridor.

"No, it's all done."

"Surely not," Marjory queried, until she spotted the camera crew going towards the exit. "You should have been on-set for two hours at least." She stopped as the flamboyantly dressed stand-in passed by.

"I didn't know you were working today, Harold?"

"I was replacing Hubert, either that or someone got our names confused." He pouted, rolling bullfrog eyes.

"There was no problem with the test then?" Marjory asked.

"Apart from it being too short? Well, for what it's worth, I'd say the kid here needs a few lessons in voice projection before he does another test," Harold said, moistening his fleshy lips with a sly, darting tongue. He crashed open the door of the Wardrobe Department, grumbling to himself about being employed by the hour and not on a daily rate.

"How d' you think it went?" Marjory asked Jake before they parted company.

"I honestly wouldn't know, but I don't want to be forced into another."

"Forced?"

"You know what I mean, Miss Dawlish. I'm here to repair damaged archive footage, not to be in front of a camera."

Chapter Seven

That night the bus was delayed, and so Jake caught another, which terminated a good mile away from the pawnshop. It meant he had to run along the coastal road to get there before it closed. He arrived just as the owner had locked the door and the closed sign was up.

After a good deal of hammering on the door, the owner opened it a crack. "We're closed, son. Come back at nine tomorrow."

"I don't want to pawn anything."

"Then what do you want?" the man said, trying to pressure the door closed.

Jake stopped it with his foot. "I'm here to pay you for the watch I pawned," he said, holding out the pawn ticket.

"That's useless. You were given a week to pay up, and now its forfeit. That's our policy. One week is all you get, so get your foot out the door, son. Like I just said – we're closed."

"You're early if the clock on the bus terminal is right, which it has to be," Jake said, as the clock chimed six.

The proprietor opened the door reluctantly and allowed him in.

"Why isn't my watch in the window where you said it would be? Have you sold it?"

"No, I have a buyer coming to collect the watch tomorrow at eight."

"Is that why you told me to call back at nine?"

"It could be."

"And why was that?"

"I called him five minutes ago to say you hadn't returned and it was his if he wanted it. He seemed genuine enough."

"And that makes everything right?"

"It does if you hadn't turned up by the time I closed."

"Do this a lot, do you? Sell on other people's property before they come back to get it?" Jake was doing his best to control his anger towards the man.

"If I think the goods are a bit suspect, I do. I'm not keen on getting the police involved."

"So why on earth would you think my watch would be suspect?"

"Because that watch has value, and the guy seemed to know some of its history," the owner said, as if expecting Jake to make a bolt for the door.

"What history? What are you talking about? It's a gold watch; what else could he tell you other than that?"

"If you are the legit owner then why don't you tell me?"

"Tell you what?" Jake was finding it difficult to control his temper. "Who was this guy? A dealer?" He wasn't going to budge an inch from that spot until the exchange had been made.

"Fact is, I've never seen him before. He came in off the street, turned up the day after I put that watch in the window to attract a bit more trade. He didn't try and haggle on the price, not like most would have done."

"You put a price ticket on my watch?" Jake said, horrified.

"Why not, if it got folk taking more of an interest in the window. It was easy to spot this guy was different. He just wanted to buy it. I could've made a packet if I'd sold it, but I couldn't because you had the pawn ticket."

"Did he say why he was so keen to buy it? There must be others like it?"

"The guy seemed to think it was stolen. He left me his card, and asked me to contact him if you didn't come back and collect it. And that's just what I did."

"Well, like I said, the watch isn't stolen." Jake counted out the amount they had agreed between them, to get the watch back. It didn't happen immediately, and it didn't look as if it would for a time given the pawnbroker's reluctant attitude.

"If this watch isn't stolen, like you say, why do you suppose the guy thought it was?" The unconvinced shopkeeper cautiously opened a drawer in the counter, where he rested his hand threateningly.

"I have no idea. None at all; he must have mistaken my watch for some other. I wouldn't have come back to collect it if I'd stolen it. Where would the sense be in that?"

"No, I don't suppose you would." He finally removed the watch from the glass counter, but still he held onto it.

"I don't get it. There must be hundreds of watches similar to this," Jake said in frustration. "You have the money, with interest, as we agreed. Now, I would like to have my watch back, if you wouldn't mind."

"Not yet. Sure, there are a lot of other watches that are similar, but not the same as this little beauty you've got here, son. Which leaves me with something of a problem." The owner was unwilling to take up the money from the counter. Instead, he examined the watch carefully. "You see, the problem I have is with you, and that's because the guy who came in here knew quite a bit of history about this watch, which is more than you seem to."

"Such as what, for instance?"

"Why not give me the name that's been inscribed inside?" the owner said, having opened up the back without letting Jake see. "What would you say's written here – if it belongs to you – like you say?"

"How do you want it, word for word?"

"The name that's written here would do for a start."

"To Jake," Jake snapped. "And did this guy also tell you what else is on the inscription, engraved underneath?"

"No, he said nothing at all about that. What he mentioned was the name– Jake."

"Then I'll tell you what else is inscribed there, shall I? 'Best wishes to Jake. An idealistic young man, on his twenty-first birthday, September 1949.'"

"That's exactly right," he said reluctantly. He was even more confused when Jake handed him his driving licence.

"That's me, Jake Velasquez, born September 1928, which would make me twenty-one in 1949," he said, and removed the watch from the man's grasp, barely able to contain his relief when he strapped it onto his wrist. "I need a receipt for the repayment," Jake said.

The owner duly wrote one out. "Sorry for the misunderstanding, son; I hope you understand why I was being so cautious?"

"Sure, but what isn't clear to me is how someone else could know about my name being inscribed inside the watch." He was wondering if it might have been Gilbert. "Not unless, of course, it was my friend who had the inscription done? What can you tell me about him?"

"He seemed genuine enough. He didn't seem the kind who would give up easily."

"Can you describe him? What did he look like? What age was he?"

"Youngish, medium height, dark hair, slim. He could've been an actor, but not one I'd recognise. He certainly had the looks for it though."

The description the man gave was nothing like Gilbert, but he asked one question which would resolve everything. "What about his voice? Was there an accent?"

"It was deep, and strong, and that's what makes me think he could be a stage actor. He did have a peculiar accent though, probably from along the East Coast: Pittsburgh, or somewhere very near. I came out here as a wannabe actor myself, a few years back, and I'm quite good at dialects. That's how I recognise where most folk are from. I'd say you have some connection to the Navajo reservation in New Mexico?"

"You've got that right," Jake said unwillingly, but he was nevertheless impressed by the man's accuracy. What bothered him was that everything the owner had said to describe the unknown man could no way have been attributed to Gilbert, and so if it wasn't Gilbert, then who was it?

"Did you say that the man left a business card?"

It took only seconds for the owner to produce the card pinned on a board by a wall telephone.

"The guy's name is Wesley Anderson."

"I've never met anyone of that name in New Mexico."

"What about Pasadena?"

"Pasadena?"

"The bus terminates at this terminal," the owner said, fixing Jake's notes onto a bundle of others with an elastic band. "It's my guess he was probably waiting to get back to Pasadena when he saw the watch in my window."

"He came here by bus? Can you remember if this guy was alone?"

"I wouldn't know. There might have been someone else with him but that's hard to say. You've seen what it's like out there at rush hour, with everyone piling on and off buses."

"So you think he was alone?"

"I didn't say that...there were other folk looking in the window. That's an eye-catching timepiece you've got there, son. Thinking about it, I suppose there could have been someone else, but I can't be certain."

Later, Jake tried to figure out how an unknown man from Pasadena would be so keen to purchase his watch; thoughts that didn't help him concentrate the following day.

Every time Jake collected another pile of reels, he wondered if he would ever reach the end of what seemed to be endless stacks of film stock. The memory of Malcolm Reynolds seated in the back of a Rolls Royce nursing a broken nose gave him some sense of satisfaction as he worked his way through reels and cans of subversive labelling.

He was taking a well-deserved break outside the building when a young Navajo sat on the bench against him.

"Say, aren't you the guy I spoke to recently. The day you started work here?" the man asked. "The name's Scott, I'm the wrangler" he added, as if hoping to jog his memory.

"Was that you with the sandwiches?" Jake asked.

"Sure it was."

There had been so many extras milling around that morning, Jake wasn't certain; not until Scott gave that smile of reassurance, and everything made sense.

"So you're Lone Wolf?"

"How did you know that?" He seemed genuinely curious.

"We met on the back lot when I took that jump on Firebrand. I'm Pale Horse," Jake said.

He looked surprised. "Hell! Was that you? I never would have recognised you," Scott said; the shock plain to see.

"But I thought you did?" Jake said, pleased to put a face to the young warrior. "What's so funny?" he asked, when Scott smiled broadly.

"Sorry, you've lost me, I don't understand?"

"How come you didn't recognise me from when we spoke after the shoot?"

"I honestly didn't have a clue who you were. I just thought you were the craziest rider I'd ever seen on the back of a horse."

"So are you, by all accounts."

"Yes, but I'm not a white boy," Scott said staring at him intently. "I tried to find you in the bar later."

"Sorry, I didn't go. I had to work late."

"Maybe some other time," Scott said. He rolled a cigarette, which he handed to Jake. He then rolled another for himself.

Over the following days, he saw nothing of Scott, and only met Marjory Dawlish for the briefest time. Regardless of her superior air, Jake had to admit that he did enjoy having her around. It made little sense to Jake that Scott was her brother, as Marjory had only referred to him as a wrangler, and they didn't look at all alike. Scott clearly had Navajo blood in him, dark-skinned and strong, whereas Marjory was delicate and pale, and her hair was fair.

Although he always preferred his own company, for some reason, on one particular afternoon he felt lonelier than he had in years. He assumed it was homesickness, as he'd never ventured any further than to Santa Rowena and, in comparison, the superficial culture shock of Hollywood was something he didn't particularly enjoy. The thought of staying in that town for even a day longer than necessary was unappealing; then again, he wondered, when he did eventually leave, where would he go?

Because there wasn't enough time to view another full reel, Jake selected a short piece of film on a battered spool –his attention drawn to the remains of a torn label on the canister, dated 1927. A screen test, he thought, for *The Return of Xavier Gérard.*

When the black-and-white footage was projected onto the screen, Jake recognised it immediately. He felt the hairs on his arms crawl as he realised that he was watching a continuation of the scratched tango sequence that Gilbert had given to him back at the Maxwell ranch. It was an imaginative and complex dance routine, but one that Jake knew intimately given his repeated viewings with the accompanying music. Even without sound it was riveting.

After rewinding it to play the dance again, Jake had barely sat down when Marjory came into the room. She sat to watch the sequence with him.

"How beautifully they dance together. Who are they? I wasn't aware that we had this. A musical would have been unlikely for this studio to make," she said hesitantly.

It seemed to Jake that she was about to say more but, noticing the way that she was clenching her hands, he decided not to comment.

"Where did you get this?" she asked, in a manner that was almost accusing.

"From the storeroom," he said, but Marjory was hypnotised by the performance on screen and remained silent.

The dance routine was cut short as the celluloid had been deliberately snapped: snapped in the same way as the footage Gilbert had given to him.

"I've seen a part of this screen test before, but not this section, not exactly. It was fairly recent, so it must have been here in the studio; if so, the likeliest person to know about that is Drew. I'm sure I have seen a part of that stage set stacked away in the scene dock. This studio must have made that screen test. Are you sure there isn't any more of this reel in the storeroom?" she asked.

"I've been through most of the storeroom, the short pieces anyway. I would have remembered if I'd seen anyone dance such a complicated tango routine. It's a particular favourite," he replied without thinking. "Unfortunately, the break happens just as the music builds. It is absolutely fantastic."

"This is really infuriating," she said, biting her nails. "Jake, how can you recognise what music they are dancing to without any sound? I thought the youth of America was into modern music?"

"Not me," Jake said, laughing to cover his embarrassment.

"Even so, unless you were trained as a dancer...I was, and although some of those steps and moves look familiar, what we've just watched is nothing like any routine I've ever seen."

"Maybe I'm no dancer, but that doesn't stop me from knowing the broken tempo of this dance very well," Jake said, and decided not to elaborate any more than that.

"I can't imagine which piece of Latino music would fit those incredible dance moves. There's nothing I know of which might come close." She was clearly moved by the grace and drama incorporated into that short clip, promising so much in the sequences that might lie ahead. It left the viewer wanting and needing to watch the conclusion.

It was a frustration that Jake had known himself for years, so he knew exactly how she was feeling. The new section that they'd just watched could almost have been filmed in slow motion and, although the sequence was practically a repeat of the footage he owned, there was a subtle hint of a drama about to unfold that sent chills along his spine.

"So what do you think the music is?" Marjory asked impatiently.

"Probably Argentinean," he said, somewhat reluctantly.

"No, I think it would have to be Spanish."

"Similar, perhaps, but it's different." Jake wished he'd remained quiet on the subject altogether, but was excited to have seen more footage of what he assumed had been lost forever.

"Go on, Jake, I'm intrigued to know what you think the music could be?"

"It would have to be Giuliani's 'Tango of Death'; there's nothing else that would fit those slow movements."

"Giuliani isn't a name I'm familiar with, not in connection with motion pictures anyway. Who on earth is this Giuliani person?"

Unsure how to respond, given that Gilbert had intimated his brother had composed it, Jake laughed. "I've no idea. The music is probably a one-off."

"You seem awfully knowledgeable. Why do you think that's the piece of music scored for this test?"

Although Jake had been determined not to admit that he was in possession of the opening section of the dance, because of Marjory's genuine interest in the screen test, he decided to mention it after all.

"Actually, I have an earlier section of this tango being performed on an old reel of film which I was given with my projector and some other movie stuff."

"What, you have something similar to this? I thought all of your film stock was silent," she said, momentarily forgetting the dance routine in the screen test had also been silent.

"They are, but I have a gramophone recording of Giuliani's 'Tango' that works perfectly with this routine."

Marjory burst out laughing. "And you honestly think what you have at home would come anywhere close to what we've just seen? Oh Jake, you really are very sweet. You have an awful lot to learn about this industry."

He knew she was perfectly correct in making that comment and yet he wasn't naive enough not to make a disturbing connection with the tango sequence, the gramophone recording, and that end reel of a movie that Gilbert had entrusted into his keeping. Was this the screen test for the dancers in that end reel and if so, why did Gilbert have it? But equally important: who had the missing reels?

Because he had no cash to buy food, Jake decided to work late in the Projection Room. Closing his eyes momentarily during a particularly boring reel, he fell asleep.

It wasn't the clicking sound of celluloid film rattling round on the finished reel that woke him, but an intense sensation of burning from the branding on his chest. It felt as if a captive bird was inside

131

his body, pecking into his heart.

Stripping off his shirt, he checked the reflection of his naked torso in the mirror, but the scar was not inflamed, as he had feared; instead, when he looked more closely at the scar, it had an uncanny resemblance to a man's eyes. In a panic, Jake saw his own frightened features reflected back from the mirror as the pecking sensation at his heart intensified. Overwhelmed by nausea and dizziness, he passed out and crashed in a quivering heap on the floor.

Scott found him a few moments later, and hauled him outside.

"I don't know what happened back there," Jake said, sucking in the warm air.

"Well I do, pal. What you need is a decent meal," Scott said, piling him into his truck. He drove to an all-night diner where he purchased a burger and a large milkshake each.

"How come you were in the building tonight?" Jake asked.

"I saw the light on when I was passing. I thought either you or Madge had forgotten to switch it off."

"What are you doing here so late? Everyone else is long gone."

Scott shrugged. "It was nothing to do with work. I needed to clear my head so I took Firebrand for a gallop. There's something important I've to sort out which would be impossible back at the apartment."

"Are you in trouble?" Jake asked instinctively.

For a time there was no response, until Scott spoke with some reluctance. "I'm not in any trouble myself, except emotionally. It's about Firebrand. The studio wants to get rid of the stallion. Because of his temperament he'll get bought up by a rodeo or sold off for dog meat. I need cash to stop that, and a lot of it from somewhere, otherwise that fantastic horse will be a goner."

It was clear that Scott was personally traumatised at the prospect, but there was not a thing Jake could offer up as a solution. He wondered why, if Marjory was his sister, she couldn't help him out. Her position at the studio was an important one, and she would have a salary to match. But not knowing Scott well enough, he hesitated from mentioning it.

"I just can't afford to pay the studio what they want," Scott continued vehemently, "but you know what? I'll rob a bank if I have to. I can't let this happen."

"Is there anything I can do to help?"

"Not unless you've got fifty bucks to spare," Scott said with some irony.

Jake winced, knowing that even if he pawned the treasured watch again, what he got in return wouldn't even come close. "I'm sorry I don't have that sort of cash."

"Jeepers, I wouldn't accept it from you if you had, Jake. I was only talking out loud. It wasn't aimed at you, for God's sake. It's my problem. I'll get it sorted, one way or another."

"How long have you got to round up the cash?"

"About four weeks."

"If you manage to pull it off, where will you stable him?"

"Well, there's the irony, Madge has made plans. She wants me to move out. Not that I could keep a horse in that patch of garden anyway," he said with a forced laugh.

"Is Madge your wife?" Jake asked, which got an amused response.

"Hell, no, Madge is my sister. Marjory Dawlish."

"Sorry, you did mention that at the jump but I thought I'd misheard, probably because she's only referred to you as the wrangler, never her brother."

"Ah, well...there's a good reason for that. Madge doesn't like anyone at the studio to know that we're related. Admitting to having a Navajo brother would give her less credibility at the studio. She holds down a high position there, and took a lot of hard knocks to get it."

"But you live in the same house?"

"Not for much longer, it seems."

"Then why?"

"Until recently, all that most of the studio staff knew about us was that I rent out her basement. I'm becoming too much of an embarrassment for her to explain away. Therefore, I have to move out."

133

"She isn't married?"

"To a producer for a short while, in Wyoming, but he wasn't going anywhere fast and there was a quickie divorce. Madge intends getting on. She would never sell herself short."

"What about you?"

"That's never going to happen. I'm not the marrying kind. I like horses too much; that, and mixing with decent people."

When Jake began work the following day, there was a pile of viewed reels stacked against the side of his seat: canisters he'd intended taking along to Drew the day before. Almost immediately after his arrival, he received a call from Drew asking him not to deliver till later.

By late morning, Jake had finished his current pile of work and went back to the storeroom to collect some more. He was working rigidly to Gilbert's system and, because of Malcolm Reynolds's manic filing system, what should have been a simple task was, in fact, a laborious and lengthy process.

There were times when he became bored watching reel after reel of inferior quality, old celluloid, most of which would snap time and again during the viewings. There was little inspiring to watch, and because of that, he decided to deviate from Gilbert's system, just the once. He scanned over the lower and middle racks, praying he would find something slightly more entertaining or essentially different.

By mid-afternoon, his eyes were aching from concentrating on the flickering footage, having worked through two uninspiring reels; he switched off the projector. Jake returned to the storeroom and opened the door onto the fire escape, and sat back in a creaking office chair to enjoy the refreshing breeze blowing in from the ocean. He closed his weary eyes for what he intended would be nothing more than the briefest moment.

He woke up with a violent jolt when the door slammed shut. Unsure where he was, he realised he'd been having a vivid dream. There was a strong scent of pine needles that was asphyxiating, although, there were no pine trees nearby. His dream had taken place in the storeroom, where, on the top rack of the shelving along the back wall, he had found two film canisters hidden behind some piles of dusty movie magazines, close to a gaping hole in the wall; clearly, they'd been hidden deliberately.

Back inside the storeroom, Jake stared at a pile of screwed-up film clips that had been thrown onto the top shelf. Apart from those, there appeared to be nothing else there. It struck him as being odd as every other space in the room was overly cluttered with canisters, dust-covered boxes, and other junk.

There were no stepladders in the room, and because the shelving was much too rickety to climb, Jake dragged the desk up tight against the unit and balanced the chair on top. This gave him enough height to see onto the top shelf. What he saw were three piles of dusty movie magazines piled exactly as they'd been in his dream.

There was not much space between the ceiling and the shelf so Jake struggled to drag them away. Once the choking dust had cleared, he could see the two canisters of film which, by now, was exactly what he had expected to find. To retrieve these took him a while longer, as some concentration was needed to prevent the canisters from falling through the gaping hole in the plasterwork, from where they might never be recovered.

Piling these two full canisters together with a few others, Jake returned to the viewing theatre, excited and just slightly nervous.

Unlike most of the reels and canisters in the storeroom, these reels had faded, yellowing labels dated 1926. The first was falsely listed as the end reel of three from a movie titled *The Venetian Mask*. The second canister was mislabelled as *Another day in Ohio*. Both filmed at the Silver Lake Studios, presumably in 1926.

What he found inside the first canister was reel one of three reels entitled *The Return of Xavier Gérard*, dated 1927. In the second canister he found reel two: the continuation reel from the same movie.

Loading the first reel onto the projector, Jake clicked off the overhead light hoping to discover exactly why this particular movie had been hidden. He switched on the projector and sat down to watch with bated breath as the shadows flickered across the wall.

From the very first frame, Jake knew he was about to watch something special. Riveted, he could barely breathe with excitement. There again was the strong aroma of pine needles. The branding on his chest was tingling and hot, but not uncomfortable enough to distract his attention from what was being projected onto the screen.

The film had been shot in black-and-white in 1927 but, unlike any of the earlier movies he'd worked through. It was neither grainy nor poorly lit. He realised he was probably watching something that the public had never been privileged to see.

The movie opened with a travelling shot, filmed in close-up on a woman's trim ankles and neat shoes as she walked along a corridor with clipped determination. When she stopped abruptly outside a glazed door, the camera panned up to the frosted glass name panel: "Franco D. Stefano, Talent Agency".

Her face as yet unseen, the woman's knuckles rapped crisply. From inside there came the muffled sound of a man calling: 'Enter.'

The next shot was of the closed door, as seen from the man's perspective inside the darkened office. When the door swung open, the woman's slender figure was in silhouette, framed in the doorway and backlit by the light from the corridor.

Way off inside the building could be heard the sound of a rehearsal in progress. A pianist was playing a foot-tapping melody by Cole Porter, accompanied by the thunderous sound of tap-dancing feet rehearsing a routine.

"They say I need be 'ere – at three, signore?" The woman spoke in a voice that was as rich and hypnotic as it was challenging; a lovely sound, which gave only the faintest hint of her Spanish origins.

When the man at the desk, as yet unseen, responded, his voice sounded oddly familiar to Jake's keen ear.

"It's five past three already, miss... and you are late." Franco D. Stefano clicked on a desk lamp to illuminate the dramatic beauty of the woman in the doorway.

"I am – Isabella Trecheanco, and I no late,' she responded with slow deliberation.

Slowly, the camera travelled away from her face, and moved across the room towards the man at the desk. When it stopped, it focused on the back of a high chair. The occupant swivelled his chair around to confront her, smiling into the camera.

Every hair on Jake's body crept with fear. He went icy-cold and his skin crawled in disbelief. He stared open-mouthed at the figure casually seated in the high-backed chair. It was him. Jake was looking at himself.

"Holy mackerel, it's you!" Jake heard his own, unmistakeable voice saying on screen, as the actor's eyes widened incredulously, staring out into the darkened auditorium. At that moment the celluloid film snapped, and the screen went blank.

Except for the rushing noise in his ears as he passed out, the last sound Jake heard in the darkened viewing room was the endless clicking of the reel going around and around on the projector.

Chapter Eight

When Jake came around he felt physically sick and was convinced that he was going to pass out again if he didn't get some fresh air. Groggily he made his way up to the flat roof of the building where he knew he wouldn't be disturbed, and stared blankly towards the horizon, wondering if he was dreaming. It took a good half hour before he was able to stop trembling, and the same again before he got up the nerve to return to the viewing theatre.

With shaking hands he made good the repair to the snapped film, which he then rewound and played through from the beginning. He hoped that somehow the terrifying visual must have been connected to his poor eyesight, or maybe, he'd fallen asleep and dreamt seeing himself on screen.

With gritted teeth, he switched on the projector, and waited. This time, even though he was prepared for what was going to happen on film, when he saw himself again he was more petrified than before. He gripped tightly onto the armrests of the chair as if he was about to fall over a cliff. It took a superhuman effort to remain calm and objective and not to run screaming from the building.

Playing the scene through again, Jake slowed down the speed on the projector just before the man spoke. He scrutinised every detail of the actor's face in the hope he might see even the slightest difference in their features, but he saw nothing that was even remotely different.

As the scene continued running beyond the repair. Jake's double on the screen said, as though the words were directed towards Jake himself: "I can't believe this is happening; that it's actually you."

It came as some relief when the camera cut away from the close-up and focused on the young woman in the doorway who was listening intently.

"Would it make a difference if it wasn't me?" she asked.

"You know it does. Having you here will make all the difference."

"I no understand why?"

"Because, Miss Trecheanco, it is I who will have the privilege of partnering you for the tango."

"You tango, Mr Stefano?" She had a startled look in her expressive eyes.

"Yes, I do. I also understand every one of the moves required to interpret Diablo's masterpiece."

The camera re-focused as the man gave her a reassuring smile. The look made Jake even more disturbed, particularly as the actor burst into a peal of laughter, causing both of his cheeks to dimple in exactly the way that Jake's own did.

Jake's head was pounding. It was impossible for him to concentrate on anything that the characters on screen were saying, and so he shut down the projector and rewound the footage to the beginning. Succumbing to his blinding headache, with trembling hands, Jake made himself a strong coffee and swallowed two aspirin.

In a daze, he answered the jangling internal telephone. At the other end, Frank, the irate assistant from the Archive Room, was shouting down the receiver, demanding that Jake deliver the latest reels within the next few minutes because Drew Walters wanted to lock up and leave the building.

With those recent images dominating his thoughts, and being encumbered with carrying the stack of reels he'd viewed over the past two days, Jake had some difficulty watching where he was going as he hurried along the corridor too fast for his own safety but he was wanting to reach the Archive Department before it closed. Like a circus performer, he successfully balanced the stacked canisters halfway down a flight of stairs before he stumbled. Struggling to maintain his balance, the canisters tipped sideways and almost toppled out of his arms. To prevent that certain disaster he had to move a lot faster down the few remaining steps than he ought to have done. As he secured a safe footing on the half-landing, his spectacles slipped off his nose and hung down from one ear. Unwisely, in a desperate attempt to sidestep and counterbalance the pile of sliding canisters, Jake missed his footing and went crashing down the remaining flight of stone stairs, cracking his head hard against the wall on the next half-landing, where he lost consciousness.

In a daze, Jake heard a man urgently asking him if he was OK, and where he hurt most, saying that it was better if he didn't move at all, not until the duty nurse had been called to examine him. To Jake that wasn't an option if he was to deliver the reels before Drew left. He struggled to sit up, groping about the floor with distorted vision in the hope of finding his spectacles.

Even through the painful blur of his partial recovery, Jake was able to recognise the delicate scent of Marjory's perfume as she removed the film canisters clutched tightly in his arms. With her, he heard Scott urging him to take time standing as his strong hands assisted him to his feet.

"Do you feel confident enough to walk?" Scott asked.

"What the hell are you doing here?" Marjory asked, attempting to hold him back. "Jake needs to stay here until he's recovered properly."

"That's too risky, Madge. We need to get him to the Medical Room before Veronica goes home. That was one hell of a fall. He needs to be checked over properly," Scott said, checking his watch. "It's almost six o'clock. You know she won't stay on here for a moment longer than is necessary."

"Oh. I hadn't thought about that."

"Lean all your weight on me," Scott said, assisting Jake down the remaining flight of steps to the ground floor and supporting him along the corridor to the Medical Room, where the nurse was locking up.

"Scott, what's happened?" Veronica asked.

"I'm sorry about this, Vee, you need to open up. This guy might be injured. He needs an expert to give him the once-over," Scott said, supporting Jake's slumped body as Veronica unlocked the door.

Jake felt incredibly sick and woozy as he was helped onto the examination couch. He lay on his back staring blankly at flickering shadows cast by the uneven rotations of an overhead fan. The downdraft definitely helped, but even so, not enough to prevent him from twisting onto his side before he threw up into a bucket which Scott held in preparation underneath him.

"Sorry..." was all Jake could muster for an apology, before he lay back, closing his eyes, and mercifully drifted off into a state of unconsciousness.

He awoke freezing cold and shivering; there was a strong scent of pine needles. For a moment everything around him was just a blur. When his vision cleared, even though he wasn't wearing his spectacles, he was able to see more clearly than he had done in years.

Seated along both walls on either side of a communicating door that opened on to a rehearsal stage, costumed extras sat talking animatedly.

On the stage beyond, a pianist was finishing a rhythmic piece of Cole Porter's music, which brought a tap-dancing rehearsal to an end. Some of the exhausted dancers trooped out through the door.

Almost immediately, Jake heard the spine-tingling introduction to Giuliani's "Tango of Death". A man with a clipboard emerged from the stage. He beckoned to a slim young woman from amongst the crowd and escorted her through the doorway onto the set, checking her name off his list.

Although Jake couldn't see her face, he recognised the dramatic flamenco costume she wore. The man with the clipboard returned to the entrance to the stage. Checking down the list, he called out a man's name.

Jake struggled to sit more upright on the couch, which he found impossible. Lying down again, he began trembling. Momentarily, he shut his eyes not wanting to be a part of whatever was happening. The scent of the pine needles became more pronounced, and only when their intoxicating perfume was completely enveloping him, did he open his eyes.

Leaning over him was the ghostly outline of a man. Jake felt no fear as the featureless face came up close against his, whispering: "Come with me, Guy. You should meet her."

Jake needed no other prompting to get off the couch and follow the ghostly shape of the man.

"What are you doing?" Jake heard Veronica calling as if she was in another room. "You mustn't get off the couch. It's too soon, Mr Velasquez. You will fall again if you do. You are still in shock. You are much too groggy to stand."

Although Jake tried hard to focus on Veronica's white uniform across the room, it was barely visible against the light as the ghostly figure passed between them. He felt light-headed.

To begin with, Jake's steps faltered, walking unsteadily as if drunk. As he got into a more purposeful stride, the nurse reached out to restrain him; an action that seemed to pass right through his arm. He barely noticed, as he was desperately trying to remember the name the assistant had called out, as if that had been at the end of a fading dream.

The figure lay the misty grey shape of his hand across the eagle branding on Jake's chest, charging it with a rush of fire.

The nurse called after him to get back on the couch before he injured himself.

"I've been called onto the set. I can't be late for this routine," Jake heard himself say. He approached the man with the clipboard, certain that, on the other side of that doorway, something life-changing was about to happen.

"Good luck with this routine, Guy," the assistant said, checking off his name on the clipboard. "I guess you'll be in safe hands with that young beauty you've been partnered with. She's one hell of a dancer."

"Thanks, pal. I know my career's riding on this test. I only hope I'm a good enough partner for her. Is she the woman wearing the red flamenco dress?" Jake felt himself prompted to ask the question. As he spoke he felt the jolt of an electrical surge penetrate his heart.

Because Jake had moved too swiftly for either Veronica or Scott to catch hold of him on the other side of the examination couch, neither of them could stop him. Instead of going through a non-existent door onto a stage beyond, Jake crashed head-on into a wall, and knocked himself out for a second time.

When he came to again, his head was thumping unbearably and his nausea felt even worse than before. There was a dull buzzing sound in his ears, as if they had been packed tightly with cotton wool. He was aware that people were talking very close to where he lay but he didn't want their attention until he could think clearly and kept his eyes firmly closed.

"I really don't understand this at all." Veronica said, leaning over him.

"It was bound to happen, attempting to walk so soon after taking that fall," Scott said as he stood up.

"It isn't that. It's just..." Veronica began weakly, lowering her voice, and moving away from the couch.

"What are you implying? Should I get him to a hospital?"

"What's bothering me is something else, and I don't know what to suggest."

"For God's sake, what are you on about?" Scott asked her impatiently, the strain in his voice clearly evident.

"You saw what he did," Veronica responded nervously.

"Sure, we all did. The guy was still concussed from that fall, and then he walked into a wall and knocked himself out." Scott was leaning closely over him on the couch, and Jake could feel his warm breath on his face.

"There is more to it than that; what happened is a bit scary..."

"What the hell are you driving at, Vee?" Scott walked across the room and stopped by the wall where Jake had knocked himself out before he spoke to her again. "Why do you keep staring at this particular place on the wall?"

"You'll think I'm crazy...if I say..."

"Why not try? We're both listening?" Marjory said.

"You must believe me when I say that I'm not making this up. Years ago, exactly where you're standing, there was a door which led onto the sound stage."

"Are you certain?" Scott said. He tapped along the solid wall until he came to that particular section. It sounded hollow. "Do you know what – you could be right. This sounds different," he admitted.

"It would."

"Given the state of this plaster it must have been blocked up a long time."

"Years ago, I worked here as a dancer, when musicals were all the rage. Back then, this room was used as a holding area for dancers and any extra performers."

"How long ago was this?" Scott asked her, sounding pensive.

"About thirty years, I suppose; long before this room was converted into a medical station."

"This is really bizarre."

"Is it bizarre to imagine that I had ambition once?" Veronica said, with a smile.

"It wasn't directed at you, Vee, or at your past ambitions. What I meant is, I don't understand how Jake would know there was a door there. The guy can't be much more than twenty."

"He's twenty-five actually," Marjory corrected him.

"OK then, twenty-five. My point is, how could anyone of his age, and who has never been in California until just a few weeks ago, possibly known about that bricked-up doorway?"

Jake lay as still as death, unable to move, convinced he was paralysed. There were unrecognisable images of people moving in and out of the fog, clouding his vision. He knew the constructive male voice belonged to Scott, and that made him feel safe. The impatience in Marjory's nasal twang soon identified her, unlike the other woman who he had no recollection of hearing before.

"Your guess is as good as mine," Marjory said. "What scares me is not that he might have been hallucinating there was a door in the wall, but what he said."

"Jake was confused after taking that fall; he could have said anything," Scott reasoned.

"They seemed to be just irrational mumblings," Marjory added impatiently.

"I know there was a door in the wall, and what's on the other side," Veronica said.

"So what?" Marjory was checking the time on the wall clock.

"Well, if you didn't hear what he said, I did. There was no mistaking what he meant when he walked into the wall: 'I've been called onto the set. I can't be late for this dance routine,' were his exact words before he knocked himself out," Veronica said, noticing that Jake's eyes were wide open. "He's come to."

Jake had a lump as big as a duck egg on his throbbing forehead when Scott helped him sit up. He drank the fizzing liquid which Veronica assured him would help get rid of the headache.

"Do you think he's broken anything?" Scott asked.

"No, he's fine, or he will be, once he's out in the fresh air," Veronica said, looking anxiously at the wall clock. "I really must go, otherwise I'll miss the bus."

"Then we'd better get him outside," Scott said, and began helping Jake down from the couch.

Marjory helped support him from the other side, saying, "I can manage him on my own, Scott, otherwise you will be late for the appointment."

"To hell with that, this is more important. That can wait."

"No, it can't. That apartment on the beach is perfect for you. If you don't get there and lay claim to it first, someone else will snap it up."

"OK, but only if you're going to look after him?" Scott said reluctantly.

Chapter Nine

Jake had fallen asleep on the bench outside of the studio building, lulled by the sound of the cresting ocean. He was awoken by Marjory, shaking him gently.

"Jake?" Marjory said. "You can't stay out here all night. We need to get you home."

"Have you seen my glasses?" Jake asked. "They came off at the top of the stairs. I must get back inside and find them." He was nursing his thumping head.

"Scott went back to get them while you were sleeping. They were broken in the nasty fall you had. Do you remember any of what happened?" Marjory asked.

"I tripped on the stairs."

"Anything else?" She handed him the neatly taped-up spectacles which Scott had done his best to repair.

"I remember falling," Jake said, fumbling to fit the spectacles onto the bridge of his nose. "What happened to the reels I was carrying?" he asked with alarm.

"Most are OK. Three of the reels came out of their containers."

"Are any damaged?"

"Not that I am aware of."

"Where are they now?"

"Scott gathered everything together after you fell. He returned all of the film stock and canisters to the Archive Department. Apparently, Drew was pleased with your repairs, and didn't think there was any damage."

"Is he still here?" Jake asked groggily, wishing he could focus properly.

"He had to leave for an urgent appointment. Has the headache eased off?" Marjory supported him as he got unsteadily to his feet.

"It's a lot better. I'll be OK, once I've had a decent sleep," Jake said, wondering whether to catch the bus to the hostel. He thought better of it when he considered the number of travellers there would be at that time of day, most of whom would be smokers. The prospect of being crushed together like sardines inside an airless bus was too much to consider. He took the keys for the pickup out of his pocket.

"What are you doing? You can't seriously think about driving home. You would be a prime candidate for an accident after two serious bangs on the head."

"Two bangs? I only fell down the stairs once." In his fuddled mind, he sensed that something else had happened that evening of much greater importance than the crack on the head from that first fall. "I don't suppose you've got anything for a headache on you?" he asked, feeling unstable and woozy.

"The nurse gave you something she said would help."

"Well it isn't working."

"Give it time. I can't give you anything else when you've already had something the nurse prescribed."

Jake was in no mood to talk, especially to Marjory, who would most likely want to open up an interrogation about what he'd 'imagined'. All he wanted was to rest his aching back against the bench, and be left in peace to gaze into the night sky. At that moment he wished he could be with Cloud Bird, knowing that only he could allay his fears about the stability of his mind. When he considered all the weird and crazy things that had been happening to him every single day since he'd left Fort Laverne, not for the first time since his arrival in California, Jake wished he could be transported back to those early days spent in his company on the reservation.

After a long battle of wills, Jake agreed not to drive to where he was staying; but he was adamant that he didn't want Marjory to drive him back either and, by mutual agreement, he accepted the offer of being driven back by one of the teamsters.

To curb the inquisitive nature of the driver, who would doubtless have reported back to Marjory where and how he was living, Jake asked to be dropped off a good mile away from the hostel.

At the studio the following day, Jake had a thorough examination by the resident doctor and spent the briefest time possible with Veronica. He spent the rest of the day categorising reels into appropriately marked canisters.

During the subsequent days, Marjory appeared at frequent intervals, concerned about the state of his health. He found himself lying, not wanting to encourage her irritating desire to rush him off to hospital for tests, even though the studio would pay the bill.

He saw much less of Scott, who didn't push him to say how he was feeling all the time. Instead he would drop by with some fresh fruit or a sandwich, and most times with a cold drink. Then he would go without having said very much at all, only that he would drop by again when he could. What was reassuring about these visits was that Scott's interest didn't seem superficial. He had an intense way of looking at Jake, as though searching instead for the person he was inside.

Jake didn't replay the two hidden reels again. He stuck rigidly to the way he had been working before, but he was unable to shake off the anxiety about what was on them. He hadn't been feeling well for a few days and longed for the weekend to arrive when he could get away from the studio. There was a constant fluttering sensation behind his eyes, and his heart kept beating crazily. So much so, that Jake actually believed that he could be dead before the end of each day.

One morning, later that week, Jake spent most of the time being sick in a toilet on the top floor of his otherwise empty building. Every time he thought the nausea had passed, and he was about to leave, he had to run back again. After the final session of vomiting, Jake saw with horror the hideous results of bile and blood in the pan. There was also a soft downy feather as from the underbelly of a large bird. Jake had no doubt at all that it was an eagle feather.

Later, when the sickness had stopped, and feeling incredibly weak, Jake made his way cautiously down the stairs. When he reached the corridor, he went to the viewing theatre which he discovered had been locked. When he heard the clock on the nearby church strike six bells it flashed through his mind that the clock must need fixing, but when he checked his wristwatch he could not believe that he had spent most of the day locked in the toilet and that it was now evening.

Needing to regain some strength before he caught the bus, Jake sat on a bench against the stage wall and closed his eyes, trying to relax to the muted sound of crashing waves; a comforting sound, most of which had been blocked out by the studio complex.

He felt certain something devastating was going to happen, and if that meant he was going to die he had no intention of dying in a stinking hostel, or worse, taking a last agonising breath of grimy air in a filthy backstreet of Los Angeles.

What haunted his fuddled brain was the eagle feather; in fact, he reasoned, all his recent physical illness must in some way be connected to the ritual for the return of Cloud Bird's spirit. If true, the thought was acceptable, even comforting.

He heard the clock strike the half hour. When it struck seven, in the distance, a door could be heard closing amid shouting voices, and cars being revved up. After five minutes or so, everywhere became peaceful again.

Not yet dusk, there was a balmy, pleasant breeze blowing in from the ocean which was more soothing than any medication. He smiled as he thought, not too seriously, that if this did turn out to be his final time on earth, it would be a pleasant one.

Jake realised he must have been dozing – he missed the clock strike the half hour, and he jolted awake just as Marjory spoke, and the church clock struck eight.

"What in God's name are you doing here, Jake? Scott and I have been worried sick all day, and we couldn't make contact because we have no idea where you live." She was doing her best to examine him closely in the fading light.

"I've been here all day," Jake said, wishing she would go away and leave him in peace.

"Then where've you been hiding? There was no sign of you in

the Projection Room. Both Scott and I checked in there two or three times. In the end I got him to lock up." She sat down beside him. "My God, Jake, you look like crap. Your skin is almost green."

"I've not been feeling too good today. Nauseous, that's all," Jake answered, doing his best to sound normal, which was harder the longer she continued her interrogation.

"Where were you?"

"Most of the time, I was in the toilet; the one on the top floor."

He closed his eyes to fend off the pain in his head and almost immediately fell asleep beside her. He had no idea for how long when Marjory gently moved his head off her shoulder.

"I'm sorry, Jake, my shoulder is hurting. I didn't mean to wake you."

"Where am I?" Jake asked with a start, feeling for his spectacles. "What happened to my glasses?"

"I took them off when you were sleeping, in case you broke them again," she said, and fitted them onto his face with nervous fingers. "Is there anything I can get for you?"

"I'd better not—" Jake began, but broke off, not wanting to go into unnecessary explanations. "I'll be fine once this headache's gone."

"Wouldn't you be better at home than out here? It can turn very cold at night."

"The fresh air helps, and it's quieter here too. The fact is it's noisy and claustrophobic where I'm staying. There would be no point going back until midnight," Jake said, wishing she would take the hint and leave, however grateful he was for her concern.

"I do have a pull-out bed in my spare room?" she offered, resting her hand in his.

"You're very kind, but I couldn't do that. Not with this sickness that comes and goes when I least expect it," he said truthfully. It had the desired effect, as she removed her hand from his immediately.

Partially aware of an awkward silence that had descended, and feeling a surge of nausea returning, he quickly put his head between his knees, where he stayed for some time until the feeling

150

passed. He was sweating profusely when he sat back on the bench, breathing in the sea air.

"You should go, Miss Dawlish," Jake said, aware of how uncomfortable she must feel.

"I can't leave you here; not like this."

"I'll be OK. I promise I won't stay here all night. I'll get off home in a while. I need a change of clothes for tomorrow."

"There is no need. My brother is about your size. I'm sure Scott will sort something out for you to wear."

"You want me to go home with you?" he asked uneasily.

"No. What I am suggesting is that one of the bungalows opposite Stage Three is available to use overnight. I use it myself if I need to stay late at the studio for any reason," she said emphatically, removing a clean handkerchief from a shoulder bag.

"I sure would appreciate that, if it's not too much trouble."

"It's the least I can do, Jake. I'm of a mind that this reaction you're having must be connected with that tumble you took earlier this week. If you wait here, I'll arrange with security that you'll be in the bungalow tonight."

"Thanks a lot, Miss Dawlish. You and Scott have been very kind."

"Can you remember much about what happened after that fall?" she asked, possibly expecting some explanation.

"It's all too hazy," Jake said, not wanting to elaborate.

"Thank God you didn't damage your face," Marjory said, mopping the streaming sweat from running into his eyes. She looked as though she was resisting the temptation to touch the angry swelling on his forehead. "That would have been too awful for everyone," she teased.

"It's a pity the same can't be said for these, not that Scott didn't do a fine repair," Jake said, readjusting the twisted frame of his glasses onto the bridge of his nose, trying to appear as normal as he could so that she would take him to where he was to spend the night, and leave him alone.

"Would you like me bring you that change of clothes?"

Jake would have liked to have refused, but she had been very kind in offering to put him up on the studio lot; he just hoped that if, and when, she returned, she didn't stay long.

"That'd be very kind, if Scott wouldn't mind me borrowing them."

"How well do you know him?" she asked suddenly.

"Not very, I suppose. We met on my first day at the gates, and again when I made the jump on Firebrand," Jake said. "Do you mind if I stay here for a while on my own? My head's thumping like crazy."

He was feeling a lot better when Marjory returned with a key to the bungalow. She also brought a few essentials — a hand towel, a new toothbrush and a tube of toothpaste, a thermos flask of weak coffee, an orange, and a banana.

"This is the best I could do at short notice. The canteen closed at six, but I had this fruit and a spare toothbrush in the office," she said. She made an awkward attempt to help him into the car. "The results from the screen test came back," Marjory said, looking as though she expected Jake to respond favourably. "Everyone's raving about them."

"That's nice," Jake said. By now it was dusk and he needed every bit of concentration to prevent him from stumbling, or worse, falling over when he got out of the car.

It wasn't far before they came to a bungalow set apart from the others, outside which were two painted chairs and a cane table.

"Unfortunately, the bungalow I suggested you stayed in tonight is being redecorated. The other hasn't been used in quite a while, and so it doesn't have much to offer in the way of comfort. It's equipped with only the bare essentials. It might not be ideal, but there's a clean bed where you can rest overnight. It can be very peaceful here; that is, until the film crew arrive. There's an internal telephone inside. If you feel at all unwell again call through to the switchboard. They will connect you directly to Doctor Stephens. He is our resident doctor on call." Unlocking the door Marjory handed Jake the key. "I'll drop Scott's clothes off a bit later on this evening. I'll do my best not to wake you. I'll leave them out here on the table."

"Thanks again," Jake said wearily. He remembered how Gia always made up the beds at the hacienda and longed for freshly laundered sheets with the fragrant hint of lavender.

To hasten her departure, Jake said he was beginning to feel better, and Marjory left him on one of the chairs outside. To be alone was an immense relief. His legs were shaking and he felt desperately sick. He felt that at any moment his head might explode from the intensity of the shooting pains rocketing around the back of his eyes. At that moment Jake couldn't have moved an inch from his chair, not even if a bomb was to explode. It was impossible to concentrate on any of the jumbled events crowding his mind, and yet that was exactly what he needed to do. He had to figure out just how his own image had appeared in that section of old footage. Every feature and expression of the man was too exact a replica of his own for it to have been anyone else. The more he puzzled the worse his headache became.

Jake staggered into the bungalow, desperate to lie down and sleep. The torturous pecking sensation at his heart had restarted. When he stumbled and glanced up, disturbing, shadowy images seemed to flicker across the wall as he caught hold of the door frame to prevent himself from falling. He paused there until his breathing became easier and the pain in his heart began to ease.

Once he had closed the mosquito screen door and his eyes became accustomed to the gloom, it was apparent that an uncomfortable night lay ahead as clearly no one had been expected to stay in the bungalow overnight. The dank air had an unpleasant smell of old varnish and musty linen. In the dim light, he could determine the place was in need of a good clean; however, anything was an improvement to sleeping under the pier, or at the hostel, where jammed windows prevented fresh air circulating through the stuffy dormitory.

On the bed was a lumpy flock pillow and a mattress covered over with a bright floral counterpane in garish colours. Jake lay on the bed, hot and sweating. The overhead fan must have blown a fuse as it stopped just as he was getting undressed. Because both of the windows were locked and there was no key to open them, he left the door wide open. As a precaution he locked the heavy-duty bolt on the sturdily built mosquito screen. After the incident at the Hotel Czardas he needed to make it hard for anyone to open the door from the outside.

Jake woke up shivering and he knew instinctively there was someone else in the icy-cold room. Because it was so dark he could barely see, he tried reaching out to switch on the bedside lamp, but was prevented from moving by a force that thrust him hard up against the headboard. There he was held rigidly by an immense pressure which threatened to crush his ribcage.

"Who's there?" Jake croaked, barely able to breathe and struggling to get free, which was impossible. "What do you want?"

His breath was frosting and breathing was difficult in the lowered temperature of the room. Even when his eyes adjusted to the dark, he couldn't identify the force that was holding him securely against the headboard. Oddly enough, although he was angry at being unable to free himself, he felt no fear.

In the inky darkness, all that he could make out was the sweat glistening on his skin, yet he was chilled. There was no pine scent in the room. Whatever had him trapped here was different.

"What do you want?" he challenged. Angrily he struggled against the pressure, determined to get free and confront whoever or whatever it was in the room. "Who the hell are you?"

An icy blast of cold air whirled around his head, blowing his hair over his eyes, making it impossible to see, then the force holding Jake eased.

For a second he was unsure if the sudden rush of air had been caused by one of the small windows gusting open, but then he understood his mistake when a ghostly shape materialised at the foot of the bed. Cursing his poor eyesight, Jake groped about for his spectacles. While trying to switch on the bedside lamp, it toppled onto the floor.

"What in hell do you want from me? Why are you in here?" Jake called angrily, reaching towards the motionless shape in the gloom, unable to make out any more detail of the figure, other than to determine it was male.

Scrambling out of the bed, the lump on his temple began throbbing, which left him giddy and uncertain of his bearings. Recovering quickly when his bare feet made contact with the cold floor, Jake groped his way along the edge of the bed towards the shape.

It was difficult to focus on anything properly but, as he got closer, he could see the apparition was not inside the room at all, but appeared to be waiting on the other side of the mosquito screen. He reached out to catch hold of the door frame. The wood was frosted over, but his concentration was focused on the ghostly figure just a few feet outside, particularly as the figure was beckoning him to follow.

Jake's head was throbbing unmercifully as he grabbed some of his clothes from a chair near the door. Quickly he tugged on his shorts and pulled on his shirt as another icy blast whooshed through the mesh door. A ghostly hand caught hold of his arm, and yanked him.

Suspended a few inches above the ground, he was dragged forward at an infinitely slow pace. The whole of his body, right down to the ends of his fingertips, was shrieking with excruciating pain, as if he was being shredded. When the pain subsided, Jake realised that he was standing on firm ground, and that whatever had pulled him, had released its hold on his arm.

With a racing heart, he looked about him for the ghostly figure; it seemed to have vanished. He squinted into the gloom at the unfamiliar shapes of other bungalows and tall silhouettes of the stage walls, as a dense bank of mist drifted eerily across the studio buildings, obliterating almost everything. Because there was no sign of the ghostly apparition, Jake began to relax, thinking he might have experienced a disturbing nightmare, and woken up after sleepwalking. Even so, he had no inclination to go back inside. His bones were aching and his skin was prickling as if he had crawled through a bank of stinging nettles. His shirt felt wet and sticky. He was about to take it off when every ache and pain was forgotten. A slight movement against the stage wall caught his attention. The ghostly shape of a Navajo warrior moved into view. Jake felt his heart would burst as the glistening shape of Cloud Bird stepped forward.

He had no thought that he must be dreaming as the winged branding over his heart let him know otherwise. Anxious when the apparition was lost from sight in an alley between two of the stages, Jake followed quickly, forcing his aching limbs into a sprint. Running along the gravel walkway, Jake so wanted to catch up that he hardly felt the pain of stones cutting into the soles of his bare feet.

Reaching the alley, he saw the figure halfway down, waiting near a wrecked covered wagon and a cluster of fake cacti at the side of the stage. Leaning against the wall was a collection of scenic flats from a dismantled stage set. When Jake came down the alley towards him, the ghostly warrior opened a painted door on one of the scenic pieces and went through, leaving it slightly ajar.

Out of breath, he briefly leaned against the stage wall for support before he continued on after Cloud Bird. There was a patch of clearing mist at the far end of the alley. When it parted he could see the studio road. Ahead, at the end of the alley, a violent storm was raging. The slashing rain and gale-force winds were bending the decorative palm trees almost double, and yet in Jake's alley there wasn't a drop of rain.

He followed the apparition through the painted door, where he was expecting to come up against the brick wall of the stage. Instead, he passed into a damp hallway at the base of a sturdy wooden staircase inside the stage. He didn't hesitate before following him up the staircase. After climbing up three flights of stairs, it opened out onto the wooden veranda of a stage set. Painted on the wall immediately behind him was a credible façade of a rambling hacienda. Running the length of this was a long balcony that he was able to walk along, expecting to catch up with the ghostly image. He could see nothing of Cloud Bird. Peering down onto the stage floor, two figures were just beneath him, tinkering with the engine of an old truck, not dissimilar to his own, but considerably older.

His curiosity aroused, he tried to go down the steps on to the stage floor to have a closer look but instead, he came up against a wall of pressure that prevented him from going any further. A light was switched on by one of the men to illuminate the engine, which enabled him to see one of their faces. It came as a severe shock when he recognised the burlier of the two men as his late father, but not in the way he remembered him. He was exactly as he had looked in the photographs he'd found amongst his father's papers at the hotel in Fort Laverne.

His father stopped work on the engine and glanced questioningly at the other man. "Is that good enough?" he asked.

Although the other man had his back towards him, Jake was instantly aware this was no ordinary mechanic. A large, square-cut diamond ring glittered on his small finger, flashing brilliantly when he rested his hand on the radiator and leaned over the engine to peer inside.

"Are you sure it's loose enough, Velasquez? It doesn't look that way to me."

"I've done exactly what you asked."

"We've only got one shot at this, and I'm damned if I can afford any mistakes," the man with the ring said, taking the spanner from his father's hand. He savagely wrenched the nut on the steering rod by another three turns. Then he swung the spanner hard against one of the headlamps and smashed the glass.

A door on the far side of the stage opened, alerting both men as the crisp sound of a man's footsteps could be heard approaching them. Jake became aware of the faint but distinctive scent of pine needles becoming stronger as the footsteps got nearer.

"Is anyone there? I'm a bit early," a man called, his youthful voice muffled beyond a stack of scenery.

"We're checking the engine," the man with the ring called, casually lighting up a cigar.

"I wasn't sure if the run was still going ahead tonight?" the young man responded.

"We have no choice. The canisters must be there on time. If they're not at the lab by first light tomorrow, Miller's movie might never get released. That opening in New York is crucial for any hope of success."

"I'll make sure the reels get there," the man said as he came into view.

When he saw the man closely, out of costume and without screen make-up, Jake thought his legs would give way beneath him. The young man on the stage below couldn't have been anyone other than himself.

He became aware of a charge in the air and felt he was in danger. Not from the enactment being played out, but something more threatening. The inadequate overhead lighting began to fade, as did the distorted conversation between the three men. The man with the diamond ring was making certain that Jake's double wouldn't set off before the prearranged time when the sound cut off sharply, like a radio play being switched off. The overhead lights dimmed so rapidly Jake could barely see the ghostly figures.

Suddenly the air swirled about him, full of grit which stung hard against his bare flesh, as a fierce draught whipped along the balcony. It made him grip the iron handrail for support but the rail was no longer firm to his touch as it had become spongy and pliable. Jake groped his way along the balcony in the semi-darkness, desperate to reach the stairs and get out of the nightmarish building, barely able to see anything ahead of him in the gale-force wind. Nauseated and dizzy, as if he had been drinking heavily, Jake had no time to stop as he made his way along the now brittle planks of the wooden balcony crumbling beneath his bare feet. Everything was disintegrating. He felt the handrail dissolve like jelly under his grip, and as the balcony floor began to give way, he stumbled on to the rickety staircase that was also beginning to fall apart.

By this time Jake could barely breathe, struggling to get through a violent dust storm. Everything around him was closing in, and he was about to be crushed between encroaching walls on all sides. In the darkness he missed his footing and pitched forward down the crumbling stairs. He was in an airless concrete tower where he would soon be crushed and entombed. There was a tired lethargy in his joints, as if he was struggling through a sand dune.

Once again, he thought that he was about to die, and closed his eyes, wishing that Cloud Bird was there to give him the courage he needed in those final moments of his life. The pain of scorched flesh from his branding felt as if he was being re-branded. It re-energised his fighting spirit. He struggled on through the mass that was close to smothering the life from him. Ahead of him through the pitch darkness was a patch of phosphorous light; it emanated from the ghostly shape of Cloud Bird, urging him on to reach the open door, where he was waiting.

Finally, Jake staggered out through what had become a slit of the open door into the crisp night air. Gasping for breath, he glanced up as a large saloon drove at speed past the opening at the end of the alley between the stages where the storm was still raging. Moments after, the old truck spluttered past, easily recognisable as the same one from the stage, as it had only one headlamp, eerily lighting the road ahead as it drove past in a deluge of driving rain.

Chapter Ten

Jake heard someone calling his name as he caught hold of the scenery. Stumbling wildly, he was unable to steady himself and crashed hard against the painted flats before he slid, unconscious, to the ground.

The night was as black as pitch when he came around. He was agonisingly stiff and aching all over, lying on a patch of dry grass with Scott bending over him.

"Jake. Jake, can you hear me? What in hell happened?"

"I don't know," Jake responded weakly.

"You must have had another fall. You're covered in cement dust. Just lie still and don't move while I call an ambulance." Scott was about to move when Jake stopped him.

"Please don't. I'll be OK once I've rested."

"Holy mackerel – what in God's name were you doing wandering about in the middle of the night?"

"I was following someone. A guy I knew," Jake said shakily, struggling to sit up.

"You were following who, where?"

"Onto the stage set, through there."

"You've lost me, pal. I don't understand what you're saying? No one can get onto these stages without a passkey. They are all locked at night." He indicated a door at the end of the alley.

Supporting Jake to his feet, Scott released him without noticing the dark smears of Jake's blood across his own white T-shirt.

"I didn't go through a stage door," Jake said. "I went through this one here." He pointed at the painted door-flat leaning against the stage wall, and Scott's eyes widened noticeably.

"Bollocks!" he laughed.

"I did, Scott, I swear."

"No you didn't. That's impossible." Scott tapped the painted flat. "You've been hallucinating."

"No way." Jake struggled free, stumbling against the wall as he did.

"Stop being a bloody fool, let me help you," Scott grumbled, catching hold of him before he toppled over.

"Take a look for yourself if you don't believe me. Painted or not, there is a way through that door onto the stage."

"I already have," Scott said, freeing Jake so that he could lean against the wall.

"Then look again." Jake gripped on to a piece of scenery as Scott inspected the painted door. "Look a bit closer. That door must be hinged."

"Well, I'm sorry to disappoint you. It's been painted for a set. There's nothing behind it, only the stage wall. There isn't a door onto the stage behind it either. The nearest one to here is at the end of the alley."

"Then I don't know how it happened, only that it did. God alone knows how but I did go through this door," Jake said wearily.

Scott was studying the irregular shape of the stage wall carefully before he responded.

"Logically, you wouldn't have been able to get onto the stage, even if there had been a door," Scott said, refusing to be pushed away. "I've had enough of this horseshit, Jake. We're wasting valuable time. I need to get you examined at the hospital." He checked the time on his watch, but Jake wasn't going anywhere.

"Logic doesn't figure in what happened to me. What I should have said was that the door didn't lead directly onto the stage. I went up the staircase first. And you can forget about taking me to any hospital. I'll be fine once I've had a decent night's sleep."

"Listen. You've had a couple of bad falls. You need to be examined by a doctor."

"I'm not going anywhere – except to bed," Jake said, coughing from a cloud of dust billowing out of his clothes. "Somehow, I went through that wall. That's how I got this dust over me."

"We both know that's not possible. The fact that you are new here confirms that. You couldn't possibly know what's on the other side of this particular wall," he said, sounding less confident. "There has to be another reason why you got into this state. To begin with, what possessed you to come down this alley in the dark, or know about this painted flat?"

Jake was aching, tired, and becoming more nervous with every question, as if his new friend was attempting to peel back layers of his private life. "All I can tell you is what happened."

"Which means you must have passed out, probably as a result from that bang to your head this afternoon."

"It's more than just a bang on the head." Jake stared at the painted door.

"Two hefty bangs, if you remember."

"Even so... this is where I fell when I came off the stage."

"Honestly, Jake, you've got to put this fantasy out of your mind. There's nothing behind here. Look, I'll prove it to you." Scott dragged the scenic door-flat further along the stage wall to reveal the brickwork underneath.

"Then how do you account for that?" Jake asked, squinting at the comparison between the old and new brickwork blocking up an original stage door.

"Well, I'm damned, I never noticed that before. Even so, there is no doorway onto the stage, so you couldn't have gone through," Scott said, expressing genuine concern.

"Couldn't I?" he said, but Scott wasn't listening, instead, he was examining the patches of blood on his white T-shirt where he had been supporting Jake earlier.

"What's this?"

"You're bleeding?" Jake said anxiously.

Scott quickly stripped off but found there was no damage to his skin underneath.

"It isn't me, Jake, it's you. I've got to get you to a doctor, and fast."

"I can't. I can barely afford to buy food let alone pay some quack to tell me I've probably been sleepwalking. I need rest, that's all." Jake fully expected that Scott would eventually go away, but Scott had no intention of leaving. Jake found this oddly comforting.

In the alley, it wasn't possible for Scott to examine the extent of Jake's injuries as there was insufficient light. He lit his cigarette lighter and held it close to Jake's ragged shirt seeing clearly the amount of blood seeping through the material.

"Jake, listen to me, this could be quite serious," he said, unable to remove any of Jake's shredded clothing to examine the extent of his injuries. "For a shirt to get into this state, you must be oozing blood from every pore. You have to be examined by a doctor at the hospital. I can pay the bill if you are really that broke."

"No."

"You have to."

"I can't, and that's final. You wouldn't understand why if I told you."

"Try me?"

"A doctor could never understand what's happened to me. Why I am in a state like this. If I had to see anyone, what I really need..." Jake paused, "is a Navajo medicine man."

"Why would you agree to be seen by a medicine man, and not by a doctor?" Scott asked. He sounded confused.

"Because I do. Isn't that reason enough?"

"Not really. If I could find a medicine man in this bloody awful city, there is no way on earth he would agree to see you, even if you do know a lot about Navajo culture. It isn't the same as belonging. See some sense, for God's sake, and see a doctor," Scott insisted.

Jake wanted to scream at him, saying instead: "I've told you what I need, and I won't see anyone else."

It was almost dawn as Scott supported Jake along the alley towards the bungalow. For a time, neither spoke. It was only when they neared Scott's battered truck that he broke the silence.

"You might think that I'm being difficult about finding a Navajo medicine man, Jake, but seriously, I'm not, and the reason I say that is because I'm of mixed-race, and even I am not fully accepted by the tribe. For a white boy like you, well, you wouldn't stand a chance." Scott helped him into the passenger seat of the truck.

"Where are you taking me?" Jake asked weakly, in too much pain to struggle against the stronger man. "I don't want to go anywhere. All I need is to lie down and sleep, and certainly not in any hospital."

"There are no doctors where we're going."

"Are you taking me to a reservation?"

"I've already explained why I can't, and even if I could, the nearest one is more than a two-day journey from here. I'm taking you to a quiet place I know of further along the coast where you can bathe in some saltwater pools. No one else ever goes there." He told Jake he was concerned by the bloodied state of his clothes. He had scribbled a hasty note and was crossing to pin it on the bungalow door. "This'll let Madge know you're not feeling well when she comes looking for you. I've said not to expect you back until this afternoon at the earliest."

"What about a change of clothes? All I have is what I'm wearing?" Jake called after him, but Scott didn't answer. He was trying to remove something caught in the mesh of the mosquito door.

"She asked me to drop off a few of my own clothes. That's why I came over tonight," Scott said as he opened the door of the truck, but he didn't get back into the cab.

"I wondered why you were here."

"It seems lucky that I was. Is there anything you need from inside there before we setoff?"

"My wristwatch, I can't leave that behind."

"Where is it?" Scott asked, taking a flashlight from the glove compartment.

"On the bedside cabinet," Jake said, getting out of the truck to join Scott who was now rattling on the mesh door.

"I don't understand this," Scott said, focusing the beam onto the unmade bed and the wristwatch on the bedside table. "How come the door is locked from the inside?"

Jake was falling asleep where he stood, and didn't want to get into complicated explanations with Scott, knowing there'd be no way he could evade the inevitable barrage of questions that would follow.

"That's because I locked it before I went to bed."

"Then how did you get out? Climb through the window?"

"No."

"Then how did you manage it?"

"I don't know for sure. That's why I asked to see a medicine man. Both of the windows are jammed. Check them yourself. I couldn't open either of them from the inside."

Scott tried, but failed, to open them. "What the devil's going on, Jake? I don't understand any of this." His hand began trembling as he shone the beam on a shred of bloodstained material from Jake's shirt that was clearly embedded in the mesh.

"And you won't, because neither can I. Only a spiritual guide from the Navajo tribe could fathom what happened tonight, even though it happened to a white boy," Jake said, repositioning the torch in Scott's hand to examine the bloodstained fabric more closely.

"What are you suggesting? That this is something paranormal?"

"It has everything to do with that. Everything that happened tonight at the stage was exactly the way I told you. But worse; what happened here in the dark is even scarier."

"What do you think did happen here tonight?" Scott asked cautiously.

Jake was in no mood to hold anything back. "I definitely left here through this doorway."

"That's bloody impossible."

"Didn't you want to know what happened?" Jake challenged.

"Yes, but—"

"OK, then how else would you explain how this got here?" Jake indicated the shredded fabric from his shirt trapped inside the wire. By a quirk of fate, there was also a broken button attached to the material; it was impossible to dispute. "To be honest, my life has gone out of control since I arrived in California, and it scares me to death, particularly now I've seen this."

The shock in Scott's eyes confirmed that he too could hardly come to terms with the facts of what must have happened.

"Jeez...I don't know what to say. How could that happen?"

"I honestly don't know, but I will be eternally grateful if it did happen."

"How can you even think that?"

"I would have given anything to make contact with my dead friend, and I did last night."

"Who was it you saw, Jake?"

"My Navajo blood brother, Cloud Bird. We were always together until he was murdered by a gang of white kids when I was fourteen."

"Has he appeared to you before?"

"No, never."

"Then why would he appear now, here. What's so different? What's changed?"

"This, I suppose, is what started things happening," Jake said. Gritting his teeth against the pain, he tore open that part of his shirt to uncover the winged branding.

"Holy cow! You went through that ritual – for him?"

"And I would go through it again, willingly."

"Is this true? You're not feeding me a load of bullshit?" Scott asked.

"Of course not. Why should I lie?"

Shock and disbelief were registering on Scott's face as he undid the tobacco tin and rolled up a cigarette. "You're serious about this, aren't you?"

"Wouldn't have shown you the branding otherwise."

"I guess not," Scott said, re-examining the perfect symmetry of the eagle burnt onto Jake's chest. "What puzzles me is why a perfectly logical man like you would have subjected himself to that ordeal. Have you any idea how many real warriors died trying to call back the spirits, let alone an inexperienced young white boy like you?"

"No, and I don't care. Cloud Bird came back for me tonight for a reason, and I followed him onto the stage to find out why."

Tentatively, Scott rested his fingers lightly on the brand and pulled away immediately. "Holy mackerel, Jake, this brand is scorching hot. How can you bear such pain without screaming?"

For the first time in a while Jake was able to smile. "That's because the brand doesn't hurt me."

Instead of commenting, Scott slit open the mesh screen with a penknife, unbolted the door and went inside to collect Jake's watch.

Neither of them spoke much on the journey along the coast. Scott was concentrating on not missing the turning off the narrow road. Ignoring the blaring car horns as he slowed down to almost a crawl, he turned onto a dirt road and continued on beyond a pair of rotting gates, driving towards the ocean through neglected orange groves.

The sun was just rising when they reached the cliff top above an isolated cove. Even so, it was difficult for Jake to see much of anything, and he stumbled often on the uneven surface until Scott went in front of him, steadying him down the steep incline of a narrow path. Below them on the rocks was a deep lagoon, and beyond that, a stretch of pale sand and an idyllic bay. It was a picture-perfect scene. Alongside the lagoon was a large rock pool which Jake was guided to.

Scott quickly stopped him from removing his clothing. "It might be better if you get in the water fully clothed. Some of the material might be stuck onto your skin. Don't risk it."

Once Jake was in the pool the water around him turned a reddish brown. For a long time, a light sheen of grey cement dust floated on the surface before drifting to the edge or sinking. When he had been soaking for a while, Scott helped Jake get out and into the deeper lagoon.

"Why do I need to get in this?"

"Because the rock pool was filled with rainwater, this is fed by the ocean."

Wincing from the stinging saltwater, Jake examined the severe grazing to his arms and legs. The oozing blood had finally stopped, and he was able to fully relax, knowing that someone else was close by. Floating on his back, he stared at the dark-bellied gathering clouds, the forerunner of an imminent storm.

Jake was staring into the slow-moving clouds when he fell asleep, dreaming that Cloud Bird had returned and was lifting him out of the water, taking him to whatever place he inhabited beyond the storm clouds, and he was blissfully happy. The rain felt as light as a kiss on his mouth as the first splatters of a heavy downpour hit the water. It woke him.

Scott was in the water beside him, supporting his head firmly, keeping him afloat. He stooped over, and kissed him gently. "Welcome back my friend. You're feeling better, I hope?"

They sheltered beneath the cliff for an hour or so, watching the storm until it moved out to sea. Although it was a magnificent sight, the wind was wild, and it was impossible to hold a conversation until the storm had finally passed over.

"What have you been thinking? You look very... serious," Scott asked.

"Do I?" Jake said, confused and uncertain. To avoid Scott's intense stare, he inspected the grazes on his arms and legs. Apart from the redness and minor soreness, they'd stopped bleeding and the pain had all but gone. "I thought I was dreaming," he said.

"Then I'm sorry. The last thing I want is to upset you."

"You haven't. I wasn't sure if that kiss actually happened. It's shaken me a bit, that's all."

"Thanks," Scott responded, adding. "I just care. By the way, I almost forgot to give you the clothes I brought over last night." He collected a bundle of clean but-worn clothes from a bag. "I'm sorry I didn't have anything better to offer you." He laughed. "There was no time to get to the laundrette."

"These are fine," Jake said. The shirt was a size bigger than he was used to, but the jeans were a perfect fit.

"I keep them on standby for when I get called to do extra's work."

"I'm surprised that you aren't getting acting parts," Jake said.

"There are no acting parts in this town for someone with my skin colour. I can only pick up work as an extra in Westerns. My father came to California from a Navajo reservation in Taos."

"Then he must have got work if you were born here. How did he get by?"

"He worked as a stunt rider with a Wild West show; a skill

168

which, thankfully, he passed down to me."

"Did your mother come from the same reservation?"

"Hardly." He laughed bitterly. "My mother was the seamstress with the show: a white girl. When Madge came along, my father bought this cheap plot of land here and did his best to make a living from planting the orange grove — but they didn't fit in with the locals. There was too much opposition. You must know yourself mixed marriages aren't accepted. Not here, and certainly not on the reservation. That's what split them up not long after I was born."

"Where are they now?"

"I have absolutely no idea where my dad is."

"What about your mother?" Jake asked.

"My mother is the head seamstress at one of the big studios, but uses her maiden name: Dawlish. Marjory has adopted the name too. She sees her from time to time."

"But you don't; why's that?"

"It was mother's choice," he said, without animosity. "She accepts Madge as her daughter because of her fair skin; unlike mine, which is taboo. Madge looks a lot like her, but as you can see, I take after my Navajo ancestors — which I'm very proud of." He ran his fingers through his mass of dark hair. "I kept my father's name of Chinook."

"Doesn't that make for complications if you and your sister have different surnames?"

"It helped getting the tenancy for somewhere decent to live. The flat we share was taken out in the name of Dawlish."

"And you don't mind?"

"Of course I mind, but how could I expect a white boy to fully understand what it's like for someone like me?"

"Well I think it's a lousy way for people to behave."

"In my opinion, no mixed-race couples give a damn about what their children will have to cope with growing up. Not if they haven't a true culture." Scott was angry, and for a time he paced about. Finally, he said: "I'm going for a swim. You'd best stay here, and don't try and follow. The current out there can be treacherous if you're unsure about where it's safe."

He plunged into the surf and swam powerfully against the incoming tide.

When Scott returned, his earlier pent-up frustration had gone, and he was his charming, amiable self. He apologised profusely for being grumpy and leaving Jake alone. He was genuinely pleased to find the injuries to Jake's skin were showing signs of recovery.

"Do you feel like talking over what happened last night? If you want to give it a try, you'll find I'm a good listener," Scott said. He opened a tin of tobacco, and rolled up a cigarette.

"Where would I even begin?" Jake opened his shirt in the sun.

Scott stared at Jake's eagle brand. "Anywhere would be a start."

"You won't believe me. No one in their right mind would. What happened last night is so improbable it makes no sense, even to me."

"Perhaps you could start with that ceremonial brand on your chest. That's got to be recent, and I'm guessing it must still hurt?"

"Now and then. How much do you know about this branding?"

For some time Scott sat on his haunches debating what to say before he answered. "I've come across that particular symbol only once before, which I remember clearly. It was on a parchment that belonged to an old medicine man at the reservation in Taos."

"How do you know it's the same?"

"That symbol can't be found anywhere else. There's no trace of it in a book of primitive customs in the museum. I read up on it as much as I could. Did you do know the branding you were subjected too was banned by the government more than half a century ago?"

"Yes, I did. I knew it was probably foolhardy for me to try."

"'Foolhardy' is hardly the first word that springs to mind," Scott said with disbelief.

"Then what would it be?" Jake asked, agitated by what was becoming something of an inquisition.

"Well, incredibly dangerous, for starters, risking your life so needlessly."

"So what, it was something I had to do. I wouldn't expect you to understand."

"But I do understand, and maybe more than you. After all, it is a part of my culture," Scott said hesitantly.

Jake was beginning to wish he hadn't got into this discussion and wondered how long it would take him to walk back to the hostel, if he set off on his own.

"There's more," Scott continued.

"And I'm sure you're about to tell me."

"You're damned right I will, if only to make you see sense. Throughout the entire 1800s, thirty-five warriors attempted to open a void into the spiritual kingdom and make contact. Thirty-three of those braves died in agony when they were consumed by a mass of flame."

"What happened to the two that survived?"

"One went crazy, and threw himself off a cliff."

"What became of the other?"

"White Bear was the medicine man with the scroll who I met in Taos. Until now, I suppose, I didn't think it was possible, but you are proof. What I can't reason out is why an innocent white boy would risk an agonising death in an attempt to bring a Navajo spirit back home," Scott said, rolling up another cigarette. "What was his name?"

"Cloud Bird. He was the chief's son."

"And the woman in the ritual, who was she?"

"You know about that too?"

"Mating is an integral part of the ritual. There must be a host body where the travelling spirit can lodge, otherwise the ceremony would count for nothing. It would be just earth, wind and fire."

"She is called Moon Spirit, my childhood friend."

"Were they related?" Scott asked tentatively. "If not, it couldn't work."

"She was his sister."

Although Jake only intended to rest for a short time, he fell asleep for a good two hours. When he finally woke, Scott had prepared a light meal of avocado and oranges.

"What time is it?" Jake asked, panicking when he realised his watch wasn't on his wrist.

"Half past eleven," Scott said, handing him his wristwatch.

"This is a fine timepiece you've got here, Jake."

"It was a gift for my eighteenth birthday."

"I saw. You were one lucky guy; it's a real beauty. Was it from your dad?"

Jake laughed. "No way, he never gave me anything. This was from a great guy I've known since I was a kid. He was more like a father to me than my own. He was always there for me while I was growing up."

"He did a good job. What's his name?"

"Gilbert. He lived at a nearby ranch. I worked there for a time until he decided to sell up and move away."

"And where is he now, this Gilbert of yours?"

Jake laughed with embarrassment. "I only wish I knew. He moved back to California almost ten years ago. I suppose he must still be here, but I've no idea where."

Scott rolled another cigarette. "Is that why you came here – hoping to find him?"

"Not entirely, I came to Los Angeles for another reason. Part of what I experienced last night must be connected, but I can't figure out what."

"What a man of mystery you are Jake Velasquez."

"I would hardly say that." Jake smiled. "If you don't mind, I'd like to get back to the studio. I'm feeling a lot better now, and there's quite a bit of work to be done."

"Marjory won't be expecting you there today. I left her that note."

"Even so, I ought to get back if I'm being paid."

Driving back through the orange grove, Jake asked: "How did you know about this place. It must be almost impossible for a stranger to find?"

"I suppose it's way off the beaten track. Madge and I grew up here as kids. You're welcome to come here anytime and get away from city life. The old place hasn't been used much since mother's parents died. There's hardly enough of the old homestead left to regard as a house anymore, but the roof and the walls are sound enough."

Chapter Eleven

As Scott had agreed to look at the reel with Jake, before he arrived, Jake set the reel going on the projector and readjusted the focus on the woman's ankles as she walked along the corridor. He had expected to feel less intimidated by the footage he was about to show, and yet he felt nervous and worse than ever.

He was trembling at the prospect of seeing himself again on screen, listening to the rhythmic beat of the woman's clipped heels advancing steadily along the corridor, which suddenly seemed to increase in sound as if they were approaching along the passage outside. His nerves worsened when the door into the viewing theatre swung open with a dramatic crash. Marjory Dawlish was standing in the doorway trying to unhook her cardigan, which had caught on the catch. She was backlit, and framed in much the same way as the actress about to be viewed on the screen.

Jake switched off the projector.

"What are you watching?" she asked. When Jake didn't answer, she switched on the overhead light. She stared into his ashen features. "Jake? What is it? What the hell is wrong with you?"

"It's nothing. Nothing at all," he said, wanting her to leave; not wanting to be forced into watching any of the film with Marjory Dawlish present. He wasn't mentally prepared for anyone to see the face of the man in the chair, except for her brother.

"You're spending too much time in here. You need some fresh air," she said, and she took his arm as if to lead him outside, but Jake wouldn't budge.

"I've only just got here. I wasn't well this morning, but I'm OK now. I've had plenty of fresh air."

"I got the note Scott left. It said you probably wouldn't be in again until tomorrow. By the look of you he was right. You should be resting. You're probably still concussed from that dreadful fall. I hope you got checked out at the hospital. Veronica should have referred you there yesterday. What did the doctor say?"

"Nothing, I didn't see one. Honestly, I'm fine. It's just a headache." Jake spoke through gritted teeth. He wanted to be rid of her and her overpowering sickly perfume.

She handed him two aspirin from her bag and got him a glass of water from the cooler before settling expectantly into the cinema seat next to him.

"The footage you were watching when I came in...what movie is it from?"

"It's been mislabelled, like most of the others, so it's hard to say." He decided not to mention what had been written on the reel.

"Where did Scott take you earlier, if not to the hospital?" she asked, catching him off guard by changing the course of her questioning.

"We went to a place further along the coast. I was feeling pretty rough when he came by with that change of clothes. Thanks, by the way, for arranging that."

"You must have been sleeping for quite some time. I was worried."

"There was really no need; I was in safe hands."

There was something going on in her mind; he could tell by the way she wouldn't look at him directly. "I hope you won't be led astray. Scott isn't like you, Jake. If you decide to embark on a movie career, an association with him could reflect badly on you, and jeopardise any prospect of getting to the top of this profession."

"Although I am enjoying this archive work, Miss Dawlish, I honestly have no intention of making this a career."

She burst into laughter. Catching hold of his arm, she said: "You are such a dear, sweet boy. You have no idea what I'm talking about. What you need is for someone to look after you in this city. Where are you staying?"

"Oh, you know, here and there." He wondered what her reaction would be if he mentioned the Salvation Army Hostel. "There didn't seem any point getting somewhere permanent for the time being."

"Then I might have a proposition that would suit us both. I've a self-contained, one bedroom annex on the ground floor at my place in the hills. Scott's been staying there recently, but he has decided to move out. It would suit you perfectly."

It wasn't that Jake disliked the idea of moving in, in fact he was interested in finding his own place, but he knew she was lying about why Scott was moving out.

"I see I've caught you a bit off balance. Think about it, and let me know tomorrow before I advertise." She touched his arm lightly before she settled back into her seat. "In the meantime, why not rewind this reel back to the beginning, and run it again."

"Wouldn't you prefer to see something else?" he asked, draining the last drop of water from the glass.

"No, I would not," she said, squeezing his arm affectionately as he got up to switch on the projector. "Rewind it."

"Right...I'll do that," he said, fumbling with the controls. He rewound the film back to the beginning, praying the celluloid would snap, or something would happen to prevent him running the reel at all.

He switched off the lights and started up the projector. As he sat next to her he could hardly breathe with the foreboding of what lay ahead. His nervous fingers dug into the arms of the seat when the scene opened again with that luxuriously slow tracking shot following the progress of the neatly shod feet along the corridor. As the actress stopped outside the office door, Jake desperately wanted to close his eyes but he couldn't. When the camera panned up the door to the frosted glass panel, Marjory Dawlish murmured her approval as the scene cut to the actress dramatically silhouetted in the doorway like a phantom.

"Why have I never seen this before?" she whispered. "This is beautifully shot."

"Have you any idea who that dancer is?" Jake asked, purposely switching off the projector to delay her from seeing himself in the chair, and dreading the inevitable interrogation which would follow; questions he could never answer.

"You mean actress. Now I hope that you're not going to make a habit of switching the projector off every time someone makes an entrance. Carry on."

"I'm sorry, Miss Dawlish. I thought you might know who she was."

"Hardly, all I've seen of her so far has been her ankles and a silhouette," she said. She reached across him to switch the projector on again, and became immediately engrossed.

There was barely any time before the chair swivelled around to reveal "Jake" seated there, staring at them both in the darkened theatre. The effect on Jake was exactly the same as before. He felt desperately sick and started to shake when he heard his own voice speaking on screen.

Marjory Dawlish leapt out of her seat in a second, staring wide-eyed at the screen, and then back at Jake in a flaming temper.

"So, you're just another bloody out of work actor. I knew I should never trust anyone as handsome as you. Why couldn't you have been honest, and just said you were an actor wanting a job."

The turmoil in Jake's head felt explosive. The venomous reaction from his boss wasn't helping a bit.

"Well, what have you got to say for yourself?"

"I'm not an actor. I have never wanted to be an actor, and God knows I didn't do this."

"Then why else would you be up there. That isn't any lookalike."

"I don't know, ALL RIGHT." Jake did his best not to shout, but it was impossible under the circumstances. Her perfume was overpowering and made him nauseous. His life had been turned completely upside down in the short time since he had driven to California. At that moment, he wished with all of his heart that he'd never left Fort Laverne.

"You would do well to mind your manners, Jake Velasquez – or you will find yourself out on your ear. I am not without influence in this town, and I'll make damned sure that you never work here again. You can depend on it."

"Quite frankly, I don't give a bull's arse what you think, Miss

Dawlish. That isn't me up there on the screen – that's a fact, believe it or not."

"Of course it's you. Who else could it be?" She was really angry, and it showed clearly in her face when she clicked on the light.

"I've already told you, I DON'T BLOODY WELL KNOW how the hell I got in this footage. I only wish that I did."

"That's bullshit," she snapped. "After all these years, I still can't believe what lengths a guy will go to get noticed." Contrary to the way she was talking, Jake could see that the woman was close to tears and was trying hard not to show it. "It's all very clever I must say. It's no wonder I didn't recall seeing any of this footage before."

"You think I'm not as horrified as you are to see myself up there? Why else do you think I tried to stop you from seeing this section?"

"Because, you must have found out I had a movie contract typed up for you; signing me as your agent. But not any more. I should fire you here and now for splicing yourself into this archive footage. No doubt it was all done on company time. Thank God you will be finished up here at the end of the week."

There was nothing Jake could possibly say that could defuse the situation. He was in too deep and so he decided to say nothing more and allow her fury to run its course. When Marjory Dawlish was all fired up, the old movie cliché about "how beautiful the girl onscreen looked when she got angry" did not apply in her case.

Because Jake was angered by her continuing insinuations, which did nothing but aggravate his nightmarish situation, he had no inclination to listen to her histrionics, and said so.

"Before you set off on this ridiculous crusade to have me either lynched or burnt at the stake for something that actually never took place, I suggest, Miss Dawlish, that as you're here, you examine this footage as closely as you like. If you imagine it's been spliced then let off steam if you need too, because I really don't need this."

"Where do you think you're going?" she demanded.

"As you said, I need some fresh air. After listening to your false accusations about me, I damn well need it." Jake gripped hard onto the back of the chair. His knuckles bleached as he steadied himself.

"Why should I bother examining anything when we both know how damnably clever you are at splicing bits of old movie stock together?" she shouted after him.

"Because if you can be bothered to look you will find only one repair on that reel up to this point; you will discover nothing, Miss Dawlish, or whatever your real name is. I'm not that good. Nobody is." he said, praying as he left the viewing theatre there were no old repairs in that opening sequence.

"The name is Marjory Dawlish, whatever you've heard," she screamed after him.

With Marjorie's scream ringing in his ears, the last thing Jake wanted was to get caught up in the frenzied world of moviemaking, and he was grateful he'd been fired. Since he'd arrived in California, except for Scott, and Ray, the security guard, no one else at the studio appeared to have any sense of reality. The bizarre events which had been happening in his life recently were light years away from anything close to reality.

He sat on the bench seat outside. Wearily he closed his eyes, recalling the events of the previous night, and the reassuring peace Scott's companionship had offered him at the cove.

When he thought about being unemployed by the end of the week, he was annoyingly no closer to finding out about his father's connection to the studio. The photos of him on the canyon road and seeing him on the stage, reminded him that he must take extra care who he asked to get that information.

Jake was almost asleep when he heard rapid footsteps approaching, which he knew could only be Marjory Dawlish. Then he caught the waft of her perfume mixed with the tobacco smoke.

"Let me guess," Jake said wearily, sitting up when she sat on the seat. "You couldn't find anything, could you?"

"No, I couldn't, but I was convinced that I would," she said, sounding deflated. "I've checked every damned frame before and after your appearance on that footage and there is no sign of any tampering; just one repair. But that doesn't mean I'm convinced."

"You didn't damage the film?" Jake asked urgently, shielding his eyes from the glare of the sun as Scott, thankfully, came into his line of vision.

"Hi," was all Scott said. He leant against the wall as Marjory Dawlish cut in, purposely not acknowledging his arrival.

"Damage the film? What do you take me for, some brainless idiot who makes accusations at young men based on absolutely nothing?" Miss Dawlish smiled wanly.

"And that, my young friend, is the nearest you will ever get to an apology for whatever she's done," Scott said, handing her a pair of sunglasses.

"Thanks for bringing these. Where did you find them?"

"They were under the front seat."

"What are you doing here anyway? I thought you had the day off to check out that apartment on the beach?"

"I had to change a flat tyre on the truck; that's why I'm here a bit late. I can view the apartment later."

"But why have you come here? My sunglasses could have waited until I got back."

Because Jake had asked him not to come over if anyone else was at the viewing theatre, Scott neatly avoided the problem, saying: "I altered the time of the viewing, which gave me some time to kill. I thought I'd drop by and watch some of the old footage Jake here's been getting from the storeroom."

"But why show an interest now? You weren't interested in any of the old reels when I offered you the job."

"I did say at the time the work wasn't of any interest because I didn't think I could do it well enough. You know how particular I am about organising stuff, Madge."

"I wish you'd stop calling me that. You know I don't like it."

"Sorry, it's just habit. Well, anyway, I didn't think that anyone would be able to make any sense of that storeroom. It was a complete shambles, and yet your man here has been cataloguing most of it, I hear."

"Who told you that?"

"Drew. Who else? He was well impressed."

"I do wish you wouldn't get involved with this side of the

production, Scott; you know Adelaide's feelings about that."

"I didn't seek Drew out if that's what you're thinking. It came up in conversation at the catering truck. There was nothing more to it than that," Scott said confidently.

It was a relief for Jake that Scott didn't mention the prearranged plan to view the reel together.

"So, why are you both sitting out here in this sweltering heat?" Scott asked, shielding his eyes from the glare off the white building.

"That's a good question. We should go back inside and take advantage of the overhead fan. It's much too bright out here." She stared witheringly at her brother. "If there's nothing else you need, Scott, then Jake and I must get back inside. The reel we are reviewing will take a lot of concentration. I can't have you in there with us if you intend chattering your way through it," she said, clearly expecting him to take the hint and leave.

"I will be as quiet as a mouse," Scott said adamantly, and followed them into the viewing theatre, where Jake reluctantly switched on the projector.

"Are you sure you've nothing else to be getting on with rather than sitting here in the dark? Haven't you got a horse to wrangle or something?"

"No, I'm afraid not," Scott said, making himself comfortable a distance away from the projector. "There is one thing, though. Can we go back to the beginning, Jake?"

"Do we have to?" Marjory Dawlish asked tersely as she re-settled herself in the seat next to where Jake had been sitting. "You don't need to do that," she said, checking the time on her watch.

"I've already started," Jake answered, rewinding the reel carefully. After he clicked off the overhead light, he switched on the projector.

Jake was trying to sense Scott's reaction to the footage, and Scott was remarkably quiet until he saw the actor in the chair.

"Holy mackerel...It's you!" Probably because Scott knew what to expect when the chair turned around, he didn't make a scene the way his sister had; instead, he laughed. "That comment just about sums this up. That's got to be you up there, Jake. How the hell did you pull that off?"

"So you agree it's Jake, too?" Marjory asked quickly.

"Of course, that goes without saying. Who else could it be? I've never seen any movie actor in this town who gets even close to Jake's look. It's incredible. There isn't a hint of difference between the real thing and what's up there. It must have been spliced in," Scott said moodily. "I didn't expect trickery from you, Jake. How did you manage it?"

"Examine the footage yourself. Nothing has been spliced in, contrary to what either of you think." Jake growled. "I never set my eyes on this reel until the day I fell down the stairs, and that's the truth. I'm damned if I know how this all came about; but one thing is certain, I'm no cheat. I expected better from you, Scott."

"Of course I don't think that."

"Then why make out I am?"

"I suppose because I honestly didn't know what to expect – except to see you up there on the screen. How could it happen?"

"How the hell do I know? I'm as confused as both of you."

"Don't you think it's incredible, though?" Scott asked, staring back at the image of Jake on the screen.

"It's bloody scary that's what it is," Jake said, and slumped into the seat.

"Maybe if we continue watching we might have more of a clue?" Scott asked, settling back into the chair.

"I thought you'd agreed not to talk?" Marjory said, but waited expectantly, like Scott, to see more of the footage.

"If we play it through until the end credits come up, we can find out exactly who he is, and the actress too. I can't say that I've ever seen her on or off screen, and that's quite extraordinary given her looks," Scott suggested.

"She does look familiar. I might have seen this actress before," Marjory said. "But I can't be certain. It was nothing more than a clip from a movie, or perhaps a screen test, but that was some time back, and I can't remember where."

When the scene continued playing, neither Scott nor Marjory passed any comment. They didn't light up a cigarette or chew any gum. Every developing scene of the movie had a riveting cocktail of brittle one-liners which none of them wanted to miss, all of which were delivered to great effect along a very credible plot. The moody look of the shadowy photography was not only dramatic, but plausible. The foot-tapping musical score had been perfectly orchestrated. It was, in fact, a monumental piece of moviemaking.

Jake's attention was transfixed by the hypnotically exotic partnership of the masked dancers in "The Tango of Death". It was an extraordinary exhibition. The difficult routine flowed as smoothly as silk. It was as if their dance was not performed by a couple but by a fusion into a single person. Of course, Jake knew the musical score intimately from the recording Gilbert had given him, so he couldn't help but express his admiration at the faultless grace of the dance.

When "Jake" was on screen, it was impossible for him to concentrate on anything else. He examined every facial expression; the shape of the teeth; the walk; even the annoying habit he had of scratching his chin when something puzzled him. It was all carefully scrutinised in the hope of finding anything different to prove that this replica wasn't him, and yet he couldn't see anything different at all. By the end of the second reel he could have screamed with frustration.

Needless to say, there was nothing about the production that any of them could fault. The direction was flawless, moving effortlessly from one scene through to the next. It was distressing for Jake to watch himself and hear his own voice speaking from the screen and, although it was shocking to see, it was a tremendous relief when the tango ended and the actor's lifeless body lay sprawled across the flagstones in a widening pool of blood.

The actress gave a truly emotional performance. The depth of her grief was absolutely convincing, not only to Jake, but to Marjory and Scott as well.

When the second reel ended, Marjory was so upset that she could barely contain her frustration. "That has got to be you up there, Velasquez – and don't you dare to say otherwise. No one in their right mind would dispute that you are in this movie," she snapped.

"Except for me," Scott said. "What you seem to have forgotten, Madge, is that what we've just watched is a very old movie, so how can you explain Jake being in it?"

"I can't, but he's a great editor. Even Drew could barely detect where he had pieced the test reels together. I know that it's him. It can't be anyone else – only Jake Velasquez."

"So what do you suggest?"

"Get me the actor's name from the end credits on the final reel. When we have that it'll be easy to match the name with a face in a back issue of *Spotlight*, whatever year this movie was shot in. Any actor who wants to get known advertises in that bloody magazine. You can be sure our star will be no exception."

"And what if I can't find his name?" Scott asked.

"You can forget the word 'can't'. That doesn't apply to either the missing reel, or the name of that actor. What I want is that you find both."

This exchange might have bothered Jake had he been listening, but his mind was occupied with another issue: trying to reason why he was up there on the screen. Maybe he had been filmed in a past life? It didn't bear thinking about. He remembered the previous night, when he had walked along that balcony on a stage set; the set below him was the same courtyard where the tango had just been performed on screen.

Jake was told to forget about reviewing any more of the old stock, and was directed to search every inch of the storeroom until the end reel had been found.

"But what if it isn't there?" he asked Marjory, convinced that his earlier suspicions about the reel Gilbert had entrusted into his care must be the missing end to the movie. However, not wanting to implicate him unless he was absolutely sure, he decided to keep those thoughts to himself, at least for the time being.

"Then it must be somewhere else in this studio, and it needs to be found," Marjory snapped. "And that includes you, Scott. Do whatever is needed to find it...but don't breathe a word to a soul about these other two reels; not to anyone."

Jake was about to tell her to get lost, but thought the better of it. To find out the actor's name in the credits, providing it wasn't his own, might clear up their doubts about him and, hopefully, it might help resolve his own nightmarish riddle.

"Do you remember seeing either of the actors before?" Scott asked.

"Not the man, that's for sure," Marjory said pointedly. "I've seen that actress before, in a minor role, but not recently. It could have been years ago for all I know."

"Who in the movie industry could forget a woman with bone structure like that?" Scott urged.

"No one" Jake agreed. "Miss Dawlish saw her dance once in a fragment of a damaged screen test."

"How could you possibly think that was her? From the bit I saw, you couldn't see their faces; they were both masked."

"Even so, you saw how amazingly they danced together, and again in what we've just watched. It was the music that made me realise this first," Jake said.

"We've talked about this before, haven't we?" Marjory said.

"Yes, we did. I brought this same recording with me. It's in my things."

"It was extraordinary music. I don't recall hearing anything like it before. Was it Argentinean?" Scott asked.

"All I know for sure is that it's called 'The Tango of Death', and it was written by a guy called Giuliani."

"I've never heard of him; how about you, Madge?" Scott asked.

Jake felt it sounded as if he wanted to clear the air with his sister.

"Once, when Jake spoke about it before," Marjory answered begrudgingly, her mood lightening. "Well, if you do have any more of that screen test, we'll get Drew to take a look. No one knows more about what's been made here than he does. If he's seen that dancer before then he'd most certainly remember."

"Do you think she was a professional dancer?" Scott asked her.

"Most actors were back then. Dancing was a prime requisite for an audition. However, what we trained for was nothing like that exhibition," she said. "I've not seen anything quite like it before. It's

185

something I shan't easily forget."

"Was she partnered in that screen test by the same man?" Scott asked.

"Yes, I'm sure, and that begs another question," Marjory said, staring more with admiration at Jake than with her earlier aggression. "How could that not be you up there, Jake? Who are you really?"

"I am exactly who I said I was: Jake Velasquez from Fort Laverne," he said, putting his driving licence between them on the table. "It says so, right there. And before you ask, I've never been to California until the day you met me at the gate with my truck."

Even so, it was clear that she wasn't convinced, and she barely glanced at the document. "You're very quiet, Scott. Aren't you going to support me in this?"

"I'd just like to say, before we go into that, from what I've seen so far, this movie is too good to be lost in the archives. You mustn't show it on the small screen. Play it at the cinema and give TV a miss for once. This could be the end of the rainbow you've been looking for, whether Jake is the actor or not," Scott said good-naturedly.

"Thank you, Scott. I'm not interested in your opinion of these two reels. This is not your area of expertise. Yours is wrangling. That's what you do best. Just tell me what you think about this actor being Jake?"

"What is it you want me to say, Madge? If Jake says that it isn't him on screen then I'm inclined to believe him, but that's not what you want to hear, is it?"

"Then you are even dumber than I imagined. No one else could look so alike," she said. She removed the reel carefully from the projector and put it into its canister, holding on to those two reels like a miser with a pot of gold.

"Where are you going with those, Madge?" Scott asked.

"Somewhere they will be safe, just for the time being, until you come up with the end reel."

"Jake can take them down to the Archive Room, if you're busy?"

"No, he damned well can't. I don't know if he can be trusted—

not after this."

Jake was slighted, and there was nothing he could do to stop her taking the reels away with her. He'd wanted to stay on late that evening and watch them through more carefully to see if they gave any clue to how he could have been photographed for the screen.

"You can't just up and walk out of here, Madge. Think about the logic of what you've just seen. If Jake was that guy then who was the woman? And when was it shot, and where? Jake has to be telling the truth."

Marjory left without another word, closely followed by Scott, leaving Jake to sort through the storeroom, where, for the remainder of the day, he industriously checked through a mountain of reels, but found nothing that even resembled the final reel.

Chapter Twelve

Unable to sleep, Jake paced along the beach until he knew exactly what he must do that morning, to either prove or disprove the idea that what Gilbert had entrusted into his care

Was the missing third reel, and he needed to find out for sure. If he was right then he had to find Gilbert and get some answers.

Jake arrived at the studio gates early, but had to wait until the night security guards changed back to the dayshift before he could gain access. When Ray arrived, he let Jake into the back room where he collected the battered tin trunk, thinking that it was unlikely that anyone might see him.

Even though there was hardly anyone else about at that time, just as an added precaution, Jake re-locked the door to the viewing theatre before he removed the reel from the trunk. With the reel were the film clips from the hacienda in Fort Laverne that Doctor Maxwell had told him to destroy. For a moment, he wondered if he was mad to think there might also be a connection with the other two reels.

When Jake opened the neatly wrapped canister, marked clearly on the lid was the film title: *The Return of Xavier Gérard*. It was dated 1928. Scribbled onto a temporary label he read "Keep on indefinite hold". Inside the canister was a reel of film in pristine condition, marked as the "end reel." The acting between the two leads was faultless in every scene. The film was a rollercoaster of suspense which had him gripping the arms of his seat until the screen went black and the end credits began to roll. For a while, Jake was too shaken by what he'd just watched, and the credits went through too quickly for him to check the actors' names, so he rewound the reel.

Because light had filtered onto the negative, when the credits came up and the principal actors were listed, it was difficult to read their names. From the blurred shapes Jake shuddered when he was able to make out the faint name of "Guy". He remembered that it was the name the apparition had called him when it had whispered in his ear. It was impossible to decipher the surname, though. Likewise, he was only just able to make out the actress's surname as "Cordova". Fortunately, he had better luck with the name of "Jon Miller" which, although faint, was attributed to the director. This was a name Jake knew from the past; a name he recalled having seen written down, although right at that moment, he couldn't remember where or when.

Despite the fact that this reel, Gilbert's reel, was the reel missing from the footage he'd been tasked with finding within the storeroom and Archive Room, it didn't present Jake with any sense of duty to the studio, and he had no intention whatsoever of handing it over to Marjory Dawlish. As a precaution, after making a note of the names on the credits, Jake rewound the reel and replaced it back inside his tin trunk, which he then locked away.

There had never been a doubt in Jake's mind about Gilbert's honesty, and he was not going to acknowledge the existence of the missing end reel to anyone. Not even to Scott. It was a decision that made him slightly uncomfortable. However, he felt sure he had to keep quiet until he'd located Gilbert and heard from him why he owned this particular reel of film, and why he'd entrusted it to him.

With a strong lead on the names of the principle actors, he returned to the storage area, and after reaching onto the top shelf, Jake returned to the viewing theatre with an armful of movie magazines from the 1920s.

He had been thumbing through most of the pile when he found an article that might have given him some information on the two actors, had someone not spilt coffee over it. All he was able to read of a press release issued by the studio was:

The principle actors have completed the final week of shooting on a supernatural murder mystery, filmed by a first-time writer & director on location and at the Silver Lake Studios. The Return of Xavier Gérard was expected to outshine anything else filmed in 1928.

And that was the end of the press release. There were no publicity stills of any scenes from the movie, nor were there any photographs of the actors.

Scott called by later that day to help Jake search through the remainder of the reels in the store.

"What did you honestly think about that guy on screen, Scott?"

"Well, for one, although you do look identical, there is a difference. Not much, I grant you, but it's enough to know that the guy in the movie isn't you."

"But he looks exactly the same."

"Facially, perhaps, but what he doesn't do is squint his eyes the way you do when you aren't wearing your specs."

"And that's all? It's something, but Miss Dawlish would never buy that."

"Well, it's a very endearing trait you have, but since you ask, this character comes over as being more confident. He's more in control of his life than you are." He mused for some time before he continued. "Another thing is, I don't get the innocence you project. Nor does he have the warmth in your smile. Like now, when you're embarrassed."

"No, I'm not," Jake protested, a little too strongly.

"The question that obviously comes to mind, because of your uncanny resemblance to this character on screen, is what do you actually know about your parents – about your family?"

"Apart from them not wanting me you mean?" Jake said, which he immediately regretted. "I'm sorry, I shouldn't have said that."

"What I'm saying, Jake, is, if that guy on screen isn't you then he has to be a blood relative. Is it possible that you were adopted?"

"If only. Then, all my rotten childhood would begin to make sense; except, I have my birth certificate, and it's no forgery. My parents are clearly stated as Ivan and Louise Velasquez."

"Even so, there's got have been a mistake," Scott said rather lamely.

"There's no way round it, Scott. I wish there was. They were hateful parents, but it's their names recorded on the certificate. I'll show you if you want?"

190

"There's really no need," Scott said. He was watching Jake clenching his knuckles. "I gather he must have been quite a bastard?"

"They both were, but I don't want to go into that."

"Did he have a profession?"

"When he wasn't drinking his way through the stock, he ran a bar. When he wasn't pissed, he ran a hostelry. He could also keep any old banger on the road years after it should have been scrapped," Jake said, unhappy to include any memory of his father in a conversation he had with Scott.

"What was he like apart from that? He must have had some redeeming features to have produced a son like you, Jake."

"The fact is, Scott, I can never remember liking the man."

"What, not at all?"

"If you'd had to live with him, you would understand, otherwise you wouldn't be asking me this. Perhaps I did miss something decent about him, but I don't think so. He was a man of low intelligence with absolutely no interest in music or art. He certainly had no interest in movies."

"Why would that be important? A lot of men don't. He wouldn't be alone in that."

"Then why, for as long as I can remember, did he receive a regular cheque each month from the old Silver Lake Studios – for years?"

"Are you sure about that?"

"Definitely."

"Have you any idea why?"

"Knowing him, it's odds-on that he was being paid to keep quiet by someone important. I've an idea it might have been Maurice Stanford," Jake said, and immediately wished he hadn't.

"What? You think he was blackmailing him?"

"It's a strong possibility, particularly as some of the things I keep coming across are beginning to make sense. If Maurice Stanford was in league with my father it would all add up; except, it wasn't his signature on the letter, telling him the cheques had to stop when the studio was sold."

191

"Where did you get this information?"

"I came across the letter after he died. It was hidden in his bureau. After I read that, I decided to come down to California and find out for myself what he'd been up to."

"Well, if it wasn't Stanford who signed the letter, whose signature was it?"

"Barbara Jeffords, Head of Accounting."

"Stanford's sister. Then he is involved for sure. When you came across this letter, was there anything else you found that might be relevant?"

"There was a reporter's camera belonging to a guy called Tom Brice. There was also a collection of black-and-white photographs."

"What were they?"

Jake related the incident of the ghostly visions on the canyon road, which he guessed were somehow relevant to the photographs Tom Brice had taken. He waited expectantly for any sign that Scott that might not believe him, but he needn't have worried.

"I'm convinced all that is connected to what I saw happening on stage."

"You never told me you saw anything that night, except for the spirit of your friend."

"I was led there for a reason. I'm certain of it."

"So what did you see?"

"My father on the stage when he was a young man; to be perfectly honest, if I hadn't come across early photographs of my Pa, I would never have recognised him."

"Are you certain it was him?"

"Positive. He was there with another man, rigging the steering rods on a truck."

"Have you any idea who the other man was? Anything you remember about him?"

"He wore an ugly diamond ring, square-cut, in a thick gold band. There was nothing modest about it."

"Then it was definitely Stanford. He wears a disgustingly flashy ring like that. Do you think they were being filmed? It could have been a scene from a movie?"

"No, most of the set had gone. It was for real, Scott. They intended to get rid of the driver, permanently."

"Do you know who the driver was?"

"It was me – or whoever it is I resemble."

"Do you have any idea why the other man was there? Did your father say anything?"

"No; he was too busy rigging the engine; although, the ugly ring guy did tell the driver he had to deliver two reels of film for processing."

"Then he would drive via the canyon pass to get to the old lab."

"The canyon road is where the photographs were taken. What if those are the same two reels we both watched?"

"It's possible, but…like all 'theories without substance – one blink and they're gone'. We need to find the missing reel. When we have that actor's name, we can take it from there."

Having begun his working day so early, it was only nine o'clock when Jake returned alone to the viewing theatre. He was about to relock the door again when it swung open and he was confronted by Drew Walters.

"What are you doing here so early?" Drew asked him.

"I couldn't sleep," Jake responded, appearing calmer than he felt. He started to re-stack the magazines into an orderly pile.

"What is it with the youth of today? You expect to get paid overtime by coming in early just to read?" Drew eyed the magazine covers with growing interest, and began to flick through them. "Where did you get these? Some of these are very collectable."

"I found them bundled up in the storeroom."

"So how come I didn't see any when I went in there?" Drew asked.

"Probably because you weren't asked to clear the place out; they were piled at the back of the top shelf. I almost missed them myself," Jake said, wishing the man would get back to his neat and orderly Archive Room so he could get on with his work.

As it was set apart from the pile, and open, Drew picked up the magazine in which Jake had read the review for *The Return of Xavier Gérard*.

"What do you find so interesting in old movie reviews?" Drew asked.

"I've been doing some research for Miss Dawlish."

"You've been working here no time at all, and now you are doing research? For what movie was that exactly?" he snapped, peevish, scouring through the pages with the eagerness of a bloodhound.

"Miss Dawlish asked me to find any information on two unknown actors in the footage we watched here yesterday. Didn't she mention anything about them when she dropped the reels off?"

"She didn't leave any reels with me, and I was here until quite late."

"Maybe she'll call by later this morning," Jake suggested, but felt in the pit of his stomach that she would not.

"Are you sure that's what Marjory said?"

"No, not exactly, I just thought that she might," he admitted.

"And what are these doing here?" Drew asked, holding up a strip of the edited film which Jake had taken from the Maxwell ranch. "These clips should never have been in the storeroom."

"They weren't. They don't belong to the studio. They were given to me years ago, in New Mexico."

Drew wasn't listening. Instead, his rapt attention was focused on the frames of a close-up. Switching on the projector, Drew fitted the short length of film onto the locating sprockets and wound the strip down manually until the actress's face was projected onto the screen.

"Dear God in Heaven! What a wonderful face this woman has. Who the hell is she?" Drew asked, staring obsessively at the face that Jake recognised instantly.

It wasn't the actress that troubled Jake; what concerned him more was why those clips of film, cut from Gilbert's reel, had been amongst the jumble of others Doctor Maxwell had asked him to destroy.

"I can't be certain, but I think this actress could be her," Jake said, handing Drew the magazine opened at the film review.

"You're kidding me, right? Coffee's been spilt all over it. I can't read anything from this," he said, angling the page into a better light.

"I think her surname is Cordova," Jake offered, only then realising the error.

"How can you make that out from this mess on the page?"

"I must have come across it in another article, not this. I can't remember which one."

"Cordova, you say? So why have I never heard of her before?" Drew seemed genuinely puzzled. "Having said that, I might have come across that incredible face in the past. It's not one that an editor would easily forget; so why the hell can't I remember when?"

"Miss Dawlish felt the same. She had no idea either. That's why she asked me to do some research."

"Marjory saw this clip?"

"No, and neither had I; not until you projected it onto the screen. What Miss Dawlish saw was her performance in the two reels she was taking over to your Archive Room."

"Two reels. Are you saying the footage is incomplete?"

"Yes. Without the end reel, we couldn't identify the actors by name."

"Well, you might do well to scan through some of the earlier casting manuals. I'd say begin with the ones dated around 1922 and 1923. Drop by the department later today, Jake, by then she'll have delivered the reels. Till then, I'll have a search around to see what I can find out about this actress." Drew chuckled happily.

Drew hadn't been gone for more than an hour when he rang through, asking that Jake come to the Archive Room as soon as he could.

"I found it on a fragment of a screen test for some movie called *The Return of Xavier Gérard*. There's not much of it here, but you'll see why I couldn't scrap it. The tragedy is that it's silent. I would have loved to hear her voice."

"Where did you find it?" Jake asked.

"Oh, a while back, one of the cleaners came across it with two reels of film she found at the back of a drawer when Maurice Stanford moved out of his office to make way for the new boardroom. She brought this clip along when I took over the archive."

"So you only have this clip – what happened to the reels?" Jake asked.

"Malcolm Reynolds, that's what. He denied any knowledge, of course, when Stanford held an inquest on the missing reels. In the end, the cleaner got booted out. After that, nothing more was said about them."

"So why is Maurice Stanford still directing here if he sold out?"

"Stanford came with the studio package. Nobody thought it was a good idea, but from what I hear, they would never have been able to take over if that old bastard wasn't included in the deal."

"So why move him out of his office?"

"Because it's the best space for production meetings; the table inside that room is big enough to seat twenty-five people at one go. That's when the heads of each department all get together for the next production, and directors like Stanford rewrite their own version of the script. Generally, it comes out nothing like the original story on its release. He was renowned for it. That's why the studio collapsed, if you ask me. It had nothing to do with the arrival of television, just his mediocre interference."

"Doesn't he have an office here anymore?" Jake asked.

"He's had one of the luxury bungalows converted opposite Stage Three. We don't see him much, but we hear him bawling sometimes and know to avoid going that way. That's a tip to remember during your stay here. Just keep out of his way and you'll hang on to your job."

Jake was about to make his excuses and return to the viewing theatre when he asked: "Have you any idea who worked here when the movie was filmed?"

"Definitely Stanford and his sister, but neither of them would help even if they could."

"Is there no one else I could ask?"

"There's Veronica, the nurse. She was here through the transition from silent movies into talkies. I guess she could help with information on the actors who were here back then. Sadly, it was their voices that finished off a lot of careers. In the silent movies, all an actor needed was to look good on screen. It was the foreign accents that screwed most of them out of a job when the talkies came in."

All the time Drew was talking, Jake was mentally kicking himself for not having remembered that Doctor Maxell had told him that Gilbert had once been an actor, which hadn't made sense at the time; of course, Gil must have been an actor on the silent screen.

"If you get nothing from the nurse, you might take a look through the studio library. I'm sure they must hang onto casting books that probably date back from forever. I'd say skip any 1922 and 1923 editions. Start looking from around 1924."

It was late in the afternoon by the time Jake made his way to the Medical Room but, finding no one there, he asked directions from a nearby office and carried on to the studio library. En route, he met Scott on the stairs.

"Hi. I was just on my way over to see you. What are you doing here?" Scott asked.

"Drew suggested I should look through some casting directories in the library."

"Shall I tag along and give you a hand? That's going to be a long job for one person if you don't have any names to go on."

Jake told him about the film's publicity release in the magazine, and the coffee stain, including the part names of Guy and Cordova. He didn't say the information hadn't come from the magazine, having decided against mentioning the end reel– at least for the time being.

The studio library had highly polished parquet flooring. It was a light and airy space. Row upon row of reference books lined the walls. There were four sets of wooden filing cabinets containing several files of photographic stills, and a plan chest stuffed with early stage designs.

There was something about Scott that everyone seemed to warm to, and Jake took great comfort in being seen as a companion. As soon as they entered, he could see that Monica, the librarian, would do anything Scott asked, and they were soon taken to where the casting directories were filed by year.

"This could take us forever," Scott said, settling cross-legged on the floor to go through the weighty volumes.

Eventually Jake found the headshot he was looking for in the 1926 edition of the *Actors Manual*. There was no doubt it was the right actress: her name was Alicia Cordova, listed as a dancer. Her film credits, which were few, listed her as a bit-part actress in *The Venetian Mask*, filmed in 1926, directed by Maurice Stanford. Her single leading role was for *The Return of Xavier Gérard*, filmed in 1927, directed by Jon Miller.

It was Scott who came up with the publicity shot of Guy Maddox. The photograph gave Jake the creeps. The face they were looking at could easily be his own. Guy Maddox had a triple listing as a musician, an actor, and a dancer. His film credits listed him as a bit-part player in *A Masked Ball* and *Another day in Ohio*, both filmed in 1926. There was another title which caught his eye entitled *The Devil of Fontainebleau*, filmed in 1925; a title he remembered having seen when Gilbert handed over a copy of this to Doctor Maxwell at the hacienda. All three movies were directed by Maurice Stanford.

There was only one other listing for Guy Maddox and that was as a leading actor in *The Return of Xavier Gérard*, filmed in 1927, and directed by Jon Miller.

Scott said to Monica that it would be helpful if they could see any reviews for any productions filmed at the Silver Lake Studios during the years 1925, 1926, and 1927.

"They aren't kept over here but we can arrange a time and I'll take you there."

Scott checked the wall clock. "Thanks all the same, but not today; anytime tomorrow would do. Whatever would suit you?"

"It would have to be in the morning: between nine thirty and ten?"

"That's fine, where should we meet?"

"They're kept in that derelict office block by the West Gate. I'll let Ray on security know to expect you, and he'll let you through.

The route through the studio is blocked off for filming all this week, so you'll need to drive there."

"Great. We'll look forward to seeing you there in the morning: nine thirty."

"Don't be late, Scott. I must open the library by ten thirty. Anthea isn't here this week to cover for me."

"Anthea?" Jake asked, seeing the fleeting look of embarrassment in Scott's face.

"Anthea Clare Baldwin. Sometimes I do occasional work for her company."

"Then why did Monica imply that she works here?"

"Not full time. She runs her business from home."

"Oh you mean for extras?" Jake asked.

This was a question which Jake noticed Scott neatly avoided by glancing again at the clock. "Say, is that the right time?" he asked, listening to his wristwatch as if it had stopped.

"Sorry. It's an hour and ten minutes slow," Monica reassured him.

When they were outside, Jake sensed that Scott was trying hard not to let his anxiety show. He said: "Listen, Jake, I have to get off now." He checked the time on his watch.

"Could I tag along?" Jake asked, unsure of what to do before he made his way back to the beach for the night.

"Any other time I'd be more than happy, Jake, but I can't; not tonight. Time is running out to keep Firebrand, and I need to raise a lot of cash pretty damned quick to save him."

"Have you been able to raise the fifty dollars yet?"

"If only that was all I needed" Scott mused. "I managed to scrape that much together, but that amount was for a down payment. The full amount was a hell of a lot more, and I only have a month to get the rest together."

"How much more do you need?" Jake asked.

"Four hundred bucks," Scott said, rechecking his watch nervously.

"You're not thinking about robbing a bank, are you?" Jake asked, trying to lighten the situation.

"It isn't a joke, you know," Scott snapped.

"I'm sorry. I didn't mean to sound crass. I just want to help if I can."

"Well, you can't, and I wouldn't let you. I have a plan, but the less you know about it the better. What we should arrange is where to meet up tomorrow. I could pick you up from wherever you're staying or, if you prefer, we could meet up at the studio gates in the morning? I don't mind which."

The following morning Scott arrived at the studio gates much later than arranged. He was dressed in a crumpled tuxedo, and looked as though he was suffering from having been out all night.

"I'm sorry for turning up like this, Jake. There was no time to get home and change, I need a short diversion before we make a start," he said.

Instead of driving into the town, he drove to a section of the beach quite close to the pier where Jake slept.

Scott had a short swim, dried off on his shirt, and changed into his jeans and T-shirt he kept folded inside the cab. "Did I keep you waiting long at the studio?"

"Hardly any time at all." Jake was curious to know where he'd been, but Scott didn't offer any explanation.

There were two stubbed out cigarettes in the sand-bucket where Monica had been waiting. She was seriously agitated and lit another cigarette when they got out of Scott's truck.

"You promised you'd be here on time, Scott. You're half an hour late."

"I'm sorry. I couldn't get away any earlier. I had an all-nighter, working for Anthea's agency."

"She told me you'd given up the escort business?"

"Not last night, unfortunately," he said. "Now we're here, any chance of seeing those reviews?"

"I've already set them out on the table. I'll make you boys some coffee while you look through them. You'll have to be quick though. We need to be out of here in half an hour."

"I can guarantee it. The coffee will be a great help."

Spread out were three bulging folders and six box files of press cuttings, all of which they searched through carefully.

"Any luck?" Monica asked, glancing at her watch.

"Nothing yet," Scott said, without looking up. "Can you remember anything from that period of moviemaking?"

"Nothing much, I'm afraid. Anthea might know more than I do."

"Didn't you say that she's not here this week?"

"Yes, but I can ask when I get home; she may remember something. She had a better grasp of English when our family came to America. She was the first to get work here on one of the musicals. They were damned good too; most of them, anyway, until Maurice Stanford took control of the studios. I'm darn sure it was that change of management policy which financially crippled this studio."

"What do you know about an actor named Guy Maddox?" Jake asked.

"Sorry, that name means nothing to me," Monica answered.

"Is there anyone else who might know about this actor? Anthea, maybe? It's imperative that we trace him, Monica," Scott urged with his winning smile.

"There's no one else working at the studio that I know of, except Maurice Stanford, and I'd sooner face a firing squad than ask him. Your best option would be the records office at City Hall. If this guy was a resident of Los Angeles, he would be registered there."

They were running out of time when Scott came across a bitter review of the 1925 box office flop entitled *The Devil of Fontainebleau*, starring Gilbert Renaldo as Napoleon; a movie which had been withdrawn from the circuits after the first week of its release.

In a news cutting from 1927, there was a lot about the much-anticipated release of *The Return of Xavier Gérard* by first-time director, Jon Miller.

In another article referring to that movie, there was a sour insinuation from Maurice Stanford that the movie was completely "un-viewable" and that it would never be released until he'd re-shot many of the scenes and re-edited the whole movie. Naturally, his own directorial credit was to replace that of the unfortunate Jon Miller.

"Where could we get more information on the actors and director who are named in this?" Scott asked when they stopped making notes.

"If they were under contract to the Silver Lake Studios, and as there are no other write-ups about them in over twenty years, I can only suggest that you boys check their names out at the Public Records Office at City Hall. Now was there anything else before I lock up?" Monica said, wanting to close.

"Actually, yes, there is something," Jake said, stopping by a framed publicity still on the wall. "Who is that?" He was scrutinising a dramatically lit publicity still of a partially naked young man.

"Oh, Gilbert Renaldo," she said. "He was quite something to watch on screen in his day. There's a close-up of him over there." It was a publicity still of the same actor as a young Napoleon, from *The Devil of Fontainebleau*, credited to the Silver Lake Studios in 1925.

There was no mistaking his features. The languid eyes, although heavily made-up for the movie, were less haunted than Jake remembered. The youthful face was immediately recognisable. The charisma generated by that quirky smile could have belonged to no other man. This was his Gilbert. In some way, he figured, Gilbert Renaldo must have had some connection with his late father, and Doctor Maxwell, too, might have been better acquainted with his father than he'd previously thought.

"Quite a handsome devil, wasn't he?" Scott commented, returning to the truck.

Instead of answering directly, Jake showed him the inscription on his wristwatch. "Believe it or not, that is the same Gilbert who gave me this watch."

"What? That guy in the photograph Monica was raving about. He gave you this, out in the middle of nowhere?"

"The very same, and now I have a surname to trace him."

It was a busy time of day when they arrived at the grand Municipal Building in the heart of the fashionable district. They had some difficulty parking, and required a lot of footwork to reach their final destination. Jake's brooding good looks attracted a lot of curious stares, but Scott steered him through the crowds without incident.

"When we come out, it may be better if you wait here while I go and get the truck," Scott suggested, and that was a relief for Jake to hear.

"How would I have managed all of this on my own, Scott? What if we hadn't met?"

"You'd have muddled through, Jake. There'd always be another guy like me willing to help out."

"It wouldn't have been the same though, would it?"

"No, I don't suppose it would."

Away from the oppressive heat, the inside of the building was noticeably cooler. The décor of the entrance hall was clinical and crisp, featuring a magnificent art-deco staircase. A uniformed commissionaire escorted them through a roped-off area to one of the four elevators and ushered them inside. On reaching the third floor, he directed them along the appropriate corridor. On this floor, unlike the splendour below, the decoration was minimal. The squeaky floor covering was of polished industrial linoleum.

Inside the records office, a mass of shelving and cabinets could be seen through the frosted glass screen behind the long counter. Behind a caged section of the counter was the person in charge. Clipped in front of her was a sign naming the woman as Miss G. Crowthorn. Duty Officer.

"This is an irregular request if neither of you are related to the gentleman," Miss Crowthorn said, peering at them over her glasses.

"We are here for research purposes, Miss Crowthorn," Scott said.

"Are you from a newspaper?" she asked suspiciously, closing the official register in front of her.

"No, Miss Crowthorn. I'm a member of staff from the Silver Lake Studios. All I require is a small amount of your time," Scott reassured her, showing an official business card he'd taken from

Marjory's office.

"And for what purpose, might I ask? Because if this is about filming inside these offices, I can tell you right now, that would never be allowed. The council policy here will not condone anything of an inferior nature."

"That is not our intention, ma'am," Jake said.

At the sound of his voice, Miss Crowthorn seemed to relax. "Whatever the nature of your request, sir, I can't let either of you gentlemen into the records office if neither of you are related to the person you want information about."

"I can't say how very important this is, Miss Crowthorn," Scott insisted.

"I only wish I could help you both. There's a strict code of practice in force. Its sole purpose is to prevent information being given to anyone other than a close relative."

"Then we do have a problem, Miss Crowthorn," Scott said winsomely. "I wonder if you've been watching the new TV series?"

"I don't watch much television. I prefer motion pictures at my local theatre."

"That is a great pity then. The storylines are compelling to follow; quite believable too."

"Which series would that be?" she asked dismissively.

"*The Heart of a City*, the show has a popular appeal?" Scott said.

"Oh, that programme. I love that show," Miss Crowthorn warmed a little.

"Well, this is our dilemma, Miss Crowthorn. One of the new characters in our latest storyline has been named as Guy Maddox." Scott spoke with some conviction.

"But surely you can change the name?" she asked logically, which Jake was sure would crumble Scott's argument.

"Generally, yes, but, unfortunately, in this instance, neither we nor the company can afford to get sued for libel. We can't use an artist's name without first obtaining his written permission."

"Very well, but only this once," she conceded, reluctantly. She ushered them into the main office which contained row upon row of filing cabinets, all stuffed with official documents.

They were instructed to sit opposite her in a smaller room lined with more filing cabinets, and linoleum-topped tables. It was a room shaded by slatted blinds at the many windows, ably deflecting the intense rays of the sun. A ceiling fan cranked the musty smell of varnished oak, swirling particles of dust through the air.

Seated opposite, they could do nothing but watch Miss Crowthorn systematically go through two of the larger files, where she found nothing. After consulting another volume, she cross-referred to a faded register for the year 1928. It was from this she got a result.

"There are two entries here for the name of Guy Maddox, which is surprising. I'm sorry, my mistake."

"Are you saying there are two men living in this city with the same name?" Jake asked.

Miss Crowthorn turned the register for him to see. "Unfortunately, that is not the case. This volume I have here is only for the registration of deaths."

"That must be a first, even in Hollywood. Two men with an unusual name, and both of them dead?" Scott observed, but when they read the two separate entries in the register, they understood the significance.

Guy Maddox / Male, aged 32 years. Actor, Musician, Dancer.
Cause of death: Crash victim.
Date: January 12, 1928.

To have found the second entry in the register would have taken considerably longer had it not been for Miss Crowthorn's cross-filing system. Five pages on from the last entry, she came to another.

Guy Maddox Junior / Male, aged three weeks.
Cause of death: Pneumonia.
Date: September 18, 1928.

"If Guy Maddox was married then perhaps his wife is still alive.

If so, there is a good chance we might find her," Jake said, as they walked to the truck. "Do you think she was an actress?"

"It's possible she was a would-be starlet, but more likely an ex-hoofer. Whatever she was, it's my guess the mother didn't survive the shock of losing both her husband and her child within the same year. If she did get through it, I guess she would have gone back to wherever she came from and not stayed on here. It would have been tough to survive in this town during the Twenties, even getting work as an extra. With no husband for support, I can't see how a widow could have survived here in this rat-race of a profession, or would want to after that."

"Even so, there is a slim chance that she might still be here," Jake said.

"No one is interested in failure here. Either she died, or went back to her home town. That's what most of them do. That's what I'd do, except this is my home town, and so for me there is no escape," Scott said.

"So, do you think we should give up on the search?"

"We must. We've reached a dead end. I'm afraid the search for Guy Maddox is over. Having said that, all's not lost– not when there is a decent telephone directory in Marjory's office, and we have an ace up our sleeve with the name of that movie's director."

As Jake climbed into Scott's truck, he picked up a business card off the floor, which he guessed must have fallen out of Scott's tuxedo jacket. On the card was printed:

Dream Lover Escorts.
Intelligent, articulate men available for private functions, social events, and companionship. Please contact Anthea Clare Baldwin. Telephone 310 555 392 (Absolute discretion is assured.)

"Is this yours?" Jake asked.

"You know it's mine. Who else would it belong to? But thanks, anyway."

"I didn't mean to read it."

"What the hell? It's better you know everything about me now.

You heard Monica refer to my working for Anthea's escort company. I don't do it on a regular basis, not anymore."

"Then why get involved in a job like that now?"

"You know why. I need an input of cash, quick."

"Then I hope it was worth it." Jake spoke with more feeling than he intended, regretting his words immediately. The hurt in Scott's eyes had gone in a moment, but it made Jake wish he hadn't picked up the card.

"As it happens, the client was a two-bit chiseller. What he wanted wasn't on offer, and so all I got for an unpleasant night's work was a measly twenty bucks."

"I'm sorry about what I just said."

"I know that, this is not the sort of town where a guy like you ought to be hanging out, Jake. Find yourself a nice girl and settle down. I wouldn't want you to finish up like me at twenty-seven. Washed-up and selling what bit of morality I once had for the price of a few bucks."

"You're worth a lot more than that," Jake said, desperate to make amends and get their friendship back onto an even keel, but he could see by the determination in Scott's face it might take a while longer.

"Jake, I'm well able to take care of myself, but you're not. When we're through tracking down this director, promise me you'll get the hell out of this town. It's no good here for a nice guy like you. Go back to Fort Laverne while you can. Do it for my peace of mind, if not for your own." A dull flush of colour returned to his handsome face, and he gave Jake the benefit of his winning smile.

"I wouldn't have anywhere to live, even if I did."

"What about where you were brought up? You must've had a home."

"That place we lived in was big, but it was never a home. It was falling apart around our ears. It could have collapsed in the first decent storm for all I know."

"What sort of a place is Fort Laverne?"

"It's little more than a ghost town at the end of a narrow canyon. The canyon itself belongs to the Navajo reservation. We lived in a habitable section of a crumbling hotel that was left to rot like the rest of the town when the railroad didn't go ahead and the planned resort failed."

"Couldn't you sell that and buy something else? Any hotel must be worth something, whatever the state."

"It might have been, if my parents had owned it. All my pa owned was a run-down bar. They had the place on a tenancy agreement. I saw—" Jake stopped mid-sentence. "Holy cow, that's it. That's where I saw that name before."

"What name?" Scott asked.

"His signature on the rental document I saw. The owner of the hotel was Jon Miller."

There was silence as both men absorbed this fact.

"You think it's the same man as the director for *Xavier Gérard*?"

"It's got to be."

"Miller is not that uncommon a name, and neither is Jon. In America there must be at least hundreds, if not thousands of men with the same name."

"Perhaps, but it's too much of a coincidence. Everything that's happened recently seems to be connected. It's becoming more and more like a huge spider's web, and I am the fly in the middle."

"Do you have the agreement for the hotel with you?"

"Yes. It's with my things in a trunk at the studio."

"Why are you keeping it there? Wouldn't your personal things be safer where you're staying?"

"Not where I'm staying," Jake said reluctantly, knowing that it would need qualifying. "There's no point looking at me like that, we all have secrets."

"Secrets are not a good thing. You must be staying somewhere, for Pete's sake," Scott said.

"After that disastrous start in Czardas Street, I slept rough for the first week, and then I made the best of it at a Salvation Army Hostel."

"You're staying at a Sally Ann Hostel?"

"Not now. I decided to get away from there and camp out. I

found a sheltered place along the beach."

"Are you crazy? You can't stay there. Any young guy sleeping rough in this town is prey to all kinds of horrors, even the police."

"There's no alternative until I get my finances straight."

"Yes, there is, and before you even think of objecting, I'm taking you there now. Most of my stuff at Madge's flat is packed up, ready for moving. I should have collected the keys to my new pad this morning, but forgot. I can get them first thing tomorrow on the way in, so if you don't mind crashing out on the couch for one night, you can move in with me."

"I've just told you, Scott, I don't have the cash to pay for a room."

"Madge won't mind; not once you sign the contract for her to represent you as an actor."

"What are you talking about? I don't want to be a bloody actor. I've already told her that."

"Then more fool you for agreeing to that screen test."

"I only agreed to gain more time at the studio. The only reason I came to California was to find out what my pa had been up to, why he was being paid off."

"Well, if you take my advice, I wouldn't tell Madge. She thinks you are already hooked and landed."

"Geez. What can I do?"

It took some time before Scott answered, and when he did, it was accompanied by that wonderful smile of his. "The best I can suggest is that you move into her apartment, and break the news gently. If I was in your situation, I'd play Madge at her own game and agree, but with conditions."

"Even though you know it's the last thing I want to do?"

"If you've been offered a window of opportunity, Jake, then use it. If you are broke, just consider this before you stride off into the sunset. If Madge represents you, you could probably earn enough from making one movie alone to put into something that you really care about. What you need to consider is this: it's Madge, and Adelaide Williams who are desperate for you to sign, not the other way around. But one word of warning before you do, you've got to read through the small print very, very carefully before you sign any contract. I've seen what she's drawn up already; that's why I'm telling you this."

"I honestly don't think I can do that," Jake protested.

"At least promise me you won't turn the idea down flat. Say you'll think about it; at least that way it will keep you around here a while longer."

On their way to the apartment in Santa Monica, they called in at the studio for Jake to collect a few clothes and paperwork from the trunk. Fortunately for Jake, Ray was working the late shift, and let him out with his duffel bag.

"What will Miss Dawlish say when she finds that I've moved in without speaking to her about it first?" he asked Scott.

"She might grumble to begin with, but everything will settle down after that. I'll slip a note to say I've persuaded you to move in after all."

"But you can't do that, not while you're still living there."

"You seem to forget – I've been kicked out. Well, more or less."

"I don't feel good about this; it's your home."

"It's a place to sleep, nothing more. Anyway, I'd feel a lot better if you moved in there rather than with someone else. At least I'd know you'd be safer there than on the beach."

"But you said she had plans?"

"And so she has. You, my friend," Scott said grimly, pulling into the drive.

Once inside the ground floor of the building, without disturbing his sister, Scott wrote a note which he slipped through her mailbox on the upper level. It gave Jake time to search through his father's paperwork for the tenancy agreement. As he rightly remembered, the document for the Grand Hotel, which his father had signed, was countersigned by Jon Miller.

"You've got to be right about this man, Jake. There are too many coincidences for this not to be the same Jon Miller," Scott said, examining the contract in detail. "And get this, for Pete's sake? The contract was drawn up in 1927. That's the same year Jon Miller directed the Guy Maddox movie."

"Agreed," Jake said, shivering in his thin shirt, unused as he was to the coastal climate which could alter in a matter of hours.

It turned into a bitterly cold night and, after a time, at Scott's suggestion, Jake abandoned the couch and got into the single bed with him.

It might have caused a great deal of embarrassment for everyone concerned when Marjory walked in with a cup of coffee. Fortunately, Scott was still in the bathroom where he'd been showering.

"Did you make one for me?" Scott asked, as he came into the room, towelling himself dry.

It startled Marjory so badly that she very nearly dropped the cup she was holding. "Why are you still here? You should have moved out yesterday."

"It was too late when we got back last night. I'll move into the new place later."

Suspiciously, Marjory Dawlish eyed up Jake in the single bed; he had done his best to cover himself up when she came in.

"Where did you sleep?" she asked Scott accusingly, staring at the narrow bed.

"On the couch; where d'you think?" Scott responded quickly.

It seemed to satisfy her when she saw the crumpled sheet on the couch, but did nothing to alleviate the shock of finding her brother naked.

"For goodness' sake, Scott, do put some clothes on."

Scott wrapped a bath towel around his lower half and sat on the bed. "Well, it seems to me that we might just as easily be shocked by seeing you in that cover-nothing whatever- you-call-it," he said good-naturedly, chuckling with amusement as she pulled the semi-transparent garment tightly around her slim figure before making her way to the door. "Did I hear you offer to make me a coffee?" Scott called after her.

"If you want one, make the bloody thing yourself," Marjory responded angrily, slamming the door.

"I really don't think it would be a good idea if I stayed here,

Scott," Jake said, unsettled by the embarrassment of Marjory Dawlish finding him in her brother's bed. He was more embarrassed at the prospect of Scott commenting on the burning topic of what had happened between them during the night, and he wasn't mentally prepared to enter into any conversation about that.

"You're kidding me, right?" Scott said, taking a drink of Jake's coffee. "You'd be a damned fool if you turned this place down. It's ideal."

"Not if your sister's going to come in when she likes, and... dressed like that."

"There is absolutely no need to bother your head about Madge. I'll have a word when she's had time to cool down. She's always been tetchy first off in the morning. Mother was exactly the same. It must be a blonde thing," he said. He stopped as he was about to go into the bathroom. "How do you feel about what happened between us last night?"

"Truthfully, I honestly don't know," Jake said, which made him feel even worse when Scott averted his eyes swiftly.

"That's absolutely fine. There's no need to get into a sweat. Most guys experience it once in their lives. Just put it down to experience. It's something I won't bother you with again."

Chapter Thirteen

An awkward silence had developed between them on the drive into the studio that morning. When Scott dropped Jake off at the gate, he mentioned casually that he wouldn't be around much for the remainder of that week as he would be moving into his new digs, but he purposely avoided saying exactly where that would be.

With the thought of moving into Scott's flat for the remainder of his stay, after the disturbing but comforting intimacy they had shared during the night, Jake went into the studio faced with an unexpected dilemma, wondering how to get free of the arrangement of staying there at all, particularly with the possibility of early morning visits to his rooms by a semi-naked Marjory Dawlish.

Work-wise, Jake had plenty of viewing to get on with until Marjory Dawlish was due to arrive by 10a.m. When she hadn't turned up by mid-morning, Jake began to wonder if he had misheard the time. By lunchtime, he was sure that something had happened, and he would have called Scott to ask if he'd had a number to call.

When Marjory Dawlish did eventually arrive, it was just after 3p.m.

"I'm sorry to have kept you waiting for so long," she said, just a little too cheerily, as she breezed into the room wearing dark glasses. "I've been in a long meeting with Adelaide all morning, discussing the result of your screen test with Hugo Page, the cameraman."

"That's a relief. I thought there was a problem with Scott."

"Have the two of you had a quarrel? Well, have you?"

"No, we hardly spoke on the way in here."

"Well, something's sparked him off. He's called me three times already this morning about collecting the rest of his stuff, but only when you aren't there."

"Actually, I wanted to talk to you about that, Miss Dawlish," he began, but Marjory wasn't in the mood to listen.

"You don't have to. I know what this is about. He's been like a bear with a sorehead about saving that bloody horse. He just won't listen to reason when a horse is involved," Marjory ranted. "What the hell does that man take me for, some dimwit just in from the sticks. I couldn't possibly have that renegade horse prancing all over my lawn. What would the neighbours think if I agreed to his demands, even for one week?"

"Where's Scott now?"

"Where do you think? He's exercising that wild piece of horseflesh along the beach."

Not only did Jake need to calm her down, he also had to put a stop to the emotional strain she was creating inside his head, and the only way to do that was to get away from her. Therefore, he suggested he went to the canteen and got them both coffees.

"That's a wonderful idea, darling. Get me a bagel too, I'm famished," she said, taking off the dark glasses, and relaxing into the chair.

When he returned with the coffees, the projector was switched on and ready for running.

"I thought you should see this," Marjory said, switching off the light, and setting the reel in motion.

Jake remembered the scene well enough, and the unfortunate way Harold the stand-in had delivered his lines. When Harold stopped speaking, Jake had turned to face him on camera. He felt his skin crawl in exactly the same way as it had the very first time he had been confronted by the face of Guy Maddox, only this time the man up there was himself, Jake Velasquez. It was the strangest thing not to think it was Guy Maddox there in his stead. Unquestionably, the two of them were identical in every conceivable way.

"What do you think?" Marjory asked, wiping a smear of lipstick from the cup before lighting up a French cigarette.

"It's hard to be objective as I knew what was happening next,"

Jake said, needing time to gather his wits.

"Even so, Jake, you must have an opinion on just how good you look on film?"

Jake realised that Marjory Dawlish was up to something, otherwise, why had she bothered showing the screen test?

"It's hard to believe that it isn't Guy Maddox up there, but me," Jake said.

Marjory Dawlish removed a "Motion Picture Contract" from her bag, which she put on the table between them, and asked him to read it through so he could get the gist of the content. She then laid a second contract on the table and, with a fountain pen, signed her name on the document, which she then passed over to Jake.

"What is the reason for two contracts, Miss Dawlish?" Jake asked, wanting more time to remember what Scott had said about reading the small print on the contract his sister was preparing.

"As you can see, the bottom one is the standard studio contract."

"What about the other?"

"This one on top is an annual contractual agreement between you and me. This states that I will be your Personal Manager, which means I will be negotiating any movie contracts for you in the foreseeable future."

Jake's stomach lurched at the very thought of committing himself to any such deal. On the one hand, he loathed the very idea of parading himself on screen; on the other hand, he detected that there was an amount of leverage here, which he could put to good use.

"OK," he said.

"You'll sign?"

"Possibly, after I've read both these contracts through."

"What, you don't trust me?"

"I didn't say that. Would you agree to sign anything without first carefully reading it through?"

He couldn't understand why he felt the need for Scott to be there to advise him, but when he read the small print Scott had referred to the night before, Jake was adamant that he would only agree to a one-picture contract with Marjory Dawlish, otherwise the deal was off.

It was clear that she was annoyed at having been sidestepped so easily but, as she readily agreed to write up a new draft that same afternoon, Jake recognised that he still had a lot of bargaining power to get what he really wanted, which was why he had agreed to sign in the first instance.

"Is that it? If so, I'll have my secretary get onto it immediately."

"Actually, no, there are two things I need included."

"And they are what, exactly?" Marjory asked, her tone cooling.

"Well, first off, I need an advance."

"How much are we talking about?"

"I would need five hundred dollars, in cash, by the end of the week."

"What? You have a nerve. You think you can bargain for that amount of an advance when I'm offering you a bloody movie contract." Marjory exclaimed.

"That's not all, Miss Dawlish. The second thing is that I want Jon Miller to direct me. That is, if we agree to go ahead." To begin with, Jake thought she was going to faint with apoplexy at the suggestion.

"Who in God's name is Jon Miller?"

"Jon Miller was the director for *The Return of Xavier Gérard*. We both know what the Silver Lake Studios did to his career by shelving that. I'd like to make some amends; besides, if I'm that similar in looks to the actor Guy Maddox, then, perhaps, if your company is prepared to distribute Jon Miller's first movie…" Jake began, but then thought it wise not to pursue her with his next request, at least for the time being. It was evident her thoughts were engaged on other, more immediate matters.

"If we ever locate the final reel," she cut in, feverishly lighting another of her foul-smelling cigarettes.

"Which we will," he said, in such a way that she knew he was onto something. "Then perhaps, if that happens, and his career gets resurrected because of it…"

"What are you suggesting?"

"Only this: if things work out for him then Jon Miller just might be persuaded to make a sequel to that movie."

Jake had shocked her.

"What do you take me for? No unknown actor would risk a promising career on a mere principle. Not here in Hollywood."

"Those are my terms, Miss Dawlish, accept them or not," he said, unstrapping Gilbert's watch. "I do have an alternative way to get the cash, so there's no need for me to negotiate any further on this."

When the shock of his request cleared from her eyes, she didn't get wild, as he'd expected; instead, she said nothing, deep in thought. She inhaled her freshly lit cigarette several times before she smiled, and he knew there was more than just a chance of getting his way.

"D' you know what, your suggestion about having this Miller guy make a sequel with you as the lead isn't such a bad idea. Let me run it by Adelaide and get her reaction."

"Does she know about the two reels?"

"Yes. She also knows that the final reel is missing and, as she says, without having that there would be no way to reshoot the remainder, as we have no idea of the story's outcome. There isn't a trace of the shooting script anywhere."

"Then you will be pleased to hear that, although I don't know where the shooting script is, I do know where the end reel can be found," Jake said with some relief, not wanting to deceive her any longer.

"What, you know where is it?"

"Yes."

"Then where the hell is it?"

"The reel belongs to someone who I am trying to locate somewhere in this city."

"Are you certain this is the final reel, Jake?"

"I couldn't be more so, Miss Dawlish," he said, wondering if he had done the right thing in mentioning this before he had asked Gilbert's permission.

"Who is this person?"

217

"I'm not able to say at this juncture, miss."

"Presumably we are taking about a man living in California?"

"Yes, we are."

"And this is someone you know well? Presumably who was connected with your editing work in New Mexico?"

"It is."

"And how come this guy has company property in his possession?"

"I can't answer that. Not yet, but I'm close to finding out." He omitted to reveal that the end reel was safely in his possession, where it would stay until he had spoken to Gilbert. To accomplish that, his hopes hinged on tracking down Jon Miller, who, he hoped might know Gil's whereabouts. That is, if he couldn't be found in the telephone directory.

"Then make sure that you keep me informed, Jake."

After Marjory Dawlish had gone, Jake realised he hadn't told her he wasn't going to take up the offer to stay at the flat and, as he was completely out of cash, it presented him with a glaring problem. It left him with no alternative but to get the salary he was owed from accounting.

When he eventually located the accounts department on the top floor of the white building, he could see why the elevator wasn't working, as the gate had been wedged open with a coat stand. Inside, every inch of space was packed solid with paperwork, folders, and ledgers.

Likewise, the space inside the secretary's office was equally restricted, leaving barely enough room for the door to be opened. Her office didn't seem to be much bigger than a broom cupboard as every conceivable space was jammed with filing cabinets, typewriters, and box upon box jammed full of office supplies and disused telephones.

"Can I help you?" the secretary asked from behind her cluttered desk.

"I sure hope so, miss. I need to speak with Barbara Jeffords."

"Do you have an appointment?" she asked, opening the office diary.

"No. I'm afraid not."

"Then you must make one. Miss Jeffords will not see you otherwise. It's company policy," she said. "Have you completed a payroll form?"

"Not that I'm aware of," Jake said.

"You must fill this in first," she said, nervously fiddling with her hair as he scribbled the relevant information in pencil. "Now that's done, I can make you that appointment," she said, taking the form from him.

"I'm afraid this can't wait, miss."

"Unfortunately, Miss Jeffords makes the rules here, and they must apply."

"When do you expect her back?" he asked, and caught the nervous look she gave towards the communicating office door.

"Miss Jeffords, she...she isn't..." The woman faltered as Jake took two strides to reach the door. "Sir, I seriously advise you against that," she squeaked as he rapped on the door, and took hold of the handle. "Sir, you can't just go in there unannounced." She lowered her voice into a whisper: "Whatever you've got to say to her just keep it brief."

Shunted away into a space that was a quarter of the original size needed, the interior of Barbara Jeffords grand office gave the impression of belonging to a deposed dictator. Taking up almost half of the room was a gigantic desk, decorated with gilt ormolu. In its present surroundings, it was grotesquely out of place, an item of furniture that one might expect to find at the Palace at Versailles, and not unlike the one used by the Emperor in the 1927epic,*Napoleon*.

Behind this desk sat Barbara Jeffords. She was a big woman with a thick squat neck and round shoulders. Her dyed hair was cropped short and did nothing for her lack of charisma. Neither did the Cupid's bow painted onto the flesh above her thin lips; along with the pencil-thin eyebrows and heavy make-up, her appearance bordered on the grotesque.

"Yes?" she snapped, re-angling the venetian blinds at the window to see him better than squinting at him through a bright

219

shaft of sunlight. "What do you want?"

"I apologise for intruding, Miss Jeffords, but I need information."

"Who are you and what are you doing in my office without an appointment?" she peered at him against the intense rays of the sun.

"I came to collect my pay cheque," Jake said. "I've been employed here for almost a month and, so far, I've only received a small advance."

"Name?" she asked in a brittle voice. She opened the payroll ledger on her desk with a resounding thud.

"The name is Velasquez, ma'am." He waited for some kind of reaction but, apart from a slight tightening of her slack jaw, there was none.

"Initial?"

"That would be 'J', ma'am; J' as in 'Jake'."

"And you've been employed here for how long?"

"Approximately one month, ma'am," he said, thinking it seemed more like a year.

"I have no one on the payroll with that name," she said, snapping the volume shut with a sense of finality. "If your details aren't entered in here, I can't pay you anything. Close the door quietly on your way out."

"Would you mind looking again, ma'am? I must be entered in there."

"I would mind. I do not make errors of that kind. Your name isn't entered in the stand-in's register, and therefore it is out of my jurisdiction. You must take it up with the person who engaged you. Ask them to sort it out before you come barging in here again."

"Excuse me, ma'am, I'm not a stand-in. I've been taken on in a temporary capacity. I'm assisting Drew Walters in the Archive Department. Call him, if it will help confirm who I am."

"That is highly irregular." Her voice quivered with controlled indignation. "There's no union rate for such a position. By whose authority were you employed? Mr Stanford has mentioned nothing about this."

"I was employed indirectly through Adelaide Williams. Her assistant, Marjory Dawlish, arranged it."

"I see," she responded icily, squinting over the rim of her spectacles. She flicked on the intercom. "Marcia. I've got a man here claiming to be a temporary assistant to Drew Walters in Archives. Is there any paperwork on him? Jake Velasquez." There was silence, then: "very well, bring it in with you, if you have the payment ready."

The secretary, Marcia, came into the room with the form Jake had completed on his arrival, which she handed over to the grim executive.

"Well, this seems to be in order," Barbara Jeffords said, glancing through the document. "Call here on Friday. Marcia will have your paycheque ready for you to collect."

"But I need something to live on until then, Miss Jeffords."

"That is not my problem. I can't pay you out of petty cash. I go to the bank on Friday. Good day, Mr Velasquez."

As he was leaving, she called after him to go back into her office.

"Yes, ma'am?"

"You've filled this form in pencil. I can't accept this. Go and fill it in again. This time use ink." She said, re-reading a section. "Wait a moment —You've put Fort Laverne, New Mexico on this form? Is that where you're from?"

"Yes, ma'am, it is."

"And your family name is...Velasquez?" she hissed, as the connection was made.

"Yes, my late father was Ivan Velasquez. You may remember the name, ma'am. You posted him company cheques on a regular basis; one every month, I believe," Jake said. Having not closed the door properly as he left, he heard Barbara Jeffords on the internal telephone, and was barely able to concentrate on filling in a new form with ink, when the one-sided conversation began.

"Maurice, get over here now. We have a major problem. Ivan Velasquez isn't done with us yet. That blackmailing snake has a son."

"No, damn it, I didn't see what he looked like. The sun was shining directly into my eyes. If the desk had been moved like I asked then, of course, I could describe him. What did he want? Well, money, of course. He made out he came here for his pay cheque, but it was easy to see what he was really after as soon as he mentioned his father's monthly cheques. I can only assume he has those incriminating photographs. Well, I don't know. Get Malcolm to do something about him, and get rid of him pretty damn quick. Frankly, I don't give a brass fart about what you might be doing. This is more important than that dull wife of yours. Get over here before we have another Velasquez leech bleeding us dry."

Chapter Fourteen

When Marjory hadn't returned by early evening, Jake was feeling more uncertain about the outcome of his demands than he had been earlier. Meantime, his search had uneven results. While he was unable to find any listing in the telephone directory for Gilbert Renaldo or Doctor Eugene Maxwell, he did strike lucky with the name of Jon Miller, not in a telephone directory, but in a worn studio contact list from the period. A man with that name was listed as living at an address in Pasadena.

As Jake was about to leave for the day, Scott came into the room. He was clearly angry and didn't smile as he faced him.

"Madge called. She asked me to drop these off," he said, sliding the keys to the apartment across the table. "You'll need them to get in. She has to work late, and she can't be there."

"That's kind of you to bring them over," Jake said. The very last thing he wanted was for Scott to move out, particularly on his behalf.

"Well, good luck," Scott said, about to leave without saying more.

"Actually, Scott, I've decided against staying there," Jake blurted out, hurt by his friend's strange mood, and wanting to make right whatever was troubling him. "I won't need these keys, but thanks all the same."

"Does Madge know you're not moving in?"

"No, I haven't seen her, not yet. I've been waiting for her to come back so that I could tell her in person."

"Well, she won't be here for a while, not after the spanner you threw into the works this afternoon."

"I've no idea what you're talking about, unless it's about the contract?"

"You've got it in one," Scott said coolly. "From what I hear, you are becoming quite a business tycoon; at least, that's what Madge said, but not using those exact words."

"So what were her 'exact words'?"

"Screwed is one that comes to mind."

"I don't understand why you're so uptight about this contract. I took your advice, and checked the small print. Where did I go wrong with that?"

"I didn't suggest that you should hold her to ransom for an immediate five hundred dollar advance, and insisting on some unknown guy directing you. What the hell were you thinking of, Jake?"

"You think I want that amount of cash for myself? Sure, I saw an opportunity in the contract, and I took advantage of it."

"I know you're broke but, even so, five hundred dollars right now. Hell, Jake."

"D' you think I'd sign up to act in any movie if there was another option? I said five hundred dollars to save Firebrand from the knackers yard. You told me five hundred dollars was the amount you needed to save him, and that's what I asked for."

"Yeah, but," was all Scott could say.

"Yeah, but nothing," Jake said, pushing the keys across the table. "The deal was done to save that horse and for no other reason, and, like I said, I won't need these."

"Darn it, Jake. Where are you staying?"

"As if you give a damn, that's my business."

"Don't be so bloody-minded and secretive." Scott retorted but with the faint hint of a smile.

"I might well ask you the same question about where you're staying if I thought you'd give me a straight answer."

"OK, I'm working on my parents' old place. It's my plan to keep Firebrand there until something better comes along."

"Well, that's good," Jake said emphatically, not wanting to show how unsettled he was by this exchange.

He was about to leave, taking the Pasadena telephone directory with him, when Scott caught hold of his arm.

"Where are you going, Jake? You can't leave like this. What if you take ill again?"

"I wasn't ill. There's a lot more to it than that."

"Sorry, wrong choice of words. What I meant was, if you…travel again, who's going to look after you when you get back?"

"No one and I prefer it that way," Jake lied, realising then how badly he had responded.

"Isn't there anything I can do?" Scott asked, releasing his arm.

"Well, since you ask, yes, there is: if you wouldn't mind telling your sister who the cheque should be made out to for the purchase of the stallion. Oh yes, would you also thank her for the offer of a place to stay, but I've made alternative arrangements," Jake said with conviction, knowing full well he would be sleeping rough under the pier again, and quite possibly for a while longer if his outstanding pay cheque didn't come through.

"You can't just clear off and leave a situation like this. You save Firebrand by shelling out a small fortune, and yet you expect me to accept that huge amount without even talking it through."

"You don't want it?" Jake asked irrationally.

"That's not what I'm saying and you know it. Why are you being so damned unreasonable?"

It was a question that Jake couldn't have answered given his emotionally charged sense of injustice, particularly when there was none at all.

"You're the one with all of the answers, Scott, not me. Go figure it out."

"This conversation is obviously heading for disaster, so I'm calling it a day," Scott said calmly, though he looked anything but calm. "I'll swing by the studio tomorrow. We'll talk again then. By that time I hope you'll be in a more approachable frame of mind."

"There's nothing wrong with my attitude, nothing at all."

"Sure, if that's what you believe. Anyway, before I go, I want to say how much I appreciate what you did for Firebrand. Thank you for that."

"Any horse lover would have done the same," Jake said unreasonably.

"You can be so bloody exasperating when you like. You know damned well that no one else on this planet would have made that choice. Even you must accept that," Scott said with an attempt at controlling his own temper. "By the way, you need to contact the Transport Captain about your truck. He didn't say why. He only asked me to pass the message on."

Because it was getting late, Jake contacted the Transport Captain to release his truck for the evening, which he agreed to do.

"Thanks for helping out with your truck when my guys couldn't get it started. I thought heads would roll when I got back, mine included, but thanks to you our jobs are safe. Give me a call if you're ever in need of a job. I can always do with a good on-site mechanic," the captain said, handing over the keys.

"Thanks all the same, but I don't plan staying on in California any longer than I have to," Jake said. It made him wonder exactly where he did want to be as he climbed back into his truck. "Which road do I take for Pasadena?" he asked, and was grateful for the man's clear directions.

"If I'd known you were collecting the truck tonight, I would've filled up with gasoline," the captain said. "I'm sorry about that, because the tank is probably a bit low but, with the fuel gauge not working properly, it's hard to tell how much is in there for sure. We have a company account with the filling station opposite the South Gate. They'll still be open if you set off quickly," he said, handing Jake a gasoline voucher.

Jake had been a bit uneasy about leaving the old tin trunk in the viewing theatre and, as it was much too heavy to keep lugging about everywhere, he removed all of his father's documents, plus the incriminating photographs, and Gilbert's precious end reel. He put all of these into his duffel bag, which he slid under the passenger seat for safety.

The filling station was already closed by the time Jake arrived. Although he was uncertain if he would have enough fuel to reach his destination, he decided to go ahead anyway, following the directions to Pasadena.

He couldn't be certain but, for most of the journey, Jake suspected he was being followed by another vehicle. Through his rear-view mirror he knew the vehicle behind him had a near-side headlamp that was much dimmer than the other.

He was directed towards Valley Lane by a lone passer-by walking a dog. He could see very little of what he assumed was a large house numbered 3290, most of which was obscured by a dense planting of trees. This imposing dwelling had a high-railed perimeter fence and was accessible through a pair of tall, heavily padlocked wrought-iron gates.

To get attention, Jake tugged on the bell-pull. He waited for some time before he heard the sharp clunk of a door being closed. Soon after, someone came down the drive towards him.

"Yes?" a manservant asked suspiciously when he eventually appeared through the gloom.

"I'm here to see Mr Jon Miller, if that would be convenient?"

He could see the distrust in the man's eyes as he peered through the decorative ironwork.

"No, that is not convenient. Mr Miller has given definite instructions that he will not give interviews to anyone. Is there anything else?"

"I wouldn't be here if it wasn't important," Jake said with determination, unwilling to be dismissed so easily.

But the manservant was equally as determined. "What you fail to understand, Sir, is that Mr Miller will see no one at all, not without a prior appointment. He gives no interviews to the press whatsoever."

"Before we go any further, sir, we should get this clear. I am not from the press, nor do I want to interview the gentleman."

"Then why are you here?"

"What I came here to see him about is a personal matter," Jake said, not wanting to discuss Gilbert's end reel with anyone other than Jon Miller.

"Then what I suggest, young man, is that you write to my employer, stating whatever it is that is so devilishly important, regardless of whether you are from the press or not. It would be pointless for you to call here again uninvited, and very inappropriate."

"Then would you be good enough to mention to Mr Miller that I have called here on the off-chance that he would agree to see me? I do honestly have something very important to discuss with him."

"So you have said, but I cannot trouble my employer this evening. Mr Miller is otherwise engaged. I suggest that you would be good enough to respect his privacy, and return to wherever it is you came from."

The manservant turned, about to return to the house, when Jake asked: "Would it be more convenient if I telephoned Mr Miller instead?"

"How come you have the private phone number for this address? Mr Miller gives it out to no one." His voice verged on threatening.

"It was purely by chance. I came across the number in an old contact list," Jake said, deciding not to mention any connection with the studio until he had spoken with Jon Miller in person.

"There would be no point in telephoning here as I intercept all the calls. As I said before, put what you have to say into a letter and post it, as you obviously have the address."

Uncertain of what to do next, Jake moved closer into the beam of light from the lamp to consult the time on his watch, and when he looked back at the manservant again, his demeanour had undergone a strange alteration.

"Do you mind if I ask where you got that watch?" The manservant moved closer to the gates to see it, and also, Jake presumed, where he could see Jake's face more clearly under the light. There was a heady scent of pine needles and wood-smoke clinging to his clothing which Jake hadn't noticed at first.

"Sure, the watch is mine. Why do you ask?"

"Because it looks identical to one I enquired about very recently," the man said. By now he seemed more preoccupied in getting a closer inspection of Jake – waiting in the pool of light cast by the wall lantern.

"Was that in a pawnshop at the bus station?" Jake asked,

troubled by the manservant's intense examination of his face, and wanting him to stop.

Even so the manservant said nothing. In that half-light and shadow, he appeared to be hardly breathing at all; although his eyes were open, in that partial light, they appeared to be glazed over, fixed on the face before him. It was as if the manservant was searching for something that could open a door on a long-forgotten memory. But whatever it was, Jake wanted it to stop. What had, at first, seemed unnervingly intense was becoming scary.

"Where did you see the watch?" Jake asked again.

But again he got no reaction. Through the shadows cast over the manservant's face, it seemed as if trails of smoke were beginning to wisp out of his mouth and nostrils as if he was smoking.

"Why are you staring at me?" Jake asked sharply, uncertain if he should stay talking with the man, but the high gate separating them gave him the confidence to persevere. "Do I know you from somewhere?" he asked, knowing perfectly well that he'd never seen this man before in his life.

Fortunately, the challenging tone in Jake's voice brought the manservant out of his dream-like state. He was a deathly white and appeared very unsteady on his feet. At first, it seemed as if he was about to collapse, but then he rallied strongly.

"Forgive me, sir, for staring at you in such a manner. I've no idea what came over me. It was unforgivably rude." he said, clearly disturbed.

"Are you Jon Miller?" Jake asked. It seemed the most logical explanation for the man's peculiar behaviour.

"No, sir, I am not. And please allow me to apologise to you once again." He was struggling to reassume an impartial manner, blinking furiously until the pupils of his eyes had closed to their normal size.

"That's OK, there's no harm done."

"Would you be offended, sir, if I asked how you were able to buy that watch from the pawnbroker when he was so adamantly against selling it to me?"

"So, it was you?" Jake said.

"Begging your pardon, sir, but you didn't answer the question?" the manservant said, probing again for the information.

"Actually, there was no need for me to buy this watch, because I am the person who originally pawned it. When I came back to redeem it, the owner mentioned your interest."

Jake backed away with understandable reservation as the manservant unlocked the gates, anticipating that he would enter the grounds.

"I think, because of these unusual circumstances, Mr Miller might well forego his earlier directive and agree to meet with you this evening. Would you care to bring your vehicle inside the gates?" he asked.

"I would; except my old truck won't fire up again until the engine's had time to cool down. Apart from that, it might not start at all as the fuel tank is close on empty."

The manservant secured the gates behind them. Jake was about to follow him along the curved drive when he noticed the parked truck further along the lane. He knew then for certain he'd been followed.

Irritated, Jake crossed into the courtyard of the grand hacienda.

"Mr Miller is generally indisposed at this hour, exercising in the pool. He could be with you within fifteen minutes. If you would wait out here, sir, until then, I'll enquire if he will see you. Who shall I say wishes to meet with him, sir?"

"My name wouldn't mean anything to him. Just say that I am here from the Silver Lake Studios."

The frosty expression that immediately appeared on the manservant's face told Jake it was a mistake to have mentioned his connection with the movie studio.

"I see. Then I will pass on that information as soon as possible, sir, but you should be aware that Mr Miller is no devotee to anyone connected with the motion picture industry, and in particular to that studio. Had you said as much when you first arrived, you would never have been allowed access."

230

For almost half an hour, Jake sat in the courtyard sipping the iced tea the manservant brought out. He couldn't help being impressed how perfectly relaxing it was in that tranquil place. It seemed to be cut off from the rest of the world. He couldn't hear a sound of any traffic outside. Not for the first time since his arrival in California, he longed to be back in the familiar surroundings of the hacienda on the Maxwell ranch.

There were showers of bougainvillea climbing rampantly over an arched colonnade to shelter many potted kentia palms from the blistering heat of the sun. At the very centre of the courtyard was an iridescent fountain carved from white marble, which was not functioning. At the end of the far wall was a set of worn granite steps leading up to either a studio or an apartment, along the front of which ran a long wooden balcony, shaded by a terracotta roof.

The moment he arrived at the inner courtyard, the thought crossed his mind this would be a perfect set for a movie. In fact, the more he dwelt on the detail surrounding him, in both shape and texture, he realised it was remarkably similar to the stage set he'd ventured onto the night he had followed Cloud Bird and witnessed the scene of his father fixing the old truck. It was clear to Jake that the stage set would have been constructed for Jon Miller's movie. A director with a keen eye for beauty, this hacienda in Pasadena couldn't belong to anyone other than the man he was seeking.

Jake's attention was caught by a damaged base-relief plaque hanging on the wall opposite. It depicted a shepherd and his dog, and it seemed to be uncannily familiar. Even at such a distance, Jake thought how closely it resembled another that he had seen countless times before. Wanting to inspect the plaque in more detail, Jake was crossing to the wall when the manservant coughed to attract his attention.

"Mr Miller has agreed to see you," he said, and made way for a tall man wearing only a pair of wet swimming trunks to pad into the courtyard, leaving a trail of wet footprints on the flagstones behind him.

He was industriously towelling his hair dry, so it was impossible to distinguish the man's face as he approached. When Jake stepped into the light, the man stopped dead in his tracks.

"Guy." Jon Miller cried hoarsely, grabbing onto a column for support.

"No, sir, you are mistaken. My name is Velasquez, Jake Velasquez."

Jake was disturbed by the effect he seemed to be having on everyone that night, but only until the swimmer removed the towel from his face. Then it was Jake's turn to be shocked, as both he and the swimmer continued to stare at each other in disbelief.

"Jeepers...Gil, what on earth are you doing here?" Jake began.

"If you're not Guy, then who in God's name are you?" Gilbert hissed aggressively.

"It's me – Jake. Don't you recognise me?"

Chapter Fifteen

For a few moments the tension between the two men was dynamic, until Gilbert strode over to Jake and gripped him forcibly by the arm.

"You aren't Guy. That's impossible."

The way he caught hold of Jake's arm couldn't have felt worse if he was clamped by an ever-tightening steel band. Gilbert's eyes were boring into him like burning coals, and there was no way Jake could shake free, not until the manservant intervened.

"Sir, you, you must release the young man before you break his arm," he said, but he was prevented from making any effort to get Jake free by Gilbert's menacing response.

"Get away from here, Wesley. This is between this fraud and me." And he thrust the manservant to one side.

"Who the hell are you?" Gilbert hissed, shaking Jake like a rag doll. "What are you doing here you evil bastard?"

"Please Gil...you must remember me. I'm Jake – Jake Velasquez. I grew up with you in Fort Laverne," Jake pleaded, but as the pain in his arms increased, he swore. "Let me go, damn it." He was acutely aware that he might easily end up with a bad injury, or worse.

Momentarily, Gilbert relaxed his grip, allowing him to grab Jake by the throat with both hands. It was a situation which might easily have put an end to Jake's short life had it not been for the quick thinking of the manservant. His swift intervention forced his employer's hands off Jake's windpipe with great difficulty, but it enabled Jake to steady himself against the wall and catch his breath.

"Get away from here while you can and whatever you do, don't come back here again." the manservant shouted at him, forcing Gilbert up against the wall in a rigid arm lock.

"I'm not going anywhere, not until Gil tells me what this is all about," Jake responded, bracing himself for another onslaught by his demented friend if he managed to get free.

"If you don't get out, sir, I won't be held responsible for what might happen to you," the manservant hissed, struggling to prevent his employer from getting away. "Why are you still here? Are you crazy?"

But Jake would have none of it. He was ready to defend himself against any onslaught, even though he knew he would be the one who would come off worse. He had to make Gilbert understand who he was.

"Gil, it's me, Jake Velasquez. I know it's been a few years since you left New Mexico, and I don't look the same as you remember me. I've grown up."

"You god-dam liar, you're not Jake," Gilbert snarled. "I'd know that kid anywhere." With a tremendous surge of strength, he forced his manservant away from him. The manservant very quickly and firmly positioned his body between the two men.

"You're way off course, Gil. I might look the same as Guy Maddox, but that's all. I'm not pretending to be him. Why the hell should I?" Jake said. "Ask me anything you like about Fort Laverne, the reservation, and the Maxwell ranch. I can answer any questions you aim at me. All I'm asking for is a chance to prove who I am."

This seemed to have the desired calming effect, but Jake remained wary, and was well prepared for another assault.

"Bollocks! Do you think I'm bloody stupid enough to believe you're that skinny kid from back home? You're a bloody impostor, and I want you off my property, now." Gilbert threatened hoarsely.

"Please hear me out, Gil. I am Jake, and I'm not going anywhere until you can accept me for who I am."

Gilbert was shaking his head as Jake was speaking. His eyes were wild and staring. "Don't make me laugh. You're not him. Not in a million years. You couldn't be that wild kid. You're a lousy opportunist. So who the hell are you? I know you're not Jake, and Guy's dead. I buried him myself. So, who the devil are you? And why are you here?"

Gilbert's handsome face was gaunt and drained of colour; his tanned skin looked yellow. There were tears welling up in his wild, glaring eyes as every ounce of aggression seemed to have drained out of him. He was in a bad mental state, and Jake knew that he was responsible.

"You really must leave now, Sir," the manservant pleaded with him. "Get out of here. If not for your own safety, then do it for the master. You can see how badly your presence is affecting him."

"I'm sorry, sir, but I can't leave. I have to make him understand who I am, or I'll never see him again, and I couldn't bear that. Not now that I've found him. Causing him grief is the last thing I want. I had no idea that he was living here."

By now, Gilbert was in a pitiable state, staring at Jake as if he was a ghost, unable to look away from him. He began gasping for air. Even though Jake thought that all of his anger had gone, Gilbert's large hands bunched into fists as he once again lurched at him. Wesley quickly intervened and forced his master bodily against the wall. But this time Gilbert gave only the slightest resistance before deflating.

"Why can't you recognise me, Gil? There must be something about me that's familiar after all the years we've known each other. You watched me grow up on the ranch, darn it. I've not altered inside. I'm still the same person who idolised you," Jake said, adding sadly: "It's inside where it hurts most. And I'm real sorry my looks have changed in such a way that affects you so bad."

Gilbert continued to stare at Jake intently but he was no longer struggling, submitting freely to the manservant's efforts to keep them apart.

"Let me go, Wesley," Gilbert said to the manservant in a voice that was barely audible. Like an invalid, he allowed Wesley to assist him onto a bench seat. "Why persist with this lie?" he spoke wearily, his rage draining from him. "There were moments when I caught a slight resemblance to Guy, but nothing more."

For a while neither spoke, and Jake was happy to bide his time and remain quiet. Eventually, Gilbert reopened the conversation. Still ashen, and looking exhausted, his red-rimmed eyes remained intense and hard.

"Who are you really?"

"I am exactly who I said, Jake Velasquez from Fort Laverne."

"Then, perhaps you can answer me this —what was Jake's Navajo name?"

"Pale Horse," Jake responded without a second's hesitation.

"How could you know that?"

"How else would I? Other than I am who I say I am."

"I don't understand this, not at all." Gilbert buried his face in the towel, wiping away the sweat.

"It is me, Gil. I just got older, that's all." Jake removed the friendship bracelet given to him by Moon Spirit which covered the brotherhood scar on his wrist. "You must remember the day I came to you when this ceremonial wound got infected. You treated it for me." Jake got closer so that Gilbert could examine the scar and the beaded strap.

"I remember the day when Jake and Cloud Bird became blood brothers," Gilbert said faintly, tracing his finger along the irregular scar.

"You remember."

"Of course I remember. How could I forget when Jake became Pale Horse?" Gilbert was still confused. "Apart from this scar, I can't associate that wild boy with you. Not in any way. The change is too great for me to accept."

"Even after you've seen this scar, you still don't think it's possible that I'm Jake Velasquez?"

"Jake's folks were Mexican, dark-skinned."

"But I was never swarthy, not like my father. My skin was always pale. You must remember my hair was almost white until I got older. If anything, I probably resembled you more than I did my own folks."

"Did I ever comment on that to you?" Gilbert asked. It was a trick question, which Jake saw through immediately, and would have found amusing had the situation not been so critical.

"How could you? You never spoke to me until the day you left for California."

"You know about that?" Gilbert's voice was barely audible.

"Of course. You never spoke to anyone, except perhaps to Doc Maxwell, and maybe Gia on occasion. But you never once spoke one word to me, not in all those years I knew you."

"How do you know all this?"

"I know because I'm Jake. Who else could know these things except me?"

"Well, if I'm wrong, how could this have happened? It's impossible to recognise the Jake I knew. You're too like Guy for me to see anything other than him."

Wesley spoke curtly to Jake as he pressed a damp cloth against his employer's forehead." If you insist on remaining here, Mr Velasquez, would you take a seat more at a distance, over there, in the shadows? It would be less upsetting for the master."

Gilbert seemed to rally his spirits, and sat bolt upright before he spoke. "If you are young Jake, why in God's name do you bear such an uncanny resemblance to Guy? Except for that scar on your wrist, you are identical to him in every way. Even your voice has the same quality as his." He was trembling now. "Excuse me. I need to go and dress."

Once the courtyard was empty, Jake tried to focus on the wristwatch, but that was impossible. Removing his glasses with trembling hands, he made a disastrous attempt to wipe away the smears from inside the lenses, and dried his eyes. He was convinced he was about to be sick. His body was ice-cold under the T-shirt that was damp with sweat. At that precise moment he missed Scott's presence more than ever. Apart from Cloud Bird, he was the one person who would have known exactly how to behave in that situation, and yet bizarrely, Jake resented him even more for not being there when he needed him most.

Half an hour had passed when Gilbert eventually returned to the courtyard. Although he was dressed, his ashen features emphasised even more that his eyes were red and swollen, failing miserably in his attempt to appear normal. He was carrying a bottle of whisky in one hand, and two tumblers in the other.

"Here, have a drink. You look as if you need one." Glaring at him, Gilbert filled up both tumblers before pushing the other towards Jake across the table.

"No thanks. I don't need that," Jake said. His throat hurt from the strangulating pressure of Gilbert's hands, and he wouldn't let that happen again.

"You're in my home, damn it. I insist," Gilbert said, menacingly, draining his own drink before filling the tumbler again. "Drink up. After that I expect some truthful answers. Don't toy about with that bloody glass, man, drink it."

"I don't want a drink," Jake said, determined not to be intimidated. It was obvious there was going to be trouble, and he needed a clear head.

"Then what the hell do you want? You come barging into my home unannounced, trying to pass yourself off as some kid I once knew. Looking like Guy resurrected from the dead. Who the devil are you?"

Jake knew the more that Gilbert drank, his situation there was not going to improve. It could only get worse. But this wasn't a confrontation he was prepared to walk away from. "You know exactly who I am."

"I know nothing of the kind, but I swear I'll get to the bottom of this before you leave here." he growled.

"Everything is exactly like I've said. My name is Jake Velasquez. I grew up in Fort Laverne."

"That's total bullshit!" Gilbert lurched away from the table with the bottle in his hand. "All I want is the truth, is that too much to ask. Well, is it?"

"I wouldn't lie to you, Gil, why should I?"

"There you go again: you open your mouth and spew nothing but lies. Do you think I would confuse you with that kid?" Gilbert took a long swig from the bottle before he turned on him again. "Opportunists like you make me sick."

"I'm no liar or an opportunist, and I won't be treated as such, not even by you." Jake stood up, ready to trade punches if necessary.

"Go to Hell." Gilbert shouted vehemently.

"I think I'm already there, Sir."

"You think this is Hell? Then try seeing the face I'm looking at now."

"Well, I've got news for you, Gil. This face is mine and it belongs to no one else." Jake refused to be humiliated by anyone, not even Gilbert. "You're drunk, sir. There's no point trying to reason with anyone in this state. There never was with my pa, and there certainly isn't with you tonight."

"Oh yeah, and if I asked you his name, you'll no doubt give me that same old line it was Ivan Velasquez?" Gilbert slurred.

"Of course I would, because that is the truth."

"And who in their right mind would nominate that wicked old bastard as their father except for a liar who didn't know any better?"

"It wasn't my choice. I had no say in the matter. Ivan Velasquez was my father, like it or not, that's how it is."

"And you expect me to believe that?" Gilbert laughed bitterly, trying to regain his balance.

"Quite frankly, Gil, you can believe what the hell you like. I waited for nine and a half years to hear from you after you left Fort Laverne. Anything at all would have done, but there was nothing, no telephone message. Not even a postcard. I know you must have been in contact with Gia. Even then you didn't care enough about me to send a message through her, and the joke is – I would have been happy enough just to get that. So who's the liar now? Try and explain why, when you promised faithfully you would be in touch with me as soon as you got settled, and you never did?" Jake was fuming, both with himself and Gilbert. He had never intended to blurt out all of those nagging thoughts he'd kept hidden for so many years, but at that precise moment everything he'd said seemed justified, and, given the distressed look on Gilbert's face, every one of them had hit home.

"I did say that, didn't I?" Gilbert slurred, allowing the manservant to support him into the hacienda.

"Yes, you bloody well did."

"Wesley, don't let this kid leave. Not until I've had the chance to speak with him in the morning," Gilbert said, clutching onto the doorframe to prevent him from stumbling.

"Very good, sir, I will attend to that. All the gasoline stations will be closed at this hour, and the young man's truck is out of fuel. He can stay here in the studio apartment."

Staying there for even a moment longer was the last thing Jake wanted but it was only after Gilbert had gone that Jake realised Jon Miller's name hadn't been mentioned, neither had he said anything about the missing reel of film and yet, finding himself caught up in a seemingly impossible situation, there had to be some way of resolving this. Meeting up with Gilbert after so many years, the last thing he wanted was to become a stranger to him, which now seemed unavoidable, unless, of course, he could come up something that only the pair of them could have known about. It was a dilemma that he would think about later, once he'd found somewhere to sleep, and with no manservant to distract him.

"I really must get back to the city," he said, uncertain about how he would do that without any transport. But Wesley wouldn't hear of it, insisting that he stayed overnight in the studio apartment, to meet up with Gilbert the following day.

"The master would be very angry tomorrow if he came down and found I had allowed you to drive back to the city."

"But I can't stay here tonight, however tempting your offer."

"I do see how difficult his attack on you must seem, and I understand that you must be eager to leave here as soon as possible, but what I ask is that you do not."

"I'm not afraid of Gilbert, not in the least. That's not the reason I have to go."

"But you must sleep somewhere, so why not here? Come morning, he will need to speak again with you."

"Sure, but—" Jake began, but he was cut short.

"I can't give you any explanation for his unreasonable outburst. All I can ask is that you offer his troubled soul your compassion, and stay."

Jake's throat was hurting, and after experiencing Gilbert's strength at first hand, he now understood how he had been capable of seeing off all three of his attackers in Fort Laverne so many years ago.

"If you think it would help. But I need to be on my way back to work early in the morning."

"About what time would that be, sir?"

"I should leave no later than 7 o'clock."

"The master is an early riser. He swims lengths in the pool for an hour– from five."

By the time Jake had followed Wesley up the steps to the studio he was convinced the building was an exact replica of the stage set he'd seen in the studio on that night Cloud Bird had taken him into the past.

Wesley led him into the apartment where he was to spend the night. The furnishings were perhaps somewhat old-fashioned but, to Jake, the highly waxed wood and subdued rich colours of the upholstery represented the best of a bygone era. Everything was carefully chosen for the comfort of the occupier with no thought to impress. Jake recognised why he had always felt so much at ease at the Maxwell ranch, as the style was undoubtedly Gilbert's personal choice.

"I hope you find everything here is to your satisfaction, sir, "Wesley said. "If you require anything more, just ring through on the internal phone."

"Would it be OK for me to take a swim?" Jake asked.

"Would that be in the morning? The master wouldn't appreciate anyone in the pool while he does his own laps. He's a dedicated swimmer."

"No, I just wondered if I might use the pool before I turn in for the night?"

"Of course," Wesley replied amiably. "Is there anything else you require of me, sir?"

It hadn't been Jake's intention to ask for anything, but as Wesley had presented him with the opportunity he took the chance.

"Wesley, can you help me with some background on Guy Maddox? It'd be difficult to ask Gil anything about him. I ask because of my resemblance to this actor. I know nothing about him."

He got a strange reaction from the manservant, who stared at him oddly though not as intensely as at their first meeting at the gate. His pale eyes appeared translucent and glazed over, as if he were going into a trance. Fortunately, when the longcase clock in the studio chimed, it shook him out of it.

"Forgive me, sir, what was the question?" Wesley asked, as the normal focus of his eyes returned, and colour replaced his eerily translucent skin.

"It doesn't matter, honestly." Jake was eager for the manservant, who now showed no sign of going, to leave.

"Forgive me, Sir, but it does matter."

"I just wondered why Gil reacted so violently when he thought I was trying to impersonate Guy Maddox."

"That's hard for me to say, sir. I didn't meet the gentleman. The accident happened before the master and I became acquainted."

"Then there's nothing you can tell me about him?"

"All I can offer you is that when something triggers the memory of how that gentleman died, it affects him badly. It's my understanding that is the reason why the master moved away from Hollywood in the 1920s, and why he stayed away for so long. No one ever thought he would come back."

"You knew Gil back then?"

"Not then, but soon after, at the Fairfax Sanatorium," Wesley answered hesitantly.

Jake didn't press him to divulge any more about that. It probably explained some of the odd hang-ups that Wesley had. Instead, he continued with his original question.

"But why would an actor's death trouble him so badly after all these years. What would make him react like that?"

"That's not for me to say, "Wesley said, as if he expected that to put an end to Jake's questions.

"But you do know, don't you?"

Wesley seemed to have gone into another of his unnerving

vacant trances. He was leaning over the balcony handrail and staring down into the courtyard as if he was expecting someone to appear, or waiting for something to happen. Suddenly the fountain switched on automatically and water gushed out of the top, cascading down the white marble. Jake could have laughed in sheer relief, but what prevented him was the look of despair in the manservant's eyes when he turned to face him.

"I am reasonably sure they were related," Wesley said.

It was a shock to hear, but when Jake considered the violence of Gil's reaction when he first saw him, that fact, if it was a fact, could well account for his aggressive behaviour.

"So, if that's true, why did Guy change his surname from Renaldo to Maddox?"

The slightest flicker of amusement crossed Wesley's otherwise tortured features, though, it didn't make him seem less creepy.

"I couldn't say. The name of Guy Maddox is carved on the headstone."

"You actually know where he's buried?" Jake asked with unconcealed surprise.

"There's a Catholic church on the far side of town. I drive the master there every Sunday."

To Jake this sounded most unlikely. "Gil would never attend a Catholic Mass, not anywhere. He's an atheist."

"He told you that?"

"Well, no..." Jake began, "it's only an assumption. Gilbert never spoke a word to me about anything at all until the day he left Fort Laverne."

"I can assure you, sir, that is the way it is."

"It just seems so unlike him. In all the years I've known him, I can't ever remember him attending a religious service of any kind."

"Well, I can vouch that he is a religious man, but he never attends mass. He waits in the car until the service is underway, and then he tends the grave. These visits give him peace when he's troubled. I'm grateful for that."

It was an unpleasantly humid night but, after a lengthy swim, Jake came up with the one memory from Fort Laverne he hoped

Gilbert would remember too. Having slept rough for so many nights since his arrival in California, to get into a comfortable bed was a luxury indeed, so much so, that he overslept, making him late to catch the early bus into the city.

Jake breakfasted alone, and was almost through when Gilbert appeared. He looked distressed and haggard, looking as though he'd slept little. It was confirmation that enough time hadn't elapsed for him to accept the alteration in Jake's appearance.

It was apparent that he was not prepared to sit and talk any longer than necessary, saying only that he needed a lengthy swim, but Jake had no intention of allowing Gilbert to erect a defensive barrier between them, just because the man either couldn't, or wouldn't accept who he was.

"Before you do that, Gil, I want you to think back to the time just after my mother died."

"Oh yes, and what would your mother's name be?"

"Louisa."

"Go on, I'm listening," Gilbert said, and warily sat opposite.

"I'm thinking back to the time when Doctor Maxwell arranged for me to be taught at the reservation school."

"Sure, I remember that time well enough. What about it?"

"Then you might also remember the distance was too far away for me to walk there. That's when you brought over the child's bike you'd found at the ranch."

This had obviously taken Gilbert by surprise, and for a few moments he occupied himself by inspecting his hands.

"The flaw in this otherwise plausible piece of information is that although it would have been difficult to get hold of, it would not have been impossible," Gilbert said cautiously with renewed interest.

"What I also remember is that because my pa refused to pay anything to get the bike roadworthy, you paid for two new tyres and a chain. You fitted all three before bringing it over. When you did, you oiled and tightened the chain, and lowered the seat until my feet reached the pedals." It was clear Gilbert remembered everything from that time, but he was not totally convinced, not until Jake added the most important piece of information he'd been saving for that moment. "I don't suppose you can remember what I asked you about the bike that day?"

"Something does come to mind, but I doubt your informer would have found you the answer to that unimportant piece of trivia," Gilbert said, appearing completely in control of what had become an unsettling situation.

But Jake knew different. He'd snared Gilbert at last. "OK, my question was this – I asked if you knew who the initials belonged to that had been scratched into the crossbar."

"Oh my God, how could you possibly know about that?"

"How d' you think? I know because I saw J.M.'s initials in the paintwork."

"OK, if you know that then tell me: what was my reply?" Gilbert challenged in a voice that was more robotic than natural.

"You wrote down they would have belonged to the boy who lived at the ranch before Doctor Maxwell moved there."

Hearing this, every speck of colour drained from Gilbert's features, staring directly at Jake's face for the first time that morning, apparently lost for words.

"I think now would be a good time to take that swim," Jake said, smiling his relief. "You always did feel a lot better when you'd had a workout."

"That's exactly what I intend doing, but – Jake, that is only on the understanding you will promise to return here again this evening?"

"If you're sure that's what you want, I would enjoy nothing more."

Because the truck was almost out of fuel, Gilbert suggested that Wesley would drive him to the studio on his scooter, and would collect him that evening. He promised that on Jake's return, they would talk properly.

Chapter Sixteen

Before he got onto the back of Wesley's scooter, Jake instinctively looked for the parked truck that had tailed him the night before. It was still in the same place, with the occupant's bare feet resting on the dashboard, indicating the driver was fast asleep, sprawled across the seats. Jake asked Wesley to wait for a moment while he scribbled a note on a scrap of paper, which he then lodged underneath the wiper blade of the truck.

Jake got Wesley to stop on the way to buy a scenic postcard of the ocean at sunset, which he sent to Gia. Addressing this to her at the Maxwell ranch, in pencil, he asked after Moon Spirit, wanting her to know that he was thinking about her. Because he had no mailing address other than the Silver Lake Studio, Jake hastily added that he'd met up with Gilbert in Pasadena, so that Gia would know where he could be reached when she had any news, even though he had doubts that she would involve her former employer with that information, given the importance of the banned "Sacred Ritual of Fire." Lastly, he gave a brief, but enthusiastic account of Firebrand, adding that his old truck had been used for filming.

As they reached the studio gates, Wesley asked: "What time would you like me to collect you this evening, sir?"

"I'll be fine making my own way back, Wesley. I won't need collecting. I know which bus to catch."

"I didn't think buses to Pasadena operated from here," Wesley said. "Are you certain you don't want me to collect you? If you need to pick up some luggage I can take you to wherever you're staying."

Until Wesley mentioned luggage, Jake had forgotten about hiding the bag of the incriminating photographs, and Gilbert's all-important end reel, under the seat of his cab. Because his truck was parked in the road outside the hacienda, Jake asked Wesley to collect the bag and keep it safe until he got back that evening.

"Yes, of course, sir. If you don't mind my saying, California isn't as safe as you're used to. Nothing of value should be left inside any vehicle overnight."

"I thought they'd be safer in my truck than leaving them here at the studio. I didn't expect to be staying at the hacienda overnight."

"If I might offer my opinion, sir, if you have anything else of value here, I could strap it onto the carrier on the scooter when I collect you this evening."

"I am grateful for the offer, but I really can make my own way back. Thanks anyway."

"It is not me you should be thanking, sir. I merely follow the master's instructions. He would be most concerned if I did not return this evening and collect you. After the upset of yesterday, I'd prefer to do as he asked, to avoid causing him undue anxiety. Please allow me to do as he asked."

"I am not being difficult, Wesley. The problem is that I have no idea what time I can get away each night. So, if you don't mind, I won't take up the kind offer of a lift tonight, but I really would appreciate it if you could take something away with you now."

At the gatehouse, Jake had a brief word with Ray, who gave him a length of rope to tie the tin trunk onto Wesley's carrier. However, when Jake arrived at the Projection Room, he discovered that the door had been forced open and all the canisters of edited film had been opened and scattered about. More disturbing was to find the padlock on his tin trunk had been smashed off, and the contents emptied onto the floor. Quickly Jake gathered his belongings together, and returned with the trunk to meet Wesley at the gatehouse.

"What happened here?" Wesley asked, noticing the smashed lock.

"Someone broke into the viewing theatre during the night and smashed off the lock. I don't know what anyone would expect to find in a beaten-up trunk like this."

"Did you keep anything of value in here?" Wesley examined the damage with the thoroughness of a professional safe breaker.

247

"Are you kidding? The watch Gilbert gave me is the only thing I own of value, and I wear that all the time."

"Whoever the thief was, he was after something you might keep in here." Wesley fingered the deep gouges chiselled into the metal. "This was no easy lock to smash off and would have taken some time, and time is something a crook on a break-in never has." Wesley spoke as though with some insight, and it made Jake wonder what this very unusual manservant's past profession had been. "It's clear this wasn't professional, but whoever did it was strong and very determined."

"How do you know that?"

Jake got the glimmer of a smile, which went as swiftly as it had appeared.

Pondering over Wesley's words, Jake tried to remember what had been inside the trunk, because he had a feeling that something was definitely not there.

"What do think might be missing?"

"I'm not exactly sure."

"Well, what is so important that you would want to keep under lock and key?"

"There wasn't much more than a reel of film belonging to Gil, and a set of black-and-white photographs which belonged to my father. But I already took them out. They're what I asked you to get out from under the seat in my truck when you get back."

"Have you any idea who might be responsible?"

"Perhaps, but it would be impossible to prove."

"Then you must be on your guard today. If the thief didn't get what he came for, and if it was important, it's odds-on he'll call again."

"You think he might come back during the day?" Jake said, wondering what he had let himself in for when he took on the temporary job at the studio.

"If it was an inside job, then yes, a determined thief would. It would be wise of you to report the incident to security," Wesley said, re-examining the damage to the trunk.

"OK."

"Before you do, what else do you have for me to take to the hacienda?"

"All I have is that trunk"

"I didn't mean from here. What about at your hotel or wherever you're living?"

"Until my first pay cheque comes through, Wesley, I'm not certain where I will be staying. Not yet anyway."

"Everything you own is in here?" Wesley asked, strapping the trunk onto the luggage carrier.

"I do have a bag of clothes, but most of that needs washing. I'll hang onto that until I can get to a launderette."

"If you would allow me to take that with me, I will have it all done by the time you return this evening."

"I'm much obliged for the offer, Wesley, but I couldn't possibly let you do that. Not wash my dirty laundry," Jake exclaimed, which brought another glimmer of a smile to the manservant's face.

"Washing laundry isn't part of my job description, sir. A local woman does that. Why not allow me to take the laundry along with me, sir? I can wait a while longer."

"You've been kind enough, Wesley. Before I do anything else, I'll take your good advice and report the break-in now. I'll bring the laundry with me on the bus."

"Then you may need this key to open the gates," Wesley said, handing him a key. "Generally I go out for a run when the master is swimming. When he is in the pool, he can't hear the bell, and so you may need to let yourself in."

On his way back to the Projection Room, Jake almost collided with Marjory Dawlish along the corridor.

"This is a coincidence. I was just coming down to give you this," she said, handing over the new draft of the contract. "There's no need to go through it out here where everyone can see," she said curtly.

However, Jake glanced through the paperwork while she lit up a cigarette, keeping abreast of him at the same snail's pace as he made his way back to the upheaval in the viewing theatre.

What Marjory had produced in her meticulously detailed

document authorised her to act on his behalf for any movie negotiations. In return, she got a fee of twenty-five percent of the agreed amount.

When they reached the door to the Projection Room, Marjory insisted he must return the signed copy to her office no later than 10 a. m. the following morning.

"Have you decided where you are staying?" she asked. She sounded pleasant enough, but was unable to conceal the steely undertone, nor the icy glint in her eye. "I will need a permanent address for you on the contract to make it legally binding."

"I'm currently staying with a friend in Pasadena," Jake responded, which seemed to satisfy her.

"Did you have trouble with the lock this morning?" Marjory quizzed, as she was about to leave. "That door looks as if it's been forced open."

"That's right, it was. The Projection Room was broken into last night."

"Why didn't you say anything about this before? Was anything taken?"

"Not that I can tell, immediately. The place was in a mess when I arrived."

"Have you reported the break-in to anyone?" she asked, surveying the damage inside.

"Ray in security had me fill out a damage report in triplicate. There might be a copy on your desk by now."

Marjory lit another cigarette from the stub, and inhaled deeply. "What do you think they were after – the two reels you found?"

"I'd say that's the likeliest motive considering the mystery that surrounds them."

"What do you mean? What mystery?" she asked sharply.

"I suppose because of the way they'd been deliberately hidden in the storeroom."

"Have you checked out the storeroom yet?" Marjory's eyes darted everywhere about the room as she anxiously paced up and down.

"Not yet, but I will as soon as this is cleared up."

"Later isn't good enough, Jake. You must check it now." When he didn't go off and look immediately, she asked crisply, "Was there something else?"

"I was wondering what you did with those two reels, Miss Dawlish?"

A flush crept into her cheeks as she answered and Jake suspected she wasn't prepared to come up with the exact truth. "They are quite safe where they are. No-one knows that I have them," she said, and flounced out.

When Jake checked the storeroom, he found that the lock had been forced, but because there weren't very many reels and canisters left inside, there wasn't much of a mess to clear up. What he did find interesting was that the top shelf, where he'd found the two hidden reels, had been cleared of everything. Even the gap in the plasterwork had been opened out wide enough for someone to see inside. It proved beyond doubt that whoever had broken into the storeroom was only interested in finding those important reels.

After Jake had reported the second break-in to Ray, and signed the appropriate form, he spent the remainder of the day attempting to organise new locks, and to have the doorframes made good. By late afternoon, because no one from the maintenance department had shown up to work on the repairs, Jake went to the studio stores and signed out the relevant hasps and locks for temporary security. These he fitted onto each of the doors himself, and left the duplicate keys with night security at the gate.

To save cash, it took Jake over an hour to walk the distance to the bus station, during which time he made a mental note that he must ask Gilbert about the whereabouts of Jon Miller. Although Wesley had previously allowed him into the house to speak with the man, there had been no mention of him since. Having lost track of time, Jake had to sprint the last hundred yards, arriving only just in time to flag down the last coach to Pasadena.

When he arrived at the hacienda, Jake checked the tree-lined avenue outside the property but the truck which had been parked there the night before had gone.

Much to his surprise, his truck was now parked behind the iron railings of the perimeter fence. He could only assume that Wesley had towed it inside given the rope lashed around the rear bumper of a gleaming 1920s saloon parked alongside it.

In the central courtyard, Wesley was putting the finishing touches to a spectacular banquet table. Gil was there too, but occupied in filleting a large salmon to go on the barbeque. When Jake arrived, Wesley lit the candelabra on the table, and poured out two glasses of wine. One he handed to Gilbert, and the other to Jake.

"I had to do something special, Jake, to make up for my atrocious behaviour yesterday, and hope that, in time, you will be able to forgive me?" Gilbert said. His high-pitched voice still seemed ridiculously out of character for such a strong and impressive man.

"Think nothing of it, Gil, it was just unfortunate that I turned up like that," Jake said, noticing that even now his old friend could hardly bring himself to look at him directly.

"I am really sorry, Jake. I've been preparing myself for this moment all day long, waiting for you to arrive, and now you are here, I'm finding it so bloody difficult to think it isn't Guy sitting opposite me."

"Perhaps it might help if you talked to me about him?" Jake said.

"Yes, perhaps. But first you must tell me what brought you out here to find me. How did you manage that? I made absolutely certain no one in Fort Laverne knew me by any name other than Gilbert?"

"Well, actually, Gil, it wasn't you that I came here to see."

"What? Then if it wasn't me, who was it? Was it Wesley here?"

"It was neither of you. I was given to understand that someone else was living here at this address," Jake said, uncertain why Gilbert and the manservant exchanged an amused glance.

"I see, and does this someone else have a name?" Gilbert asked with a smile.

"Sure, Jon Miller," Jake said. He glanced about the courtyard as though expecting the man to appear through one of the cloisters and join them at the table. What he wasn't expecting was for Gilbert to explode with laughter, like a schoolboy.

"You came in search of Jon Miller, and instead... you found me. Gee-wiz Jake, this is priceless. And you have no idea why Jon Miller isn't here?"

"No, I don't."

"Tell me, where did you pick up this man's name and information?"

"They were amongst some old files at the Silver Lake Studios."

"Ah, well that's confusing," Gilbert said thoughtfully, and sat back in his seat, expecting more. "I didn't think that you'd have come across Jon Miller's address on any records there."

"Well, that's right. I got that from an old crew list."

"So what exactly do you know about this man, Jake?"

"I know he is the most talented director I've ever come across."

"You know about his work, how come?" Gilbert asked, taking a more serious tone and appearing anxious.

"I know I shouldn't have watched the movie reel which you trusted into my care, Gil, but there was a genuine reason why I had to watch it through."

"You've kept that reel safe, haven't you?"

"That's one of the reasons why I came to California. You left no forwarding address and I was desperate to trace you, but couldn't, not without knowing your surname."

"I'm sorry, Jake. I should have thought a bit more about the effect that would have had on you. Only Gia knew where I moved, and she would never have passed that on, not even to you, without my permission." Gilbert poured himself a generous measure of wine. He gazed thoughtfully into the red liquid, swirling it around in his glass" But tell me, Jake, what was the reason you came to Pasadena in search of Jon Miller? Good director or not, what would make you of all people want to look him up? That man hasn't worked for more than a quarter of a century."

"It was to ask him why he'd given the end reel of that amazing movie to you, Gil. Can you tell me why? It must be the property of the Silver Lake Studios. I know it wouldn't be stolen, but I need to know."

"Before I explain, Jake, which I will in due course, I want you to tell me why this is so important to you."

"That's because without allowing him to have your end reel, his incredible movie could never be released."

"It couldn't be released anyway," Gilbert said, draining his wine in a single draught. "Guy Maddox was taking the two other reels to be copied at the lab when his vehicle skidded out of control on the upper canyon road and went over the cliff. There were no copies made, and that movie died with him," Gilbert said grimly, and poured out another glass of wine.

"But that's where you're wrong, Gil. Those two reels exist."

"You're mistaken, Jake. What remained of those two containers was found amongst the wreckage. That was the only way Guy's charred remains could be identified."

"But, Gil, they do exist. I know that for a fact, because I came across them hidden in the storeroom at the old Silver Lake Studios."

"That's impossible. They went up in flames in the crash. I saw what was left of the film in the charred canisters." He was becoming angry, and again drained his glass of wine in one go.

"But why were you there, Gil? I don't understand?"

"Jon Miller is my real name," Gilbert said. He poured himself another glass of wine, which he drank in moments. "I acted under the name of Gilbert Renaldo only because the producers thought that name had more appeal. When my career crashed with the introduction of talkies, when I would have been laughed off the screen, I was offered the chance to direct, and so I used my real name of Jon Miller. I'm using it now."

"You're Jon Miller."

"I am. So tell me, Jake, why do you imagine that you could have found the two reels that I know for a fact were destroyed? There were never any copies made. Those two reels were the only ones in existence, and they went up in smoke."

Jake could see that Gilbert would take some convincing that the two reels had survived, so he went through the action as he had seen it played out on the screen. He described very methodically every scene, and Gilbert was intent on not missing a single word or description. Jake knew that Gilbert was almost convinced when he began to question him about specific details of the plot and some of the exchanges between the leading actors. Then he asked Jake to describe how the dramatic final scene of reel two had ended, after which, instead of getting the jubilant reaction Jake expected, Gilbert's mood was something more ferocious and deadly.

"That evil twisted bastard." Gilbert ranted, pacing the floor like a man demented. In his fury, he hurled the wine decanter against the wall, shattering it on impact. As if by divine intervention Wesley appeared from the shadows and caught hold of Gilbert's arm before he could destroy everything else breakable.

"You had better sit down, sir, before you hurt yourself with flying glass or injure your young companion," Wesley said, quietly.

The mention of Jake seemed to have a partially calming effect.

"Don't you understand what this means, Wes? It means that evil bastard sent Guy off on an impossible mission that night. He must have known that something was going to happen." Gilbert ranted, outraged.

He shook so violently with the intensity of his distress that it created a chain of events which had an astonishing effect on the ridiculously high pitch of his voice. As he raged aloud, his prepubescent voice began to fracture, as it ought to have done thirty years earlier when he was a teenager.

"Stanford knew. That bastard knew all along Guy didn't have those reels with him." Gilbert ranted, unaware of the dramatic alteration to his deepening voice.

"But why would he have lied to you about that?" Jake asked.

"I don't know, but I'll get to the truth." Gilbert glared into the darkening shadows of the courtyard. "What I don't get is why the hell Stanford would have been so insistent it was Guy who must drive to the lab in that god awful storm if those reels were not the ones in need of copying. Guy was no fool. He would never have agreed to anything as crazy as that. Not unless there was an emergency."

"Maybe Maurice Stanford had his own reasons to send Guy up the canyon road," Jake said, remembering clearly the black-and-white photographs of his father and Maurice Stanford blocking the road with the fallen tree. "Wouldn't he have taken the coast road instead? That would have been a lot safer."

"That was exactly my question at the time, which now makes me wonder if the accident was indeed no accident, but planned," Gilbert growled.

Standing on a chair, Gilbert got down a worn folder from the top shelf of a bookcase. He took out a yellowed newspaper, which he held under a lamp for Jake to see. On the front page was a photograph of the mangled wreckage of the truck at the bottom of the canyon and, with it, an inset photograph of a fallen tree straddling the upper road.

"If you look closely, Jake, you can see the skid marks confirming it was this fallen tree that caused the vehicle to go out of control and force it off the road."

"Can I see that?" Jake asked breathlessly, examining not the wreckage in the canyon but the position of the fallen tree, and that narrow section of the road in particular, which he recognised immediately because of its relationship to the silhouette of another tree, stark and gaunt against the skyline, on high ground at a sharp bend in the road.

The article underneath the photographs named the driver as "unknown" and, instead, concentrated on the death of Tom Brice, the newspaper's ace photographer. The article also stated that the newsroom was unclear why his body had been recovered from the wreckage, as his own car had been parked a short distance away. It also questioned what had become of his folding bellows Kodak camera – something that Tom Brice would never have been without – and why neither the camera nor its remains had ever been found.

"You seem mighty interested in that article," Gilbert observed over Jake's shoulder.

"Well, that's because this article confirms Guy Maddox was murdered, together with Tom Brice," Jake stated emphatically. "I'm sure I know what happened that night. I've got proof."

"Impossible. How could you?"

"When I was clearing out pa's things, after he was buried, I came across a collection of photographs he'd hidden in his roll-top desk. Tom Brice, the reporter named here, must have taken them on the night Guy's truck went over the cliff," Jake said, indicating where the fallen tree straddled the road. "One of them was of this exact spot and, what confirms that, is the tree silhouetted on that ridge of high ground. The photograph I have shows that same tree, stark against the skyline on the curve in the road."

"You have that photograph?" Gilbert asked.

"Yes, that and a few others, amongst them is a picture of a tree straddling the road; it's taken from a different angle sure, but, nevertheless, it's almost an exact match to this photograph in the newspaper. That same tree was felled by my pa and another man."

"Do you know who the other guy is?"

"No, but you can see in the photograph that he wore a huge diamond ring. The only other photograph in this collection shows my pa and that other guy positioning the felled tree across the road, exactly where it is in this newspaper photo."

"So you think Tom Brice must have taken those photographs?"

"It would make sense."

"And that would be a good enough reason for Tom Brice to die?"

"It's a sickening thought that my own pa would be party to any of this, and that's how he got hold of the reporter's camera."

For some time Gilbert said nothing. He poured himself a glass of whisky and downed it in one go. "If the photographs are the way that you remember them then I guess you're right about this. Tom Brice was probably spotted taking those stills, and he was killed for it. Where are these pictures now?"

"They're in the apartment here. I had them with me in my truck last night, for safety. Wesley took them up to the apartment after he dropped me off at the studio."

"Wes mentioned that your stuff at the studio got broken into last night. It's my guess it's those incriminating photographs they were after," Gilbert mused, but Jake wasn't convinced.

"Perhaps they had something to do with the break-in, but I'm more inclined to think they were after your end reel. It's been generating too much interest lately for it not to have been that. Whoever broke into my trunk knew exactly what they were after," Jake said. He gave him a detailed description of the Projection Room with the scattered film canisters, and related how every one of them had been opened. He also mentioned the recently opened up section of wall in the storeroom where the other two reels had been hidden.

"Did they take anything of yours?"

"Not that I can be sure of, except for that camera which belonged to Tom Brice."

"Do you know the camera belonged to that reporter though? A decent camera could have belonged to anyone, even an expensive bellows camera."

"Not that one. This Kodak camera had Tom Brice's name scratched into the casing."

"Can I get Wesley to collect the stills from your room?" Gilbert asked impatiently, getting out of the chair. "If those photographs are like you've described, they could be evidence against Stanford's involvement, and bring that old bastard to justice."

Jake thought about telling Gilbert everything that he had been witness to on the stage when his father and Maurice Stanford had rigged Guy's pickup for the crash. He decided against it because he felt only Scott understood the complexities of the ritual he had survived and which had allowed him to witness that event from the past.

"If those photographs were not what they were after, why the hell would the end reel to my movie matter to anyone else?" Gilbert asked, indicating to Wesley to collect the photos.

"After I discovered the two hidden reels in the storeroom, the two other people who watched those reels with me were as astounded as I was by what you had achieved."

"Hang on for a second, Jake. Rewind a bit. What exactly are you employed to do at the studio?"

"It's only a temporary position. Because I'd been a

projectionist, and was able to edit old movie footage quite well, I was taken on to sort out their storeroom of old film stock. I named and catalogued everything as best as I could. Generally, it was all black-and-white, run-of-the-mill stuff. That is, until I came across those two reels of your movie, and played the opening sequence between Guy and the flamenco dancer."

"That would have been one hell of a shock when Guy turned around to face Alicia in the doorway."

"You have no idea."

"It'd be enough to send most men screaming to the sanatorium. You seem to have come through remarkably well."

"Not immediately," Jake said. "There were a few sleepless nights in between."

"So, who are the other people who've seen reels one and two, apart from you?"

"Marjory Dawlish. She gave me the job."

"That makes sense. And who was the other?"

"Scott, he's her brother. I'd trust that man with my life," Jake blurted out, not wanting him to have any doubts about Scott's integrity.

"I've heard about Marjory Dawlish, but who is this brother of hers. Scott Dawlish?"

"No, Scott kept his father's surname of Chinook, or Grey Wolf."

"Aha. I know exactly who he is. He's that wrangler who gets talked about quite a lot in the trade magazines. The boy has quite a reputation for breaking in wild horses. I would imagine the two of you have a lot in common." Gilbert smiled.

"You know him?" Jake asked.

"No, I can't say I do, not in person. All I can hope now is that it's young Scott, and not his sister, who knows about the end reel?"

With a sinking heart Jake owned up, but hastened to reassure him that no one other than himself had watched the end reel. By this time, Wesley had come down from the apartment with the photographs and the film canister. Jake carefully laid out the photographs on a table and switched on the lamp.

"This still was definitely taken where Guy's accident occurred,"

Gilbert confirmed, after he examined the first of the photographs with a magnifying glass. "It's the one used in the press coverage."

Gilbert's mood changed noticeably when he peered closely at the second image showing the two men felling the tree. He was barely able to contain himself when he saw the third photograph of the men dragging the tree into position across the road. Jake thought he would explode with fury. His face was grey, and his brow deeply furrowed. His eyes appeared to have sunk into their sockets, narrowing into slits.

"Forgive me, Jake, if I leave you for a minute," Gilbert said. He pulled his shirt off in a fury, and made his way quickly to the pool. Wrenching off the remainder of his clothes he dived into the pool with barely a splash, swimming up and down endlessly like a power-steamer.

Remembering this habit Gilbert had of burning off his problems in the pool, and expecting it would be some time before he re-emerged, Jake took the opportunity to go to the apartment and take a shower. He changed into the clothes that Wesley had laid out for him. It came as no surprise that both the linen shirt and the shorts fitted him perfectly. As Jake was almost ready to go back down, Wesley knocked on the door.

"The master sends his sincere apologies, Mr Velasquez, but hopes you'll understand that he needs to be alone this evening. He'll not be joining you for supper."

The next morning, Gilbert was already downstairs, dressed and waiting for Jake to appear, but when Jake walked in Gilbert shied away from him like a temperamental horse about to bolt.

"Hell, Jake, even the way you walk is so bloody creepy. How can you look so like him, and act like him too?"

"I'm sorry it affects you this way, Gil. I just want everything between us to be the same as it was back in Fort Laverne."

"I've lain awake all night, Jake, thinking how improbable it is that you and Guy could be so incredibly alike. All I can come up with is that you have to be closely related. There is no other explanation."

"Believe me, I really have considered that, too, but I know it isn't possible. I have seen my birth certificate, which names Ivan and Louisa Velasquez as my parents."

"Even so, Jake, there has to be some way you are connected to Guy. I've never seen two men so much alike before, except identical twins."

"The birth certificate isn't a fake; I only wish it was. That would have explained a lot about why my parents treated me like an outcast."

"There has to be a connection between you and him. I mean, the way you bite at the inside of your lip when you're nervous. Guy did that too. But there are a lot of things you do, Jake, there has to be an explanation." Gilbert sounded exasperated.

"I know that Guy Maddox had a son also named Guy but he died soon after he was born. His name was recorded in the register of deaths."

"I know that well enough, having buried them both. But that doesn't mean he didn't conceive another child, by another woman."

"Would he? He was married, wasn't he? I suppose another son could have been possible."

"He wasn't that sort of guy in the least. I guess I'm just clutching at straws. Anyway, that scenario does nothing for your mother's reputation. He was my friend; he would have told me."

Jake refrained from saying that he could remember nothing about his mother that was remotely warm or loving, a "cold fish", his father had often described her. Her shrew-like tongue would have kept any would-be lovers well at bay.

Checking his watch, Jake realised that he was going to be late to the studio if he didn't leave immediately, as he had yet to get fuel for his truck.

"Gil, I'm really sorry, but I've got to get off for work." Before he went, however, he told Gilbert about having taken a screen test, and the movie offer, and that he'd said he would only agree to appear in a sequel to *The Return of Xavier Gérard* if they got Jon Miller to direct.

"That's quite a lot to take in, Jake," Gilbert said. "Can you stay here today to talk this through?"

"I can't, Gil, however much I'd like to. I've got to be there today. I've a lot of work to be getting get on with."

"Wesley can take you in, and collect you after work. I'd like you to stay overnight again. This time, I promise I won't let you eat on your own."

"Sure, that would be great. There is one thing I would like to know before I set off."

"Fire away, what did you want to know?"

"It's about that bike you gave me..." Jake began, and Gilbert laughed.

"J. M.'s initials were mine, and yes, the bike belonged to me. Now get off to work before you're really late."

Chapter Seventeen

When Jake arrived in the Projection Room, not quite everything seemed to be in order and as he had left it the evening before. The first thing that caught his attention was that the cupboard where his damaged trunk had been kept was firmly closed. It was something he didn't remember having done the previous night, although he couldn't be certain. What confirmed his suspicions that someone had been in there was how very neat the contents of the cupboard were.

There were other things, like the way the film canisters had been stacked, which looked wrong. What clinched it was the repaired length of film that he remembered leaving in the machine to bond overnight. Although it had been carefully returned after being examined, it hadn't been locked back into the same position.

Jake made himself coffee, and was outside taking a break on the bench seat when Marjory Dawlish appeared and sat beside him.

"Well?" she asked, as if expecting him to read her mind.

"Well what?"

"You know exactly what– the contract, of course. Have you read it through, and signed?"

"No, I haven't, not yet. I meant to but I didn't get the chance."

"Why ever not?" she asked frostily.

"I'm sorry, Miss Dawlish, I guess I was more bothered about the break-in, and it just slipped my mind. I'll get onto it tonight."

"I would hope so. I've upheld my end of the bargain. The advance payment you wanted has been arranged. However, you'll not be getting any cheque until the contract has been signed."

She had a strange look in her eye. Reaching across him, she removed the cup from his hand and sipped the coffee before handing it back with a gesture of assumed intimacy.

"The cheque shouldn't be made out to me, Miss Dawlish," Jake blurted out.

"Why?"

"I asked for that amount because I need to help someone out of a jam."

"Then who do you want it made out to? This is an awful lot of cash we are talking about here."

"I would like it made out to Scott, your brother."

Marjory looked shocked at the request. "You can't be serious. Why in hell would you do that?"

"It's not for him personally. It's so he can purchase Firebrand."

Momentarily lost for words, Marjory took a powder compact from her pocket and clicked it open, examining the reflection of her flawless make-up in the mirror, and giving herself time to consider his words.

"You're buying a horse – together? In God's name why would you get involved with that? It's a completely wild and uncontrollable animal – at such a diabolical cost? Forgive me for saying this, Jake, but I can't for the life of me understand why you'd embark on such a crazy scheme. Why would anyone in their right mind do that?"

"I'm sure Scott will explain everything when he collects the cheque."

"What is it that I am being excluded from? I know something happened between you. He's been like a bear with a sore head these past two days. I can hardly get a sensible word out of him and now you're proposing to do this?" She snapped the compact shut for theatrical effect. "Would you care to tell me what's going on?"

"Nothing I know of," Jake said, wishing that she wouldn't probe any deeper. He was feeling embarrassed as it was. He just wished that she would leave him alone and allow him to get on with his work.

"Well – there is something, and don't you dare suggest that I'm imagining it."

"You should know your brother well enough to realise that he's crazy about saving that horse. Unless he gets the cash to buy it, it'll end up at a rodeo in Vegas. Neither of us wants that. Do you?"

"It's a horse, for God's sake. What's wrong with you guys? It's not going to be the end of the world when that nag is sold off. Scott can go to Vegas any time and see it perform at the rodeo." She then began probing again. "It might be the horse that's bothering him, but I doubt that. It's something else. He never broods like this. In fact, he was never like this until you began working here."

"I've absolutely no idea, unless it's because he's been evicted from his apartment," Jake said, unable to resist the comment. However, Marjory's questioning had set his mind whirring over what other reasons there might be: reasons more closely connected with him, reasons he didn't particularly want to consider.

"I don't know what my brother said about why I asked him to move out. I can only tell you it was unavoidable. We have differing views on just about everything imaginable. I can't live like that, and neither could he."

"Scott didn't say much about it. Having to move out just might be the reason for the change in him," Jake said, which seemed to pacify her.

"If the place where you're staying doesn't work out, Jake, then the offer for you to move into Scott's old rooms still remains open." She lit a cigarette.

"Thanks. I really appreciate the offer," he said. "Have you had any word on the break-in?"

She said that she hadn't, although the question seemed to unsettle her. Moments later, she made her excuses and left him to return to his work.

Jake was halfway through watching yet another uninspiring reel of the old stock when Scott came into the room looking as if he was spoiling for a fight. Jake switched off the projector and stood up to face whatever was about to happen.

"Hi," Scott said awkwardly, contrary to his outward appearance. "I dropped by to ask if you would keep an eye out for Madge. I'm a bit worried about her safety."

"Sure, what makes you think she might be in trouble?" Jake moved the empty canister from the seat beside him, making a space for Scott to sit. Scott declined.

"I've got this idea she's trying to make some kind of a deal with that old bastard, Stanford. If Madge gets involved with that scumbag, she can only come out of it badly, whatever it is she's trying to arrange. Apart from his dragon of a sister, no one ever gets the upper hand with Stanford. I suppose she's safe enough in the newer block, but not in this part of the building. You're too cut off up here."

"Why would you think something might happen here? She doesn't come up to the Projection Room that often."

"Maybe not, but that doesn't alter the fact I saw Frank Clark snooping about in here earlier."

"Frank who?" Jake didn't recognise the name.

"The guy works for Drew Walters."

"Oh him, I know who you mean. When was it you saw him?"

"About an hour ago; I was just passing," Scott began hesitantly. Jake noticed how he managed to avoid mentioning why he was there. "The fact is, Jake, I was hoping to find you here. The light was on and the door was unlocked. Instead, I collided into Clark on his way out. He was clutching onto a movie canister."

"Well, that sure explains what's been happening in here," Jake mused.

"Say, he wouldn't have got his hands on that end reel you and Madge have been arguing about, would he?"

"No, I've got that somewhere very safe."

"Where would that be, in Pasadena?" Scott's subsequent embarrassment revealed that it was a comment he regretted.

"You came up here to find me, Scott, why was that? And why did you follow me to Pasadena?"

"Well, first off, I just wanted to say thanks for the generous offer, but I can't accept that cash from you. I couldn't borrow that amount of cash from anyone. It's way too much."

"But if you don't accept it, what then, what happens to the stallion?"

"He'll be sold off to that rodeo in Vegas, as the company have agreed."

"Let me get this right, Scott, because, quite honestly, none of this makes sense. What you're saying is that you would prefer to rent out your time, and God knows what else, to any takers who come along rather than accept an offer from me, a friend, for the exact amount you need – without any strings attached?" Jake was barely able to control his anger.

"It isn't like that, Jake, and you know it," Scott said.

"Then exactly how is it? It seems perfectly clear to me what you mean."

"You're impossible. The fact is, I don't know why I can't take that amount of cash from you, but I can't. It just feels wrong, that's all." He sat down abruptly on the seat next to Jake, drumming his fingers on the wooden arm with frustration.

Jake wasn't about to stop until Scott agreed to accept the cash. From his point of view it was only because of the sale of the stallion that he had agreed to sign up for a movie contract in the first place.

"Well, I sure couldn't live with myself if I'd made that decision, not if I'd been offered the money with no strings attached."

"It's too much of an obligation, that's why. Why would anyone offer that kind of help to a virtual stranger?" Scott growled. "Because that's what I am."

"This is nothing to do with what happened between us the other night, Scott, far from it. This is a genuine offer to save the horse. It's not a personal handout."

Scott was silent.

"Instead of putting up obstacles, Scott, why not consider how your refusal would affect the horse? How will you feel when its spirit's broken? Or drops dead from bucking off an endless convoy of bronco riders? What good will your bloody misguided pride have done for him then? He'll be no damn use to anyone other than the glue factory."

There was an uneasy shift in Scott's manner as Jake's argument struck home.

"Very well then, but only on the clear understanding, Jake, that if I do take up your offer, I will pay you back every dime, however long it takes."

"You think I care about the cash? I just want that stallion to be given a decent chance, that's all."

"Isn't that what we both want?" Scott said pointedly.

"Then you'll accept the offer and buy him?"

"Yes, I will. Thanks," Scott said grimly as he left.

When he'd gone, the room felt dull, leaving Jake unable to concentrate properly for the rest of the day.

Jake finished his work a bit earlier that afternoon and was waiting at the studio gates to be collected by Wesley when he was hailed by the Transport Captain, who was driving into the studios.

"Hi there, Jake, boy am I glad to see you this evening. Something's only just come up and I thought I'd missed you. Can you bring your truck in tomorrow? They want it on the back lot first thing in the morning. It's needed for a reshoot."

"I thought all the filming was done?"

"Apparently not; the sequence with your truck got screwed up and it needs to be shot again. They're very insistent, so I made sure Frazer cut you a better deal this time for the rental. I must say I enjoyed that. He's one of the nastiest pieces of work I've come across and, believe me, I've met quite a few in my time." he chuckled.

"Sure, Mr Jones, I'll bring it along tomorrow" Jake said, breaking into a run as Wesley pulled up on the scooter a short distance from the entrance, where they had prearranged to meet.

They had barely reached the end of the road, when the sound of squealing tyres made Jake look back from his position on the pillion seat before they rounded the bend.

As the Transport Captain drove through the security gate, he narrowly avoided a collision with a gleaming blue convertible being driven at a lunatic speed from around the side of the stage. Beyond that Jake saw nothing, given the amount of rush-hour traffic crossing the junction ahead. As Wesley waited for the seemingly endless vehicles to clear before he turned into the slip road, the same dark blue convertible cut them up on the inside. The driver was Maurice Stanford. The woman passenger tried to get Stanford to pull over and stop. Instead, he shoved her hard against the passenger door, yelling abuse. Amid the protest of grinding gears, blaring horns, and the squeal of brakes, the convertible lurched out into the traffic and roared away from the junction.

At Gilbert's hacienda, Jake went up to the apartment, showered and changed. As he was getting dressed, he noticed there had been a few subtle changes to the room. There were potted plants, and light, billowing curtains at the open windows. There was a neat counterpane, and his bed had been newly made up with crisp linen sheets. Extra furniture had been added to offer more comfort. Particularly welcoming was the gentle aroma of wax-polished furniture. It crossed Jake's mind that Gilbert might be preparing for him to stay there for a while longer.

After they had eaten, Gilbert was eager to show Jake part of the building that was new to him.

"You must spend most of your time shut away in that viewing theatre, but I want to show you the one I've had built in here, "Gilbert said, opening the door.

Although it was a plain room, the equipment was new and clearly much more up to date than that used by Jake at the studio. He began to wonder if all the editing equipment, projector and library of movies given to him after the death of Doctor Maxwell was simply a parting gift from Gilbert himself, and not, as he had been led to believe, as a bequest of the old doctor. Jake's mind was racing. Had everything that had helped him survive in Fort Laverne been a parting gift from Gilbert?

"Don't you like it, Jake?" Gilbert asked. "I would have thought, given your interest in old movies, this set-up would be right up your street?"

"Oh, it sure is. It just got me thinking."

"About what, exactly?"

"I was wondering about all the movie equipment and film stock you said Doctor Maxwell had left me in his will. I'm wondering if all that really belonged to you and, if so, why you made out they were from someone else?"

Gilbert was embarrassed but admitted to having done just that. "They were no use to me, Jake, and you were a movie nut. I just thought you might be in need of some escapism after I'd gone."

"Well, there's another thing. It's about the break-in at the Maxwell ranch after the funeral. What were those men after when they ransacked the place? Was it the end reel of your movie?"

"I believe it was. That's why I left it with you."

"Before the break-in at the ranch on that day, have you any idea why they beat up my pa, and smashed up a memorial stone in the backyard?"

"It might have been to get information out of him about where I was living."

"I get they might want to find Jon Miller if they were after the end reel, but why go to Doc Maxwell's ranch? And you were living there under a different name? I can't make sense of that."

"Your father was connected with the studio. He knew who I was, and where I was. That's why they put the pressure on him."

"But why would they leave it so long to go there in search of you?"

"If Ivan was being paid his blackmail money from Stanford, that's how they knew where to find him. They'd be after those incriminating photos. So, apart from one of them returning home with a broken nose, they had a wasted journey on both counts," Gilbert said, which made them both laugh.

"But pa said that he'd been trying to protect me. Why would he protect me from anything? He'd never bothered about me before, so why take a beating on my account?"

"Sorry, Jake, I can't help you on that one. I'm equally in the dark."

Gilbert opened up the canister of film and carefully loaded it onto the projector with a look of satisfaction. "It would be interesting to get both yours and Wesley's reaction to this reel. Let's watch it together. I know you've seen it already, but maybe now that you know all about Guy, watching him on screen performing might be less disturbing."

"Sure, I'd love to sit through it with you."

"Be prepared for the inevitable reaction when Wesley sees the likeness between you and Guy. Will you be OK with that?" Gilbert asked.

"I am well prepared to see Guy on screen, unlike the first time when I thought I was going mad." Jake shuddered. "If Scott hadn't been there to point out the differences between us, I don't know what the hell I'd have done."

"I'm glad there was a friend sensible enough to help you through that. I can't begin to imagine how weird it would be for anyone to see their double on screen. I doubt I would've handled it as well as you did," Gilbert said.

"I didn't, not to begin with."

"Well you did eventually. The fact is, Jake, I'm a little nervous about seeing Guy up there on the screen, even after so many years have passed. You wouldn't think it was me who directed him in the damned thing. Look how my hands are shaking." Gilbert held out his trembling fingers for Jake to see as he poured himself a generous whisky before calling Wesley in.

"Once you get over the initial shock, Gil, the rest won't seem so bad," Jake attempted to reassure him.

"What floors me is how in God's name such an unpleasant character as Ivan Velasquez could sire such a decent young man as you. I'll never understand that."

"I didn't realise you disliked pa so much?"

"I disliked both of your parents from the moment I began to hear the reports about how they treated you. A stray dog would have got better treatment."

Shortly after, Jake was settled into his seat and Wesley was preparing to set the film running. Having muttered a vague excuse about getting his new spectacles, Gilbert left the room, saying he'd return in moments, and Wesley should get the movie started.

The overhead light had been switched off, and there was only the whirring sound of the projector running. Apart from an intense humidity in the room all seemed to be perfectly normal, but when the flickering images were projected onto the screen, the room temperature plummeted rapidly. There was a stillness in the air, and Jake had the creepiest feeling that something weird was about to happen.

He took off his spectacles to clean them when the now familiar scent of pine needles filled the room, bringing goose bumps along his arms. For a moment, he was tempted to call for Gilbert to come back on any pretext, but he couldn't bring himself to do it.

Jake fumbled badly with his spectacles and they slipped from his hand and slid down the side of his seat. Unable to retrieve them easily, even though the image was blurred, he couldn't take his eyes off the screen, and was still groping about for them when the movie began.

As happened with his previous viewings on the first reel, Jake became instantly mesmerised by the opening sequence. For this, the director had used a similar, hypnotic beginning, featuring the lithe young dancer as she advanced towards the courtyard of the hacienda. The drama of her progress was glimpsed through a series of arches as the camera tracked her movement, intensified by the swish of her red flamenco skirt. Accompanying the rhythmic clip of Isabella Trecheanco's neat Cuban heels was an unseen guitarist playing the dramatic introduction for "The Tango of Death".

Still groping for his spectacles, Jake's hand got stuck which caused him to look away momentarily from the screen just as the camera angle changed to focus on the slender silhouette of the dancer waiting in one of the arches expectantly, poised with the castanets.

At the precise moment she stepped forward into a strong shaft of light to illuminate her features, the oddest thing happened. Jake looked towards Wesley who was staring transfixed at the screen. Hampered by the darkness and by not wearing his glasses, it was difficult for Jake to see anything clearly. Blinking furiously, Jake cursed his eyes for not focusing properly. Through a distorted haze, he could tell the woman's presence on screen had affected the manservant badly.

Jake felt that Wesley wasn't riveted so much by the woman's beauty, but seemed to be more of recognition. He was in shock, gawping open-mouthed in the way he had been when he met Jake on the first evening of his arrival. His hand was resting on the hot metal of the projector and must surely be burning.

Jake knew Wesley wasn't smoking a cigarette but there were

definite wisps of greenish smoke being exhaled through his seemingly frozen mouth and nostrils. The woman's face was perfectly framed and remained motionless on the screen. Even though the aroma of pine needles had intensified, it didn't eradicate the stench of scorched flesh from Wesley's hand. But the man gave no outward sign of his suffering. He remained completely motionless, as though a switch controlling him had been turned off.

Jake stumbled towards him in the darkness, where, incredibly, it seemed to him, the wisps of green smoke coming from Wesley's mouth began thickening into the shape of a man's head, neck, and shoulders. Before Jake was able to reach him, the smoky green outline of a man's arm strained desperately towards the woman's face on the screen. Rubbing his eyes in an effort to see better, Jake tried and failed again to focus in the dark, although he had the impression that, as he got closer to Wesley, the manservant inhaled deeply, and the vapour-like shape of the man was sucked back into his mouth.

When Jake reached him, he was desperate to prevent the machinery from overheating, and to stop the celluloid from melting Gilbert's precious film. It took a few seconds before he was able to unlock Wesley's ice-cold hand. As his tenacious grip was released, the manservant was jolted out of whatever trance he had been locked into, his breathing returning rapidly to normal, as too was his awareness just as Gilbert returned.

"Can you wind back to the beginning?" Gilbert peered into the gloom suspiciously. "Is there something burning in here?" he asked, switching on the light.

"The reel jammed and Wesley's burnt his hand quite badly by the looks of it," Jake said.

"How did you do this, Wes?" Gilbert asked, inspecting the burn.

"I'm not sure, Mr Jon. I guess I must have held it too long on the projector."

"Let's get something onto this immediately. Jake can set up the reel while we're gone. Then you must sit down with us, Wes. I want us all to watch it through together," Gilbert said, ushering Wesley out ahead of him. "See to the reel, Jake, this shouldn't take too long. Why is it so damned cold in here?"

Later, as they sat and viewed the end reel, Jake was unable to relax, not after the strange incident with Wesley. By now he had recovered his spectacles and kept an eye on Wesley, who nursed his wrapped hand throughout the opening sequence. This time, when the woman featured on the screen, there was no reaction from him at all.

When the screening was over Gilbert switched off the projector. Instead of asking Wesley his thoughts of the content, he seemed more interested in what Jake had to report on what Scott and his sister had had to say after they had watched the first two reels.

"Wes, would you set out a few snacks and drinks by the pool, nothing fancy. Be careful of your hand, then come and join us," Gilbert said, before turning back to Jake. "Was their reaction good or bad? Please don't say they were indifferent. I can take any opinion except indifference."

"Marjory Dawlish seemed quite overwhelmed, and Scott too, although his opinion was more positive, saying that, if this movie was released, properly, even after all these years, it could become a modern-day classic. Unusually for her, Marjory actually agreed with him."

"Well, Jake, I like the sound of your young friends." Gilbert smiled, but for some reason, Jake resented his tone

"Scott has more of an acquired taste than the usual Hollywood crowd I've come across," Jake said uncomfortably.

"Did they make any other comments?" Gilbert asked.

"There were plenty; too many to remember. But there wasn't a single negative comment amongst them."

"So, what was their reaction when Guy first appeared on screen? That must have been one hell of a shock. That surely wouldn't have passed without comment."

"There was a lot of comparison between myself and Guy. In fact, Marjory Dawlish refused to believe it wasn't me up there. She got the notion into her head that I was an out of work actor and had edited myself into that particular reel." Jake laughed. "I don't think she has any idea how long that would take an expert, never mind me."

"It's a novel idea I must say. This Marjory Dawlish sounds a shrewd cookie."

"She is, but she's nice enough."

"You mean she's nice enough when she wants to be? And what about her brother, did he think the same?"

"Maybe at first, I couldn't tell. He made a few jibes at the beginning, but that didn't last for very long."

"That's interesting. He was prepared to believe you?"

"I suppose, because there were a couple of things he noticed about me that were different to Guy."

Gilbert was smiling. "Let me guess. Maybe the way you squint into the light when you aren't wearing your spectacles?"

Jake laughed. "Sure, it was partly that. I suppose everyone would notice that except for me."

"I only picked up on it because it's something you always did when you were a boy."

"Scott just notices things more than most, I suppose," Jake responded defensively.

"But not so the ambitious Marjory Dawlish. What did she have to say when she realised that it was someone else on screen, and not you?"

"It put the cat well and truly amongst the pigeons, but she recovered. Scott and I were ordered to track down the missing last reel at all costs. She needed to track down who the unknown actors were. You can understand why. It was great direction and going on her reaction, the best she's seen too. It's different, exciting."

"So what do you think might happen next?" Gilbert asked.

Jake remembered the bargain he'd struck with Marjory, and that he had the contract that still needed to be read and signed in his pocket.

"I've probably done something very stupid, Gil, but there seemed no other way out. You see, there's this wonderful wild stallion at the studio that needs saving from being sold off to a rodeo in Las Vegas. I had to help scrape the necessary cash together with Scott. He's been hiring himself out as an escort."

"You're not saying that you've been selling yourself too?"

"No way, I was offered a much better option. A few days back Marjory made me take a screen test."

"Which no doubt amazed them all," Gilbert said, barely able to keep the irony out of his voice.

"Marjory and her boss did seem impressed."

"And...?"

"She wants to represent me."

"That figures. Please don't tell me the woman has sweet-talked you into selling yourself off cheap?"

"Not in the least. It didn't all go her way. She was eager for me to sign an actor's contract with her. So I came up with a proposition. I asked for a cash advance up front."

"You did? And she agreed?" Gilbert asked with unconcealed amazement. "I can hardly believe it, Jake. It has got to be unheard of in this town. I'm astounded. Only a kid from the sticks could get away with it."

"Well it sure looks that way, because she gave me a contract to sign."

"Did you sign?"

"Not yet. I brought it with me," Jake said, which brought a sigh of relief from his old mentor.

"Then we should look it over together. I must confess, I never would have imagined a kid like you would be even remotely interested in acting."

"Actually I loathed the very idea, so I drove a hard bargain with her. I honestly didn't think she'd go for it and I'd be off the hook. But it didn't work out that way."

"Not much you plan ever does, at least, not for me. So, what else aren't you telling me, Jake? I know you've been up to something. Your eyes always gave you away when you were a child, and they still do."

Jake told Gilbert about his suggestion that, if he was going to be cast because of his identical looks to Guy Maddox, it should be put to good use, maybe in a sequel to *The Return of Xavier Gérard*, but only after the original had been released onto the movie circuits. He then spoke of his other request: if that was agreed upon, he wouldn't accept any role unless the same director, Jon Miller, was engaged to make the sequel.

"You actually said that?" Gilbert laughed. "Only someone who had no desire to work in movies at all would ever have dared to say that in my day. I'm surprised the woman didn't have you kicked out."

"I suppose it was a bit much." Jake cringed at the thought of Marjory repeating what he'd said to her brother, or to anyone else come to that.

"You could say that," Gilbert said, laughing uproariously. "Well, I'm damned if I've heard anything like it, except perhaps, by some big star back in my heyday. And you're telling me this Marjory Dawlish actually considered your terms?"

"Well I think so, although I haven't read through the second draft of the contract," Jake said.

Gilbert looked at him with unconcealed admiration. "Are you telling me that you had the nerve to question the first draft?" he asked, roaring again with laughter.

"It seemed the best way. I wanted to get out of doing the job anyway. It was like a living nightmare. The more I demanded, the more she agreed to go along with what I asked." He pulled the crumpled contract from his back pocket and passed it to Gilbert.

There was a long silence while Gilbert studied the paper.

"Well, you seem to have covered just about everything in this. My only suggestion would be that you sign up to make just one movie, Jake. Don't agree to make any others until you've spoken with me."

"Scott advised me to read the small print in the first draft. That's one of the reasons I wouldn't sign it to begin with."

"Well, Scott sounds a really smart guy. How did he react when you mentioned the idea of a sequel?"

"I didn't get a chance to say much about it. He'd gotten the wrong idea about why I was pushing for the advance. We had a bit of a falling out."

"Just a lover's tiff," Gilbert said, with underlying amusement, in a tone to which Jake took great exception. He visibly bristled at the suggestion.

"I'm sorry, Jake. That was a foolish comment. I meant you no offence. I rather like the sound of this guy. I am, though, curious about your relationship with him."

"He's someone I got to know at the studio. We're just pals. He's Marjory Dawlish's brother so I see more of him than anyone else there, that's all." Jake grumbled, fearing this line of questioning wasn't going to go away.

Gilbert changed the subject. "So... Marjory Dawlish appeared to be taken with the idea of making a sequel?"

"Very much; in fact, I'd say she was excited by the prospect. That's probably why she caved in to my demands so easily."

"Guy and I had exactly the same thoughts about making a sequel a few days before he was killed. Until you reappeared into my life, that prospect was unthinkable, but now, all that could change drastically."

Chapter Eighteen

When all three of them were together in the courtyard, Gilbert asked Wesley his opinion on the third reel.

"To offer you an accurate opinion, sir, I would need to have watched the other reels – which I assume you don't have?"

"Quite right, Wes, but regardless, I'd appreciate your opinion on what you did see. I know you will have one," Gilbert teased, and poured out three drinks. "Therefore, I would ask you to break with tradition, just for once, and join us for drinks." He indicated a vacant seat.

"Thank you for the offer, Mr Jon, but I couldn't possibly," Wesley responded.

"For God's sake, man, just for once sit down." Gilbert said brusquely, and the manservant obeyed. "Thank you. Now then, what were your thoughts on that reel?"

"To say that I enjoyed what I saw on the screen would be a rather inadequate way to express my true feelings, sir. However, I shall do my best," Wesley began awkwardly. He was perching uncomfortably on the very edge of the seat rather than sitting, and began fidgeting with his neat bowtie, clearing his throat before he spoke. "Perhaps the only piece of constructive criticism I can offer would be that, perhaps, the ending was just too abrupt for my own personal taste."

"I see. And why was that? Did the ending leave you wanting more?"

"That was precisely it, sir. I feel certain I will speak for many people who might see this reel when I say how anxious it made me. Needing to know what happened to Isabella Trecheanco after she was deported would be an understatement. But more than that, I was disturbed by the shock ending of the biplane crash. Anyone that had become so involved with the Franco D. Stefano character would need a glimmer of hope that, by some miracle, he had been able to survive. But I cannot see how that would be possible."

"Was there anything else apart from the talent agent?"

"Well, yes, sir. Would it be impertinent of me to ask if Franco survived the crash?"

"Quite possibly, but that is all I can offer you at this precise moment, Wesley. I'm sorry. I don't even know myself, not for sure. However, there could be a slim chance. Nothing more than that if I'm being completely honest. Is there anything else which springs to mind?" Gilbert asked, expecting more. He wasn't disappointed.

"Well, yes, as a matter of fact, there is. What I cannot understand is how you were able to make this movie without my knowing anything about it. I had no idea you were involved in any such project, not during the entire four years since you came back to California. But what I find more puzzling than anything else is a query I have regarding the young gentleman here?"

"What about him?"

"What I don't understand, not being educated in the skill of moviemaking, is this: how was it possible, even with exceptionally good make-up, to age Mr Velasquez so well? This must have been filmed some time ago, because looking at him today he looks too young for the part."

"Anything else?" Gilbert pressured him, wanting to extract every observation that Wesley had.

"In my humble opinion, I have to say that your protégée is, without doubt, destined for a great career in the motion picture industry."

"Then, do you think that a sequel should be made?"

"Oh yes, sir, without a doubt. A sequel would be a compulsive must-see after this movie has been released," he said.

Having concluded, Wesley got to his feet as though his legs were spring-loaded. Collecting a silver tray, he busied himself gathering up the empty glasses. "Will that be all you require of me for the moment, sir?"

"No, not quite, there is one last thing I need you to do for me tonight, Wesley. Would you unearth an old manuscript from the study?"

Although Wesley's mouth was closed, a strange hissing sound seemed to come from him before he looked up. He gave the oddest smile.

"The Tango of Death," Wesley said.

"Whatever would I do without you keeping me in order, Wesley?" Gilbert said, and the manservant went back indoors.

"Pardon me for asking, Gil, but...?"

"How did Wesley know what I was going to ask him to find? Well, the answer to that one is that I have no idea. I don't suppose I will ever work out what goes on in that brain of his. Maybe he is psychic, which would explain quite a lot. Wesley has an inbuilt knowledge about me from my odd preferences in food and drink, to my tastes in my reading material. Can you imagine what it was like when a complete stranger, as he was back then, knew exactly how I preferred to construct the outline of a script? No one else in this business could follow me in the way I do that, except for Guy."

There was much more Jake wanted to ask, but he didn't. His eyes had become heavy with the need to sleep, and so, before Wesley returned with the manuscript, Jake made his apologies, and retired to the comfort of his bed.

Although he was desperately tired, he slept uneasily into the early hours. He had vivid dreams of being in the back of an out of control vehicle, racing along the same stretch of the canyon road where Guy Maddox had lost his life. It was a nightmarish scenario which kept repeating over and over again. When Jake awoke, the sheets were saturated with sweat.

Getting a cold drink from the fridge, he tried to reason that any dream, vivid or not, would invariably involve people he knew. He had the impression that there was someone in the back of the pickup with him; a woman who'd been clinging onto the side rails of the truck as the rapidly accelerating vehicle hurtled off the edge of the road and propelled into space, high above the ravine. What had disturbed him more than anything else about that dream was that

Scott was badly injured, lying crumpled, at the edge of the canyon road.

There was no chance of trying to get any sleep, not until the fearsome images had had time to fade. He was sitting on the balcony, bathed in moonlight, desperately wanting to clear his mind of his dreams, when he heard the introduction of the now familiar tango, perfectly played on a classical guitar. Listening intently to the magic of that passionate rhythm, all Jake's earlier fears evaporated into thin air.

The slow opening movement came to an end and the guitarist stopped playing. Irked by the overpowering silence that engulfed him, Jake paced back and forth along the balcony, needing to hear more music, wondering who the guitarist could have been.

As he paced, he was more certain than ever that the balcony outside the studio apartment was the original idea for the stage set – the balcony he had ventured along on the night he had followed the ghostly apparition of Cloud Bird.

When he gazed into the courtyard, he was convinced the area below him was what had been replicated as a stage set. In the final reel of Gilbert's movie, it was the setting for that all-important "Tango of Death".

Intermingled with the distant sound of the ocean, he heard again the distinctive opening of the tango, but not played on the guitar, instead it was being played on the piano, even so, it was a compelling, magical sound on the night air, with the added intoxicating perfume of jasmine. The night was warm and comforting. It was a perfect place to relax and absorb the music, blanking out completely the nightmarish trauma of his dreams.

Without any warning, the temperature around him dropped, leaving him shivering with cold. Captivated by the music, Jake had no thought to go back inside to the warmth of the studio apartment. He began to feel again the pain burning in the branding scar. This developed quickly into a pain so intense that he was convinced his heart would explode.

Oddly, he felt no fear, only a calming reassurance that Cloud Bird's spirit was close by. He was aware of his friend's indistinct image, leaning over the balcony, beckoning to him to do the same as if something important was about to happen. Jake did this, and just as quickly as the pain had begun it eased off until, thankfully, it had gone.

At first glance, Jake didn't notice the figure standing in the cloisters below. It could have been a statue, except that it cast an unearthly shadow, not dark, but vaguely phosphorous and, by this light, he recognised the shape of Wesley. About to call down to him, he instinctively paused.

The extreme cold was something that Jake associated with the returning spirit of Cloud Bird, but, this time, he noticed a difference. The powerful aroma of pine needles made him nauseous and giddy. He gripped tightly onto the handrail to prevent himself from falling when the ghostly character of Isabella Trecheanco appeared, twirling fascinatingly beside the fountain to the clicking of castanets and the staccato clipping of her Cuban heels.

Jake became aware that another ghostly figure had emerged from the gloom of the cloistered courtyard from where Wesley had stood earlier.

Continuing with the flamenco rhythm, the dancer hardly acknowledged that her ghostly companion was Guy Maddox. Keeping pace to the rhythm of her snapping heels, the dancer swirled through the mist until, as naturally as day follows night, he moved in and partnered her.

As the slow, dramatic tempo increased, the powerful introduction to "The Tango of Death" began. Fascinated, Jake could hardly breathe, watching the precise, integrated movements of the dancers below in the courtyard: two artists consumed with the passion of partnering each other in those incredible movements.

As the couple began rhythmically weaving the difficult steps through each of the cloistered arches, it gave the impression that, although these two people were interpreting the music perfectly, the timing was such that he could have been watching a lone dancer, which made him wonder if this was the woman who'd given birth to Guy's son, the infant who had tragically died so soon after his birth.

As this thought flashed into his mind, the woman glanced up in his direction and stumbled, bringing the dance to an abrupt end.

When the dancers broke apart, Guy walked a few paces away from her, where his shape began to fade away, merging into the darkened cloisters, leaving his partner desolate and isolated. As the music came to its tragic end, she turned her masked face away from where Guy had disappeared and gazed up at the balcony. Unlike in the movie when the dance ended, Isabella Trecheanco quite deliberately did not remove the mask to reveal her exquisitely beautiful face. She became quite still, statuesque, soon to be engulfed within the swirl of lingering mist. Her hair was neatly coiled into the nape of her neck, exactly as he remembered it. It was no longer the lustrous jet black but shining with streaks of silver. Her ghostly image was staring directly at Jake. The grey mist thickened around her trim ankles and swirled up in a rush of gusting wind that howled across the courtyard, carrying with it the heartrending sound of a woman's voice screaming the name "Guy" over and over again.

This tormented cry chilled him to the bone; the anguished sound resonating through every arch of the courtyard, ending in a final, haunting cry as the moon slid behind a passing cloud, allowing Isabella Trecheanco's ghostly figure to fade into the shadowy cloisters, the way Guy Maddox had done a few moments earlier.

When the cloud had cleared, there was no trace of her. Even so, Jake was convinced that what he had witnessed that night in the courtyard had not been a dream. There was still music being played on the piano, but now it was coming from a candlelit room on the ground floor on the opposite side of the courtyard from where he was standing.

Jake was no longer feeling the perishing cold, only the warmth of a balmy night, when his nerves were set gratingly on edge by the jangling sound of a telephone, an incredibly intrusive noise, destroying entirely his reflective thoughts. The ringing brought a stop to the music.

Beyond the French doors, he could see Gilbert talking animatedly into the telephone and, during the short, but intense conversation that followed, he saw Gilbert lean forward to get a clearer view of the balcony where Jake was standing.

As if to qualify something to the caller, Gilbert nodded in response before he ended the call. Rubbing the back of his neck as if to ease some tension, Gilbert poured out a drink and he came out into the courtyard.

"Feel like joining me out here, Jake?" he called, without looking up. He lit a cigarette.

When Jake came down, Gilbert didn't refer to the telephone call; instead, he apologised if he'd woken Jake up with his playing. "I'm unused to having anyone else here, apart from Wesley. That man could sleep through an earthquake. In fact he has – on two occasions," Gilbert concluded with a laugh.

"It wasn't the piano that woke me, Gil. I couldn't sleep. By the way, does Wesley play the classical guitar?" Jake asked. He assumed that Gilbert would say yes, knowing there was no one else staying there, and was surprised when he said that Wesley didn't.

Gilbert laughed. "That man has no musicality in him at all. Believe me I've tried many times with the piano, and the guitar. Wes can barely strum a cord without it sounding abysmal. But then I wouldn't be the best teacher for the guitar. The piano is my instrument, and he's no better on that either."

"Then why keep a classical guitar in the music room?" Jake asked.

"That belonged to Guy. He was a gifted musician. He was an absolute master. In fact, his composition for "The Tango of Death" was written specifically for the guitar, and I will always regret not having stood my ground with the producers. They insisted on having an orchestral score recorded for the tango. I should have insisted they treat the score the way it was written." He looked about him. "Wesley will be dead to the world by now, otherwise he'd be out here, fussing about like an old hen."

"He wasn't asleep a short while ago. Just before you called me down from the balcony, he was smoking in the cloisters."

"Then you couldn't have been wearing your glasses. Wesley doesn't smoke. And, he usually retires much earlier than I do. He's an early riser. It was probably a shadow. On a moonlit night such as this, sometimes the shadows play havoc with my own vision."

"I was wearing them, and it was definitely him," Jake said, deciding not to mention anything else he had seen.

"Where was he?" Gilbert asked curiously, looking around him with interest.

"Standing in the cloisters, over there."

Almost before Jake knew it Gilbert was on his feet striding quickly towards where Jake had indicated. "Quick, Jake, give me a hand over here." Gilbert called back urgently. He knelt beside Wesley's body crumpled against one of the columns.

"There's hardly a sign of a pulse. I guess he must have passed out." Gilbert spoke calmly enough but there was panic in his eyes.

"What can I do to help?" Jake asked.

"Nip into the music room and get me a large brandy. Make it as quick as you can," Gilbert said, as Jake helped him to angle the manservant into a better position. "Just get the brandy Jake, and be quick. I can manage Wesley from here," Gilbert said, seating the manservant onto a stone bench.

"Where in the music room?" Jake asked, already on his way.

"It's decanted on the bureau. Pour a decent amount. That should bring him around."

When Jake returned, Wesley was vomiting into the shrubbery. Although he was retching violently, there was nothing but green smoke, as if the man's internal organs were fermenting. Combined with this, was an almost overpowering smell of pine needles.

Once the brandy had been administered, Wesley began to recover. After a short time, although he was unable to communicate, with Gilbert's help he was able to make a few staggering steps back into the building, where Gilbert insisted on helping him to his own bedroom, being nearest. A good half hour later, Gilbert returned and reassured Jake that Wesley was comfortable and sleeping normally.

"This is proving to be quite a night," Gilbert said tentatively, relaxing into a seat beside Jake. "Everything seems to have kicked off after that call I had earlier. You were up on the balcony at the time."

"You mean the call that interrupted you on the piano?" Jake began, realising that Gilbert was in need of some prompting if he was to learn more. "I saw you through the window. You seemed upset?"

"Not upset exactly. More confused, I suppose. That call was from a relative. Apparently, she had just woken from a disturbing dream."

"Why would she call you after midnight, Gil? Couldn't it have waited until the morning?"

"Not really; in this dream, she saw you up on the balcony."

"We all dream about odd things."

"She thought it was Guy. She told me exactly where you were standing."

"But that's impossible. It couldn't happen."

"When I asked her to be more specific, she claimed you were tugging at your right ear, the way you always do when you're confused. How could she know about that?"

"She could have been mistaken."

"No way, and, Jake, that is what you were actually doing when I looked to see."

"Did she say anything else?" Jake was gripping onto the edge of his seat. He had started to tremble and needed time to absorb what Gilbert was telling him.

"Yes, she did. And this is where it's a bit crazy. She thought there was a 'figure' up there with you on the balcony."

"What figure?" Jake felt the goose bumps begin to spike along his arms.

"Like a ghost, the shape of a Navajo warrior, as if that makes any sense. Apparently, it was at the far end of the balcony. All I saw, apart from you, was mist. No shapes. It doesn't seem likely that someone could dream up such an implausible scenario as that," Gilbert said, more to himself than to Jake.

Jake said nothing, but he did want to know more about what else Gilbert's relative had seen in her dream. Had she also been witness to that extraordinary tango?

"Did she mention having seen anyone else in the courtyard? Dancing, or anything?"

"Dancing? What are you talking about? There's only the three of us here. She had a dream. There was nothing more to it than that."

"That was no ordinary dream, Gil, if she saw me up there on the balcony. Is this relative of yours psychic?"

"I very much doubt it."

"It's odd isn't it, during all the years when I was growing up, I never thought about you having a family, not until you said that you had a brother."

"Guy was my half-brother," Gilbert corrected.

"What about the relative who called you tonight, is she a half-sister?"

"No, she isn't, and that's all you need to know for now. There are some people I don't want to talk about, not yet anyway."

"Sorry, Gil, I didn't mean to pry."

"Don't worry about it, Jake. If I was in your position, I would be curious too." Gilbert stood up. "I'm going to make us a coffee."

He returned with a coffee percolator, a bottle of milk, and two cups. Having poured the coffee, he said "God alone knows what's going on tonight. What is more disturbing to me than any dream is this wretched business with Wesley. What happened out there just now is a continuing mystery about the man."

"What do you mean?" Jake was curious.

"Well, the fact is, and I can say this hand on heart, I was sure Wesley was dead when I first got to him."

"But he wasn't."

"And praise the Lord for that..."Gilbert hesitated. "The unnerving thing is, I was certain Wesley wasn't breathing at all. In fact, I'd go as far as to say that I'm convinced he wasn't."

"He might just have appeared that way, if he was unconscious," Jake suggested, trying to be objective and to keep his mind away from the mystery woman's dream. He had every intention of finding out more about her before the night was over.

"I've seen men unconscious before, Jake, but this was different. There wasn't a spark of life in him— nothing at all. And why did the place reek of goddamn pine needles? Here in Pasadena, of all places? I'm telling you, this has got to rate as one hell of a weird night."

"Does it really matter, Gil, if Wesley has recovered from whatever it was ailing him? And he did recover very quickly."

"No one could be happier about that than I am. Fortunately for him, Wesley has no recollection about what happened."

"Did your mystery caller mention Wesley in her dream?"

"No, she only asked about the figure looking down from the balcony."

"Did she see anything else in the courtyard, apart from me?" Jake asked cautiously, wondering if the caller had witnessed any of the broken tango.

"Like what?" Gilbert asked curiously.

"Well, if she saw me up on the balcony, did she comment about the music you were playing? Or see anyone else?"

"She didn't say, and I never thought to ask. Her call came as quite a surprise, ringing me up out of the blue." Gilbert sat upright and rolled his shoulders to ease the tension building up at the back of his neck. "We haven't been in contact for a very long time, years, in fact. What I find so bloody uncanny is that, after so long, she actually chose to call me on the night that you were staying here. It can't be a coincidence. Don't think I'm going nuts, Jake, but I really think there are supernatural forces at work here, considering what she saw, and what happened to Wesley."

"I agree with you, Gil, but it's not just about tonight. There is something strange going on. Not only in your home. There have been several weird incidents which have happened to me since I arrived in California."

"What happened here tonight is different to the break-in at the studio." Gilbert clearly misunderstood Jake's meaning so Jake decided to leave it alone, at least for now.

"Considering how late it is, you must have been close to this woman if she felt OK to call you in the middle of the night. I don't think I'd have the gall to do that."

"She lives just a few miles away, on the far side of the canyon, with a swine of a husband. He doesn't know that I moved back to California. If he did, he certainly wouldn't allow her to make any calls to me. So, it was strange to hear her voice again."

"Who is she?"

"You wouldn't know her, Jake." Gilbert checked the time on his wristwatch. "I think we've spoken enough tonight, and you need to be at the studio in a few hours. Get off to bed for some shut-eye. I need to look in on Wesley, anyway. We can talk more about this when you get back from work."

"Sure, if you're not too tired."

Chapter Nineteen

The following morning Jake came down earlier than usual, needing to fill up at the gas station on his way to the studio. He could hear low voices talking intently in a nearby room. He didn't have time for breakfast, but he needed to thank Gilbert for his hospitality. He didn't want to interrupt the conversation, and so he waited for a lull to happen before he entered through the partially opened door.

"If you will forgive me for saying so, sir, that doesn't make sense. And you did say that she was hysterical."

"And yet, how did she know the exact piece of music I was playing? I haven't played Guy's tango in years—" Gilbert stopped speaking as Jake knocked lightly on the door before entering.

"I'm sorry, Gil, I didn't mean to break up your conversation. I just wanted to thank you for allowing me to stay here again. I'd have waited longer, but I need to stop for gas on my way to the studio."

"I hope you'll come back again after work?" Gilbert asked.

"I know you offered last night, but I wasn't planning on doing so. I've been living on your generosity for long enough."

"Nonsense, I love having you here. Besides, there is too much we have to catch up on. Surely you wouldn't deprive me of that? Come back tonight, please, unless you have somewhere else to be?"

"No, no I haven't." Jake smiled, remembering the draughty nights sheltering under the pier; he had little enthusiasm to repeat those experiences.

"Then sit down and eat something before you go. Five minutes isn't going to make a difference." Gilbert slid over a freshly boiled egg and the toast rack. "Wesley just made that for me. He'll rustle up another in no time, so eat it before it gets cold." He poured out a cup of steaming coffee before sitting in the chair opposite Jake.

"Did you overhear any of the conversation I was having with Wesley when you came in?" he asked casually, as if they'd been talking about nothing of any importance.

"Not really. Why?"

"No reason in particular." Gilbert smiled a winning smile, which always seemed to put everything to rights in the world. But it didn't stop Jake from puzzling over the mystery relative, and why, as she had seen him on the balcony so clearly, she hadn't mentioned anything about the dancers, particularly now he knew that she had heard the music, and was probably familiar with the piece Gilbert had been playing.

At the studio, the morning was moderately uneventful. Jake's concentration was repeatedly interrupted. Marjory had arrived first with an interrogation about why the studio contract hadn't been signed, and why his signature was not on hers either, if she was going to represent him. But, as Gilbert had pointed out, Jake said there were two mistakes that needed to be amended before he signed anything.

Soon after she had taken her leave, Adelaide Williams summoned Jake into her spacious office in the white building.

"In all seriousness, Mr Velasquez, I simply can't understand your reasoning. Both Marjory and I are bending over backwards to accommodate you with your requests. Because of that, the very least I would expect from someone in your situation would be that you would have the good grace to sign." Her annoyance was ill-concealed as she re-angled the fan on her desk.

"Actually, Miss Williams, there was a clause in paragraph three that I was uncertain about, and another in paragraph six. It's only because of these that I couldn't put my name to the document," Jake said, as she examined the contract.

"Really, and what are they?" She put on a pair of spectacles to study the paragraphs in question. "To be perfectly frank, my dear, I can't see why any actor in your position would question a three-year contract?" Adelaide Williams said incredulously.

"I told Miss Dawlish I would only sign up to work on the sequel to Jon Miller's lost movie."

"And what if I say that is an impossible request, Mr Velasquez?"

"Then I can't sign," Jake responded with the relief of a man set free from the gallows. "I'm really sorry, Miss Williams, if I have been wasting your time," he said, preparing to leave.

"Just a moment – we aren't through talking. You do realise this decision could be regarded as a most catastrophic mistake by other people in the business?"

Jake assumed her tone was intended to sound authoritative, but it didn't come over as harsh as her stern façade implied. There was an odd vulnerability about the way she glanced at the door, as if expecting to be interrupted at any moment, which, to Jake, didn't seem logical, as the only sound from the outer office was the industrious clacking of her secretary's typewriter. When the telephone rang on her desk, Jake thought she would jump out of her skin.

"Hi," Adelaide Williams answered, holding the receiver as she might have done with a deadly snake, purposely avoiding eye contact with Jake. "I can't speak now. I have someone in the office." She winced visibly at the grating tone of the caller. "Yes. Of course I understand. I'm dealing with it, like you asked." Her eyes flicked briefly in Jake's direction, before cautiously turning away and lowering her voice. "This is different. I can't answer that. I shall do my very best."

To see Adelaide Williams close up so early in the morning was very unlike Jake's previous encounter. She was wearing very little make-up, and Jake saw a badly hidden scar that raked across her face from just beneath her right eye, down across the cheek bone, and ending in her upper lip. But even with that brutal scar, Miss Williams was more attractive than he remembered. Without the mask of dark glasses, there was a weariness of life in her sad grey eyes, emphasised by the dark circles surrounding them.

Adelaide Williams was clearly agitated when she hung up the receiver with a sharp click. "Why don't you sit down, Mr Velasquez? I find it difficult to hold a conversation with someone towering above my desk." She lit a cigarette and inhaled the smoke deeply.

When she spoke Jake could see lipstick smudged on her teeth; the same bright red as on the stubs of the cigarettes piled up in the ashtray. Conscious of his disapproving glance, she swiftly emptied the dog-ends into a waste basket beside her chair.

"Now, where were we?" she asked through a cloud of smoke, shuffling the paperwork about on her desk with no apparent purpose except, perhaps, to apply some occupation for her trembling fingers.

"We were discussing the sequel to Jon Miller's movie, Miss Williams."

"Oh yes, of course."

"I would like to be perfectly clear about where I stand on this issue, Miss Williams. I am not an actor, nor ever wanted to be. Hoping to get even a small part in any movie was never a consideration when I came down to California," Jake said. He could tell that this information had caught her unawares when she ground out the half-finished cigarette into the ashtray.

"How can you possibly make such an outrageous statement? Mercy! Everyone I meet in Hollywood wants to be in the movies. This is a glorious profession... for anyone. She hastily put on her sunglasses, which was totally unnecessary in that office – except, Jake thought, for concealing the truth in her misting eyes.

"Then I must be the exception, Miss Williams. I have never acted in my life. If I do go ahead with this sequel, as you and Miss Dawlish suggest, surely that might prove to be equally disastrous for us both." Jake fully expected that this piece of information would get him off the hook. However, Adelaide Williams was grimly determined to get her own way.

"When the timing is right, I am always up for the challenge, and I see that in you, Mr Velasquez. The prospect of going ahead with a sequel to that extraordinary movie by Jon Miller would be absolutely thrilling. You can rest assured that I will get the wording in this contract amended immediately. When that is done, I will expect you to sign and have it returned to me by the end of the day." Adelaide Williams turned her attention to the mound of paperwork on her desk as a sign that the interview was at an end.

"We haven't yet discussed paragraph six," Jake said, bringing his most important objection to her attention. For some time she looked quizzically at the paragraph.

"Why would you question Maurice Stanford as our choice of director? The man has impeccable credentials. He was also the person responsible for allowing the original movie to be made. It is because he remembers the way that picture was shot. He would be the ideal person to make any audience believe that you are a reincarnation of the leading character in *The Return of Xavier Gérard*. Only a director with Mr Stanford's expertise could be expected to make the proposed sequel work."

"Even so, Miss Williams, because I do look like the leading actor in the original movie, I would have thought there was little need to convince anyone that it was the same character on screen?"

"The cinema-going audience is not so easily fooled, Mr Velasquez, not without using a master in the craft of subtle direction."

"Forgive me if I stick with my principles, Miss Williams. I realise what a great risk you're taking by considering an amateur like me. But I think it's unlikely an audience would question my uncanny resemblance to Guy Maddox, especially as my voice is so like his too."

Jake surmised that, because she was so unused to having her authority questioned by anyone in the building, it was a bitter pill for Adelaide Williams to swallow. Finding herself in that dilemma and, by necessity, having to keep uncharacteristically quiet, she picked irritably at the corner of the leather insert on her desk until he finished speaking.

"Having watched through the two reels in our possession, perhaps you have a valid point. However, the strong resemblance between you and that actor cannot compensate for the fact that you have never acted on screen before. Therefore, what you need is the expertise of an experienced director, a man who can fully explain the progression of the character you will be playing. Mr

Stanford will be taking the sole responsibility for writing the sequel."

Jake's jaw dropped. "What? You're saying that Maurice Stanford would write this as well?"

"We have already spoken about this. Mr Stanford is quite prepared to make time in a crushingly busy schedule to accommodate this. In fact he has already begun work on the first draft."

"Miss Williams, you misunderstand. I only agreed to become involved in this sequel if Jon Miller did it all. No one could know what is required in the script better than him. He both wrote and directed the original."

Jake thought she would either have a seizure or explode with indignation at this but she did neither.

"Young man, you are outrageous. You can't possibly expect me to agree to that. Jon Millar hasn't been heard of in the past twenty years. The man was admitted into a sanatorium for the mentally unbalanced." Clearly, she was expecting the shocking information to shake him from his request.

"You must be confusing Jon Miller with someone else, Miss Williams," he said calmly, thrusting his hands into his pockets.

"Not in the least. I know this to be a fact. I was working in the studio's publicity department when Jon Miller's attempted suicide was hushed up." She hurled the information at Jake almost triumphantly, but she was unable to conceal the full impact that youthful incident had on her. This showed clearly in her trembling hands as she lit up another cigarette.

"He attempted suicide?" Jake repeated, unable to concede that Gilbert would have tried to end his own life. "Forgive me, Miss Williams, but that doesn't seem possible."

She inhaled on the crackling cigarette again, spending some time removing the shred of tobacco stuck to her lipstick before answering. "I am not mistaken about this, Mr Velasquez. I was the person who summoned our doctor to the scene. If I hadn't, the sleeping pills would never have been pumped out of Jon Miller's stomach, nor would he have been pulled out of a car full of exhaust fumes."

"There is a doctor here?"

"There is always a studio doctor on call at night," she explained. "He might have known what sanatorium Mr Miller was transferred to from the hospital. Fortunately for Jon Miller, the studio publicity department put a blanket over any chance of the scandal breaking. No one ever knew where he was taken and, before you ask, I understand that duty doctor died some time ago in a hick township of New Mexico. If Jon Miller was ever released from that sanatorium he might very well have succeeded in his next suicide attempt. He'll almost certainly be dead now."

"But you don't know that, not for certain."

"Agreed, and I can't justify authorising the expense of such a hopeless search as your request would involve. I am sorry, Mr Velasquez, but you will have to work with me on this, and agree to be directed by Maurice Stanford," she said, grinding out the stub of the cigarette into the ashtray. She lit up another cigarette, drawing in the smoke with the smug attitude of a victor.

"Well, fortunately, I know otherwise, Miss Williams."

"You know just what, exactly?"

"That Jon Miller is alive and well. I also know that he could be tempted to work on this sequel."

"How could you possibly know that?" she asked fiercely, crushing the newly lit cigarette into the ashtray with frustration.

"Because I spoke with Jon Miller only yesterday," he said.

Flustered by this news, she turned up the speed on the desk fan which redistributed every single piece of paperwork on her desk.

"Maurice Stanford will not be at all pleased to learn about this unexpected turn of events, Mr Velasquez. Not pleased at all."

"Then I take it that you would agree to Jon Miller directing the sequel?"

"In principle, yes." Grudgingly she gathered together her paperwork. "I will have the amendments to the contract by tomorrow. Marjory will be in contact and let you know when they are ready to be signed."

It was clear that Adelaide Williams had been cornered, and that she would have happily ousted him from the studio had he potentially not been such a hot commodity. A thought which convinced him that, as soon as this project was over, the more distance he put between himself and the movie industry, the better.

That evening after dinner, Jake was relaxing comfortably on one of the chairs in the courtyard when Gilbert joined him. He said that, although Wesley had been up and about earlier that morning, he hadn't fully recovered from the previous night's events and had gone to bed. Gilbert sank into one of the comfortable chairs opposite Jake, lit up a cigarette and poured out the coffee.

"So, Jake, what is it that's been troubling you about Wesley? Don't deny it. I was watching you over dinner."

"It's just the weird impression he gives off."

"Well, out with it, what is it?"

"Well. There are times when he has this habit of not staring at me exactly but seems to be looking through me, blocking out everything around him – if that makes sense."

"Why do you think that is?" Gilbert asked curiously.

"It's as though he's got it into his head that, somehow, I'm another person in Guy's skin."

"A wolf in sheep's clothing," Gilbert said, attempting to make light of a situation that was troubling them both.

"He doesn't actually look at me, he looks into me. I think Wesley believes that I've stolen Guy's identity. He did this at the gate when I first arrived."

"Wesley can be a bit of an acquired taste, but you need to see beyond his peculiarities. He's a really good sort. He's been through a lot of emotional stuff in his life, a lot more than most, which would probably explain away a lot of his oddities. On the other hand, I can't say that I've ever noticed him look at you any differently than he does to me."

"I wouldn't lie about something like that, Gil."

"I know that, it's just that Wesley is, well, he's a one-off. I've never seen him how we found him last night. Whatever your first impressions might be, Jake, please don't react badly towards him. If I hadn't met Wesley at the sanatorium, quite frankly, I don't think I would have survived. He was the one who helped me through that wretched period in my life after Guy had been killed."

"I heard today that you were in a sanatorium for a time." Jake wished that he hadn't opened up the discussion. It would have been an emotionally difficult time in Gil's life, and Jake felt he was forcing him to talk about a subject that might stress him. "I'm sorry, Gil. The last thing I wanted was to bring this up."

"There was no secret about where I was locked up. It's more of a shock to learn that you could know anything about it. Who did you hear it from? It happened such a long time ago, I wouldn't have thought anyone would know about it."

"Adelaide Williams"

"Ah, that makes sense. I remember Adelaide very well. Although the aftermath of that episode is a blank canvas to me, I learnt afterwards that she'd been working late when she found me in the back of my car with the engine running. She hauled me out of the car and probably saved my life through her quick thinking. She called Eugene and they drove me to the nearest hospital. It was touch and go for a time."

"You mean Doctor Maxwell?"

"Yes. After the treatment, I was transferred to the sanatorium."

"And that's where you met Wesley?" Jake was sickened by how close Gilbert's attempted suicide had been.

"That was sometime later, when I was fully recovered." Gilbert reached out, gripping Jake's upper arm reassuringly. "Don't look so worried, Jake. I won't be trying that again."

"Was Wesley working with Doctor Maxwell?" Jake asked.

"No, Wesley was an inmate, like me, but not for any self-inflicted reason. His case was completely different, and all the more unusual for it." Gilbert spoke with some reservation, reflecting on that unhappy period of his life. "Knowing Wesley as he is now, a decent-living guy with an impeccable character, it's hard to imagine his earlier background in Detroit and California, until that near-fatal shooting. Before that there had been a very unpleasant side to the man's life."

"I couldn't imagine Wesley being unpleasant. Not in any way."

"Wesley is a good-looking man, and that was part of his trade, being able to combine the role of a male socialite with that of a petty crook. Once he'd been into some of the wealthier homes, it was easy for him to break in a few weeks later and rob from the rich and famous."

"You're saying that Wesley was some kind of gangster?"

"Not exactly, more of a petty crook, with the ability to break the combination of any safe."

"Surely not? Not Wesley." Jake protested until, thinking back, he remembered the professional way that Wesley had examined his trunk after it had been broken into.

"Trust me, it's the truth." Gilbert said, reflecting on past events.

"It does seem hard to believe," Jake responded, although now with less conviction.

"You'd think so, wouldn't you? But everything about him changed, and his old life was abandoned."

"How could any man, after living such a life, be able to change so drastically?"

"There's a reason. Will you accept that what I tell you is the truth?"

"Of course I would. Why would you think otherwise?"

"Probably because what I have to tell you will seem stranger than fiction." Gilbert spoke reluctantly. "The fact is that Wesley, the opportunist, died on the operating table. A surgeon was attempting to remove a bullet which had pierced his heart. He was pronounced dead by two surgeons, but when his body was being taken down to the mortuary, a good twenty minutes later, Wesley began to breathe again. What is so bloody unbelievable about this miracle is that Wesley's previous character disappeared, and the Wesley that you and I both know replaced it."

"That's an incredible story."

"It is. But what is more incredible is that what happened to Wesley that night was exactly the plot that Guy and I had devised for the sequel to *The Return of Xavier Gérard*.

When Jake turned in he lay awake for some time, pondering over Wesley's previous life, his apparent death, and the change of character. On the verge of sleep, the thought came into his mind that if Los Angeles was known as the City of Angels, then perhaps Pasadena might also be a City of Spirits.

The next day, Marjory made a brief appearance in the viewing theatre to say Jake was required to be in Adelaide Williams office at 10a.m.the following morning to sign the contract, and that he was not to be late.

"I understand you've located Jon Miller?" she snapped accusingly. "Have you any idea what a devilishly awkward position that's put me in? Have you no concept of loyalty at all? Why couldn't you have told me about him first? Instead, I'm given that information from Adelaide."

"I'm sorry, Miss Dawlish. It wasn't intentional," he said, wondering why she was so edgy about it.

"I don't understand why. D' you think I'm some sort of ogre that you're unable to confide in?"

"I didn't have the opportunity of speaking with you yesterday. Jon Miller's name was mentioned because it came up in the conversation, that's all."

Her attitude changed, and she said just a little too graciously: "Well, it's done now. There's no need to dwell on it any longer." He noticed that not once throughout the exchange had she looked him directly in the eyes. He decided to find out just how much Marjory did know.

"Do you think Miss Williams was surprised Jon Miller had been living so close to the studio all this time?" he asked.

"Pasadena came as rather a shock to both of us," she said.

"I didn't mention where Jon Miller might be living."

"But you must have."

"I was very careful not to mention where he was living."

"You must have said something, Jake."

"I've said nothing to anyone. Only one other person could have told you, and that's Scott." Jake was deeply distressed by this, and the rush of scarlet into her normally pale cheeks confirmed his suspicions.

"If you wanted to keep Jon Miller's whereabouts a secret, why tell Scott?"

"I didn't tell him, or anyone else. He followed me."

"Why would he do that?"

"I don't know."

He knew that he needed to pay more attention to what Marjory Dawlish was saying rather than try to analyse his own confused feelings.

"What difference does it make who the hell told me, or where this man lives? All that interests me is that you think Jon Miller would be interested in directing a sequel," she said annoyingly, giving Jake the impression that she believed, as always, that she had the upper hand.

"Yes, I believe he's interested. But he'd want to view the first two reels of the original."

"Jon Miller intends to come here to view them at the studio?"

"No, Miss Dawlish, what Mr Miller was suggesting is for him to view the reels privately, at his home."

She clearly wanted to say no, but was smart enough to realise that, if she did, she would also use Jake as a spur to her own career by representing him in the proposed sequel.

"Unbelievable. Who the hell does this Jon Miller think he is?"

"For a start, I'd say that he is an incredibly talented director who has every right to review his past work. It seems logical to me."

"But why would he want to review them in Pasadena and not here?"

"That would be because he leads a very private life, and perhaps, more importantly, because he has access to the end reel."

Saying that clinched the deal.

"Well, it's against my better judgement but I might allow them out of the studio but only on the condition that I hand them over to him in person."

"I'll see that he gets your message." Jake doubted that Gilbert would agree to see anyone at all.

"Ask him to call me on this number," she said, and paused. "It isn't my intention to scare him off. The way I understand it is that Jon Miller wants first to review the original movie before agreeing to direct the sequel. See that you persuade him to meet up with me, Jake, otherwise we'll all lose out."

Chapter Twenty

Jake was partially hidden behind the seats repairing a speaker cable when the Projection Room door creaked open and a man entered. Jake was in an awkward position and, as he had a screwdriver clenched between his teeth, he was unable to call out. It was a cramped space and impossible to move without losing hold of the junction plate he'd been struggling with for the last half hour, and so he chose to carry on working, assuming the visitor would be Scott –that was until he heard the unseen man lock the door and proceed to rifle through the filing cabinets, littering the floor with discarded files and paperwork during his search.

Jake gave up the job in hand, and stood up angrily to confront the intruder, facing not one man in his Projection Room, but two.

"What in hell are you doing in that cabinet?" Jake demanded of Drew's Archive Assistant when he spun around to face him. He was clearly shocked that, apart from himself and his companion, anyone else was in the Projection Room.

"Drew asked me to come over," Frank Clark lied. His eyes were wild and desperate, like a rabbit trapped in a car's headlights. Unlike him, the other man carried on clearing the shelf in another cabinet, indifferent to Jake's challenge.

"So what is he doing in here?" Jake asked, which got no response from Frank Clark or the second intruder, who was hard to distinguish from Jake's position in the gloom. This was a brute of a man with a severely broken nose, who Jake recognised as the same man who had attacked Gilbert in Fort Laverne some time before.

"You, whoever you are, can stop what you're doing right now and gather up that frigging mess, or you'll have security to contend with."

Because Jake was so angry, he was ready to tackle both of the men, but what he wasn't prepared for was the other man's reaction when Jake stepped forward into the light. Instead of attacking Jake and beating him into a pulp, as Jake was expecting, this giant of a man began wrenching frantically at the locked door handle as if he was being plagued by all the demons of Hell. Shaking with fear, he yanked again at the locked door and physically forced it open with an almighty splintering of wood and disappeared along the corridor.

In his haste to prevent Frank Clark from getting away, Jake stumbled over the seats, which gave Clark the opportunity to land him a hefty wallop to the side of the head, bringing Jake to his knees. Just as the Archive Assistant was about to make good his escape, he in turn was stopped with some force.

"What the devil's going on here, you jerk?" Scott grabbed Frank by the throat and slammed him hard up against the splintered doorframe. "Are you OK there, Jake?"

"I think so," Jake said groggily, getting unsteadily to his feet, holding onto one of the seats for support. A trickle of blood was beginning to run down his cheek.

In his dazed state, the room seemed to be swimming around and he could taste blood in his mouth. It was important that Frank Clark didn't get away before he got some answers about what they had been after, and he thanked God that Scott happened along when he did.

"Are you sure about that, because you don't look it from where I'm standing."

"Give me a minute, Scott."

"Good, then I'll be with you after I get a few answers. Did this heap of horse shite say what he was doing here?" Scott asked as if the intruder didn't exist; all the time, tightening the grip on his throat as he gurgled for him to stop.

"All he said was that Drew asked them to come by."

"Drew wouldn't have sanctioned this," Scott said, looking about him at the state of the room. "Did you say there was someone else in here?" He wrestled Frank back against the door, clamping an iron grip on the man's arm as he tried to squirm free.

"Yeah, there was another guy with him."

"Were they threatening you? Is that why you wouldn't let them in?" Scott asked, referring to the shattered doorframe.

"They let themselves in and locked the door behind them. They didn't see me working behind the seats."

"Then why is the door hanging off its hinges?"

"It was the guy with a broken nose. He had a panic attack when he saw me. He smashed the door open to get out. He bolted off down the corridor like a scared rabbit."

"Was it that creep Malcolm Reynolds?" Scott challenged, slacking the hold he had on Frank Clark's neck. "Answer me, damn it. Was Reynolds the guy with a broken nose, tell me, unless you'd like one yourself?"

"Sure, it was Malcolm Reynolds," Frank croaked.

"Well, that would explain a lot," Scott said with annoyance, looking over the chaotic state of the room.

"What do you think they were after?" Jake asked.

"It's got to be the two Guy Maddox reels," Scott said, trying to get a clear look at Jake's injuries without releasing his hold on Frank's neck.

"Well they were wasting their time if that's what they were after. They're not here. I don't know where they are."

"Well I do. Madge asked me to collect them on my way in. Apparently, like the jerk here, she needs them urgently."

"So they're safe?" Jake said. He clamped a handkerchief on his temple to prevent the stream of blood going into his eyes.

"Jeepers, you're bleeding," Scott said, venting his pent-up anger on Clark by slamming him repeatedly against the doorframe. "What did you do it for, you twisted moron?"

"Let him go, Scott," Jake insisted, wanting him to release his tightening stranglehold before the man choked to death. "Please, he isn't worth it."

Further along the corridor they heard a door being slammed hard. This was followed by the clatter of high-heels approaching. The sound of the clattering heels paused only momentarily just a few yards away from the door, before continuing on.

Marjory barged in between them before she became aware of her brother's hands around Frank Clark's throat. "For goodness'

306

sake, Scott, what are you doing? Let the man go." She failed miserably to disengage Scott's fingers from the man's throat. "You don't know your own strength. Look at his face, he can't breathe."

"Not before I get some answers."

"You won't get any at all if you don't let him go. He's choking."

"Do as she asks, Scott," Jake urged, remembering Gilbert pinning him up against a wall with a similar strangulating hold. "I'm OK now, honestly."

"Well..." Scott released his grip, but not enough to let him go.

Under interrogation, with bulging eyes and a reddening throat, Frank claimed that Malcolm Reynolds had forced him to help find the missing reels. "I had no choice," he whined miserably.

"Malcolm Reynolds was here, in this building?" Marjory questioned.

"Yes, ma'am," Frank Clark said.

"That doesn't make sense. How could he possibly get past security at the gate? He's been banned from entering the studio."

"He didn't say, Miss Dawlish." Frank's shifty eyes flickered slyly as he looked for any route of escape when Scott took over the questioning again.

"Come on, Frank, you know everything that goes on in this studio. So, how did that hulk get in here? And, what's more, who put him up to raiding this place?" Scott asked menacingly.

"I'm not sure, but I think he got through the gates with Miss Jeffords in her limo."

"Ray on security would never have allowed that, even if he was travelling with her. It's more than his job's worth," Scott said.

"They came in through the South Gate. A new security guy started there a couple of weeks back. He isn't that bright."

Marjory Dawlish was not at all impressed with Frank's explanation, but she was even less impressed at her brother assuming control of the situation, and made it perfectly clear that she wanted him gone.

"There's no need for you to hang around here, Scott, not if you have other things to be getting on with. I can handle everything," she said, placing herself between Frank and the open door. "You can sit down over there, Frank. We are not through yet."

"I'll be off then," Scott said, handing Jake a backpack containing the two reels of film. "It's probably better if Jake looks after these until you're ready for them," he said, purposely not commenting on the contents when he handed them over.

"Well, just for the time being," Marjory said, expecting him to leave. "By the way, did you remember to bring the Hasselblad camera in with you? The stills man keeps going on at me about returning his blasted camera. I'm sure it's important but I do have enough going on in my life at the moment without getting involved in that as well. If he asks for it again I swear I'll have a nervous breakdown." Marjory said, pacing the floor.

"How could I possibly forget? You reminded me about it three times in one hour this morning," Scott said, removing the bulky Hasselblad from the bag Jake was holding. "In fact, it might not be a bad idea if Jake rattled off a few shots now, just to show what a state this place is before it gets cleaned up."

"Good idea," Marjory said, as he left.

Without being asked, Jake opened up the camera and covered both angles of the room with photographs. Meanwhile, Marjory continued her interrogation of Frank Clark, but with Scott now gone, and with him the threat of any reprisals, she achieved nothing. So she asked Jake to watch him and made a call on the internal phone.

Frank Clark was insisting that he should be allowed to leave when Drew Walters came into the room and immediately noticed him pressed up against the wall. "So, what in hell are you doing here, Frank? I thought you were due for a dental appointment?"

"I... I," Frank began. He was flustered and not quick-witted enough to escape detection in the lie.

"What he's trying to say, Drew, is that he needed to get in here and trash the place rather than go for any mythical appointment," Marjory snapped.

"Frank would never do anything like this. He is too much of a conscientious worker," Drew said defensively.

"That's a load of crap. That man is a liability and a complete waste of space. It was him and that blundering imbecile Malcolm Reynolds, who are responsible for the mess in here and for doing this," she said, indicating the blood oozing from the cut on Jake's temple.

"He did that to you?" Drew exclaimed, examining Jake's face. "Why?"

"I was trying to stop them from doing this," Jake said, omitting to mention what they had been searching for.

"What shall I do, Marjory? Do you want me to fire him? Because I will, if that's what you want," Drew said reluctantly. "The problem is he'll cause a lot of trouble if he goes to the union about this, we both know they could even shut the studio down."

"Your man can complain to King Kong for all I care. I have two independent witnesses who will confirm it was Frank Clark and Malcolm Reynolds who made this bloody shambles in here," she said victoriously, tapping the Hasselblad camera. If I show these photographs at the next union meeting, I can assure you that your indispensable assistant will never work here again, or at any other studio in this town come to that."

When everyone had gone, having refused all offers of help, it took Jake a long time to get the Projection Room back in any semblance of order and was late leaving the studio and ran all the way to the bus depot. Irritatingly, Marjory Dawlish had decided to keep hold of the two Guy Maddox reels until she had finalised a few details with Jon Miller.

When Jake arrived at the hacienda, even before he had time to pass on Marjory Dawlish's message, Gilbert had her business card and began dialling out the number.

"Well, let's see about this, shall we?" Gilbert said, listening to the ringing tone at the other end.

"What are you going to do about getting the other two reels?" Jake asked.

"Whatever I can, but not on her terms – on mine. Your Miss Dawlish might be used to dictating her demands to employees at the studio, but that ends at the studio gates. It won't wash here." Gilbert said, breaking off as the telephone was picked up at the other end.

"Marjory Dawlish? This is Jon Miller. I understand you were expecting my call? Likewise, it's good to make contact with you," Gilbert said with a raised eyebrow. "Yes, Jake is with me. Now, with regard to this proposition, I'd like to review the two lost reels. I understand perfectly, but that's not practical. Why? Because those reels went missing before I got to see the result. I'm sure you will appreciate that a period of twenty-five years has elapsed since that movie was completed, which is why I don't think a meeting is necessary at this stage. Not to begin with; it is imperative for me to watch the entire movie through, independently."

He smiled, listening to her response. "Yes, of course. I will most certainly give you an answer about the suitability of casting an unknown like Jake Velasquez in the sequel. So, shall we say – first thing tomorrow, at about 7a.m.? Yes, you have my word on it. Once I have viewed the reels, they will be returned by your courier immediately."

Gilbert then gave directions to the hacienda. "Ask whoever you send to ring on the bell twice, and then wait a minute before giving one further ring. My man will escort them into the house and I'll sign for the delivery. Good evening, Miss Dawlish. Likewise, we'll speak again tomorrow."

After dinner, Gilbert poured himself a stiff drink before he mentioned the sequel.

"Now the missing reels have turned up, the more I think about finishing the story, the more excited I am," Gilbert enthused.

"Then you'll consider making the sequel?"

"Let anyone try and stop me." Gilbert responded with a laugh. "Even before we had the end of Guy's movie in the can, he came up with a great idea that could make a sequel even more interesting than the original. There's a draft of his screenplay, but it probably needs some work."

"Is that what you sent Wesley inside for last night?"

"He found it after you went up to your room," Gilbert said.

"But you gave me the impression that you hadn't read it through since you and Guy wrote it?"

"That's right. I haven't. I want to get your reaction to the storyline first. This project is too important to charge ahead on my own. Because Guy was in on the original from the very beginning, that's why I believe the movie came together so smoothly."

"Where's the manuscript now?" Jake asked, curious about what Gilbert, and Guy Maddox, had come up with, and hoped that the storyline would give him confidence to go through with the project, if that was what Gilbert wanted. However, the more the prospect became a reality, the more nervous he became. He was terrified, not only of having to act, but of the destructive exposure he would be committing himself to.

"It's on your bedside table. Look it over later, and let me know what you think in the morning."

"But, in principle, you've not yet agreed with Miss Dawlish to direct the sequel?"

"You should realise nothing is binding in this city unless a contract has been signed. It's all a game of cat and mouse. I'm not so rusty that I don't know how it works here. But if you do decide to work on it with me when you've read the story, I'll have Wesley type up another copy so we can go through it together. Are you still comfortable with the thought of playing that part?"

It was a great chance for Gilbert and Guy Maddox to have the recognition they so rightly deserved. Because Gilbert seemed eager to get on with it and as the last thing Jake wanted was to open up about his own anxiety, he tried reasoning. "Wouldn't it be better to find a real actor to play the part instead of me, Gil? I'm scared I'll let you down."

"You won't, trust me on that. I promise I'll coach you through every scene. This isn't theatre where you get one shot at delivering the line perfectly. Movie actors are different. Few get it right the first take, not even the good ones. All I ask is that you memorise the few pages of script we need to shoot that day, and leave the rest to me. If you don't get it right on the first take, we'll shoot it again if necessary."

"Are you sure about this, Gil?"

"I've never been more certain of anything in my life. What I've learnt over the years is this. If you believe in what you're saying, the performance will be credible."

"OK then, if you're sure an actor wouldn't be better in this role."

"Your looks are identical to Guy. No one else could come close. When you've read through our script, I'm sure you'll understand what I'm driving at. You'll see no one else could do the sequel except for Guy in the role of Franco D. Stefano. He would have needed make-up in the flashback sequences. But it's easy with you, Jake, to make you appear older. Holy mackerel! The way you are staring at me right now is just the way Guy would have done. You really are scarily like him, in every way."

"But surely there must be make-up people who could make a real actor look convincing enough to pass for Guy Maddox?"

"They wouldn't be able to give him the bone structure, or the natural inflections that you both have in the voice. It would always be someone else trying to get away with it."

"But, even so, I'm not sure how any movie would hold up with me taking the lead. We'd both be nervous wrecks by the end of the first day."

"Not if I'm directing."

"I'm not trying to be difficult, Gil, honestly, but have you thought this through enough? What if I photograph differently to Guy? I know that being photographed puts on about ten pounds in weight."

"You will photograph perfectly fine, Jake. Even now that I'm used to you being here, I still find it unnerving to see you sitting opposite me in that chair," Gilbert said, scrutinising him objectively. "Look, if I can't tell the two of you apart then neither could anyone else."

"There are a few small differences," Jake added, remembering Scott's comments.

"These," Gilbert said, removing Jake's spectacles.

"How can you remember someone's face in such detail, after so long? It must be twenty, twenty-five years since you made that movie?" Jake said, wondering about the nature of their relationship when they were young men.

"It was twenty-six years ago to be accurate, and the reason I remember him so well is that I knew Guy long before that movie was made," Gilbert said. He poured himself another generous whisky. "Guy wasn't just my best friend, he was my half-brother too."

"Guy Maddox was your brother?" Jake questioned, but it was less of a shock than he might have expected. He had been unconsciously aware of marked similarities in the two men, like the shape of their noses and the depth of their dark intelligent eyes.

"I'm proud to say that he was. No one could have had a better brother. We got on from the first moment we were reunited."

Gilbert checked his watch anxiously. "Do you suppose Marjory Dawlish decided against sending those reels over?"

"I doubt that very much. She'll probably call Drew to bring them over. I don't think she'll risk sending them anywhere by courier," Jake said, which did a lot to ease Gilbert's growing anxiety.

"I'm sorry, Jake. It's just that I'm really keen to see if we did actually make a great film. It was our first and only movie together. Just imagine what a memorial it would be to Guy if the other two reels are as good as the one we saw last night."

Jake could see that Gilbert's mind was in need of another focus, given the steady rate that he was downing the whisky. He wouldn't be anywhere near sober if the reels didn't arrive soon.

"Do you mind if I make some coffee?" Jake said, rejecting Gilbert's suggestion Wesley should make it instead. "It's a bit too strong for me the way Wesley makes it. I like my coffee the way Gia made it, back home. You did too, as I remember," Jake said as Gilbert followed him through into the kitchen.

"I'm glad you reminded me about that. I suppose I've reverted back since I returned here." Smiling, Gilbert put the half-empty tumbler on the draining board. "Have I said how great it is to have you here, Jake?"

"Not in so many words. I'm happy to be here too."

"Remind me, what were we talking about?"

Jake was about to ask what had become of Alicia Cordova

when Wesley appeared in the doorway.

"Excuse me, sir, there is a gentleman at the gate with a package."

"He didn't give it to you?" he asked.

"The gentleman refused to hand it over to anyone other than you, sir. It all seems to be genuine, Mr Jon. I checked the package. It is from the Silver Lake Studios."

"Well, you had better ask him up to the house, Wesley."

"I already have, sir. But he won't come through the gates."

"Did he give a reason why?" Gilbert asked curiously.

"He seems genuinely pressed for time. I understand that he was called in at the last-minute with strict instructions that the reels must be handed over to you in person."

"Then I'd better go out," Gilbert said. However, he only went as far as the front door and shouted to the shadowy figure outside the gates. "Are you here with a package for me?"

"If you are Mr Miller then yes, I am," the young man replied.

It was a murderously humid night, and the courier was suffering badly from the heat, dressed in an evening suit. His voice sounded strained; his throat was badly restricted by a tight-fitting starched wing collar and bow tie.

"Then you had better come up to the house," Gilbert said, as Wesley unlocked the tall iron gates.

"That won't be necessary, sir. All I need from you is some proof of identity, and your signature."

Gilbert laughed. "Then you can expect a long wait, because I won't be signing anything I can't see in the gloom. You'd better come up to the house where I can read the document you want signed, and check the contents of the package."

"I can't do that, sir. I am already late for an engagement in town." The shadowy figure was seemingly immovable on the other side of the open gate.

"Then suit yourself young man. As for myself, I'm going back inside."

"But, sir, what about the package?" the man called after him.

"Well, if you won't hand it to me, so that I can verify the

contents, I suggest that you take the package back to Miss Dawlish. I hope she understands your reasoning for coming out to Pasadena and not fulfilling the mission," Gilbert said abruptly, and returned indoors.

This had the desired effect; a short time later, Wesley escorted the young man into the courtyard.

"You must be an actor," Gilbert said, offering him the director's copy of his script for *The Return of Xavier Gérard*. "I believe this should prove my identity, since you have brought along the filmed reels?"

"Thank you, Mr Miller," he said as Gilbert opened the package and checked the canisters, waiting for his signature on the paperwork. "No sir, I'm not an actor. I am a wrangler by profession."

"Then forgive me for asking, but why are you dressed like that?"

"Just for tonight, I'm working as a male escort at a big Academy bash in town." He did his best to keep out of the light when Jake appeared.

"But only until the next offer comes along," Jake cut in.

"You know this man?" Gilbert asked, registering his surprise.

"Sure, this is Scott I told you about. Scott Chinook."

"My sister is Marjory Dawlish," Scott explained coolly, handing over the reels of film. "If you'll excuse me, sir, I really must be off." He glanced anxiously at his watch.

"What time does the function begin?"

"Eight o'clock."

"Then I won't keep you but, before you go, would you be kind enough to offer me your opinion on these two reels, which I understand you have already seen?"

"You shouldn't ask my opinion, Mr Miller, I'm no critic."

"I'm not asking for a comprehensive critique, Scott. Just an honest opinion, that's all."

"Then, for what it's worth, Mr Miller, I would rate this movie as the best I've ever seen, and that is the truth."

After Scott had gone, contrary to Jake's opinion, Gilbert praised him warmly.

"Now, that is an exceptional young man."

"Why say that when he's so open about what he's prepared to do for money?" Jake said begrudgingly.

"Well, to begin with, he didn't lie about being a paid escort, unlike most young actors would have done when they are reduced to that. Honesty is a virtue that I have always admired in you, Jake. And that is a rare commodity in this city, which no doubt you will find out when you've been here a while longer. I had to resort to the same thing when my own cash ran out, just as your charming friend is doing now."

Jake had been more unsettled by Scott's appearance than he cared to admit even to himself, and Gilbert's easy acceptance of him made him wish he hadn't made any comments at all to either of the men.

As soon as the two reels had been shown, Jake made his excuses and went up to the apartment, where he intended to sleep and blank out his troubling thoughts, which was impossible. Because he couldn't sleep, he read through Gilbert and Guy's unfinished script instead.

Chapter Twenty-One

"Damn the woman," Gilbert said hanging up the telephone receiver. He was already prepared for his morning swim when Jake breezed through the kitchen on his way to work. "That was your Miss Dawlish. Apparently, there's been some glitch about who's going to direct the sequel."

"Did she give a reason why?" Jake asked.

"No, but that's how it goes. One minute a movie is all full-steam ahead and then, before you know it, the project's folded. If you take my advice, Jake, you'll make a run for it back to Fort Laverne," Gilbert said irritably, brandishing the bread knife before slicing a loaf to make toast. "You can't go off to work without eating anything, Jake."

"There's no time, Gil. I've a bus to catch."

"That Dawlish woman said Scott will be arriving here shortly to pick up the reels. Why not wait and get a lift back with him into the studio?" Gilbert said.

Although it made sense, it was the very last thing Jake wanted to happen. "I can't take that chance. Scott might not be delivering them to her at the office."

"Wesley can run you in. Anything's better than the 'Sardine Run' at this hour. The bus will be packed. I've done it, trust me. Garlic breath, musty clothing and a heady mix of cheap perfume are not the best of travelling companions."

Until Gilbert mentioned it, the prospect of being crushed into an airless bus for the best part of an hour, made him think again. Maybe having Wesley run him into the studio on his scooter was an offer too good to refuse.

After eating a quick breakfast to satisfy Gilbert he wouldn't die from starvation, Jake was about to set off on the back of Wesley's scooter when Scott's truck pulled up at the gate to collect the reels of film. After that, there was no alternative other than to go with him in the pickup.

Neither of them wanted to be the first to break the silence, and so they travelled most of the way without saying a word, until Jake said: "I gather there's a conflict over the choice of director to make the sequel?" He indicated the reels of returned film between them on the seat.

"I didn't hear anything about that. Only that Adelaide Williams had a nasty fall at her place yesterday."

"I'm sorry to hear it. Was it bad?"

"I'm not sure. Madge didn't say, only that she won't be at work for a few days," Scott said, and the blanket of silence descended between them again until they were held up at the lights, not far from their destination.

"How did it go last night?" Jake asked.

"I got paid, that's all you need to know. Look I'm sorry about turning up like that at Miller's place. I didn't have any time to get back to my digs and change."

"I'm sure he wouldn't mind. Aren't you working here today?" he asked.

Scott pulled up at the studio gate just slightly ahead of a coach that began disgorging the noisy workforce.

"There's talk of something happening later on in the week, but nothing definite," he said as Jake got out of the cab.

"Well, thanks for the ride. I hope it wasn't too far out of your way?"

"Not a bit," Scott responded, revving the engine as though he was impatient to be off.

"By the way," Jake said, as Scott put the truck in gear, "do you remember I told you about that guy who helped bring me up on the ranch back in Fort Laverne?"

"Gilbert? Why, have you got a lead on his whereabouts?" Scott asked, unable to quell his interest.

"Well, actually, you just left him. Gilbert's real name is Jon Miller." As Jake spoke, the clock on the gatehouse chimed 7 o'clock, prompting him to make a quick dash to get through the gate ahead of the crowd, as each one of them would need to show their pass.

"Wait, you can't just say that and leave," Scott called after him, but Jake was already lost amongst the throng of employees passing through the security gate.

Jake saw nothing of Marjory Dawlish that day or the next. Therefore he had nothing to report back to Gilbert about the possible change of director.

When he got to the hacienda on the second night, Jake could only comment on the canteen gossip about the injuries Adelaide Williams had sustained, which seemed to get more speculative as little new information emerged. She and Marjory Dawlish were rumoured to be joined at the hip on a mystery sequel somewhere away from the studio. As Jake never went anywhere without wearing the battered hat and spectacles, he seemed to be just another scruffy technician waiting to be served, and with whom the canteen staff could air the most recent studio gossip.

Both evenings, after they had eaten, Jake and Gilbert immersed themselves going through the script, which needed little improvement. It was a passionate and heartrending story of love and loss. It repeatedly brought goose bumps along Jake's arms, as Gilbert coached him in understanding the lead character who had died tragically at the conclusion of the original movie, and who now grappled to find solace in his distressing resurrection.

There were long conversations about the way Guy Maddox would have portrayed that situation had he lived, amongst these, Jake asked Gilbert to enlighten him about a comment he'd made some time earlier.

"You've told me that you and Guy got along together from the first moment you met. Why would you say that if Guy was your half-brother?"

"For the first eighteen years of my life, I didn't know Guy existed. He was illegitimate and I wasn't, and because my father was a bone-headed jerk, he refused to acknowledge either Guy or his mother, Sophia Maddox."

"So that's why your names are different?"

"Sophia was a French Canadian, living in Quebec. It was years

319

before I had any inkling about their existence."

"What was your father doing in Canada if you lived in New Mexico?"

"At the time, my old man was on the lookout for investors to construct a dam in the valley beyond Fort Laverne."

"I thought the idea of creating a lake to build a luxury resort around was just folklore?"

"Not a bit of it; the old man was convinced it would make him and the investors into millionaires. He went to Quebec to sell off some railway property he owned over there to finance his investment. He needed a quick sale to complete the building work on the Grand Hotel, expecting the hotel would bring in a good return once he got the building completed in time for the proposed railroad between Fort Laverne and Santa Rowena. What he, the rail barons, and the investors didn't foresee, was the Navajo council rejecting their plans to bring a railway through their reservation."

"Your father was a part of that?"

"It was a greed-fuelled notion from the start, and if it had gone ahead, the track would have divided that narrow passage of land in the canyon, that so-called reservation; the Navajos could barely survive on that strip of land back then, so who could blame the tribe elders for turning down their scheming proposal? When that project fell apart, my father abandoned all work on the hotel. Not long after that he died, then a few years later your pa took the tenancy over."

"So, Gil, if you didn't know you had a brother, how did you actually meet?"

"It happened purely by chance. We were both in Santa Barbara to sign up for a place at Madam Thelma's Academy for Speech and Drama."

Gilbert smiled at the sound of his deep voice, obviously relishing every syllable. Had it not been for that great change in Gilbert's voice, Jake would never have asked: "An academy for speech and drama? What was it you were hoping to do on stage?"

"It wasn't the prospect of an acting career which made me enrol. I thought, or rather I hoped, there was a remote chance of my voice breaking with proper coaching. At the time, Madam Thelma was regarded as the very best voice coach and, for a time, I believed the woman genuinely thought she could help me. But in the end, she couldn't do anything. She recommended that I return home as soon as I could, to save what cash I had left, and get myself an office job close to home..." Gilbert paused. Jake didn't speak. "Fate took a hand, I suppose. Guy and I became acquainted during my last week in town. Like me, he was working as a waiter in a bistro, to earn some cash. We got talking, and he learnt I was returning to Fort Laverne. Guy knew his father's name was Miller, and also the town where he lived. But even so, it was a shock to discover that my father had actually sired us both."

"So why would a Canadian travel so far to wait on tables in Santa Barbara?"

"Guy needed to earn cash to pay Madam Thelma. He had to because her fees were so high. Guy was there to get rid of his French accent, so that he could audition for the stage. What was so great about him was that he never once ridiculed me about the pitch of my voice. That alone would have endeared me to him for life, but to discover that we were related came as a huge bonus."

Jake poured out more coffee. "So how did you both get into the movies? Particularly you, if you were so against doing anything like that? You were on your way back home."

"Madam Thelma's Academy was a big draw for a lot of theatrical agents. We were both scouted in the bistro, and moved to Hollywood in the summer of 1924. To begin with, because the movies back then were silent, I did better, getting cast in bit parts and then I got my big break in *The Venetian Mask* for the Silver Lake Studios. It was crazy, because Guy was the best-looking man to arrive in Hollywood in years and yet that seemed to go against him. He could get no work in this godforsaken town, not even as a waiter."

"But why would his looks hold him back? I'd have thought it would be completely the opposite."

"You would think so, wouldn't you? Not in his case. The motion picture industry is a money-making machine. Most of the major studios had invested heavily in promoting their own leading actors. The studio bosses were against employing Guy in case he damaged the careers of some of their major stars."

"But, how could an unknown like Guy Maddox be a challenge to their box office stars?"

"Apart from his extraordinary looks, he could not only act convincingly, but was also a gifted and athletic dancer. Word gets around this city like a forest fire. You can imagine the sensation he created when he first arrived here, and the interest some of the reporters took when his career was blanked not only by the studios but all the casting agencies. Guy couldn't get any work. And he wouldn't accept any handouts, not even from me, and God knows I tried."

"Then how did he survive?" Jake asked.

"He did what most out of work actors of his generation did when they couldn't get a job. He hired himself out as a dance instructor. What I didn't know was that Guy was a great gymnast with a talent for creating inventive moves into any dance. His version of the tango, as you've been witness to on the screen, was introduced with great dramatic effect, especially when he partnered Alicia Cordova in the tango he composed for that screen test. The rest you know."

"Did Guy compose the music on the recording you gave me in Fort Laverne?" Jake asked.

"He did." Gilbert beamed with immense pride. "I knew you'd like that."

"Like doesn't even come close. It is electrifying. I love that music. Anyone who sees your movie, Gil, couldn't help but do otherwise," Jake said, wondering if he should go on, seeing tears welling up in Gilbert's eyes. "It was magical for me to watch that piece of music being so beautifully integrated into the dance. I couldn't get the tune out of my head for days after. I still can't. What puzzles me is why you would part with such a treasured item by entrusting it into my care."

Gilbert laughed. "Actually, I do have another copy of the record. I'm not that much of a dope."

When Jake arrived at the studios the following day, he found a scrawled note from Adelaide Williams had been left on the work table in the Projection Room where he couldn't fail to see it. In the note, she asked him to look over the pages she'd sent over. Underneath the note, was a typed synopsis for a new screenplay entitled *Mail Order Murder*.

There was something vaguely familiar about the opening, but within one minute he was revolted by the sentimentality oozing like treacle from the pages. When he came across the name of Xavier Gérard, he felt physically sick, realising this turgid, botched attempt at creating a sequel to the Guy Maddox movie violated every subtle nuance and creative twist in the characters Gilbert had brought onto the screen in the original movie.

After reading the uninspiring synopsis, his opinion of it was that it was fit only for burning – it was a diabolically poor substitute for Gilbert's script of *The Return of Xavier Gérard*. It was clear this was nothing more than a third-rate attempt to cash in on the intended release of the original movie, a bewitching story that had been created so carefully on screen. His thoughts were disrupted by the harsh jangling of the internal phone. When he picked up the receiver, a nasal twang summoned him to Adelaide Williams office.

On his arrival, the secretary informed him that her boss had returned from sick leave for a few hours, and wanted to speak with him in her office as soon as he had read the pages of the synopsis.

Even in the poor light filtering through the almost closed blinds, Jake could tell the woman was suffering from her many injuries. He thought that she must be desperate to have bothered coming into the office at all. Although she was wearing sunglasses, he could see the yellowed bruises that spread out from beneath them. Her cheek was swollen and what couldn't be covered completely by a layer of thick make-up was severe bruising around her throat. Nor had it been possible to disguise her swollen and cut lips.

With the draught created by Jake closing the door, a wooden crutch that had been leaning against the wall slipped over and crashed noisily against a metal filing cabinet. Adelaide Williams almost jumped out of her skin.

"Can I get you a painkiller, Miss Williams?" Jake asked, as he propped the crutch where it wouldn't fall over again, and where she could easily reach it.

"A whisky would be preferable," she said, painfully, through swollen lips, where he saw that one of her teeth had been broken.

"I'm sure it would, Miss Williams, but you're in a lot of pain, so I think a painkiller would be better." Without waiting for a response, Jake went through to the private bathroom suite where he found the bottle he needed, and returned to her desk with a tumbler of water and two aspirin.

"Thank you, darling, I'm more grateful for these than you could ever imagine. You really are very sweet." Adelaide Williams swallowed the tablets gratefully.

"You should be at home, Miss Williams," he said, wondering why she had been allowed to get out of bed, let alone come into work.

"I have unfinished business in need of my attention."

"Is there anything I can do to help?"

"Yes, there is, and that is precisely the reason you were asked to my office."

"I see. So was it about this?" Jake asked, laying the synopsis on her desk.

"Have you read it?" She tried to stand, but thought better of it and slumped back into the chair.

"You shouldn't be at work today, Miss Williams. Surely your doctor has advised you against it?"

"I haven't seen a doctor. It was only a tumble in the garden."

"Really, someone mentioned you fell down the stairs?"

"No, I tripped and fell in the garden," she insisted.

Jake was more concerned with her injuries than getting into a lengthy conversation about the tripe he had been required to read. "If you don't mind going in my truck, I can take you into the hospital." Jake offered, but she persisted with the earlier conversation.

"I can't go anywhere, not until this situation has been

resolved," Miss Williams said, trying to get more comfortable in the high-backed office chair.

"We can talk about whatever you want on our way to the hospital, Miss Williams," Jake persisted.

"Oh, very well, but I insist you drive my car," she said, sliding the keys across the table towards him.

"I came in by cab. Hopefully, my car is in the car park where I left it. I couldn't have driven home, not after that fall," she said.

She realised that Jake had picked up on her blunder. However, she didn't make any further comments, and allowed him to assist her to her car and drive her to the nearby hospital.

Jake waited with her for almost three hours until she was attended by a Norwegian intern who was not much older than he was. He then waited for another hour before she was wheeled back to the waiting room. Once the two men had Adelaide Williams settled in the car, the intern took Jake aside and apologised for the long delay, insisting that X-rays had been necessary, given the extent of her injuries.

"I have given your mother a sedative," the doctor said. "Because of that she is going to be drowsy for some time, but hopefully that will induce the sleep she is so badly in need of. I'm sure I don't have to tell you that under no circumstances should Mrs Stanford be left unattended overnight."

"I'm sorry," Jake said with some confusion. "Her name is Adelaide Williams, not Stanford."

"My apologies, I stand corrected. Your mother was suffering acute pain when she was admitted. I administered a light dose of morphine to ease her before we took down her notes. She was registered with this hospital a few years ago," he said, checking the document. "Adelaide. That's what was written down here on her medical file," he said, flicking through earlier notes, until he found the reference he was looking for. "Ah yes, I'm sorry. I mistook her maiden name for that of her marital one. Ask her to make the necessary changes to the medical card she carries with her when she's feeling up to it." He amended the notes in the file. "Have you any idea who did this to her?"

"No, none at all, all I was told this morning that she had taken a bad tumble in the garden a few days ago."

"Her injuries are from no fall, I can assure you of that, sir. Your mother suffered a severe beating a few days ago. It's as well you brought her in here today and had her checked over. I've put stitches into three of the nasty gashes on her back and hip. Those might well have turned septic."

"But she will recover?" Jake asked, expressing his concern.

"The injuries she has sustained will heal soon enough but I can't be as optimistic for her mental state. Whoever gave her that beating should be reported to the court."

"Did she give you any idea who it was?"

"She denied that anyone else was involved, and insists this happened when she fell."

"Surely, if you're a doctor here, there must be some leverage you could put on her to say who it was?"

"I'm not a doctor, sir, I'm an intern. I know those injuries she's sustained could never have been caused through a fall. I can put that into my report, but without the name of her assailant I can't do anything more." The intern handed Jake a business card. "If she does mention the person responsible, please give me a call."

Adelaide Williams directed Jake through a maze of streets to the exclusive residential area of Bel Air.

"Is there someone at home who can take care of you?" Jake asked. He turned off the road into a sweeping avenue of Cyprus trees, but got no response from his passenger who was now sound asleep in the back seat.

The driveway opened out onto high ground with a million-dollar view of the glistening ocean. When he pulled up beside the mausoleum of what was her home it seemed, on closer inspection, in desperate need of renovation and in danger of being reduced to a heap of rubble by the next big earthquake.

Jake woke her as gently as he could. "Is there anyone here who can help you, Miss Williams?" Jake asked, repeating his earlier question.

"Unfortunately there is not. My butler is no longer employed here."

"If you have a contact number for him, I could make a call and ask him to come over," Jake suggested.

"He is no longer available, otherwise I would give you his number gladly. He's now in England." Tears were welling up as she spoke.

Jake offered a handkerchief which she took gladly, before helping her into the building and, despite all her protestations, he insisted on carrying her up the grand staircase she could never have climbed on her own. Once on the landing, he carried her through a massive archway which gave access to the door. Jake switched on a light and surveyed the small but modern interior of her apartment.

"This is very different to what I expected from the outside," he said, smiling gently.

"It's a home for me." She bit down on her lip to prevent herself from crying out when she attempted to get to her feet again, and fell back into the chair.

"Let me help you," Jake said, attempting to get her to stand again, but she wouldn't.

"You can't," she answered tearfully.

"Please, you can't manage alone. You must allow me to help you."

"How can you? I need the bathroom."

"I'll help you to the door. Just tell me where it is. I'll wait outside until you call for me."

"I don't want you carrying me again." She was emphatic.

"That wasn't my intention. Not after climbing those killer stairs." He sounded a lot more jovial than he felt, but he was well rewarded by her glimmer of a smile between those misshapen, tortured lips in a seemingly bloodless face.

Offering little resistance, Adelaide allowed Jake to assist her through the neatly furnished, comfortable room and into a small corridor where she asked him to wait for her. But, because his back was aching, he wandered back through the living room and gazed out at the staggering view from what had once been a palatial mansion.

When he'd helped her back into a comfortable chair, Jake asked if he could make a short telephone call to Gilbert to say that everything was fine but not to expect him back that evening. When Jake asked, contrary to what he expected, a glazed look of panic came into her eyes.

"You can't stay here. No one can. It isn't allowed." Adelaide Williams exclaimed, her voice verging on hysteria.

Jake was completely taken aback by her reaction but, nevertheless, based on her frail condition, he reassured her that, on the advice from the hospital, someone had to stay with her overnight. If not him, it would have to be someone else.

"I didn't mean to alarm you, Miss Williams, but the intern was adamant that you shouldn't be left alone this evening. If you're unhappy with me staying here, I can wait around until someone else arrives?" Glancing at the clock, he wondered if she would be able to get anyone over to stay at such short notice.

Having a similar thought in mind she said, "I would ask you to call Marjory, but it's getting rather dark out."

"Gil will worry if I don't make that call home. I really don't mind staying over."

She reluctantly agreed, but then suddenly asked, "Is Gilbert your lover?"

"No, he damned well isn't," Jake protested vehemently. "He virtually brought me up. It was Gilbert who first got me an interest in the movies. He lives just out of town. I'm staying with him temporarily until I can get a place of my own."

"I do apologise." She spoke with such sincerity that it pained him for having shouted.

"I am the one who should apologise. I guess I'm just not used to the way people speak their mind in California."

"It's been a hard day for us both, I think," Adelaide said, resuming some of her earlier authority. "I think what we both need is a very large drink."

"Alcohol would really be unwise for you, Miss Williams, since you're on some strong medication," Jake blurted out the warning, which brought back the glimmer of a smile.

"I thank you for your concern, Jake, but what I was offering was a cup of imported camomile tea. I find it very relaxing, as I'm sure you will too."

For some time they sat opposite each other in silence, although the way she stared at him was discomforting. She eventually spoke.

"I once saw Guy Maddox at the studios, on my seventeenth birthday."

That made Adelaide Williams no more than forty-two years old, which came as a shock to Jake, having thought that she was considerably older. On the bookshelf behind her, in a plain silver frame, was a photograph of Adelaide Williams on the arm of a young man at a glittering Hollywood occasion.

"Would you like me to call the man in the photograph and ask him to come over?"

"He was only my escort for the Awards evening, nothing more than that."

She allowed Jake to assist her into her bedroom, stifling her groans of pain and embarrassment, as he helped her remove her outer clothing.

"The couch in the sitting room pulls out into a bed if you insist on staying," she said wearily, as helped her into the bed.

"Thanks. I'm going to leave the door ajar so I can hear you call out if you need anything in the night."

"I didn't expect this kindness, not from anyone." She seemed tearful.

"Think no more of it. It's the least I can do. Is there anyone I can call that can be with you after I leave in the morning?" he asked, before switching out the light.

"There's no one," she said drowsily, but then sat bolt upright in the bed as a thought took hold. "If I'm not up before you leave in the morning, I'd be grateful if you would tidy the bed back into the couch, and please make sure that you leave no evidence that you stayed over tonight. He mustn't know anyone was here, and in particular, you."

Once Jake had prepared his bed, he examined the framed photograph under the light. It had been taken some time in the past when Adelaide was young and undeniably pretty. Her fresh, enigmatic features had no trace of the disfiguring scar she now tried so hard to disguise beneath make-up. He wondered if the photograph had been taken at an Academy Awards ceremony. It must have been taken at least twenty years earlier; he smiled when he contemplated that her paid escort for that evening would have been someone like Scott.

When he scrutinised the face of her companion, to his astonishment, he realised he was staring at Wesley, Gilbert's manservant. It was clear that Adelaide was enthralled at being escorted by a mature and good-looking man such as Wesley. Strangely though, in this photograph, Wesley would have been aged no more than thirty-five, perhaps even younger. Incredibly, although Adelaide Williams had aged, perhaps more rapidly than most, Wesley didn't look a day older in the photograph than he did today.

Above the mantelpiece was a large oil painting on canvas, depicting a woman and child reclining on the window seat at a grand country house. There was no doubt in his mind that the child was Adelaide in the arms of an attractive woman, who, he assumed, was her mother.

From his low position on the pull-out bed as he leaned over to switch off the lamp, he could see painstaking repairs that had been made to the canvas, which, except from his obscure viewpoint, successfully hid the vicious slashes from some time in the past.

Adelaide's terrified screams roused Jake from a deep sleep, and he was out of bed in an instant, afraid that he would find her beating off an intruder; instead, he found her threshing about under the bedcovers reliving a vivid nightmare. She was deeply asleep. Jake clicked on the light so that she wouldn't be alarmed when she woke. As there was little hope of getting back to sleep, he poured himself an iced tea from a jug in the refrigerator, and sat in the darkened living room in a comfortable chair and gazed out across the ocean. In the breaking light, he thought over the recent events, ever more sure that he had no desire to remain in this crazy city any longer than was necessary.

An hour later, he tapped lightly on Adelaide's door until he heard a movement inside. At her request, he helped her into the living room that was now filled with the warming light of dawn. He made them both a glass of her camomile tea, and sat in comparative silence watching a sailboat glide across the shimmering orb of the sun as it lifted above the horizon.

Over breakfast, when they were both dressed, he asked:" The portrait over the mantelpiece, is it of you and your mother?"

"Yes, it is. That's the only likeness I have of her."

"She's lovely," Jake said, with genuine admiration.

"Isn't she just too divine for words? Mother was the actress, Valerie Costello. In her day, Valerie was regarded as a great beauty when she first arrived in Hollywood." Her voice then hardened as she continued. "Unfortunately for her those features were her downfall. My father took a fancy to her and had to possess her for himself, which he did."

"Why do you say that?"

"Because he had an eye for any young starlet that came to this city in search of a career; the more talented they were, the harder they got chased. That is, until he got what he was after. I think he did genuinely care for my mother, in the beginning, and that's why he married her. More is the pity. It was the other girls who got off lightly, not having been served with a life sentence."

"Would you like me to contact her for you?"

"Valerie is dead. She was attacked by an intruder at the house. This happened when my father was supposedly away on a business meeting. She never regained consciousness, and died from her injuries a week later."

"That's terrible. Was the intruder ever caught?"

"No, he never was, but now I'm older, I have my suspicions." She spoke as if to herself, not acknowledging that Jake would have heard.

Before Jake left for the studio, he put everything away just as she directed, leaving no trace that anyone had stayed there overnight.

He drove to the studio in Adelaide's car.

Throughout that working day, Jake saw nothing of either Scott or Marjory Dawlish.

When he'd finished work, he placed a call to Gilbert, who wasn't available, and so he left a message with Wesley that he wouldn't be home again that evening. When the manservant asked, Jake took care not to mention where he was staying.

Because he didn't have much cash, Jake called at a local market and bought a few supplies and a bunch of fresh flowers before making his way back to the crumbling mansion in the ridiculously luxurious area of Bel Air. After getting lost a few times on the way, he eventually turned Adelaide's expensive car into the drive.

It took a while, but eventually a shocked and wary Adelaide received him at the door with a dustpan and brush in her hand.

"You came back. I didn't expect you," she said, flustered. There was a new bruised swelling on her forehead, and a fresh cut on her cheek.

"I'm sorry. Didn't I say I would come back?"

"Yes, you did, but I didn't expect you would." She tried to avert her face when she saw that he was inspecting the new injuries. "I've been having great difficulty getting about on these crutches. I fell."

"Then that just proves what I said earlier. You shouldn't be here on your own, not in your condition. Anything could happen."

"What have you brought?" she asked, in a successful attempt to deflect any more of the interrogation by allowing him inside, taking more notice of the flowers than of the paper bag he was carrying.

"I brought along a few supplies for the week, just in case you didn't have enough in," he said, taking the groceries into the kitchen. "I got enough to make dinner for us both."

"What, for the two of us?"

"Sure, unless you're expecting someone else, in which case, I'll make myself scarce."

There was an empty whisky bottle, and a partially drained glass on the worktop. Before she could prevent him from going into the living room, Jake went inside with the vase of flowers, and saw the destruction. The portrait of Adelaide and her mother had been wrenched off the wall and dumped against the open grate. The broken gilded frame had been used to shatter the collection of porcelain ornaments she'd carefully displayed on the shelf beneath it.

Although the wall safe, previously hidden behind the painting, had been jemmied, gouged, and battered, it was still unopened. An antique chair had been smashed hard against a splintered standard lamp, both of which were irreparable. The shade from the lamp had been crushed almost beyond recognition and wedged into what remained of a palm, lurching over in the remains of an oriental jardinière in the far corner, which Jake had admired the previous evening. Had the destruction of Adelaide's living room not been so tragic, it would have seemed almost farcical.

The silence that followed the unasked question hung like a lead shield between the two of them. Jake did his best to restore a semblance of order to the room. He carefully detached the portrait of her mother from the remaining frame. Luckily, the only harm to the canvas was a small tear in the lower corner. Otherwise, apart from a nasty coating of grey ash from the grate, the painting was in good order.

"Why would anyone in their right mind do this?" Jake asked, assisting Adelaide into the seat beside him to examine the painting.

"This is what he does when he doesn't get his own way."

"Who are we talking about here?"

"That twisted bastard I have of a father, who else?"

"What would possess someone to do something like this?" Jake asked, wondering if it was connected to his having stayed there overnight, but she said nothing.

He collected a few things he needed from the bathroom. "I should never have left you alone today. There should have been someone here to protect you."

She allowed him gently to bathe the fresh cuts on her face and apply some antiseptic ointment.

"It's better that you weren't here," Adelaide said, bitterly. "I would hate to think that you, of all people, would end up like this, or even worse. Any future you might have in movies would be ruined forever. Your life would be all washed-up and going nowhere, just like mine has been for all of these years."

"Was it your father who also did this to you?" he asked, lightly touching the old scarring on her face.

"Who else but that vicious animal? You must have suspected by now that Maurice Stanford is my father."

"I thought you might have been related from the mix up of your name at the hospital. What I can't understand is why a father would inflict something like this on his own daughter. It's unthinkable."

"His defence for doing this was to say that I got in the way, trying to defend mother from the attack." She realised what she had unintentionally revealed. "Please forget I said anything, Jake. I lied in my statement to the police."

"Don't worry, my lips are sealed," Jake said, more calmly than he felt. He didn't want to burden Adelaide Williams with the fury welling up inside him. Instead, he propped up the painting where it was safe and where she could see it clearly, before he carried on clearing up the mess as best he could.

Before he went into the kitchen to prepare the meal, Jake switched on the undamaged radiogram and placed a well-played LP onto the turntable– it was obviously a favourite recording – by a velvet-voiced female vocalist crooning her way through the delectable words and music of Cole Porter.

It was only after they had eaten that Jake broached the subject again. This time he was more specific, and asked: "Would any of this attack be connected to me? Was it because I didn't agree to him directing the sequel?"

"It was, but it was also about me, because I had failed to convince you."

Hearing this posed a real dilemma for Jake. Primarily because he wanted to protect her from any repeat attack he said: "If I agree to Maurice Stanford's demands, will that prevent him from making another repeat of this? If so, then I'll do what he asks, but only on the condition he uses Gilbert's screenplay."

"I assume that your friend Gilbert is acquainted with Jon Miller?"

"Yes, I suppose he is."

"You suppose?"

"When *The Return of Xavier Gérard* was in the final stages of filming, they came up with the idea of a sequel and wrote the screenplay together. I'd prefer not to say any more about this until I've spoken with Gilbert about the possibility of not having Jon Miller direct."

When Jake drove away from the house the following morning, he was determined that Maurice Stanford would pay for his involvement in the death of Guy Maddox and, quite possibly, for that of Adelaide's mother too.

Jake called Gilbert from the studio, saying he might not return to the hacienda again that evening. He didn't give any reason why, and Gilbert didn't ask. Twice during the day Jake was harassed by Marjory Dawlish, urging him to sign the contract. Both times he managed to avoid responding to her questioning, particularly when she asked why he hadn't been home with Jon Miller for the past two nights, but only because he didn't want to involve Adelaide Williams.

"I've called his number to make contact with you on both nights. I thought you were lodging there?" she said peevishly.

"I am, but not at the moment," Jake said wearily, wishing that she would go away and stop prying into his life.

"Then it's fortunate for us both that Adelaide is off work at the moment, otherwise the entire project would grind to a halt. Subterfuge doesn't come to you naturally, Jake. You need to work at it more. By the way, how is my brother?" she asked.

"I wouldn't know, Miss Dawlish. I haven't seen him recently."

Jake's reply brought an end to the conversation.

Chapter Twenty-Two

That same evening Jake was driving through the elaborate iron gates to Adelaide's home when, rounding a blind corner of the drive, he narrowly avoided colliding with a delivery van.

"Hey pal, d' you know if anyone lives back here?" the driver asked, once apologies had been exchanged. "I've been ringing the bell, but no one came to the door."

"Sure, the name's Williams. You probably got no answer because she's on crutches. It's quite a way to the front door."

"Did you say Williams? That's not the name I've got a delivery for," the driver said, referring to a sheaf of paperwork.

"You might find her listed under the name Stanford. It could be either. She uses both in her profession," Jake explained.

"Are you here to see Miss Stanford?" he asked, anxiously checking his watch. "I'd normally call back later, but the other driver's off sick and I've got too much to deliver today. If you're going up to the house, would you mind dropping this off for me?"

"Sure, I can sign for it," Jake said, and added his signature to a list of others.

The delivery man took a large cardboard container from the van, which had been dispatched from a theatrical costumier in Santa Monica.

Jake laughed. "A fancy-dress costume is the last thing this lady needs right now."

"Well, it's signed for now, pal. I can't take it back to the warehouse; besides, it's already been paid for."

"What's this bash in aid of?"

"I'm not sure, only that it's a masked ball. You know the sort of thing: big hair and crazy frocks. If you ask me, it's just another mad spending spree for movie stars with nothing better to waste their dollars on." he said caustically. "It's gonna be one humdinger of an

336

event. I've delivered three van loads of this stuff today, and there's a ton more back at the warehouse that I've now got to deliver on my own before the weekend," he grumbled, and got back into the cab.

"Well, good luck with it anyway," Jake said.

"That's one hell of a place back there. It spooked me out when I first saw it. Good luck, pal, I'm sure glad it's gonna be you and not me going inside there." He gave a cheery wave and roared off round the sharp bend in the drive, disappearing in a cloud of dust and exhaust fumes.

Jake was pleased by the way Adelaide's authoritative attitude towards him had mellowed after their return from the hospital, appreciating the way he had managed to get her apartment back into a semblance of order. He had also made a call to Gilbert for his recommendation of a restorer of fine art, and arranged to have the painting of Adelaide's mother collected by an Italian company the following day.

As he waited for Adelaide to answer the door, Jake understood how the delivery man would have assumed that no one lived there.

"Did you pass anyone on the way here, Jake? Someone was hammering on the front door for an eternity before I got there. I just hope that it wasn't the art restorer you've arranged."

"They won't come for the painting until tomorrow afternoon, around three o'clock. Their collection service couldn't do it any sooner."

"Then who on earth could that caller have been?"

"It's no mystery, Miss Williams. I met the van on the drive with a delivery from a theatrical costumier. I signed for it." Jake placed the box on the kitchen table. "He said it was pre-ordered and already paid for." Adelaide seemed to be confused ."He said it was for a masked ball."

"Hell and damnation! I'd forgotten all about him arranging for another of his bloody freak shows. Why in hell's name my father chooses to arrange these events for that incestuous band of yes-men is beyond me. They hang on his every word, including the film crew. I can't imagine why they never want to celebrate the end of his movies."

"Surely you won't consider going to this function, Miss Williams?"

"I must, otherwise he will be even more insufferable. All the cast and crew members are expected to be there. No exceptions. No excuses."

"That's bordering on dictatorship. Not everyone can go surely?"

"Although he's no longer the head of Silver Lake Studios, he still holds considerable sway in the industry. He could destroy even an established career with a few words in a single phone call, whether it be true or not."

"He'd go that far?"

"That, and worse," she said vehemently.

"Even so, no one's going to expect you to attend a fancy-dress ball on crutches?" he said.

She began unpacking the box to reveal a pirate costume, a stuffed parrot, and a wooden leg. If the contents hadn't been so cruelly chosen, Jake would have laughed.

"You see what a bloody monster he is." She hurled the stuffed bird at the wall, giving vent to her frustration. "Who else would find this funny?" she screamed at the top of her voice, and Jake was thankful that he hadn't given in to laughing.

Much against her demands for a large Scotch, Jake made her a camomile tea.

"Where is the whisky I asked for?" She scowled. "I'll need to get through a whole bottle before I attend this farcical ball."

"You're not really considering going?"

"What choice do I have?"

"Plenty, I'd say."

"Dear boy, how naive you are. There is never a choice. You have absolutely no idea what the consequences would be if I didn't attend."

It was easy to see that she was dreading the prospect, and Jake wanted to do whatever he could to ease her fear.

"Well, if you are going you must let me escort you, in case you might be in need of some moral support."

Adelaide Williams gratefully accepted his offer.

"But Jake, you mustn't stay here this evening. I must be here on my own. My stepmother rang through earlier, warning me that my father intends coming over here this evening. He mustn't find you here."

"What do you take me for? I can't leave you alone with that animal."

"But you must. You don't understand the implications. You're the image of Guy Maddox, and my father loathed him. I fear for your safety too, Jake. If you agree to go ahead and work with him on the sequel that he wants to direct, at least you'd have the security of being on set with a film crew. It's too risky for him to see you here with me."

"Why did he hate Guy so much?"

"I can't go into that now. I need you to get away from here before he arrives."

"How can you hope to protect yourself if he attacks you again?" Jake asked, but her mind was made up.

"He is probably calling by to make sure that I attend that blasted function," Adelaide said, standing unsteadily on her crutches. "When he sees I've a problem walking, it'll make sense even to him that I'm engaging an escort. He won't be seen in the company of men who hire themselves out for an evening, so he'll keep well away." She walked with some difficulty to where her mother's portrait had been hung, which now exposed a safe behind. From this she removed a battered tin box containing a small pistol. It brought the briefest smile to her lips. "The derringer is my protection for this evening, so there is no need for you to worry, my dear boy. The only things that my father fears are death and retribution, so this is the perfect instrument to keep him at bay."

"Is it loaded?"

"Of course, and yes, I am prepared to use it, if necessary, to defend myself. I do know how to use it. I wouldn't kill him. A flesh wound would suffice as a painful warning. When his inevitable assassination happens, I shall leave that in the capable hands of someone else," she said coolly. "Can I trust you to look after something very important until I can get another safe installed?" She removed a locked metal box from amongst the many jewellery boxes piled in there.

"Of course you can."

"I'm sure there's some dark secret in here connected to my father. But now I can't keep it hidden in my safe, knowing that he would eventually find it."

"But why would you hand this over to me for safekeeping, Miss Williams? You hardly know me."

"Under different circumstances I wouldn't need to ask you or anyone for help. For years, William, our butler, took care of mother and me after one of my father's irrational rages, but now that he's gone, I need someone I can trust to take his place."

"But why me, Miss Williams, you know nothing at all about me?"

"I appreciate why you question my motives, and to be perfectly frank, after working for so many years in such an insidious industry, I hope that I am a better judge of character than I might have been otherwise."

"But even so, Miss Williams, I would feel uncomfortable being entrusted with something of your late mother's that you value."

"There is no one else I can ask, Jake. Valerie's box must be kept out his hands."

"Then I will keep it safe. However, I would strongly suggest that you arrange for a safety deposit box at your bank. Until then, I would be happy to do as you ask."

"As soon as I'm feeling better, then I will do exactly that, but before that can happen, I need this box opened. There must be some incriminating information inside which I can use against my father. After the last beating I took I don't think I could survive another. I need to protect myself. The only way I can do that is by getting information on something rotten he's been involved with and use that against him." Adelaide said, urging Jake and the strongbox towards the door. "I'm hoping that the answer to my prayers will be in that box. What I want is for you to open it."

"I honestly want to help you Miss Williams. I will take the box with me, but you should open it yourself."

"I don't have the combination for the lock, and you are a man with initiative."

"It seems like prying," Jake said uncomfortably, wishing that she hadn't asked.

"Not if I've asked you to do this as a favour to me," she said, enclosing her hands gently round his as he held the box. "Because of Valerie's infatuation with Guy Maddox, I suspect there might be something inside, linked with his death. Surely that alone must be an incentive?"

"I might look like him, Miss Williams, but that's where it ends, I can assure you. There is absolutely no connection between us, none whatsoever."

Jake felt sick to his stomach. He couldn't believe that a dead man continued to infiltrate more and more into his life, and he needed it to end before he went mad.

"You must tell me who this box belongs to if it isn't yours," he said, suspicious of her insistence that he, and not a locksmith, should open a box that obviously belonged to someone else.

"I would never ask you to tamper with something that didn't belong to me, Jake. This box was my mother's, which she kept hidden. I believe the contents of this box are the reason why an intruder broke into our house all those years ago and brutally assaulted her. Whoever the man was, he was after something in particular, and I'm convinced it must have been what is inside this box."

"It could just have been a routine burglary that went wrong," Jake said.

"I think that very unlikely. This box is the only item of mother's belongings that was never tampered with on that dreadful night, and that was only because mother kept it well hidden. I only came across it by accident a few weeks ago, concealed inside the window seat. I'd no idea anything was in there. The police investigation came up with no explanation why it was only her bedroom and sitting room in her private apartment that got ransacked, and nothing was taken. Whoever it was went too far in his efforts to make mother talk. She never recovered from that dreadful beating."

Once in his cab, Jake examined the sturdy metal box carefully. In the poor light he noticed a small engraved brass plate under the folding handle. When he examined this more closely his blood ran cold as he identified the inscribed name as "Eugene Maxwell, MD".

Until he saw Dr Maxwell's name, Jake had thought it unlikely that the contents of the box would be connected with Guy Maddox. But that was a name that seemed to crop up at every twist and turn: a name that seemingly had influenced the lives of everyone who knew him. Jake resolved to try and lay the ghost of this man to rest, once and for all, and he thought the best place to begin would be to visit the place where he was buried.

Once Jake had examined the street map of Los Angeles, and located the Catholic cemetery in Santa Monica where Guy Maddox was supposedly buried, he drove directly to the churchyard. After a long search he came upon two plain headstones cut from grey slate. They were positioned a distance away from the main burial ground, alongside a low wall and sheltered by the overhanging boughs of an ancient cedar. Beyond the wall was an uninterrupted view of the ocean.

On the first headstone was a short inscription, dedicated to the memory of Guy Maddox, "a loving husband and father". On the other was an inscription to Guy Maddox Jnr. "A transient spirit, and a loss not easily borne by those he left behind." Although it had been twenty-five and twenty-four years, respectively, since father and son had been laid to rest, both graves were lovingly tended with fresh flowers on them. Despite the intense heat of the California climate, shaded or not, none of the flowers were showing any sign of wilting. The grass had been neatly clipped.

"Is she still alive?" Jake asked, almost immediately he arrived back at the hacienda.

"Is who alive?" Gilbert asked, confused by the abruptness of

Jake's question.

"Guy's wife. I've just come from the cemetery. The grass on his grave is newly cut and the flowers are fresh. They must have been put there today."

"Did you see anyone tending it?"

"No."

"Then how d' you know it wasn't me?" Gilbert asked evasively.

"I know because you don't go there that often. Wesley told me. So, is she alive?"

It was a while before Gilbert answered, but Jake was in no hurry. He would have waited all day if he'd had to.

"Yes, she is. She remarried, but I don't see her that often." Gilbert then noticed the metal box that Jake had placed on the table between them. "And what is this, Jake?"

"It was given to me by Adelaide Williams. According to her, it might have something inside which we might find interesting."

He sat back in his chair and lit up a cigarette, seemingly hypnotised by the box. "Do you know who Adelaide Williams is related to?"

"Yes, she's Maurice Stanford's daughter." Jake began relating the details of his time spent with her, and of the injuries she had sustained from her father. "Aren't you interested in this box she asked me to unlock?" Jake asked.

"If I wasn't before, I am now. But why have you brought it here to open? Aren't the contents private?" Gilbert reacted badly when he saw the inscribed name of Doctor Maxwell. "Have you any idea where she got this from?"

"Apparently, she came across it recently by accident, hidden away in a window seat years ago by her mother. The reason I've been given this box is that she wants me to try and unlock it. She has no idea what's inside, except there could be a connection to Guy Maddox." Then Jake explained Adelaide's theories concerning the death of her mother and her own ill treatment.

"This becomes more curious by the minute."

"It sure does, Gil; except, why would Doctor Maxwell have given this box to Miss Williams' mother if it was so important? I didn't know they knew each other."

"Adelaide's mother was born Valerie Costello. She and Eugene grew up together in a small town on the outskirts of Kansas," Gilbert said, failing in his first attempts to open the combination of the sturdy lock. "This must have been hidden in a safe place for quite a few years if Valerie hid it. She died less than a year after Guy."

"Maybe that's why Miss Williams thinks the contents might be connected to Guy." Jake also attempted to find the combination, but without success.

"I know that Eugene made a deal with Stanford to stop him beating Valerie, but it wasn't long before he reneged on the deal and the abuse started over again. It only stopped when Eugene played whatever trump card he was holding. Possibly that trump card is what he kept inside this box."

"Did Doctor Maxwell ever mention what that deal was?" Jake asked, as Wesley came in to switch on various lamps.

"He hinted that he'd done something unforgivable, and he would be struck off the Medical Register if the truth ever got out, but that was all he ever said about it. He only mentioned it after his apartment at the hospital had been ransacked. A few days later, Valerie was beaten senseless by that intruder. I've always thought that it must have been Stanford, trying to extract information from her."

"That's exactly what Miss Williams thought. But why would her mother hide this box where she was living? It doesn't make sense."

"It does when you consider the first place you'd look for something deemed to be so important would be in that evil bastard's own lair."

"So you're sure that Stanford was the intruder?"

"If he wasn't, by God he must have set it up. Stanford must have been behind it. My guess is that Valerie took that last beating by refusing to offer up information on the whereabouts of this box."

They worked until midnight to release the lock mechanism when, by shear fluke, Gilbert coded in his own birth date. When the lock was released, they emptied out the contents onto the table.

"So, what was it that you didn't want anyone else to see, Eugene?" Gilbert murmured.

He went meticulously through the sheaf of official paperwork until he came upon the death certificate for Jake Velasquez. It was issued to Jake's parents in September 1928 and signed by Doctor Eugene Maxwell on the date Jake knew so well from the memorial headstone in Fort Laverne.

"Well, Jake," Gilbert said, handing the certificate over to Jake. "According to this, you don't exist."

"This must have been made out for my twin brother," Jake said, staring at his name on the certificate. "What he must have done is to mix up my Christian name with that of my brother's on here." But Gilbert was reading a written report attached to the death certificate.

"Eugene was dedicated to his work, and very thorough. He would never have made such a mistake."

"But I found my birth certificate amongst my father's belongings after he died. I can show you. I've got it with me. I've got all his paperwork. I'll go and get it." Jake got out of the chair, but Gilbert restrained him.

"Jake, the name on this death certificate is genuine. There's nothing in this report to indicate that your mother bore another child. What it does state is that there were complications incurred by the premature birth and that she would be unable to have any more children."

"I don't get it. Can you make sense of it, Gil?"

Gilbert continued to stare at Jake's name on the document, until he said: "Let's see what else is in here."

His hands were trembling as he laid the death certificate aside, and one by one carefully removed the contents from each of the remaining envelopes. When he began reading the last document, the colour slowly drained away from his face, leaving him ashen. Tears began to form in his eyes as he scrutinised every word for a second time.

"That wicked bastard. How could he do such a thing? All he

seemed bothered about was being struck off the Medical Register." Gilbert thumped his fist down hard on the table. "God Almighty, it's no wonder he kept this bloody secret from me. If I'd known anything about this, I swear, I would have strangled the evil swine with my bare hands."

Gilbert was on his feet now and raging like an animal. It brought Wesley swiftly from the cloisters, not running, but gliding out of the shadows with an already prepared glass of brandy.

With Gilbert outraged, it was impossible for Jake to learn what had triggered such an outburst, as the document was still clenched in his hand. Eventually, when some time elapsed and another brandy was consumed, the rage burnt itself out, and was replaced by a long and morose silence.

Unsure of what to do for the best Jake retired to his room. He returned later with all the documents and paperwork that had been hidden in his father's desk.

"I'm sorry, Jake. It's just that...it's just that..." Gilbert repeated hesitantly, before he broke off and excused himself to go inside the hacienda. "There is an urgent call I need to make. She needs to know about this."

"If you're calling Adelaide Williams, she doesn't know any more than I've already told you," Jake called after him.

Gilbert went through to the living room, where soon he could be seen talking animatedly into the telephone. It was clear the call was an extremely emotional one, and he seemed to be on the verge of breaking down. Jake was about to go inside to comfort him when Wesley beat him to it.

Chapter Twenty-Three

Exactly how long the telephone conversation went on and how long it was before Gilbert reappeared in the courtyard was something Jake didn't know, but the wait seemed like a lifetime. When Gilbert did return, it was with two mugs of fresh coffee.

"I hope this is the way you like it. Not too strong but not too weak." It was an effort at joviality that didn't work. "Jake, I offer my sincere apologies for leaving without a word of explanation." Gilbert spoke with such controlled emotion that Jake wished he would just go and sleep off whatever was upsetting him.

"Don't give it another thought, Gil. You were distraught. I should never have brought that damned box here in the first place. I wouldn't have if I'd thought for a second that you'd have gotten so upset by the contents."

"You did right bringing it here, Jake. It was the best thing you could have done – for everyone's sake. That call was probably the most important one I shall ever make..." Gilbert paused, uncertain how best to continue. He began to shuffle through the other paperwork from the box until, inevitably, he re-examined the contents of the final envelope.

"What's in that envelope that's so upsetting?"

The answer was muttered as Gilbert continued to stare at the document. "What I can't come to terms with is why in hell didn't Eugene report Stanford to the police about the abuse Valerie was being subjected to, instead of resorting to this?"

"Gil, what did Doctor Maxwell do exactly?"

"Do? Where the hell do I begin? So many lives have been ruined and you, Jake, are one of the two people most affected by this." He laid the birth certificate between them.

"Why are you showing me this?"

"Guy had a son." Gilbert almost choked on the information.

"I already know that. Scott and I saw both of their names entered in the register of deaths at City Hall."

"Yes, but this document proves that his son isn't dead."

The way Gilbert was staring across the table at him caused the hair on the back of his neck to crawl. "But he is, Gil. His name is clearly carved on the headstone in the cemetery. They would never bury an empty coffin. There had to be a baby inside."

"The infant buried there isn't Guy's son. It's a stillborn: Jake Velasquez."

Jake's chair hit the floor with a crash. He was on his feet leaning on the table. "What in hell are you saying, Gil? I'm here, right in front of you."

"Jake. Jake. Sit down and hear me out," Gilbert said. "This birth certificate in Eugene's box, the one he made out for Guy's son, isn't a copy. This is the original." Then he placed the death certificate next to it. "Likewise, this death certificate for Jake Velasquez, also from Eugene's box, is the original. The birth certificate made out to your so-called parents, for you, is a fake."

"That's impossible."

"Is it really so unlikely? Think about it for a second. You're not remotely like your parents, not in any way at all. Your skin was as pale as ivory when you were a child, and your eyes were the deepest green. What are the odds against a blond child being born to Mexican parents? More than a million to one, I'd say."

"So what you're actually suggesting is that I was swapped at birth?" Jake asked incredulously.

"I'm saying precisely that, Jake. That's why you are the image of my brother."

"But if Doctor Maxwell had done that deliberately, he must have known that my parents would've suspected there'd been an exchange." Jake remembered the awful treatment he'd received from both parents, and he recalled how very uncaring they'd been.

"Oh, they knew all right. They had nothing to lose by taking you on." Gilbert rifled through the paperwork and picked out an old chequebook and glanced through the entries on each of the stubs. "Here we have the evidence which proves that theory is right." He showed Jake the regular withdrawals from Doctor Maxwell's account, paid to Ivan Velasquez at the beginning of every month, starting the date Jake had been born to a Mrs A. Maddox, in September 1928. The payments ended abruptly at Doctor Maxwell's death in 1948.

"But why would my natural mother allow that to happen?"

"Because she was duped by that swine Maxwell. She would have believed her doctor when he broke the news that you were dead. The infant would have been the real Jake Velasquez."

Jake felt giddy and nauseous. The room he was in suddenly seemed to be underwater. However hard he tried, he couldn't absorb anything that Gilbert was saying. He strained to hear every word but nothing intelligible came through. He closed his eyes for what he imagined was just a second but when he opened them again he was seated on a stone bench near the fountain.

As he regained consciousness, there was a strong, soothing scent of pine needles. A hazy green mist was blurring his vision. He felt a pressure at his temples, manipulated by fingers penetrating deep into his skull. He felt perfectly safe with the warmth of well-being.

He became aware of Wesley supporting him and holding a damp cloth against his forehead.

"You had us worried back there, Jake. You passed out." Gilbert rested his hand lightly on Jake's arm as he offered him a tumbler of fizzing water. "Drink this back. It'll help you feel better. All this has been quite a shock for everyone, but more so for you. You couldn't have seen this coming."

Once Jake was sitting upright, Wesley removed the cloth, which, in the evening light, showed wisps of the now familiar phosphorous green mist drifting from it. Jake drank down the fizzing liquid, which soon stopped his queasiness. Some time passed before he was able to ask questions that were in need of answers.

"If I was swapped and everything appeared to be legal, why would my pa and ma need to leave California? Why would they move so far away to resettle in New Mexico? And why choose Fort Laverne of all places. It's little more than a ghost town."

"Because they needed you to be as inconspicuous as possible, I suppose. Wherever you grew up round here, people would talk. Fort Laverne being so cut off from everyday society must have had some appeal."

"But if their own infant had died, why bother with this subterfuge?"

"You were a meal ticket, and that ghost town was as good a place as any to settle. We know that Ivan Velasquez was a participant in Guy's murder, and that he was blackmailing Stanford with those photographs you found. That was one hell of a reason."

"But why chose Fort Laverne?"

"Eugene would have had a hand in where they relocated. He was desperate to get away from the Los Angeles area. So was I. After what he'd done, his conscience probably got the better of him and he needed to keep an eye on you."

"But why did you hand over the tenancy of the hotel to my parents if you didn't know anything about what he was up to?"

"All I was told was that Ivan Velasquez and his sick wife had an ailing child and no roof over their heads. I was living in Los Angeles when this came up. I never met either of them. That white elephant was no use to me, and I felt sorry for them; Eugene brought back the contract for me to sign. Because I also owned the hacienda and ranch, when we moved back, it made sense to live out there and stay a good distance away from the town and the inquisitive old timers who still live there."

"I always assumed the property belonged to Doctor Maxwell."

"Both my grandparents were big cattle barons in the early days. Even after my father's disastrous speculation on the railroad, he was a very wealthy man."

Jake was feeling a chill in the night air and began to shiver. He wanted to move away from the water spraying from the fountain but he was uncertain if his legs would support him if he stood up. Wesley had left, so Gilbert helped Jake out of the breeze.

When Wesley returned to the courtyard, he was accompanied by Scott.

"Didn't you know your buddy was coming over?" Gilbert asked, registering Jake's surprise.

"No. I've no idea why he's here." Jake felt nervous. "Please don't say anything to him about what we've found out. It's all too new, and way too complicated for me to talk about it to anyone yet."

"But you will tell him?"

"When the time is right, yes I will. Not now," Jake whispered as Gilbert stood up to receive the newcomer.

Scott, being the type of man he was, made his apologies for arriving so late in the evening and came directly to his reasons for being there. "I've been mighty anxious about what might have happened to you, Jake. Madge has been trying to make contact with you for days," he said in a rush.

"Well that's odd, because I've been at the studio most of the time, repairing stuff in the Projection Room after the break-in."

"So why haven't you answered the phone when she's called?"

"Because the internal phone was ripped off the wall during the break-in and it hasn't been fixed," Jake said wearily. He was exhausted by the recent developments, drained of energy, and feeling utterly wretched. The last thing he wanted was to be interrogated. "If she was so bothered about why I wasn't answering, it wouldn't have been too far for her to walk over and find out."

"Well, it's a decent walk to make if you're overloaded with work in the office. In case you hadn't heard, Adelaide Williams has been off sick for days, leaving Madge to cope on her own with sorting out Stanford's end-of-picture party." This fired Gilbert's immediate interest.

"What did you say your sister is busy with?" Gilbert asked.

"A masked ball; it's going to be another lavish affair. He plans to hold it on the Tsar's Grand Ballroom set on Stage Three. To which you are both invited."

"It sounds very unlike Stanford. What's it in aid of?"

"It's to celebrate the end of shooting on *The Escape of a Renegade*. But the other reason I called here, Mr Miller, is to alert you that Stanford is intending to announce to the press that he will

351

direct the sequel of the movie you made with Guy Maddox. He's written the script for it: *The Death of Don Juan*. Madge says that it's being promoted as a musical extravaganza."

While he was talking, Scott only briefly referred to Gilbert, for the rest of the time he was studying Jake.

"You sure you're OK?" he asked doubtfully and moved closer to see him better in the fading light.

"I'm fine, Scott, honestly."

"Well, I doubt that very much. You look goddamn awful," Scott said.

It brought a glimmer of a smile to Jake's face. He fumbled to fasten his open shirt, which prompted Gilbert to ask the question which seemed to have been bothering him for some time.

"That scarring looks very recent. How long ago did you get that ceremonial branding of an eagle in flight?"

"It was a few days before I left Fort Laverne."

"It's very beautiful, but why put your body through the pain of being branded?"

"I would prefer not to go into the reasons why at the moment. My head is still reeling from all that other stuff."

"I knew it, you are unwell" Scott said, who had been studying the strain in Jake's face.

"I'm not unwell in the least. Just a bit tired that's all"

"Well I think you are, and you need to rest."

"For Pete's sake, leave me alone. I'm perfectly fine" Jake said irritably, wanting nothing more than a quiet place where he could close his eyes and not think about anything else.

"Well I'm not sure that you are, Jake. Scott's right, you look washed out. Why don't you go up to the apartment and rest for an hour?" Gilbert said. "We can talk about the ceremonial branding later."

"Sure. I don't mind talking about whatever you like, but not tonight. It's too complicated."

"Then let's make it tomorrow, shall we?"

Jake knew by the look in his eye that Gilbert was too curious not to be put off, but the idea of trying to explain why he and Moon

Spirit had risked their lives by taking part in the outlawed "Ritual of Fire" was more than he was prepared to deal with, at least on his own. "I'm OK with tomorrow, but only if Scott can be here too."

"You want Scott here. Why?"

"There's really no need to involve me in this Jake," Scott said.

"There's every need; you're part Navajo and can explain what the branding was about. You've researched this ritual. You can go into more detail than I ever could."

"Hang on a minute you two. You're saying this was more than a branding ceremony, that you were involved in some obscure tribal ritual. What the hell have you been up to, Jake?" Gilbert exclaimed.

"It's complicated, like I've said. That's why Scott needs to be here" Jake answered, which seemed a logical request. However, deep down, he knew that he would have felt too exposed if Scott wasn't there for support.

"If that's the case then you're right to ask Scott to be here, that is, if that's OK with him?" Gilbert said.

"Tomorrow, I'm on call all day for a reshoot on the back lot. I'm not sure what time I can get away."

"Just come over whenever you can. If it's getting late, give me a call and we can arrange it for another time."

"I'll do my utmost to get here early, sir."

"Then you will come?" Jake said, expressing his immense relief.

"You can rely on it, Jake. But for now, you should do as Mr Miller said and rest. You look beat."

Moments after Scott had gone, instead of going up to the apartment, Jake made preparations to leave.

"I thought you were going to rest. Where are you off to now, Jake? It's getting late."

"I promised Miss Williams I would call in tonight, just in case anyone showed up."

"And when you get there, what will you tell her?" Gilbert asked.

"Tell her...about what?"

"Don't you think she's going to ask if you've opened the box, and if so, what was inside?"

"Well if she does, then I'll tell her what she wants to know."

"OK. And exactly what will you tell her about the contents? I would advise you to think very carefully about this before you get there. If not, do you want her to know who you really are? Jake, remember who this woman's father is," Gilbert said through gritted teeth, and more passionately than Jake thought was really necessary, as if there was another reason for Jake not to tell Adelaide everything.

"Is there something I'm not getting?" Jake asked and, given Gilbert's facial reaction, it was clear there was.

"All I'm saying is this. Consider your answers well before you tell her anything she doesn't need to know, anything at all."

"But she has a right to know about the contents. The box belonged to her mother."

"Correction, the box was only left in Valerie's safe keeping. The box didn't belong to her at all, but Eugene Maxwell."

"So when she asks about what was inside, what shall I tell her?"

"A watered-down version about some of the contents would probably do for now. Later, she can be told everything, but trust me, now really isn't that time."

The balmy California evening was still light when Jake drew up at the house. Inside he found Adelaide Williams fast asleep on the balcony. Before waking her, he made a fresh pot of herbal tea and scrambled three fresh eggs he'd bought on the way ;serving this up with a finely chopped salad, he took them out to her on a tray. She woke refreshed and gratefully ate every scrap of the meal. As Gilbert had predicted, it didn't take long before Adelaide enquired after the box.

"Did you manage to open Mother's box for me, Jake?"

"Yes, Miss Williams, I did."

"And what about the contents, what did you find inside?"

"Most of it was Doctor Maxwell's paperwork, which related to his work at a hospital in Pasadena."

"Doctor Maxwell? You must surely be mistaken. Why would Mother have his papers in her box? It doesn't make any sense."

"Actually, it does, given the box really belonged to the doctor. There was no mistake. His name is inscribed on the side, although the lettering isn't very clear. That's perhaps why you didn't notice it. I'm sorry to disappoint you, Miss Williams. The box is definitely his."

"But why would Mother have hidden something which didn't belong to her. I hope you're not implying theft?"

"Certainly not, Miss Williams, there must be some perfectly logical explanation why."

"Where is the box now?"

"That and the contents are safe at the place where I'm staying. As soon as you are feeling better, I will drive you over there so that you can go through everything yourself."

The information had obviously come as a shock, and so Jake made her some herbal tea. Giving her time to readjust her ideas and, as expected, when he returned from the kitchen, Adelaide, had more questions.

"Tell me, honestly, did you come across anything at all that I might use as a lever against my father's violent behaviour?"

"That's possible, but only you can decide that, Miss Williams."

"And was there any mention of Guy Maddox?"

"Yes, there was some, but as the documents related to family matters, I don't feel it is my place to comment on those or anything else. Any information on that could only be released through Guy's older brother," Jake answered cautiously.

"What? Guy Maddox had a brother?" Adelaide asked in astonishment. "Why was I never told about that?" she complained as if she ought to have known.

Throughout that humid night, sleep came and went with every passing half hour. He set off for the studio at dawn, having left Adelaide a light breakfast on the balcony for when she was eventually up and dressed.

Having so much on his mind, it was difficult to concentrate properly on his drive to the studio, and he had two near misses with the early morning traffic. He saw nothing of Scott during that day, which he was partially grateful for, given that he was still undecided about telling him about his real birth certificate, and more so, that he was the son of Guy Maddox. Although this confirmed their identical looks, after twenty-five years of believing himself to be the son of another man, it was hard to grasp the information himself.

Marjory Dawlish came in and out of the viewing theatre a few times during the day, each time asking if he'd signed the contract yet.

"I don't have it with me, Miss Dawlish, so I can't sign anything."

"But you will, won't you, and before Adelaide gets back to work?"

"You know I will, once this question about the director for the sequel has been resolved."

"Well that can't happen until Adelaide returns, and that defeats the objective in having you sign sooner than later. God alone knows when she will back to work. I've never known any woman as accident prone. It's impossible to reach her at home now that William the butler has gone back to England. I would go to the property myself, if only I had the time."

"I'm sure Miss Williams will be back at work soon," Jake said, concerned that she might arrive unexpectedly while he was there.

"And until she does return to the office, I'll be holding down two jobs on a single salary," Marjory said with annoyance, as if without her own Herculean effort the entire studio would shut down.

"I'm sorry you're finding it so difficult, Miss Dawlish."

"What would help get me through this crisis, Jake, is if I could get you to sign that contract. It would be a huge weight off my mind."

When the telephone rang, Drew's timing couldn't have been more perfect, saying it was imperative that Marjory went up to the editing department immediately.

Collecting the reels Jake had finished working on, she suggested that he might want to leave early and consider her request, adding they should resume their conversation the following day.

Before going to Pasadena, Jake called in on Adelaide only to find her asleep. He tidied up the sitting room and left her a tuna salad on the table, which he covered with a plate. On this he scribbled a note saying he would call back later. He left Gilbert's home telephone number, in case Stanford made an unexpected call and she needed him to come back.

Because he'd had very little sleep on the previous night and, it was quite early when he arrived in Pasadena, Gilbert suggested that he took a nap in the apartment, saying he would wake him the moment Scott arrived.

Jake awoke to the sound of voices in the courtyard, and saw Scott in conversation with Gilbert through the window.

"I don't wish to appear rude, Mr Miller," he heard Scott say, "but I really ought not discuss anything about the ritual until Jake is with us."

"That's fine by me, Scott. Anyway he's awake now," Gilbert said, as Jake approached. "I'll get Wesley to make some fresh coffee before we make a start. That will give this sleepyhead time to wake up properly."

After Wesley had brought them coffee, Gilbert asked him to join them, which he did, but even at a distance, Jake could feel the intensity of the manservant's penetrating gaze. To begin with, not wanting to go into any great detail about the Navajo ceremony, Jake thought Gilbert would be satisfied with what little he was prepared to tell him, but that was not to be.

After a few questions, Gilbert realised that the ceremony was a lot more complex than he had at first assumed. He asked for more details, which Jake, reluctantly, gave him, until he understood the exact nature of the ritual, and what it had entailed.

"What in hell were you thinking of, Jake? I've heard about these attempts to reincarnate a dead spirit. You're goddam lucky you didn't die, you crazy kid."

"I didn't though, did I?" Jake said. He tried to avoid Gilbert's penetrating stare, and that of Wesley, who was listening attentively, almost invisible in the shadows. Wesley's eyes had the same chilling, disconnected stare Jake had seen the night he first arrived at the hacienda.

Gilbert then asked the name of the woman who had agreed to share in the ritual, and Jake had no choice but to tell him. It was clear from the look of total disbelief on his face that Gilbert was not prepared for the answer he got.

"Moon Spirit agreed willingly to take part," Jake said, placing a hand protectively across the eagle scar above his heart.

"It's unheard of, Jake. In all the years I lived there as a child, and during the twenty years after I returned, the elders of the tribe would never allow the chief's daughter to be involved in a ceremony like that. She was his only remaining child. It's unthinkable."

Jake shifted his position on the seat uncomfortably. As an outsider to tribal law, he wondered just how much Gilbert could know of the highly secret details of ritualistic ceremonies. "I didn't arrange it, Gil. I couldn't have stopped it from happening, even if I'd wanted to. The ceremony had to be consummated by two people who loved Cloud Bird, to open the passage to earth. We both had to be there, you must understand that."

"Consummated, for a branding?" Gilbert persisted.

"How can you think I put Moon Spirit through that ceremony just for a damned branding? A branding? What the hell d' you take me for, Gil? We did this because we both believed we could return Cloud Bird's spirit to earth. It was something that he was convinced was possible, and so was I. When Moon Spirit was close to death from a snake bite, Cloud Bird told me that if old Nykodema couldn't save her with his potions, he was determined to evoke the "Ritual of Fire" himself and return her spirit home. Don't you understand, Gil? It was foretold on the day she was born that Moon Spirit had a spiritual purpose on earth. We both believed this was it."

"And what about Cloud Bird's future, was there any mention of that?" Gilbert asked.

"Chief Oglala said at his birth too, it was told in the casting of bones that his son was destined to achieve greatness in the Navajo Nation. Given that he was taken before his time, and that we were blood brothers, it made perfect sense that I should be the one to instigate his return. Both Chief Oglala and Nykodema agreed that if all of the predictions were correct, then I was the only one who could guide Cloud Bird back to fulfil that destiny."

"I'm sorry, Jake. What I said earlier about the branding came out wrong," Gilbert said, as Scott poured out more coffee.

"Drink some of this, Jake, "Scott said, as he began to explain the ceremony to Gil.

To Jake's immense relief, Scott explained that the only way that Cloud Bird's spirit could be returned to earth was by puncturing the heart of the male, in this instance, Jake. Once the spirit had been successfully absorbed into the host's body, it must then be passed into the womb of the second host: a woman who could only have been chosen by a medicine man.

"You can't alter a traditional ceremony, Mr Miller. What these two young people were doing was not about enjoying sex together. There was the possibility that the transference of the spirit could have resulted in either one or both of their deaths. It's about making the ultimate choice. There's certainly no American Indian woman amongst my acquaintance who would have considered such a thing."

"I see," Gilbert said.

Scott had more to give. "Moon Spirit would have known she was risking her own life in the transference of semen. If her womb hadn't been the perfect host for the ritual, I shudder to think what would have happened to her internal organs. It would have taken tremendous courage to go through with it. Particularly after seeing what Jake's body had been subjected to during the ritual."

"I didn't know any of that," Gilbert said.

"There are not many white men who would, Mr Miller. What is said in the description of this ritual is very basic."

"The fact is, I've only heard scrappy details of this firebird ritual. I thought it was just a load of hogwash," Gilbert said.

"Well, it isn't. Whatever you might think, Jake had tremendous courage to do what he did."

"But why would two intelligent people attempt such a thing in the first place, that's what gets me. It couldn't possibly work."

"I strongly suspect that it did work given that both of them are still alive, Mr Miller. I believe, and I sincerely hope, that one other survived to come through the ordeal."

"So it's possible that Moon Spirit is with child?"

"I think it's very likely."

"Jake, you should marry the girl," Gilbert said, out of the blue.

Scott continued speaking with convincing authority. "If a child was conceived during that religious Navajo ritual, it will have a high status on the reservation. For one, because his father has undergone and survived that ordeal in order to give him life, and two, because of his mother's willingness to conceive the ritual was fulfilled. Because of that, the child will receive immense respect from the elders of the tribe, and so will its mother."

"Do you think that's possible? The child won't be one hundred percent Navajo. Whatever the sex of this child is, it will, nevertheless, be regarded by most as being of mixed-race."

"Mixed blood will not be an issue, Mr Miller. I know that because that's what I have. Whether or not the spirit of Cloud Bird returns in this child will never be proven, but this child will be honoured as such."

"So why are you against Jake making the child legitimate?"

"This was not a normal conception, and the parents should not feel forced into marriage for respectability. It would demean the spiritual association of the birth."

"But that's crazy, Scott. You're suggesting that the sanctity of marriage could be unacceptable?"

"What I'm saying is that if they commit to each other in marriage they could possibly find themselves in a no man's land. A marriage of convenience made to legitimise a normal conception is one thing, but for a child conceived through this ritual, it might cast doubt in the minds of sceptics amongst the Navajo tribe."

"There's more for a child than to begin its life on a reservation," Gilbert retorted.

"Well, I know what I would prefer."

"But it isn't your choice, is it, Scott?"

"No, sir, it isn't."

Scott stood up in preparation to go. "I'm sorry, Jake, my other reason for calling here this evening is that the Transport Captain dropped me off on his way to a location. He needs your truck back at the studio tonight. It's something to do with fitting it out for a reshoot, if that's OK by you?"

"Sure," Jake said, handing him the keys. "I thought he'd forgotten."

"Not a chance. Apparently, the director wants brighter headlights. It's for a night shoot sometime this week. They insisted that you must drive. It's for continuity. You'd better get some rest. It could take all night." On his way out Scott added: "Don't be surprised if you see me there. I'm going just in case you need some support."

"I can manage, honestly, there's really no need."

"Ordinarily I would agree, but not for this shoot. That jerk Frazer will be directing the night filming. When he's involved anything could go wrong, particularly if he dreams up any action shots. I plan to get there early, just to make sure your truck has been properly overhauled, that the brakes work, and the lights are functioning properly. Otherwise, I'll keep out of the way."

"Thanks," Jake said, but by then Scott had gone. However, the clarity of his recent exchange with Gilbert had left Jake with a lot to think about.

Chapter Twenty-Four

The following day Jake journeyed by bus into the studio. Within half an hour of arriving, he was confronted by Marjory Dawlish, enquiring if he had brought in the signed contract with him. Completely against his character, Jake managed to avoid telling her that, on Gilbert's sound advice, he hadn't done so.

He asked her when the reshoots on his truck would happen, so that he could get it back. With a volatile gesture of raised hands, she said that she hadn't been informed that any reshoots were needed.

Adelaide Williams called, but when she understood that he had no means of transport, she arranged for him to be brought to the house by a member of the teamsters. On the way out, Jake enquired after his truck at the teamster's office, but, strangely, they had no information about the reshoots, or of the whereabouts of Jake's truck.

On his arrival, Adelaide's unkempt appearance suggested that she was neglecting herself, until he saw new bruising on her arms, and the smashed contents of her china cabinet. At first, she insisted this had been done previously, but as Jake had cleared up the room when he was there before, he knew otherwise. He made no comment when Adelaide said that she had fallen again and didn't venture any further information.

At her request, Jake set up a small projector and folding screen in one of her other rooms within the huge mansion. After that, he made her a light meal of scrambled eggs with a side salad of grapes, tomatoes and kiwi fruit which she ate hungrily, leaving a clean plate.

She allowed Jake to help her through to the dusty mausoleum of a room where he had set up the projector, a room crowded with furniture draped over with dust sheets. When he removed one of the covers to help her into the comfort of an armchair, a cloud of dust enveloped them both, which she found more amusing than anything else.

"You must think some of the rooms in this house are very Dickensian," Adelaide commented as she made herself more comfortable. "If you enjoy reading, Jake, there's a well-stocked library along the corridor. There are some very good novels amongst them. Mother had a passion for books. You're welcome to browse through the shelves any time."

She relaxed into the seat as Jake switched off the light and focused the projector lens onto the blank screen.

"What are we watching?" he asked curiously.

"I'd forgotten this existed until I came across it yesterday in mother's old room. Although it was an obsession of my father's, I'm sure you will find it interesting."

Jake watched the blank screen with rapt attention, expecting maybe a feature film. Instead, he was shown a reel of screen tests that had been spliced together, including out-takes of unwanted footage from a variety of movies.

The reel opened with a newsreel segment of a bathing beauty contest where, amongst the many contestants, he recognised Adelaide's mother from the portrait. After this, there was an interesting screen test, again of her mother, devoid of make-up and without the trappings of any Hollywood glamour. She gave a riveting performance, which albeit short, proved her to be an excellent actress. There was another section of newsreel footage with her looking incredibly glamorous, but unhappy, on the arm of her escort, Maurice Stanford. The edit flickered and Jake thought it had reached the end.

"Don't switch off yet, Jake, there's more on here that I want you to see."

What he wasn't prepared for next was a screen test of Guy Maddox. The actress playing opposite him was again Adelaide's mother. By now, her bloom of youth was well on the decline, which was compensated for by the use of heavy make-up. In comparison, Guy had a look of youthful innocence, fresh and alive.

In this particular clip, Guy was very close to Jake's own age. Even in that short scene, it was apparent that Adelaide's mother found him very attractive. There was a natural majesty about the way Guy's presence commanded the screen and, watching him, Jake could understand why it was a tragedy for the movie-going public to have missed out on seeing him.

Throughout this, Adelaide was making comments and comparisons about Guy and himself. But Jake was much too interested in the next footage to hear her. His father was now in preparation for the dance sequence for Gilbert's movie. Another screen test followed on.

His heart skipped a beat the moment the enchantingly fresh face of Alicia Cordova turned towards the camera, readjusting the Cuban heel of her shoe, before positioning herself in readiness with her partner to commence with the screen test.

Unfortunately, there wasn't enough time to absorb her lovely features before the tango began. In this, she was partnered by Guy Maddox. However the dance lasted only seconds before the film clip became erratic and cut off, even before the dance itself had begun. There followed a compilation of other shots, all of them featuring Alicia Cordova. There were no others featuring Guy Maddox.

"What caused the damage to that earlier dance sequence?" Jake asked, examining the badly crumpled footage.

"It happened during a family argument with my father, if you hadn't already guessed." Adelaide said vehemently. "What I have here is all the footage that could be saved with Guy on it. My mother was so very much in love with him. Most women were. I was, too, at the time. That's why my father did his best to destroy every inch of footage with Guy on it."

"If that's the case, why would he want to resurrect the movie that Guy made with Jon Miller, and choose to direct the sequel?"

"Well, now he sees the potential of having a box office smash on his hands if *The Return of Xavier Gérard* is released. If that can be followed up with a sequel, he would be financially set up for life."

"So how did he overlook that section of Guy preparing to go into the dance?" Jake asked, careful not to let on that he also knew the actress.

"Because Alicia Cordova was also featured in that section, he took great pleasure in destroying every scrap of footage of him on screen with mother, except when she acted opposite him in the screen test. What my father hated more than anything about Guy Maddox was that Alicia was in love with Guy and not him."

"I'm sorry, I must have misheard, I though you said that-that Alicia Cordova was in love with Guy Maddox?"

"Well, yes, of course she was. They were inseparable. It was inevitable they would marry. Everyone in the studio expected it. It came as no surprise to anyone, except my father, when she became Alicia Maddox."

Jake wanted desperately to ask more about his mother but he couldn't. Instead he asked if he could rewind and rerun the reel to absorb every beautiful detail of her.

Because of her repeated beatings, Adelaide had become very unsteady on her crutches and was in need of someone to be with her, and so Jake telephoned Gilbert and arranged for Wesley to meet with him at the studio in the morning with a change of clothes, explaining that he would be staying overnight at the mansion.

What Jake hadn't anticipated were her nightmares and sleepwalking episodes, during which he only just prevented her from falling headlong down the stairs. What he'd intended would be one overnight stay, he extended until a live-in nurse could be engaged who would stay with her until she was no longer in need of the crutches. By Jake's estimation, that could be a long time if she didn't rest properly, as she was obsessed by the thought of not being able to attend the masked ball.

After the first night of his stay, Jake set off for work in Adelaide's car later than he expected, having to wait for the gardener to show up. When he did, the man agreed to keep an eye on the invalid. Jake had also arranged for the cleaner to temporarily change her routine from one day a week into four and, in doing so, to keep an eye on her employer.

It was clear that Jake's work in the Projection Room was almost at an end, and he was told in no uncertain terms that, if he hadn't signed Marjory's all-important agreement by the weekend, he would not only be out of a job, but would not get the cash Scott so badly needed to save Firebrand.

During the next couple of days at the studio, Jake saw nothing of Scott. It presented him with a problem of locating his missing truck, as the Transport Captain was taking a late vacation in Europe and no one else in that department could tell him what had become of it. Only Scott could answer the question, and he was nowhere to be found. Even Marjory seemed to be genuinely concerned by his absence. Nevertheless, this didn't prevent her from asking Jake to accompany her to the ball.

"I'm sorry, Miss Dawlish, I can't."

"You are going to be there though? It will be a huge event." she said peevishly.

"That was the idea. I'm not sure now."

"If this is connected with my brother's absence, I can reassure you that he's probably gone off to wrangle some stray horse or another for the new Western series. He will be back in time for the ball. His contract here depends on it. We can both meet up with him there."

Although he was partially reassured by this information, Jake wasn't totally convinced. What he wanted was for her to leave him alone. "I've already agreed to go with someone," he said, deliberately avoiding naming either Gilbert or Adelaide Williams, aware that if he did go, he would need to let one or the other down. Since his arrival in California, his life had become increasingly more complicated.

By the afternoon on the third day after Scott had gone missing, Jake was determined to make contact with him, and planned to make a long search for the orange grove where Scott had taken him to help him recover. But he needed Adelaide's car to search for him.

On his way to the mansion Jake took what he expected would be a short detour, calling at a couple of places where he thought he might find Scott, but because his knowledge of the area was limited, he got lost a few times on the way. His first stop was at a forge where Scott helped out from time to time, repairing wheels for stagecoaches on a TV series, and where he also did a lot of re-shoeing on some of the more difficult horses. He hadn't been seen there either, so Jake spent more time going from one hostelry to another, asking anyone remotely acquainted with the wrangler for any information at all, but no one had seen him that week. It was the same story at the escort agency. By now, Jake was becoming increasingly worried about Scott's safety.

Although it wasn't dusk when he arrived at the mansion, there were so many lights burning that Jake panicked. Had something had happened to Adelaide during his long absence?

"Jake, is that you? Where the hell have you been?" Adelaide called from inside the living room. "I've been worried half to death for the past hour in case something awful had happened."

"I'm really sorry," Jake said, relieved that she sounded OK, if perhaps a bit grumpy, probably because she was hungry. Because of the diversion he'd made, he'd forgotten to call in at the grocery store on his way back as he'd promised. He would need to go back out again. "I clean forgot to call in at the store and get the groceries. I'll get off now. It won't take long."

"Don't go anywhere, Jake, not now. There's no time," Adelaide said, balancing on her crutches as she appeared in the hall. "Have you forgotten? We need to be at the masked ball in less than an hour. If I'm not there before my father arrives, there'll be all hell to pay."

"I'm sorry, I guess it just slipped my mind," Jake responded, trying to appear positive but knowing there was no way he could get out of going.

"Your friend, Gilbert, rang while you were out. He said that he and his manservant would meet up with you at the ball. He did offer to drop off a costume and mask for you on the way there, but I told him that was all taken care of," she said.

In defiance of the pirate costume, strap-on wooden leg, and stuffed parrot which her father was expecting her to wear, Adelaide had chosen comfort instead, and was wearing a baggy Perrot's outfit, which didn't look at all out of place with the crutches. Her glittering mask included a fake nose so it was doubtful that anyone from the studio would ever recognise her, which was precisely what she wanted.

"That's a brilliant choice of costume, Miss Williams."

"Do you really think so? Well if you like this, wait until you see what I have arranged for you."

"About that, Miss Williams, I'm sorry to disappoint you, but I can't attend this function. There is an important issue I must deal with this evening."

"You can't be serious about pulling out of our arrangement? I can't go on my own, Jake, you know that. I need you to be with me."

"I've been thinking about that. I can call for a taxi cab, and arrange for someone to accompany you in my place."

"Don't be ridiculous. You couldn't get anyone to cover for you at this hour."

"There is an escort agency my friend worked for recently. If I called that number and mentioned his name, I'm sure they would help out."

"Have you taken leave of your senses? Think of my position at the studio. Everyone I know will be at this gathering. Gossip spreads like wildfire in this town, and I certainly have no intention of being the brunt of anyone's jibes, being seen on the arm of a male hooker. It would only take one person to recognise him, and my reputation would be minced meat."

"I was only suggesting that your companion might be engaged from an escort agency, Miss Williams, nothing more."

"There is absolutely no difference between an escort and a male hooker in this town, except, possibly, the hint of respectability that comes by renting a man in a tuxedo for the evening from an agency. However charming the man is, I would certainly never subscribe to that. I made an error of judgement years ago being seen with a male socialite from Detroit, never again."

"Then I'm at a loss of what to suggest. I'm sorry to have put you in this situation, Miss Williams. It's not that I don't want to go. It's just that I can't. The friend that I mentioned has been missing for days, which is so unlike him. I need to find out where he is, and make sure he's all right," Jake said, determined to find any way to get out of attending an unimportant event like a masked ball.

"If you haven't been able to locate this friend of yours after a lengthy search, three hours spent at the ball will hardly alter the predicament you seem to imagine he's in. This isn't New Mexico, Jake. There is no honour in Hollywood that can compete with the power of a dollar bill. Given your friend's chosen occupation, he's probably earning a damned good pay cheque from an aging starlet by staying longer than he planned. Some of these women would pay anything for male company."

"Three hours you say?" Jake asked.

"Give or take half an hour. I've no intention of staying any longer than is necessary. Once I'm back here, you can continue with the search."

"If that's how long you think we'll be gone, that's what I'll do."

On his makeshift bed in the sitting room, there was the familiar costume of a South American gaucho, already laid out in preparation for him to wear.

"How did you know my size?" Jake asked.

"The wardrobe girl remembered you from when she kitted you out for the screen test. They had your measurements."

"Why is it so important that I dress up?" he asked dubiously.

"Because tonight, everyone involved in making the sequel to Guy's old movie will be there, and what better way than to shock them all?" she said with a laugh. "You might think it's a crazy idea, but I thought what fun it would be if you were dressed in the same clothes Guy wore for that tango in that old movie."

"You mean these are the actual clothes he wore in Jon Miller's movie?" he asked. "How on earth did you manage that?"

"You already know that Valerie was besotted by him. I think this proves it. She got them from the costume designer at the end of filming." She glanced at the time on the mantle clock.

"I thought you rented them from the studio?"

369

"I just got your measurements from them to make sure these would fit. Please get changed into this outfit, Jake, otherwise we're going to arrive late."

Examining the outfit, he noticed a tear in the sleeve of the left arm which had been cobbled together during the filming, but which had never been properly mended. Lingering amongst the fibres of the crumpled cotton shirt he breathed in the fragrant scent of pine needles. There was a smear of red lipstick on the chest of the shirt, and another on the cuff of the sleeve. There was also actor's make-up around the neck of the shirt.

"I hope you don't mind me saying, but this doesn't look very clean," Jake remarked, but hastily pulled on the shirt when Adelaide hobbled through.

"I'm sorry, I didn't think. I just assumed it would have been washed," she said with an admiring glance. She looked away as he pulled the worn leather chaps over the tight-fitting pants. "I don't have an alternative. I'm sorry."

"That's OK," he said. It was genuinely heartfelt, as he was strangely comforted by the soiled garment – making contact with his unknown father and wearing the shirt he had worn the year Jake was born.

There had been a last-minute change of plan to the venue for the ball. Instead of the function being held on a studio set, a grand hotel in Santa Monica had been hired for the event, and it was very clear why. Scores of jostling latecomers were holding invitations aloft for the uniformed commissionaire to see before being allowed into the crush of masked and ingeniously attired crowds in the ballroom, where a medley of popular show tunes was being played.

Chapter Twenty-Six

Jake located Gilbert and Wesley out on the terrace, where they had arranged to meet.

"What an outrageously bizarre situation this is," Gilbert remarked with a bold laugh. "The three of us all dressed as South American gauchos." He looked more closely at Jake's costume. "This is the genuine article, Jake. How did you come by it?"

"Adelaide had it hidden amongst her mother's possessions." Jake turned to look for her, but she seemed to have disappeared.

"I recognise this," Gilbert said, fingering the cobbled patch on the sleeve.

"I thought you might. Guy wore this for the tango in your movie."

The conversation stopped when Adelaide Williams came out of the powder room and made her way towards them.

Before she reached them, Wesley straightened the right sleeve of Jake's jacket. Jake was surprised when the manservant removed a flat metal object from a concealed pocket on the inside of the sleeve. He seemed to know exactly where to find it. Expertly manipulating a tiny catch on the object, Wesley released a bloodied blade from the handle of what turned out to be a theatrical flick-knife. Because of the mask Wesley was wearing, Jake couldn't gauge the change to his normally impassive face as he stared at the prop dagger. He folded the blade back into the handle and returned it into the hidden pocket of Jake's sleeve. Only when Adelaide joined them, did Wesley look directly into Jake's eyes, but he offered no explanation.

When the introductions were made, Jake was at first surprised that Adelaide didn't recognise Gilbert, considering that she had discovered his attempted suicide, but he figured, given the richness of his adult voice, and because his mask also incorporated a hooked nose, it made sense. Fortunately she had no reason to delve into Gilbert's real identity, and was perfectly happy to accept him as Jake's friend, and an old acquaintance of Guy Maddox.

Jake was not so much puzzled that Adelaide didn't recognise Wesley as the man that she had been in love with years ago, but that Wesley didn't show any sign of recognising her either, even when she briefly removed her own mask to wipe her eyes.

"I don't see Scott anywhere?" Gilbert questioned, looking about the room. "He would be hard to miss, even with a mask."

"I wish he was here. I've been asking about him for the past three days, and no one's laid eyes on him, not even his sister. He hasn't been seen since he left Pasadena to drive back to the studios in my old truck. No one has seen him there either," Jake said half to himself, scanning the crowd for any sign of the young wrangler.

After Gilbert sent Wesley off to the bar for a bottle of vodka, he gave his excuses and made his way to an unoccupied table on the opposite side of the dance floor.

It was immediately apparent that this masked ball would be a glittering Hollywood event. Everyone who passed through the doors was extravagantly dressed and it made Jake's gaucho costume, and those of his two companions, seem almost drab by comparison. Apart from a couple of very colourless Keystone cops, the other flamboyant costumes blended perfectly into the ambience of the evening.

A cold shudder ran down Jake's spine at the jarring sound of Barbara Jeffords announcing the entrance of her party with a raucous greeting. Most people in the immediate vicinity of the doors who didn't know her must have wondered why on earth such a woman would be invited to that auspicious gathering.

Guffawing like a redneck, Barbara Jeffords was wreathed in a cloud of dubious perfume that even Jake could detect from the far side of the hall as she continued her brash assault on the English language. It soon had every head turned towards her and her entourage until they were all well inside the ballroom.

It was difficult to decide what Maurice Stanford had decided to wear, except that he closely resembled a sausage crammed into a very tight Pimpernel outfit. He accompanied the rowdy Barbara Jeffords, dressed as Al Capone. Following meekly behind her was her weasel-like husband, kitted out as a gunslinger.

Seeming rather out of place, and trailing a few paces behind, was a slim younger woman, her face was well-concealed beneath the veil of an authentic Spanish mantilla. A voluminous satin cloak covered everything she was wearing, except for her trim ankles and the Cuban heels of her shoes.

Even before the Stanford party was seated, Adelaide Williams insisted that Jake should get her further away from them. She was unbelievably nervous that her father would fly into a raging temper when he saw that she had disobeyed his request and chosen to wear a different costume. Jake had witnessed the aftermath of Maurice Stanford not getting his own way so Adelaide's seemingly childish request didn't seem at all unreasonable to him. Because of the crowds closing in around them, Jake helped her to another part of the room where Gilbert and Wesley were seated at a table, emptying glasses of neat vodka.

To gain access to Gilbert's table, and avoid unnecessary crushing from the crowd, Jake took Adelaide through French doors opening onto the terrace. This overlooked a garden, the larger part of which had been commandeered as an overflow car park and which was continually filling up. By the time they passed by the fourth set of French doors, Wesley could be seen reaching across the table to light Gilbert's cigarette.

Jake was about to open the door when he recognised the explosive exhaust on his old pickup. Straining his eyes in the dark he saw his truck parked with both doors of the cab flung wide open. Two figures were scrambling awkwardly out of it, as a dark shape rolled off the back of the truck and landed on the grass, where a bound and hooded figure struggled to its feet, stumbling about, and trying to wrench off the hood. The figure was swiftly laid low by a blow to the head and bundled back onto the truck and the tailgate was quickly raised. Jake was about to leap over the balustrade to investigate, when Adelaide grabbed onto his arm with the tenacity of a terrier.

"For God's sake, Jake, you can't go off and leave me exposed out here like this. What if my father comes out and discovers me?"

"He won't. He's only just arrived. I promise I shan't leave you for long. There's something going on over there which I need to investigate." But she refused to let go.

"It will only be some rednecks brawling," she said.

"You saw what happened then?"

"That sort of thing happens in downtown LA every night. There's no need for you to get involved. Security tonight will be very strict. Let them deal with that old truck," she said, and urged him towards the door.

Once they were inside they found that area too was beginning to fill up.

Because there was only enough seating at the table for Adelaide, Jake remained standing. Quite deliberately, he got into a position which made it difficult for her to exchange any comments with either Gilbert or his companion, and very soon she became silent, safely distanced from her father's group who were seated almost directly opposite them on the far side of the dance floor.

Jake hadn't been observing them at their table for long when Maurice Stanford was approached by two men in Cossack costumes. One of the men had a bloodstained handkerchief pressed tightly against his previously broken nose in an attempt to stem a flow of blood, which, judging by the state of his clothes, had been bleeding for some time. Jake recognised the man instantly as Malcolm Reynolds. He was being supported by the other Cossack, who was also suffering with a cut lip and a torn shirt. The second man was soon identified as Frank Clark when he removed his mask to whisper urgently to Maurice Stanford. Immediately, Stanford, Barbara Jeffords, and her husband followed the two Cossacks outside onto the terrace.

Only the veiled woman remained seated alone in her isolated position, some distance away from the other guests. With Stanford gone, she beckoned over the Latin American bandleader. When she spoke, her breath billowed out the lace veil of her mantilla, presumably requesting a specific number to be played by his band.

It was impossible for Jake to hear what they were saying but he felt sure that the bandleader responded in what appeared to be animated Castilian Spanish as he glanced through the sheets of handwritten music she handed to him. After the bandleader had momentarily studied the music, he smiled excitedly. Bowing away from her like a marionette, he returned to the stage from where he barked out orders to the musicians, who lowered their instruments and retreated into the wings until only the guitarist remained.

Handing the sheet music to the guitarist, the bandleader then repositioned the microphone beside his chair, allowing time for the guitarist to adjust the music stand and place the sheets of music at eye level.

Meanwhile, the bandleader announced to the gathering that the next piece of music had been composed for an exhibition dance and had never been performed in public. It was to be played by request to the memory of the dead composer. Having said this, the bandleader cued the lighting operator to dim the lights except for a single spotlight on the guitarist.

Expectantly, everyone in the room fell silent when the musician positioned the guitar in readiness and studied the music on the stand before him. A look of panic flittered across his face and he turned anxiously towards the bandleader, looking as though he was willing him to offer any excuse at all not to have to play such a complicated piece.

The unfortunate guitarist struggled miserably to get through the introduction without blundering. Sight-reading is rarely easy, and clearly without having had time to practice, he could only sound like a bad amateur. To begin with, the gathered audience were confused, but because of the theatricality of the occasion, they began to think this was the blundering introduction to a comedy act. A few amongst the crowd began to chortle, until everyone joined in and laughed.

Feeling only anguished embarrassment for the ridiculed musician, Jake failed to notice the man approaching the stage who deliberately removed his mask before he stepped into the spotlight with the performer. Calmly, Wesley took the guitar from the distressed musician, who offered no resistance before fleeing into the darkness to join the other musicians.

"What the devil is Wesley up to?" Gilbert whispered incredulously. "The man can't manage to play one decent chord on the guitar. This is heading for absolute chaos."

"Holy Mother," Adelaide exclaimed urgently, catching hold of Jake's sleeve, tugging at it for his attention, "it's him, the man in my photograph. How can he still look like that? He hasn't aged a day from the time we dated. That was a quarter of a century ago."

Jake barely heard a word she was saying. His total concentration focused on Wesley. He knew that something extraordinary was about to happen. As too did the other partygoers, who became unexpectedly hushed.

Unconcerned by the attention of the audience, Wesley moved away from the spotlight and leant against the proscenium arch, readjusting the tension of the strings until the guitar was positioned against him in readiness to be played. He was staring intently into the darkness beyond the spotlight, waiting.

A gasp rippled amongst the expectant crowd when, as though a light had been switched off inside him, still holding onto the guitar, Wesley's shoulders hunched over, his head bowed forward like a marionette. When his lank, dark hair fell over his eyes, it was the only movement within his lifeless shape. Then, with equal drama, as if the show was finally about to begin, the spotlight operator narrowed the beam of light to focus down on his head and shoulders.

There was no sound from the mesmerised gathering around the dance floor, but when trails of green smoke began to drift out from his nostrils, the enthralled audience gasped, imagining this was a controlled special effect, and part of the act. They gasped again with anticipation when Wesley's shoulders straightened and his bowed head snapped up again, as he stared out into the darkness. In moments, the riveted crowd fell silent when they too heard the rhythmic click of castanets as a second spotlight illuminated an area in the centre of the dance floor.

Like the gathered crowd, Wesley seemed also to be waiting and listening expectantly as the clicking sound of the castanets came nearer. Now this was accompanied by the rhythmic sound of clipped heels as the figure of a flamenco dancer came towards him across the darkened floor. The Cuban heels of her shoes were crisp and precise, which to Jake's keen ear sounded eerily similar to the long tracking shot in the opening scene of Gilbert's movie.

Unidentifiable, the dancer came no closer into the spotlight than to the perimeter. The staccato beat of the Cuban heels flashing beneath the swirl of her exotic red skirts, slowed down to a different pace while continuing to work their magic on a captivated audience. In silhouette, with her arms gracefully poised above her head, the castanets clicked out a synchronised rhythm as the dancer swirled about the floor. Continuing the intricate dance steps, the dancer sang a short opening accompaniment in a dramatic mixture of English and Castilian Spanish, her voice dark and sultry. It was a compelling performance, sounding all the more beautiful in the absolute silence of that grand ballroom.

Because of Jake's rapt attention to the dancer, it came as a shock when the first chords of guitar music were plucked out. Timed to perfection, the result was electrifying, and as the music intensified, so did the clipped sound of the dancer's heels as the woman became immersed into the darkness once more.

Isolated in the spotlight, Wesley's precise fingering ran riot over the strings. It was a different interpretation of the dance, which ordinarily might be classed an exceptional tango. But on this particular evening, something quite extraordinary was happening to that piece of music, perhaps even unworldly given its hypnotic quality. The way that Wesley was playing Guy's composition it seemed as if time itself had stopped to listen.

Circling dramatically around the edge of the spotlight was the flickering swish of red skirts, tempestuously flashing in and out of the spotlight. Every movement symbolically coordinated with the rapid fire of her Cuban heels.

Unlike everyone else in the room, Adelaide was not only

spellbound but, on removing her mask, it was evident that she was shocked. "I don't understand how one man with a guitar can produce such an exquisite sound. This is far better than the orchestrated backing they used on Guy's movie—" She broke off, mesmerised by the passionate movements of the partially silhouetted dancer, as if trying to recapture some half-forgotten memory. "Oh my God, if only this was being recorded on film. This dancer must be used in the sequel. Jake, Jake! We must get her agent's name before she disappears," Adelaide chided optimistically. Apart from Jake, who was standing nearest, no one else heard.

"Can't you forget that bloody sequel for once, Miss Williams and watch this? Why go on about work. What you're witnessing out there is pure genius."

"You think I'm not aware of that. I'm doing what I do best. It's my job. That's what makes me a sharp professional."

"Then take this time off, Miss Williams. I may not be a professional, but I believe you will never see anything like this again" Jake hissed through clenched teeth, alternating his attention between Wesley and the magnetic flickering of red skirts as the dancer tantalised the audience by just clipping the edge of the spotlight.

Not once did Wesley take a single glance at the sheet music. It was as though he knew every subtle change of the rhythm by heart.

"God in Heaven, what is happening here tonight? Only Guy could have interpreted his own music like this," Gilbert whispered in a daze. "This is almost surreal. They both are."

"It's magical," Jake whispered, hypnotised by the fluctuating rhythm of Wesley's incredible playing, and totally mesmerised by the dancer. He could barely breathe when at last her dramatic shape ventured into the centre spotlight in preparation of the main sequence as the introduction of the tango came to an end.

What he feared most was the maze of intricate steps that lay ahead in that next sequence and, with no sign of anyone coming forward to partner her, he had no idea how she would get through it alone. Why had such a talented dancer chosen a routine that needed a partner? Yet there she was, alone, and performing even more beautifully than he ever remembered seeing on film.

As the spotlight on Wesley narrowed down onto his long, expressive fingers, the rhythm of the guitar slowed down until there was barely any sound at all. It was then he stepped onto the dance floor, no longer plucking the strings. Instead, he lightly drummed on the wooden instrument, alternating between the palms of his hands and fingers, still in perfect synchronisation to the woman's clipping heels as he approached her.

When the dancer finally came into the full glare of the double spotlight, clearly visible on her wrist was a distinctive charm bracelet, simple, but eye-catching. Jake felt Adelaide grip tightly onto his arm.

"Holy Mother of God... it can't be her If he sees her performing like this, he'll kill her," Adelaide choked, verging on hysteria. "What possessed her to dance again in public after all these years?" Adelaide whispered in a voice so low that Jake had to strain to hear.

"Who is she?" he asked, but he got no response.

Adelaide seemed to breathe her words rather than speak them.

"I would never have recognised her, not seeing this change in her tonight. I can't believe I could have forgotten what an amazing dancer she once was, and how very beautiful she still is on the dance floor."

"Who is she?" Jake repeated, but Adelaide was not to be distracted from her thoughts.

"All I ever saw was the kindness she offered to a stepdaughter who was only a year younger than herself," Adelaide continued to mutter to herself, but Jake was shocked to learn that the woman he had assumed was a graceful young dancer had to be a mature woman in her forties.

"Please, tell me who she is," Jake whispered hoarsely. He was still unable to take his gaze from the couple on the dance floor. He was half-expecting Wesley himself to partner the woman in the main section of the dance.

"Alicia Cordova, my stepmother," she answered.

His mind reeled. "Alicia Cordova. That's her - on the dance floor."

Jake was staggered to learn that the beautiful Alicia Cordova, his true mother, was so close at that moment. He was convinced that she would turn and notice him in the crowd, if only he dared to call out her name. If only he dared.

Instead of Wesley making any physical contact with her, as Jake had expected, just as the opening had been recorded on film, he began to pluck on the strings of the guitar for the short but passionate introduction to 'The Tango of Death'. Gradually he backed away from the spotlight into the darkness leaving the dancer alone, poised in readiness to begin the dance on cue. It was a daunting routine for any dancer of her age. Even with an athletic partner like Guy Maddox to support her it would be challenging for her to even consider, but to dance as a solo performer was verging on madness. Jake knew that if someone didn't partner her within the next few moments she would enter into that remorseless routine from which there would be no escape in that relentless spotlight.

Jake's mouth felt dry and he thought that his heart would burst through his chest as he stepped onto the dance floor. He knew every intricate step and movement of the dance although he had never partnered anyone in his life. But like his mother had done before him, he paced his treads across the dance floor, keeping perfectly in time with the music, comforted by the regular clip on the heels of his boots.

At the moment Jake stepped onto the dance floor a hoarse warning from Gilbert rang in his ear.

"For Pete's sake, Jake, what are you thinking? She mustn't know who you are. Make sure the mask stays covering your face, boy. The shock would surely kill her."

Her back was towards him as he approached but, even so, he detected a slight stiffening of her posture when she realised she was not alone on the dance floor. Unable to prepare her, Jake took hold of her arm and swung her to face him, exactly the move he had seen Guy Maddox do a dozen times before on screen.

It was a powerful movement that he could see caused her dark eyes to register shock and confusion even through the mask. But as a true professional, she responded to the pressure of his hand and went smoothly into the routine.

For the first few bars of the music, Jake felt that he had two left feet. Temporarily he was glad to be led by her. He knew in a heartbeat that he was in the hands of a professional, and relaxed. Thereafter he didn't falter on a single step, and took control of the dance as she allowed him to lead.

The dance began slowly at first and became faster as they went into the first set of complex moves, prompting her to whisper into his ear: "Guy, can it really be you?" as they negotiated their way around the floor. The spotlight operator religiously followed every faultless move, ensuring that every step of the tango was illuminated as the perfectly paired dancers manoeuvred around the floor.

For Jake, this was an unbelievable experience, being in a situation where he was not only dancing before a gathered audience, but that he was partnering his own mother –the dancer he had watched on screen so many times, now thrilled by the fact she had performed this exact routine with his father. He did his utmost to convey the same concentrated passion into the dance, exactly the way that his father had until his untimely death.

Although his mother was no longer a young woman, Jake was amazed by her flexibility, moving into each of the changing holds perfectly in time, her heels clipping precisely with the continually altering pace of the rhythm, making that ridiculously intense sequence appear smooth and effortless, balanced as lightly as a leaf in his arms.

As the music began to approach the final crescendo, Jake became increasingly nervous for her safety, as the finale of the dance involved a violent death throw of his partner. Instinctively, Jake removed the fake dagger from the pocket in his sleeve. He released the bloodied blade of the flick-knife a split second before he flung his partner's body to spin gracefully across the floor, increasing his own speed to compliment hers. In a series of athletic leaps, Jake paced himself alongside her exactly as Guy Maddox had done years before on film until her body assumed the position of her imminent death as the spinning momentum ended with her inert body isolated inside a brilliant spotlight.

His father had concluded the dance with the bloodied dagger clenched in his hand as he supposedly took his own life but, for Jake, that ending didn't go according to plan.

In the void of darkness surrounding the follow spot Maurice Stanford had come up behind Gilbert. Gilbert, like everyone else in the room, was enthralled by the performance as the dance came to its conclusion and was caught unaware by a fierce blow on the back of the head with a champagne bottle. It was a crippling attack, which brought Gilbert to his knees, where he collapsed, bleeding profusely. Unseen by the remainder of the crowd, the bottle was thrown into the darkness, skidding across the floor, where it ended up directly beneath Jake's feet.

Jake had failed to notice the spinning remains of the broken champagne bottle as it skidded across the floor towards him. He only felt the glass crush underfoot as he slipped and crashed onto the floor, banging his head and knocking himself out.

No one else in the ballroom had any idea that he was concussed, having miraculously fallen in the centre of his own spotlight, in the position required for the conclusion of the dance. The bloodied dagger still clenched in his hand, Jake's body mirrored his own death to that of Alicia Cordova's – the sequence timed a heartbeat away from Wesley's final chord on the guitar.

At the dramatic conclusion, the lights snapped off, leaving the ballroom in complete darkness, and an enthralled gathering to cheer and applaud loudly their unquestionable admiration.

But Jake heard none of it.

When he came around, chaos seemed to have broken out in the ballroom. Close to the bandstand, Gilbert was nursing his bleeding head while Wesley did his very best to stem the flow of blood, cautiously removing the remaining particles of glass that were still embedded in his scalp.

Nauseous and dizzy, and unable to coordinate his movements

as he sat up, Jake saw Alicia Cordova being forcibly manhandled away from the ballroom. One arm clamped in Maurice Stanford's vice-like grip and her other by his sister, Barbara Jeffords. Unable to stand, there was nothing on earth that Jake could do to prevent this from happening.

Hardly anyone had been witness to what had happened to Gilbert in the darkened ballroom, and even less of the crowd had any idea Jake had been rendered unconscious. The masked ball faltered only briefly before the earlier frivolity was resumed and the band struck up again.

Chapter Twenty-Six

On the way back to the hacienda, Gilbert broached the subject of how it could be possible for Wesley to have performed an almost impossible guitar solo without needing to consult the sheet music, but because he was sitting awkwardly on the backseat of the jolting cab, Wesley was able to avoid responding even though he was busy tending the gash on Gilbert's head. Also, because Gilbert was in pain he failed to notice the faint mist that seemed to wisp through the fibres of Wesley's clothes.

There was a tremendous vulnerability about the way Wesley stared down at his own hands, as if seeing them for the first time. Like a blind person having regained their sight.

When the cab reached the hacienda, Jake scrutinised Wesley's features carefully under an electric light. There was certainly a noticeable change to the texture of his now vibrant skin. His normally impassive eyes, that had always seemed dull and lacklustre, sparkled with renewed interest.

"Where in hell did that dagger come from?" Gilbert asked, after recovering enough to show interest.

"It was hidden in the sleeve of Guy's costume." Jake's answer had Gilbert even more confused.

"How come I didn't know that? I was the one who directed that bloody movie."

"You must have known about it if Guy used it in the dance. The tango had to conclude with her death."

"But he didn't use it, Jake, that's my point. You've seen the footage of that dance, so you must know that it was never used for the end sequence. We intended it, but the blade jammed. I wish to God it had been used. It was a chilling moment to see it raised up at the end of Alicia's death scene. It was bloody well perfect. We must redo that dance in the sequel. We'll use it then. How come you knew it was hidden there?"

"I didn't. Wesley did," Jake said, prompting Wesley to leave and get coffee.

"Wesley? That doesn't make sense."

"None of it does, Gil. Not when you consider everything that's happened this evening."

"I'll ask him when he returns," Gilbert said.

"What will happen to Alicia after this?" Jake asked.

"Stanford will probably lock her away for the next twenty years with the rest of his valuable possessions. You must have realised by now that she was married to him?"

"I gathered, but why on earth would she marry him? Presumably she could have had the pick of any man in Hollywood?" Jake asked, not looking at Gilbert but at Wesley as he poured out their coffee, wondering what thoughts were going on behind the controlled exterior of his handsome face.

"Alicia was a complete mess when Guy was killed. She had no interest in anything, not until she discovered that she was pregnant; after that, you became her obsession. Alicia would have married anyone to prevent her from being deported back to her country of origin. She needed to protect Guy's unborn child."

"But if she was Guy's widow, surely it would be impossible for the state to get her deported."

"It wasn't that simple. Alicia was here illegally in the States. Guy was a Canadian and a resident alien here, working with a rather dubious work permit. If that had been checked, the immigration authority in Canada would never have accepted her over their border as Guy's widow, especially because he was the illegitimate child of a Catholic girl who never registered his birth. Guy was working here on fake papers. The whole thing was a bloody mess from start to finish, and it was all about to unravel."

"She could have returned to Spain. I'd have thought anything would have been preferable to anchoring herself to that vicious creep."

"What she did was born from the fear for your safety. Alicia was from a politically active family in Madrid. Back in 1926, after she began touring over here with the dancing troupe, every member of her family was arrested. Not one of them was ever heard of again. We believe they were shot. There is still no trace of them. Trust me, Jake, I haven't been idle in trying to get what information I could."

Gilbert winced as Wesley removed another piece of broken glass from his scalp and treated the open wound with iodine.

It was late the following evening when the telephone rang. Jake picked up the receiver quickly to avoid waking Gilbert who had retired to his bed.

"Hello?" Jake asked.

"Who am I speaking to?"

Jake didn't recognise the voice. "This is Jake Velasquez. Mr Miller isn't available right now. Can you call back in the morning?"

"Jake Velasquez, the extra?"

"Yes, that is my name, but I'm not an extra."

"Actually, it's you I'm looking for, Mr Velasquez. We can't get your truck started; the carburettor keeps flooding. We need you to come over to the studio right away, as soon as you can. The director begins reshooting in an hour."

"Have you any idea what the time is now?" Jake responded irritably.

"Sure, it's just coming up for 2 a.m. is that a problem for you? You were informed this would be a night shoot when the truck was collected."

"I was, but I would've expected a bit more warning than this. Being summoned to the studio at this short notice is a bit much."

"I'm sorry. I was told that a message was sent to you from the office earlier today," the voice said.

"Who was delivering this? I got no message."

"A guy named Scott. I don't have a surname."

"I can assure you, he didn't show up here."

"Well, our apologies again if he didn't show, I can't imagine what happened."

In the background Jake heard the rasping voice of a woman reprimanding the caller.

"Are you still on the phone, Frazer? That call's costing me?" The nauseatingly familiar voice snapped, unaware she was being overheard. "How long does it take to convince a two-bit chiseller from the sticks that he's needed on set?" She swiftly masked the harshness from her voice as, childlike, she called, "Hi" to someone, confirming to Jake that the voice belonged to Barbara Jeffords.

"I'm almost done," Frazer responded lamely.

"If Scott's there, he can get the truck started. Can you put him on the phone? I'd like a word with him," Jake argued, in an attempt to get any information on Scott's whereabouts.

"I just said, didn't I? I don't know where he is," Frazer blustered unconvincingly, which made Jake very uneasy.

He realised he needed to continue his search for Scott and to do that he needed to get to the studio as soon as possible.

"So, Mr Velasquez, can we expect to see you here within the hour?" Frazer urged.

"I've a question for you before I set off. If you're prepared for this night shot, where in hell have you been hiding my truck all this time?"

"When we had the truck up on the ramp, the mechanic noticed how rusted the chassis was so it was taken to the workshop to be reinforced. The artist's safety always comes first. You will be reimbursed for your cab fare."

Jake agreed to be there as soon as he could.

It was a hot and intensely humid night. Jake didn't have a clean short-sleeved shirt to wear, and so he wore a rather flamboyant Hawaiian one with a tear on the shoulder which Gilbert loaned him.

Jake was about to place a call for a cab when Wesley emerged from the gloom to say he would drive him to the studio on the scooter, and he was not going to be dissuaded from his offer. As they were about to leave, Wesley caught hold of Jake's arm, making him stop in front of the hall mirror, where he studied their two reflections side by side. With his tousled hair and torn shirt, Jake looked every inch the young movie star, but Wesley's image in the mirror was somewhat distorted. He had changed out of his uniform and was wearing a pair of linen trousers and an open-necked shirt.

387

For the first time in their short acquaintance, his features were flushed. There were beads of perspiration gathering on his forehead, and the muscles either side of his strong jaw were clenching and unclenching. Jake had a hard time concentrating on Wesley's reflection for long as he kept losing focus. Finally he caught hold of the hallstand, fearing that he might pass out.

Jake wasn't the least bit uneasy when Wesley turned him to look at him face to face, even when he passed his fingers lightly across all of Jake's features, just as the blind would have done, committing them to memory. Jake noticed the now familiar scent of pine needles which seemed to exude from the pores of Wesley's skin as his indistinct image stabilised in the mirror. In the manservant's clear eyes there was a flicker of recognition when, all too briefly, he gave Jake the most beautiful smile, a smile that a father would have bestowed on an infant son.

"Where are you off to at this time of night?" Gilbert asked, bleary eyed, wearing his silk dressing gown and slippers. He was balancing an ice-bag on his aching head.

"They want me at the studio for a night shot in the pickup," Jake said.

"Then call them back and tell them to go to hell, Jake. You shouldn't be driving anywhere in that old truck, particularly at night."

"I won't be taking any risks in the truck, Gil. I don't think they want me there for that reason at all."

"Then why not wait until morning?"

"Because there's something going on there that isn't right. The truth is, I'm worried about Scott, if you really must know. I think he's in trouble."

"Who asked you to go?" Gilbert asked, suspiciously.

"Frazer called from Barbara Jeffords' office. He said they can't get the pickup started without me. That makes sense. I'm the one who has to drive it for the shot."

"If it's a night scene they're filming, it could be King Kong in the driving seat, so why do they want you?"

"It's my truck. I know its quirks if the engine cuts out."

"But, Jake, the filming is all done now."

"They just need a long shot on the truck."

"Did they say where?" Gilbert asked suspiciously.

"Along the upper canyon road, I believe."

"That's no more than a dirt track. You won't see more than a few feet ahead with your bad eyesight and poor headlights."

"It's OK, they've been fixed, Gil."

"They won't be that good, even if they have, which I doubt. You shouldn't go, Jake, not along that stretch of dirt track at night. This has the imprint of Stanford all over it. It's the same stretch of road where Guy went over the cliff," Gilbert said, repositioning the ice pack, as Wesley stepped between them.

"There's no need to be concerned over the safety of the young gentleman, Mr Jon. I shall take as much care of him as if he was my only son," Wesley reassured him. "I have chosen to accompany Mr Jake to the studio because, like you, I feel this might well be a trap. If so, I swear on the life of my darling wife that anyone who puts his young life in danger will pay for it dearly with their own."

"You have a wife?" Gilbert called after him as Wesley drove away from the hacienda with Jake behind him on the pillion seat. "Why did you never say?"

"If I had told you who she was, you would never have believed me." Wesley laughed.

There was a delay by the night security at the gatehouse because the guard on duty was asleep in his chair. In an attempt to regain some credibility for being caught out because of the late hour of their arrival, he checked out the studio's work schedule and said that there was no mention of any reshoots. After making a call to Frazer's office, the security guard gave Jake permission to go through, but, on his own. He told Wesley he must wait outside the studio gates for him to return.

"Where will I find them?" Jake asked the guard.

"Mr Frazer didn't say," he said dismissively.

"Then can you call him back and find out?" Jake asked.

"Not at this hour. I've already disturbed them once, and Miss Jeffords does not take kindly to that. She won't answer again at this time of night, even if I ring."

"What is Barbara Jeffords doing here at this ungodly hour?"

"That isn't my place to ask," the guard said, assuming a more dictatorial stance as he was now wide awake. "And neither is it yours," he reprimanded while peering over his spectacles at a map of the studio layout. "If I were you, I'd try the back of Stage Three. They sometimes use one of the bungalows back there as an office."

"Thanks, I know exactly where they are," Jake said, and set off into the gloom.

When he looked back, Wesley smiled at him reassuringly and re-mounted the scooter. When he fired up the engine, Jake could only hope that the manservant wouldn't abandon him there. The strangest thing about Wesley as he revved the scooter was not the phosphorous mist rising through his clothes, although that was strange enough in the gloom, instead it was the intense glow of his eyes, like piercingly red-hot coals in his pale handsome face. When Jake turned away Wesley drove off not in the direction of Pasadena, but followed the perimeter wall of the studio complex in the direction Jake was going.

The studio wasn't functioning at night; everywhere was in comparative darkness with only minimal, secondary illumination. Although Jake had the feeling that he was being followed, he was too preoccupied with the way his heart was pounding. The branding over his heart felt as if it was on fire, exactly the way it did during the ritual. Jake caught hold of the stage wall, waiting until his giddiness passed and was able to continue.

Although it was a warm and balmy night, Jake felt a biting chill cut into his clothes, and he began to walk more quickly between the stages. When he turned a corner, fully expecting it to be warmer, standing directly ahead of him in the gloom was the ghostly shape of Cloud Bird, beckoning him to follow. Trustingly, Jake followed the apparition along an alley towards the row of bungalows.

Parked outside the bungalow where he had stayed before was his old pickup. Lashed against the rails in the back of the truck was something very big and, judging from the lopsided angle of the suspension, very heavy. But the state of his truck and whatever might be in it went completely out of his mind as the door of the bungalow crashed open, allowing Jake very little time to step back into the shadows.

Outraged, he saw Scott, bound to a chair, being dragged by his hair from the bungalow by Maurice Stanford. Helping him with the weight of the chair was Barbara Jeffords' weasel-like husband. Although Scott was bound and gagged, unbeknown to his captors, he was untying the rope which bound him.

With pent-up fury, Jake was about to lurch forward in an attempt to reach him when the ghostly figure of Cloud Bird stepped in front of him, restraining him. With blurred vision he saw Scott struggle free of the rope bindings but his limbs would be stiff, and there was no time to get clear before he stumbled and fell, where he was beaten unconscious by Maurice Stanford and thrown bodily into the back of the pickup by the two men.

Blinded by rage, and disregarding the debilitating burning sensation from his branding, Jake clawed his way through the swirling mass that was Cloud Bird, and charged towards the two men. In what felt like a rush of wind, he thought rather than heard Cloud Bird calling to him.

"Don't do this, Jake. I can't protect you out there. We came back here to save you both."

Jake's blood was boiling and he wanted retribution. Running as fast as he could, with Gilbert's oversized Hawaiian shirt flapping loosely about him like a pair of demented wings, Jake reached the truck and attacked Maurice Stanford with the ferocity of a raging bull, punching him to the ground. But he failed to see Barbara Jeffords' weasel-like husband, Felix, coming up behind him wielding a baseball bat. Swinging it hard like a club, the wood connected ferociously with the back of Jake's head and everything blacked out.

Jake felt himself being dumped unceremoniously into the back of the pickup near to where Scott was slumped against the cab. He could hear Stanford, and different footsteps of someone approaching. Stanford, still obviously groggy from the attack, covered Scott over with a canvas sheet. Likewise, Jake was covered with a sheet. The men were waiting for someone, Jake thought.

Instead of the night watchman, he heard Barbara Jeffords' determined stride in high-heels, her breath shallow and quick from the exertion of walking even the short distance from her office building.

"What the hell are you doing, Maurice?" she challenged suspiciously. Ignoring her husband's protests as if he didn't exist, she yanked back the crumpled sheet covering Jake.

He kept his eyes closed, lying face down on the open back of the truck.

"You've got eyes in your head, woman, what in hell do you think I'm doing? I'm taking care of this piece of crap. He came at me from nowhere. I don't know who he is, but he's going to damn well pay for this," Stanford retorted.

"Is he dead?" Barbra Jeffords said.

"Turn the prick over and let's see. If he isn't he soon will be."

Jake felt hands lifting up his head.

"What's that kid from Fort Laverne doing here, Maurice?" Barbara Jeffords said, turning her head from his.

"Fort Laverne? You mean it's that blackmailer's son, Velasquez?"

"Sometimes I can't believe that we're related at all, Maurice. You do know who this is, don't you?"

"I just said, didn't I?" Stanford snarled.

"Velasquez be damned. Don't you ever read the memos I've sent you about this kid?"

"Do you think I've got time to wade through that stack of paperwork piling up my in tray every day? Don't ask me about what I have or haven't read, because that's down to your nickel and dime budget cuts. You're the one who fired my assistant."

"Don't evade the issue. You damn well should have read them. Just turn the brat over and you'll see what I mean. Do it, Maurice."

"I've already seen one Velasquez, why bother with a younger version?" he growled, and spat out a mouthful of blood, and a couple of broken teeth.

"That's horse shite, Maurice. Only a mindless idiot would think the way you do. You've only got to look at this kid's face to know

392

that he and that old bastard aren't related. For God's sake, wake up. You've seen the screen test. Who did you think he was, Adolf Hitler?" she shrieked close to Jake's ear. "Look at him, Maurice. This is Alicia's son. The same kid you were going to cast in the sequel."

Stanford reached in to roll Jake onto his back; he peered into his face while Jake kept perfectly still. "Are you having a cheap laugh? What if he does look like Guy Maddox, I would have thought someone who's been in the business as long as you have, Babs, wouldn't be fooled by stage make-up. You know how good they are in that department." He started to rub hard at Jake's face.

"No department is that good, Maurice. Trust me, this is Alicia's son. Who else could have spawned an identical lookalike, except for that, that triple threat?"

"Triple threat?"

"That all singing, dancing, and acting machine, Guy Maddox."

"But that's impossible. It can't be him. It can't be. Alicia's kid's dead; Maxwell arranged it."

"Then that old pervert lied, as this proves. So what do you propose doing with her kid now that he's still alive, Maurice?"

"I'll just do what I should have done years ago with his blackmailing substitute of a father. I'll get rid of this chiselling little prick for good, that's what." Stanford exclaimed viciously.

"And how do you propose to do that, if he isn't dead? Dump him at the side of the road, and expect him to keep quiet when he comes round?" Barbara Jeffords asked, throwing the sheet back over Jake.

Jake let out a groan.

"I've had a much better idea. All this situation needs is some creative imagination and the drain on our finances will be ended – for good this time."

"Now I am interested," she urged.

"What better way than getting rid of this little swine in exactly the same way we did with Maddox."

"You can't seriously be considering that old trick again, Maurice? We barely got away with it last time, and God alone knows, we wouldn't again."

"Why the hell not, the plan would have worked out perfectly if that dork of a reporter hadn't been snapping us with his camera. He's dead and out of the way, so with no one else spying, then why not get rid of the kid in the same way? Well, are you going along with it?"

"I suppose there is some merit in the plan. It would do us all a favour just as long as it goes smoothly this time."

"Trust me, it will," Stanford said.

Jake groaned at a well-aimed punch into his ribs.

"So, how long have you known this kid was still alive?"

"About a week, I suppose. I made Dawlish show me the kid's screen test before I offered to release any cash. I could have thrown up when I saw that footage but it got me thinking. If the lookalike kid had presented himself at the studio as Ivan Velasquez's son, it didn't take long to figure out the connection to Guy Maddox."

"How come you saw through it, Babs, when no one else did?"

"Think of the connection with Fort Laverne where this kid was brought up," she said, waiting for the response, which never came. "It's the same dump that Eugene Maxwell moved to after he resigned from the hospital where Alicia gave birth."

"Maxwell moved out there for a good reason."

"And what was that?"

"Because, Babs, I shelled out a king's ransom for Maxwell to get rid of Alicia's brat. Whoever this kid looks like it can't be him. I know that for sure, because Maxwell was paid to suffocate the little bastard."

"Well you paid him for nothing, unless there was something else."

"Yes, but how do you explain the dead baby in the coffin? It had to be there to comfort Alicia at the service. How did he manage that?"

"It wouldn't be that hard for a doctor at the hospital to swap a live kid for a dead one."

She lit a cigarette with another match and inhaled deeply before tossing the cover back across Jake's face.

"Does Alicia know about any of this?"

"What do you think after that incident at the ball? That Spanish bitch has always been too smart for her own good. Of course she suspects."

"What can we do, Babs? If this gets out, we'll all be ruined. Alicia's bound to talk."

"Well, first, you need to keep your nerve. Everything is under control. I've made sure of that. Alicia's been heavily sedated, at least for now."

"But what do we do when that temperamental bitch comes around again? How in hell do we prevent her from going to the press?" Stanford asked, tentatively fingering the deep gauges across his cheek.

"That's already been taken care of. The Four Oakes Asylum has agreed to send over all of the necessary paperwork we need to have her committed. The only problem you will have with that, Maurice, is when the press gets to know that another of your wives has been committed to a mental institution."

"Gee, Babs. You've thought of everything, I should have done it years back. An asylum is the best place for a temperamental spitfire like her."

"Everything, that is, except for disposing of that kid of hers: for good, this time."

"Then I say we go ahead with my plan that's already in hand and ditch the freak over the canyon along that same stretch of road where we got rid of Maddox. There's no better way to cover this up than by proving we were the victims of a daring robbery," Stanford exclaimed with renewed enthusiasm. "Last time the whole plan was almost ruined by that jerk of a reporter."

"What do you mean 'almost'? We were ruined," she hissed.

The sound of Scott recovering drew her attention, and Jake heard the sound of the tarpaulin being pulled back.

"Holy cow Maurice, what in hell is this jerk doing here? This is Marjory Dawlish's kid brother?"

"So, who gives a damn? There was no choice, Babs, that nosey bastard saw what we did to the steering rods on this truck. The only way to keep him quiet is to get rid of him at the same time as the other one." Stanford spoke confidently as Jake felt Barbara rustle around inside the pickup as she examined Scott's bindings.

"Then you need to get up there and rope him up tight against the side. Even I could get free from those knots in two seconds flat."

"Don't have a go at me. Blame Felix, he did that."

"That dope can't even tie his own shoelaces properly without help," she exclaimed bitterly. "Well, don't just stand there. Get on with it now, Maurice, and for God's sake, do it quick before the wrangler comes around again." She virtually spat with anger, as Scott groaned loudly.

"I can't get up there, Babs. You know what the doc said. I'm not to climb with my bad back."

"Then you and Felix had better help me up there, and I'll do it."

She cursed loudly as the two men groaned and pushed and shoved her huge backside onto the tailgate; Jake saw a blur of her white bulging thighs between her suspenders and stocking tops as she was manhandled into the truck.

With an unskilled hand, she roped Scott back against the side of the truck as tightly as she could, before covering him over with the canvas sheet.

"Maybe this wasn't such a bad idea, after all, Maurice," she said, sweating heavily. "With any luck, the cops might think these two faggots had a lovers' tiff, and that's what sent their truck off the road, and over the cliff edge."

Before she got down off the truck she pulled back the other, larger, tarpaulin to uncover a large iron office safe.

"What in God's name is this doing on the back of the truck, Maurice? I want answers. Explain yourself," she screeched, bordering on hysteria.

"Isn't it obvious? What better way to establish a heist than for the safe to disappear? It was a pure stroke of genius."

"More like a stroke of madness. How in hell did you and that pathetic excuse for a husband of mine get it on here? It weighs a ton."

"I got Frazer and Malcolm Reynolds to get the safe onto the back of the truck this afternoon. No one saw them. You can trust me on that, Babs."

"I can't trust you to do anything, you brainless idiot. How old are you, for God's sake, three? Are you so brain-dead that you've forgotten what we keep inside? Well, have you? If the law gets their hands on any of those incriminating papers, we'll all be done for: you, me, and Felix. Even those two blundering imbeciles you employ would get slung in jail and they'd throw away the key."

"You've lost me. What imbeciles?"

"Frazer and the human bulldozer of course. That idiot with the broken nose, Reynolds."

"OK, so I made an error of judgement. I get that, but after this accident there won't be any evidence left to connect the contents of the safe to anything or anyone of us. Not when all of this goes over the cliff in the truck."

"The safe is earthquake proof, you dunderhead," Barbara Jeffords screamed at him.

Jake felt her getting onto her knees and begin a frantic attempt to dial open the combination of the safe.

"Felix, don't just stand there with your mouth gaping open. Get up here NOW and lend a hand. You are better with this than I am," she shrieked in his face, as her husband reluctantly clambered onto the back of the pickup.

Barbara Jeffords was about to get off all fours when she froze, hearing a man coming towards them through the alley, whistling.

"Stay down, Babs, and hide. You too Felix." Stanford hissed through the railings, as Jake heard Wesley come around the corner.

"Say, you there." Jake heard Wesley calling out. "Could you help me? I'm looking for someone?"

"Maybe I could. Who would that be?" Stanford asked casually.

Jake heard the puff of him lighting a cigar as if he hadn't a care in the world as Wesley approached.

"Jake Velasquez: he's a good-looking boy about twenty-five years old? I've been waiting at the gate to take him home. The security guard allowed me through to find him."

"Security let you through?" Stanford asked suspiciously as the cigar went out.

"Sure. The guard knows me from dropping Jake off at the studio before," Wesley said, offering up the visitor's pass pinned onto his shirt.

"Sorry. Looks like you've just missed him," Stanford said, playing for time.

"Have you any idea where I might find him? It's important," Wesley said amiably, reaching into his pocket for his lighter to relight Stanford's cigar.

Inhaling deeply, Stanford relaxed, having presumably taken control of the situation. "The kid went off to open up one of the lock-ups where I could drop off his truck overnight," he said, fully prepared to wait it out.

Scott groaned from underneath the canvas sheet as he started to come around.

"How about this as an idea: I can drop you off there now, if you like?" Stanford said, as though he fully expected Wesley to refuse the offer.

But Wesley did exactly the opposite.

"Let me get the tailgate up for you," Wesley said casually enough, as Jake's foot jerked out from underneath the other tarpaulin. "I shouldn't think you would want this load to get spread across the sidewalk?"

"Thanks. I'd have done it myself only I've got a back problem. I'm waiting for my driver to show up. He deals with that sort of thing," Stanford said, consulting his watch irritably. "I've no idea where the two guys I employ have got to. They should've been here long before now. They're better at getting this pile of junk started than I am. It's probably better if you don't wait for a lift. It could be some time yet before they arrive."

Breathing heavily from the exertion, Stanford forced his huge frame through the cab door and sat in the passenger seat. "When I see the kid, I'll be sure and send him back to you at the gate directly."

Wesley had other ideas. Before Stanford could protest he got into the driver's seat and revved up the engine, grating the gears into first, just as Frazer and Malcolm Reynolds came into view, running towards the moving truck.

Unwilling to swerve an inch, the truck narrowly missed hitting them both as they flattened themselves like cardboard up against the wall of the soundstage.

"Slow down, for mercy's sake or you'll kill us both," Stanford howled through gritted teeth.

Wesley drove towards the delivery gate at the back of the studios. Refusing to stop at the lowered barrier, he crashed through the bar, which splintered like dry matchwood. The impact badly cracked the passenger side of the split windscreen.

"Where in hell are you taking me?"

"Where else but up the old canyon road," Wesley announced. Jake thought he sounded calm amid the stench of burning rubber as the truck rounded a sharp bend.

The tyres squealed noisily as it turned onto the upper road, and then he accelerated hard to gain as much speed as he could before reaching the approach to the canyon road up a steep hill out of the city.

"But you can't. You don't understand. This truck isn't safe for anyone to drive. For pity's sake, whoever you are, slow down before you have us all killed."

"The truck isn't safe? How come? I thought it had been serviced for tonight's filming?" Wesley asked, yanking unnecessarily hard on the steering, making the vehicle swerve badly, and throwing Jake and Scott to the side of the pickup.

"Well, it isn't. For God's sake, slow down now while you are still able to steer."

"So that's it, is it? You've rigged the steering rods to either come loose or snap off?"

"I... I..."

"You evil bastard! How can you and any one of your cohorts sleep at night?" Wesley hissed. Jake caught the flicker of light as Wesley switched on the poor headlights as they came to the end of the street lighting and he accelerated up the sharp incline of the road into the night.

"For God's sake STOP this. I'll pay anything, anything you ask, only pull over now and let me out," Stanford shrieked, as Wesley increased speed.

"You're going nowhere. It's time for you to experience what Guy Maddox had to on the night you sent him plunging to his death. You must remember what happened that night."

"I know nothing. Whatever you've been told, it's all lies," Stanford whimpered.

"Why not allow me to refresh your memory. The way it went was like this. By the time Guy reached a certain point in the road, you were waiting up ahead for him with Velasquez, where that log you felled was blocking the road to make him swerve. Surely, you haven't forgotten how you both fixed the accelerator and steering rods before Guy set off?"

Stanford was oblivious to Barbara Jeffords' screams for him to stop the truck. Jake watched as she fought her way clear from beneath a pile of boxes where Felix remained cowed. Then she stumbled heavily in an attempt to regain her balance when the screeching tyres took a corner too severely before it diverted onto the old canyon road. This sudden swerve caused her to lurch forward where she appeared to dive headfirst into the safe with the speed of a raging elephant. She crashed head-on into the solid metal door and was immediately concussed.

"Who in God's name are you?" Stanford screeched, gripping onto the dashboard in terror as the vehicle made the sharp turn off the road and hurtled along the old dirt road that ran along the edge of the canyon.

"Take a wild guess, Stanford. Who do you think would travel back so far to make you pay for what you did to me and my family?"

"Let me out of here, you bloody lunatic," Stanford wailed, beating his fists on the dashboard with desperation. "Take me back to the studio. You've got me confused with someone else in connection with all of these twisted ramblings. I don't know you."

"That isn't true, though, is it? After all, you and your tramp of a sister should know very well who I am, having arranged my death right down to the last detail."

"You're mistaken. I have never killed anyone in my entire life,"

Stanford screeched.

"Then I suppose you naturally deny forcing my truck off the canyon road, and arranging for my new-born son to be murdered, you jerk. All that, because you just had to possess my wife for yourself," Wesley hissed menacingly.

"What d' you mean your 'wife'?" Blinded by fear, Stanford's attitude altered as he fumbled desperately inside his pocket, and he pulled out a short metal object. "No one knew about Guy Maddox, no one. There were only the three of us. So now you've got me here, why not come clean. Who the hell are you, another hack reporter after his big scoop?" Stanford snarled dangerously and clicked open the deadly blade from the flick-knife. He gave a savage upward thrust and plunged the honed steel deep into Wesley's side, while at the same time foolishly attempting to grab hold of the steering wheel.

Instead of Wesley keeling over, his hand clamped around Stanford's wrist with a vice-like grip, ever-tightening his grasp until Stanford squealed with the unnaturally high-pitched shriek of a girl as Jake heard a bone of his wrist shatter.

Stanford's other hand released its hold on the knife protruding from Wesley's strong body. Wesley didn't react at all to the deadly blade that should have been draining the life away from him.

"You swine, you've shattered my wrist," Stanford howled in agony. "You should be dead or dying by now," he screeched.

"How can you expect to kill a man who is already dead, Stanford?" Wesley said, turning to face him, his eyes like red-hot coals simmering with fury. "Your time's almost up, you evil bastard, get prepared for a journey into hell."

"I'll pay anything you ask if you'll only listen to reason. Whatever you were told was all lies. Guy Maddox's death was an accident. I swear that's the truth." Stanford gasped with agonising pain. Beside him the physical shape of the man driving the truck appeared to be gradually transforming into a pulsating green mist.

"My earthly body might have died that night, Stanford, but not my avenging spirit which is about to dispatch you to where you belong." Wesley's disembodied voice reverberated around the cab.

"I'm here to avenge the wrongs you and your sister have done to my family."

"I am innocent, I swear."

"And we both know you put my wife through a living hell, thinking our son was dead."

"I didn't kill him. He is alive – in the back of the truck. Pull over and I'll show you," he squealed.

"I know that. What I also know is that, very soon, you and your evil bitch of a sister are going to experience the same fate you arranged for me." Wesley said, the timbre of his voice becoming strangely distorted. To Jake it sounded like interference on the airwaves of a radio transmission.

As Wesley's dissolving foot pressed down hard on the accelerator, the increase of speed prompted Stanford to scream – wild and shrill – like a child under attack, tearful and wailing, as if the Devil himself was propelling him into the depths of Hades. There was the nauseating stench of urine as a dark patch spread across the crotch of his immaculate pants.

What had seemed like a sack of potatoes in the back of the pickup struggled to stand up when the petrified screams of her brother roused Barbara Jeffords out of her concussion. Horrified, she too began wailing hysterically. It was a terrifying sound causing Felix to retreat even deeper under the layers of tarpaulin as he saw the desperate shape of his bullying wife clinging onto the side rails of the truck for grim death in an attempt to sit up. She was oblivious to the fact that on the opposite side of the pickup Scott had freed himself of the binding ropes. Wesley's fractured voice seemed to gather strength as he bellowed at him through the partition window.

"We're running out of time, Scott. Before I lose control of this truck, do what you can and save yourself, and for God's sake get my boy out of here while you have time," Wesley cried with increasing urgency.

Needing no further prompting, Scott wrapped Jake in a blanket and, for his added safety, hauled him as close as he dared to the end of the truck. Dropping the tailgate, he positioned them in readiness for the first chance to jump clear of the moving truck to land anywhere on the irregular patches of narrow ground between the edge of the road and the cliff face, praying for a decent patch of grass to help cushion their fall when they went.

"You have to chance this and jump now, Scott. I can't hold this truck steady for much longer." Wesley called through the window, as one of the steering rods snapped, causing the vehicle to swerve dramatically across the narrow road towards the canyon wall and then swerve back again towards the edge of the cliff amid the sound of squealing tyres.

Holding Jake's wrapped body tightly against him, Scott jumped backwards off the swaying truck as cleanly as he could, having positioned himself underneath Jake to cushion him from injury. It would be a serious impact with the rocky, compacted surface of the road.

Inside the careering truck, the interior of the cab had filled with an acrid green smoke, which would have made it virtually impossible to see the road ahead through the cracked windscreen. Through this swirling fog, Wesley's indeterminate shape offered no resistance when Maurice Stanford reached across him, and grabbed onto the steering wheel.

Squealing like a pig being slaughtered, the truck began to accelerate even faster along the narrowing road towards the treacherously sharp bend immediately ahead. Rigid with fear, Stanford was unable to squeeze past the steering wheel to switch off the engine. With desperation, he grappled to control the wheel with his only workable hand in a final attempt to keep the truck from swerving any closer towards the edge of the canyon.

As the truck neared the deadly bend in the road the swirling green fog evaporated. Unbelievably, instead of seeing Wesley's lifeless body slumped back into the seat, all that remained was the crumpled shape of a human being with every living fibre sucked out of it, a grotesquely abandoned shell of a man, with no apparent living substance in him at all. Where the knife had been plunged into Wesley's side there was no sign of blood, only a thick green substance smelling strongly of pine needles oozing out of the wound.

With a resounding crack the damaged steering rods severed completely and the speeding truck went out of control just as it cornered that fatal bend. It swerved violently towards the edge of the canyon where it careered into space over the edge of the ravine.

Hanging for grim death onto the side rails in the back of the truck, Barbara Jeffords clung onto them like a gladiatorial soprano from *The Flying Dutchman*. For a long moment the launched vehicle appeared to glide across the canyon, the woman's screams of terror echoing those of her brother who was alone inside the cab. There was no longer any sign of Wesley's lifeless shape in the driver's seat, only a rapidly corroding flick-knife.

The terrifying screams fell silent when the truck nose-dived, plunging like a falling rock, cab first, into the rocky base of the cliff. The gasoline tank exploded on impact, erupting into a spiralling whoosh of flames.

Chapter Twenty-Seven

It took a full year before Gilbert had the sequel completed for his previous movie *The Return of Xavier Gérard* and, by that time, the reprinted original starring Guy Maddox and Alicia Cordova had been out on general release, opening to rave reviews. Gilbert's reputation as an inspired director was established virtually overnight.

It took that entire year for Scott to recover from his injuries, and that fact alone kept Jake grounded. He was agreeable enough to perform in Gilbert's sequel when asked and, at the end of the filming, he confessed he had genuinely enjoyed the experience, particularly in those sequences which featuring his mother. Jake's only insistence before the movie's release was that he was allowed to perform under his own name of Guy Maddox Jnr. When the shooting was finally over, Gilbert had insisted on signing over the deeds of the Maxwell ranch in Fort Laverne to Jake and his mother.

On the day of departure Firebrand was loaded into the horsebox. Marjory saw them off from the gates of the old Silver Lake Studio. Behind her, someone using a megaphone was shouting: "Quiet please. Action... Rolling."

Marjory grumbled something about adolescent incompetence, before she strode back through the studio gates.

Once Gilbert's lawyer had drawn up all the documents required for the transfer of ownership of the Maxwell ranch, Jake took the train to visit him in Santa Rowena and signed the relevant documents.

After spending a year and a half in California, where everything in the city of Los Angeles seemed to be either unreal or out of step with everyday living, Jake found, in comparison, that the level of traffic noise and scurrying townsfolk in Santa Rowena, made him wonder why he had ever been troubled by it in the first place.

After he had signed the deeds of ownership Jake went in

search of a decent horse from the only stables in town, which was in the process of being converted into a garage, with a range of expensive apartments for sale above. Fortunately, the property was still under the same ownership and he was able to purchase a job lot of bridles, halters, and rope, before he went in search of the local Knackers yard, to where the few remaining horses had been dispatched.

After some intensive negotiation with the run-down slaughterhouse, Jake purchased not just one of the mares, as he'd previously intended, but all twelve of the mares and two foals. In addition he negotiated a deal to purchase three overworked donkeys, a mule, and a beaten-up cart, with the irritating sound of the owner's voice ringing in his ears, telling him that if any one of the bony relics which Jake had purchased made even half the distance to Fort Laverne, it would be a miracle.

Once the mule was hitched up, and the cart had been loaded, Jake used an old Navajo method for roping the horses and donkeys individually, before setting off on the forty-mile trek across the reservation, wrongly estimating the journey would take no longer than two days and nights. In fact, it took him the best part of a week after one of the ailing donkeys got worse, collapsed, and died. Another day was lost rounding up two of the mares that slipped their halters, and then another day was lost when he went swimming in the river.

On this occasion, Jake was challenged by four young braves who seemingly appeared from nowhere in a beaten-up truck, towing a horse box, questioning Jake's right to be on Navajo land, and demanding four of the mares in payment. In a moment, still wet from the river, Jake jumped down from one of the mares, ready to fight all four of the men, if need be, to defend his property when the nearest of the braves signalled for the others to get down from the back of the pickup.

Instead, he looked on, stunned, when they fell to their knees, bowing their heads in acknowledgement to Jake's superiority. It was only when he saw each of the braves staring at the branding over his heart that he understood why. Even so, it proved to be a difficult encounter as they seemed unable to regard him as an equal while they shared a meal. Soon after they had eaten together the braves left, reassuring him that no one else would hinder his journey to the ranch.

As Jake neared Fort Laverne it was the silence that caught him unawares. When he rode through the main street it had become more like a ghost town than ever as all but three, maybe four, families of the original townsfolk had seemingly left. Something Jake couldn't have imagined when he had left there more than a year ago was that he would have felt so elated to return, and yet he did.

Parked in an open space outside of the Maxwell ranch was a large assortment of dusty and well-travelled vehicles, most of these with trailers and horseboxes attached. There were more of the same parked up the long drive leading up to the hacienda, but none of these mattered when he caught sight of Gia's solitary figure on the porch waiting for him to arrive. He was confused to see his Navajo mother-figure in ceremonial regalia befitting her position as the wife of a chief, which traditionally would only have been worn in her grandmother's day for an important ceremony. There were embroidered symbols on the clothing, similar to those she had worked into the ceremonial blanket for the ritual of Cloud Bird's spiritual return.

There was also a noticeable change of attitude towards Jake, as she came forward to greet him when he dismounted. Unlike the embrace he had expected after this long-awaited return, this woman, who from infancy had treated Jake as her own son, said nothing at all; instead, she kissed the backs of both hands with an unexpected reverence. Gia then unfolded an intricately designed cloth to reveal a beaten silver armlet in the shape of an eagle's claw. There was an inlaid, cross-banded mesh made from the finest gold thread, so delicate and pale that it could have been Jake's own hair as a child. Inset into the centre of this remarkable armlet was a piece of green turquoise, expertly carved into the shape of an eagle's head.

After Gia had fitted this about his upper arm, she smiled

warmly, welcoming him home. When he asked after Moon Spirit's whereabouts and, the burning question – if there had been a child – the only information she offered was that at exactly high noon he should arrive at Shadow Rock, where all of his questions would be answered.

Instead of Gia leading Jake into the kitchen where she would normally have prepared a meal for his return, she led him into the courtyard where old Nykodema was waiting. Unlike the last time Jake had seen him, the old man treated him with the same unnerving reverence he had displayed to the Navajo chief. It made Jake very uncomfortable indeed, aware that something important was about to happen.

A fire had been made in the centre of the courtyard, over which hung a steaming pot. A few Navajo items had been laid out on a stone bench, consisting of a loincloth decorated with mystic symbols, a woven headband, and a pair of moccasins. Added to these was a woven belt, a hunting knife in a sheath, and an empty leather pouch.

Unable to prevent it from happening, Jake allowed the old medicine man to remove all of his European clothes. This included Gilbert's wristwatch and Jake's spectacles, both of which he resisted but then relaxed when the old man put them into the leather pouch and attached it to the Navajo belt.

Seating Jake cross-legged on an embroidered blanket, old Nykodema poured some green liquid from the steaming pot, which Jake had to drink in one long draught. It was a nauseating potion that was both thick and slimy. Jake dreaded to think what the concoction contained. It was a potion, more like molten lava than any liquid, which left him with an angry burning sensation all the way down to his stomach. After that, everything around became hazy and distant.

When Jake came to, he felt cleansed and refreshed. He was aware that his face and body had been shaved of all hair. Although everything was still hazy, without wearing his glasses there was an odd clarity, as if the mist was clearing. He discovered that he was now wearing the loincloth, moccasins, and the woven headband.

Nykodema had finished painting symbols across Jake's forehead and was now engrossed in depicting a pair of eagle wings across his chest, ending with a series of tribal symbols that encircled the ritual branding.

Grunting with satisfaction, the old man fastened the belt around Jake's waist and gave a toothless smile when Jake attempted to put on his spectacles, saying: "You no need this day," indicating the courtyard around them which Jake could see with perfect clarity.

When the midday sun was almost overhead, Gia and old Nykodema were nowhere to be found, and Jake made his way to the stable block. Shockingly, every one of the many stalls was empty except one where his dappled mare greeted him ecstatically. Slipping Cloud Bird's old rope halter over the mare's head, he rode bareback towards the reservation where he hoped to meet Moon Spirit at Shadow Rock in the sacred burial ground.

It was an unusually cloudy day, hot and muggy, with scarcely a breath of wind and yet the leaves on the sparse saplings growing from the cracks on the cliff face trembled as a brilliant ray of sunlight broke through the clouds. The shadow of a hovering bird was briefly cast onto the rocks beside him. It faded immediately as the ray of sunlight slid into the gathering clouds.

As Jake experienced the first cold chill on his bare arms he knew that Cloud Bird was very near. Unlike the infrequent occasions in California when he had been visible, this time he was not. With the sole purpose in mind of finding him, Jake rode the mare carefully down the rocky incline above the burial site where he was convinced he would be confronted by his lost companion. But, when the sun broke through the clouds, instead of Cloud Bird's ghostly apparition it was Moon Spirit who was waiting for him beside the dark rock face where he dismounted. She was heart-wrenchingly beautiful and looked every inch the daughter of a Navajo chief. Cradled lovingly in her arms was their beautiful son.

Seated regally on a horse immediately behind her was her father, Chief Oglala, silent and glowering ferociously in war paint, his lance poised in readiness to hurl at any intruder. He wore a full ceremonial headdress and armlets of eagle feathers the way his forefathers would have done. On his chest hung a beaded decoration of symbols, hanging from this was a disc of turquoise and more eagle feathers.

When Jake appeared, Chief Oglala lowered his lance in respect, with a slight incline of his head. The image of her father might have been cast in bronze had it not been for the slight movement of the quivering feathers on his dramatic headdress.

Perfectly formed, the infant was unlike any child Jake had ever seen, and as the baby gazed back at him Jake knew that he and Moon Spirit had achieved the seemingly impossible by returning her brother's spirit back to earth, safe in the body of their own child.

Contrasting starkly against the infant's olive skin, the colour of its hair was so pale that it shone like strands of white gold in the sun, and only then Jake realised that it wasn't finely wrought strands of gold incorporated into the armlet he wore, but strands of the child's hair.

When Jake took hold of their son and held him aloft, he saw the same steady look of recognition in his eyes as he had seen in the eyes of Cloud Bird after any length of time they had been forced to stay apart. In such bright sunlight, the infant gave the impression that sunlight radiated from him. But more moving was the boy's welcoming smile, so like the one Cloud Bird had given him on the very first day they met. It virtually took Jake's breath away. This was not the gurgling pleasure of a contented baby but a beautiful, briefly adult, smile. It sent an immense shudder of happiness through Jake knowing he'd been partially responsible for returning his blood brother and dear friend to his Navajo tribe. It was a birth, which he hoped would one day become an extraordinary life.

Cradling the child in his arms, Jake shaded his eyes to look beyond a gap in the clouds. Wheeling high above them was the glorious shape of a great eagle. In the brilliant sunlight, it seemed that the burnished wing feathers were ablaze with fire and that its entire shape was slowly being consumed by flames as the sunlight became more intense. Then as swiftly as the dramatic shape of the bird had appeared, it was gone, swallowed up amongst the swirling clouds as the gap between them closed.

"Thank you, Pale Horse, for this precious gift," Moon Spirit said when he handed the infant back into her keeping. She looked down at the child and smiled in such a way that Jake saw that her life was complete and that she regarded Jake only as a treasured companion and a good father for their child. "At sundown there will be a council gathering to name our son, and also to honour your return."

"What name have you chosen?" Jake asked.

"I thought Diyin would be appropriate."

"Diyin? To be truthful, I'm unsure about that. It's not a name that I'm familiar with. It sounds too much like 'dying' to be right for such a wonderful child as this," Jake answered cautiously.

Moon Spirit laughed. "Idiot, the word translates as 'He that is holy,' and I believe our son is exactly that."

"Then it sounds perfect."

"So you agree?"

"Yes, I do, absolutely."

"Then my father will be content. The elders are already calling Diyin the winged Messiah."

She placed their son safely into a papoose, intricately decorated with layers of coloured bark. In the centre, worked in beaten silver, was the flight of a descending eagle through a bank of dark clouds.

Once she was mounted on horseback with the papoose strapped onto her back, Moon Spirit rode off towards the village without a backward glance, primarily escorted by her father, but immediately shadowed by four warriors forming a guard of honour. Strikingly noticeable, was the proud bearing the braves assumed on horseback; young Navajos with a purpose so altered to the indifference displayed by the tribal youth which had been so apparent when he had left for California.

Beckoning Jake to lead this war party were eight mounted braves, banded together in a protective formation, young warriors from an unfamiliar tribe who had journeyed a considerable distance to be present at the Navajo sundown ceremony. Unlike the reservation braves, many of them wore jeans and T-shirts, but none of that detracted from their pride in being invited to be an integral part of this momentous event. From the direction of the village came the sound of chants and drumming which echoed through the canyon.

In the distance, three chieftains of different tribes were gathered astride horses, waiting expectantly for the stately entourage to arrive. With them were the tribal elders of the village and old Nykodema, all of them waiting for Moon Spirit and the child named 'He that is holy' to return. The emotion Jake felt watching them was indescribable, knowing that Cloud Bird's spirit had already begun repairing the damaged pride of the Navajo nation through the birth of his son. Beyond that, who could imagine what else the child's miracle birth might achieve during his own lifetime?

On Jake's arrival at an area of religious ground where the ceremony was due to take place, the huge gathering had already parted to allow Chief Oglala and Moon Spirit access through a circle of brightly painted rocks and twelve boulders, forming the arena. Dominating the centre of this was an oblong, wooden platform. Mystic symbols had been painted around the edge. Similar to the twelve boulders in the arena, two rocks supporting this platform had been intricately adorned with painted symbols, whereas the surface of the platform was plain and had none. On the ground underneath were four incense burners. At head height, four unlit torches were staked into the ground at each corner.

Chief Oglala and Gia were already seated a short distance away, parallel to the platform. The child looked on quietly from the chief's lap as Moon Spirit approached Jake when he dismounted.

"Nykodema asked that we stand opposite each other, at either end of the altar," Moon Spirit said. When positioned in readiness, they were separated by the short platform at table height. "Whatever happens during this ceremony, I am assured that our child will come to no harm, Pale Horse."

"I want to believe that, but as this ceremony has never been performed before, it is hard not to question what danger he might face," Jake said.

"Just remember what ordeals you went through to bring my brother's spirit back, and how you persevered despite everything that happened. This is Diyin's holy initiation, and nothing must interfere with that. His birth was a sacred event and must be recognised as such. Promise me, Pale Horse, that you will do nothing to hinder these proceedings. Promise me."

"You have my word on that. How could I do any other when we have already entrusted our own lives to this holy man who helped return Cloud Bird into the body of this child. That, and the respect our son already commands, speaks volumes."

At sundown the fragmented canopy of clouds became a breathtaking sight, as if they were blazing with fire. It was the perfect herald to the opening of the spiritual ceremony. At four equidistant positions along the canyon ridge, ceremonial beacons were lit as the final rays of the sun sank beyond the canyon wall and the night sky clouded over.

When the irregular drumming began, eight teenage Navajo boys appeared, twisting and moving around and around the platform until eventually they stopped before Chief Oglala and the child, forming into the shape of a quivering bird. In the lead was the boy with a feathered headdress. Behind him were three others. The last of these wore a feathered tail attached to his waist. On either side of the second boy, two other boys formed the wings. On this final circuit, the lead boy lit each of the flaming torches at all four corners of the platform. Once each of the torches burst into flame, the chanting became even louder.

Through a break in the clouds a beam of moonlight illuminated the intricate painted symbols on the altar. When the drumming stopped and the formation broke apart, Nykodema made his way towards the platform with the child in his arms. Reverently, he laid the infant on the platform in a crucifix position with an arm extended towards each parent, its head positioned towards the east, its unblinking eyes gazing transfixed on the moon.

Following the child's gaze, Jake saw the silhouette of an eagle glide slowly across the face of the silvery orb before cloud blocked out the light. With only flaming torches to illuminate the altar,

Nykodema, unrolled a length of fine white cloth, decorated around the border with mystical symbols. Drawn in charcoal at the centre was the outline of an eagle in flight. Carefully opening out the cloth, he covered every inch of the infant's body, placing the emblem over the child's heart. Giving one end of the cloth to Moon Spirit, he handed the other to Jake, as a narrow shaft of moonlight broke through the clouds, isolating the emblem. From a pouch, Nykodema sprinkled three pinches of glittering dust over the charcoal shape and stepped quickly away.

Until Jake looked across at Moon Spirit, and saw the calm reassurance in her face, he was finding it difficult to breathe in his concern for the safety of their son when, amid a shower of sparks, a slender plume of smoke coiled up from the emblem, Desperate to get the infant from underneath the cloth, Jake glanced at her again, fully prepared to go against his promise if she was in agreement. Although her distressed features bordered on alarm, her eyes had that familiar, grim determination from their childhood, and knew that he must remain steadfast in his resolve.

Within moments the plume of smoke had evaporated as the beam of moonlight spread over the cloth. From beneath the altar, a mist filtered up from the incense burners and swirled around the base until the platform appeared to be floating on a cloud. Incredibly, the infant's body began to levitate off the platform until it was at chest height with its parents. Although every one of the symbols decorating the edge of the cloth were there, where the charcoal outline of the eagle had been, there was no sign, nor was there any scorching, nothing at all, just a pristine surface of the cloth. Both parents visibly breathed a sigh of relief as the levitated child slowly lowered down to the altar.

When Nykodema removed the cloth, he lifted up the naked infant from the platform, proudly displaying the branding of an eagle over its heart, identical to Jake's own. Accompanied on either side by Jake and Moon Spirit, Nykodema handed the infant into Chief Oglala's expectant arms. Moon Spirit sat at his right hand, Jake on his left. Once they were both seated, the final celebrations got underway.

The sundown ceremony concluded by sunrise and the decision about his own future was made so much easier, freeing him to be true to his innermost feelings.

"I will always love you, Pale Horse, for what you have done for my brother, returning his spirit back to this nation through our son."

"I would willingly risk my life again to have been instrumental in that. My only concern is the colour of my skin. Will I be allowed to spend any time with him on the reservation?"

"You can be assured of that; you are his earthly father. Without your unquestionable love and bravery, he would never have been reborn to fulfil whatever destiny fate has in store. Everyone is aware that, without you, it would not have been possible."

"Even so, because I was only a blood brother to Cloud Bird, will that not prove detrimental to the devotion of his followers?"

"Your position on the reservation has changed, Pale Horse. After meeting with the elders, my father was allowed to adopt you as his son. You can be reassured that, although this child will grow up safe in my father's care, I will tutor his education. Any mystical instruction will be undertaken by old Nykodema."

After taking his leave of Moon Spirit and his son, Jake had no doubt of his own destiny that lay ahead.

The following day, Jake scaled the rugged pinnacle of rock from where there was a clear view of the upper road where it bridged over the river, thereby avoiding the town. Wiping away the dust off his spectacles made him wonder about the contents of the miracle green drink old Nykodema had concocted, enabling him to see clearly for those few important hours.

After an hour of waiting from his elevated position on the rock, Jake saw the shooting brake with the horsebox take the left-hand fork in the road towards the hacienda. Firebrand's tail swished out of the attached box when the shooting break changed gear.

Alicia looked relaxed and happy behind the steering wheel. Bandaged, and seated in the passenger seat beside her, was Scott. He was laughing at something she had said. He raised a bandaged arm out of the window in a mock salute towards the hill where Jake was waiting.

His own future was at last complete now that Scott had finally arrived at the hacienda, where he would ultimately remain, happy to be in a place where they would both feel safe and secure, content in each other's company. With a whooping laugh, Jake mounted the dappled mare and urged her into a gallop.

Printed in Great Britain
by Amazon